PENGUIN BOOKS

The Advent Killer

The Advent Killer

ALASTAIR GUNN

PENGUIN BOOKS

PENGUIN BOOKS

Published by the Penguin Group

Penguin Books Ltd, 80 Strand, London wc2r orl, England

Penguin Group (USA) Inc., 375 Hudson Street, New York, New York 10014, USA

Penguin Group (Canada), 90 Eglinton Avenue East, Suite 700, Toronto, Ontario, Canada m4p 2y3
(a division of Pearson Penguin Canada Inc.)

Penguin Ireland, 25 St Stephen's Green, Dublin 2, Ireland (a division of Penguin Books Ltd)

Penguin Group (Australia), 707 Collins Street, Melbourne, Victoria 3008,
Australia (a division of Pearson Australia Group Pty Ltd)

Penguin Books India Pvt Ltd, 11 Community Centre,
Panchsheel Park, New Delhi – 110 017, India

Penguin Group (NZ), 67 Apollo Drive, Rosedale, Auckland 0632, New Zealand
(a division of Pearson New Zealand Ltd)

Penguin Books (South Africa) (Pty) Ltd, Block D, Rosebank Office Park, 181 Jan Smuts Avenue,
Parktown North, Gauteng 2193, South Africa

Penguin Books Ltd, Registered Offices: 80 Strand, London wc2r orl, England

www.penguin.com

First published 2013

001

Copyright © Alastair Gunn, 2013

Typeset in 12.5/14.75pt Garamond MT Std by Palimpsest Book Production Ltd,
Falkirk, Stirlingshire
Printed in Great Britain by Clays Ltd, St Ives plc

isbn: 978-1-405-92644-7

www.greenpenguin.co.uk

Penguin Books is committed to a sustainable
future for our business, our readers and our planet.
This book is made from Forest Stewardship
Council™ certified paper.

For Anna

ACKNOWLEDGEMENTS

First I'd like to thank my agent, Caroline Hardman, and her partner Joanna Swainson at Hardman & Swainson, for believing in this book, and helping me bring it to the attention of such a great publisher.

Thanks also to my publishing editor, Rowland White, and his fantastic team at Penguin/Michael Joseph, especially Kirsty Taylor, Bea McIntyre and Tim Broughton.

And thanks to all the friends and relatives who read previous drafts of this book over the years, and who provided feedback, support and encouragement.

Particular mention must go to my good friends Charlie and Dyan, my sister, Kirsty, my mum and Wendy, plus my future father-in-law, Tony, and the entire Ascott family (plus partners and dogs) and the man I met in St James' Park (no names were exchanged) who kindly showed me the cut through from Old Queen Street onto Birdcage Walk. Thanks also to Nigel Grimshaw for giving me a break in journalism, and Simon Johnston for passing on various wisdoms during my time at Emap. This wouldn't have been possible without all of you.

And special thanks, of course, to Anna, who helps, supports, encourages and inspires me every single day (although not specifically to write about murder). This book (and hopefully many more to come) is for you.

PROLOGUE

The nausea took hold out of nowhere.

He swayed, losing focus, reaching instinctively for support. As his hand found anchor, somewhere beyond the miasma of emotion slowing his thoughts, his damaged shoulder blared its distress.

Was he losing consciousness?

He rubbed his eyes, fighting the combined effects of trauma and exhaustion, then leaned over the sink and splashed water onto his face, feeling his senses sharpen as the cold shocked his skin. He straightened, confident now that he wasn't going to pass out, glancing down at the knife lodged in his left shoulder, blood spreading. His time here was limited; he needed to finish this.

He turned back to his victim.

She lay awkwardly, like a person hit by a car, already comatose before they come to rest yards from the point of impact. Except that, despite her apparent tranquillity, she wasn't unconscious.

Far from it.

She stared into space, perhaps no longer aware of his presence. Then she coughed, her automatic functions creating puppet-like movements as her body strained in response. Blood crept from the side of her mouth.

He felt the swirl of emotion. But he remained strong.

He watched her panic build. The colour drained from

her skin, her chest began to undulate more quickly, her breaths became short and more desperate.

But the real clue was always in the eyes.

Her pupils dilated, the irises flashing between rapid blinks. But, after a moment, she became suddenly still.

A few weeks before, such behaviour would have surprised him, but he had seen it before. The same futile strategy to which they all resorted in the end.

She was trying to *talk*.

He stepped forwards, into her field of vision, barely able to contain the anticipation rising within himself. In a corner of his mind, the grandfather clock ticked inexorably towards the hour.

He said, 'It's time.'

He crouched over her. 'I know what you're trying to do, but it's too late to repent now. You made your choices.' He reached for the roll of tape. 'I understand you're finding it difficult to make noise at the moment, but this may take a while, and I can't have you screaming halfway through.'

He pulled a length of tape free and placed it across her mouth, winding it tightly around her head and tearing off the end.

Then he reached into the bag for his knife.

The knife.

Her eyes widened, at once pleading with him to stop and daring him to continue.

Did she really despise him?

Suddenly something ran down his cheek. He felt dizzy, and he realized he was sweating. His thoughts clouded. Could he really do this?

To the only woman he had ever loved?

No, he would not be deterred. *How dare she use what happened as leverage?*

He wiped his eyes of his humiliation and anger. But still some part of him wanted her to understand.

'I know you're scared.' He leaned closer. 'But, one day, my actions will make sense to everyone. Things are clear now; change demands sacrifice. You have to die, for the greater good.'

Did she understand? Her eyes said no. Her eyes conveyed hatred. *But why?* He'd hidden nothing from her in the end.

She had no right.

Enraged, he grabbed her shirt, ripping it open, scattering buttons across the floor. Dropping the material, he gripped the knife hard, making contact with the tip on her torso, watching the sharpened blade threatening the soft integrity of her skin.

One last chance?

Her eyes bored into him, her revulsion complete.

No.

The knife's razor point broke the surface, blood immediately beading around the tip as it moved, slicing membrane and entering flesh.

He paused, watching the thin stream of crimson as it crept down her side, relishing the absolute panic in his victim's expression.

Here was the final opportunity to relent, although somehow he'd always known he wouldn't take it. Now was his moment of destiny.

He stole one final look at her smooth, undamaged skin.

And made the first incision.

3

Two weeks earlier . . .

MONDAY

I.

The bathroom door burst open as she lunged through.

She slumped against the thin laminate, hearing it crackle against her weight until she became still. The room was quiet now, save for her short, snatched breaths. But DCI Antonia Hawkins was still desperately willing herself not to throw up.

She took off her jacket and draped it over the edge of the bath.

Breathe.

But the text message loomed again in her mind, and she felt her stomach tighten. She stumbled forwards, tripping over the towel she had left on the bathmat earlier, dropping her mobile. It clattered to the floor, skidding into the corner out of sight.

Hawkins reached the toilet, bracing herself with a hand either side of the bowl. Two strings of saliva hung from her mouth. She fought another urge to heave, catching a glimpse of her reflection in the water below, diluted mascara already running down reddened cheeks.

Do not *be sick.*

She slumped against the bath, resting her head on the toilet seat, still breathing in quick, shallow bursts. She brought a hand to her face, pinching her temples, swallowing between breaths. Then she caught a sour lungful of rim block. Her senses sharpened and the urge to vomit left her at last.

Hawkins heaved herself up onto her knees and sat back on her heels, breathing more slowly now, wiping her mouth with her palm.

One week until Christmas.

She tore off a piece of toilet paper and stood up shakily to see into the mirror above the sink, dabbing at her make-up.

Fair enough, she reasoned with her reflection: an experienced Met Police detective – supposedly used to dealing with the ridiculous pressures of homicide investigation – should not have been reduced to this pitiful state by a simple text message. But sod's law was currently doing a fantastic job of turning her first case in charge as acting Chief Inspector into her worst nightmare.

She fought down the fear that she was completely out of her depth.

She could *do* this: she had to. Her career depended on it.

Hawkins bent down to grope in the corner behind the toilet, locating the stray handset and dragging it out. She wiped the dust off it and pressed the home button to illuminate the screen, relieved to find it crack-free. But the preview of the text was still there, beside the missed call icon.

Her phone had been on silent when it rang earlier, before she noticed the text that had sent her, reeling, towards the bathroom.

They've found number three.

She paused, unable to tell from the preview whether the text contained any further information; unsure whether she wanted to know even if it did. Apprehension flared as she began swiping the screen to unlock the phone.

Then it rang.

She jumped, almost dropping it again, cursing herself for being so tense.

The number was withheld, but Hawkins knew who it was before she answered. 'Hello?'

'Hawkins.' There were never pleasantries with Chief Superintendent Kirby-Jones. 'I hope you've heard from Barclay.'

She cringed. 'Yes, sir.'

'I was forced to contact your subordinates because I couldn't reach you directly. Your trainee detective constable was the only one who answered.'

As far as Hawkins was aware, it was still acceptable for her to have her phone on silent in her own time. She made an attempt at an apology, anyway, but he cut her off. 'As you're aware, we have a third victim.'

'Sir.' She paused, uncertain if she wanted the inevitable answer. 'Is it him?'

'The body was found two hours ago by a cleaner, so details are light, but all the preliminaries match – lone female, at home, approximate time of death, method of incapacitation. There's room for error, but do you doubt it?'

She didn't want to respond. 'No, sir.'

'If this one links with the first two, your investigation will be upgraded to serious incident status, code name Operation Charter.'

Hawkins closed her eyes. Three victims; one assassin. Which meant the perpetrator had just bagged the official designation reserved for the truly psychopathic fruit-loop elite.

Serial killer.

As soon as the press got hold of information like that, media scrutiny would turn, full beam, on those leading the investigation.

And she was in charge.

Hawkins was fighting back fresh bile as Kirby-Jones continued, and she tried to focus on what the DCS was saying.

'I've instructed Barclay to collect you, plus reinforcements, on the way to the scene. He has directions and basic information, and he'll be with you any minute. You'll need to contact the rest of your team on the way. Clear?'

'Yes, sir.' She began frantically trying to repair her make-up in the mirror with her free hand.

'Remember, Detective, the public is watching.'

The line went dead.

Hawkins stood, looking at her patchwork foundation in the mirror, with the words *chief investigating officer* repeating over and over in her mind.

After a moment, she lowered the phone and quickly finished her make-up.

She rattled downstairs just in time to see an unmarked Vauxhall pull up outside.

Shit.

She walked into the hall and checked herself in the mirror, pausing to wrestle her dark brown mane into a clip.

The car's horn sounded outside, and Hawkins moved

to the door, taking a deep breath and smoothing her crumpled suit. She picked up her bag. Vanity would have to wait. Right now, she had the biggest case of her career to deal with.

But she surprised herself with a smile as she stepped around the boxes Paul had left behind when he'd moved out a few months earlier.

They were the least of her worries.

2.

DCI Hawkins closed her front door and stood under the porch, digging in her bag for her umbrella. It was only fifteen yards to the car, thanks to a patch of communal grass outside her house, but the rain was horrendous.

She angled her brolly into the downpour and headed for the dark blue Insignia idling beside the pavement. The wind was bitter, and she opened the passenger door with relief.

'Thanks for the lift.' Hawkins dropped into the seat, dumping her umbrella in the foot well and yanking on her seatbelt. 'You know where we're going, right?'

'Yes, ma'am.' DC John Barclay revved the engine as they roared away from the kerb, tyres fighting for grip. 'Hampstead.'

'Very upmarket.' She glanced at her wiry young driver, deciding against asking him to slow down as they slewed onto the main road. Traffic was light and they needed to get there.

She was relieved to note that the trainee detective constable looked a little overwhelmed, too: his shirt collar was rucked up, and he had a thin, white line around his mouth.

She wasn't the only one who left home in a hurry.

'John.' She indicated the same area on her own face. 'You've got some toothpaste . . .'

'Oh.' He licked a finger and began wiping. 'Gone?'

'Yeah.' Hawkins edged away when his hand brushed her leg as he changed gear exiting a bend. He probably hadn't intended it.

They rode for a few seconds in silence before Hawkins produced her mobile. 'I'm just going to call Frank and Amala.'

'Already taken care of.' Barclay tapped his earpiece. 'They're meeting us there.'

'Great.' Hawkins rebagged the phone. His proaction meant she'd have her full unit at the murder scene early on: essential to secure the maximum number of witnesses. Instead she found her notepad and started making an investigation plan, resting on her knee.

'So,' she breezed, stoking the positive atmosphere, still writing, 'I hear you got a call from the chief super.'

'Yes.' Barclay said as they idled at some lights, the rhythmic thump of the windscreen wipers compounding his lack of elaboration.

She annotated a couple of tasks on her pad before glancing at him, 'What did he say?'

John looked over, almost as if he'd forgotten about her. 'There's another body, ma'am. According to early reports from Scenes of Crime, she died at some point yesterday morning.'

Sunday. *Just like the others.*

The lights changed and they moved off.

'So who was she?'

Barclay coughed. 'Ever heard of Jessica Anderton?'

'The politician's wife?'

Of course she knew of Jessica Anderton, and her

husband, Charles. The charismatic people's champion of the Labour party and his stunning young socialite, ex-model wife were never far from the headlines. A celebrity-obsessed public had battled recently to buy the Gucci handbag Jessica had donated to a charity auction; they'd queued for hours to buy *Hello* magazine when it ran exclusive photos and an interview with the couple prior to their wedding. Even the opposition's repeated allegations that the Andertons' marriage was a poll-friendly sham had tailed off in recent months.

'Blimey.' Hawkins tried to hide the trepidation in her voice. 'What about MO?'

'That's him.'

Hawkins looked across to see Barclay pointing ahead. Then she remembered Kirby-Jones' instruction to collect reinforcements on their way to the scene.

Barclay pulled over to the kerb. 'Just like the DCS said – thirties, slim, unnecessary facial hair.'

Hawkins squinted through the rain bouncing off the windscreen, trying to get a look at her newest team member. A man waved and jogged out from under the cover of a bus shelter, holding a newspaper above his head and a mobile to his ear, weaving his way through the sea of suited nine-to-fivers.

He finished his call and slipped the phone inside his suede jacket as he pulled open the rear door of the car and got in.

'DCI Hawkins?' His accent was clipped, Belfast probably. 'DS Eddie Connor.'

'Call me Antonia.' They shook hands between the seats. 'And this is our trainee, DC John Barclay. Thanks for coming at such short notice.'

'Well, your man didn't disappoint the press, anyway.' Connor pulled the rear door shut as he held up a moist copy of the *Daily Mail*.

Hawkins twisted in her seat. '*Will Killer Strike Again?*' She read the headline aloud in her best movie-trailer voice, feigning nonchalance. 'Where would we be without the great British press to stir up some decent, nationwide panic? Can't wait to see what happens when those arse-holes hear about our latest.'

'They already know,' Connor said. 'I just spoke to a friend of mine in Scenes of Crime. The media were there before *him*.'

'Fantastic.' Hawkins looked at Barclay, about to suggest they shouldn't hang around, but there was no need. He opened the throttle and accelerated back into the flow of early morning London traffic.

'So where have you joined us from?' Hawkins said over her shoulder, bracing herself between floor and armrest as Barclay swung out to overtake a meandering waste-disposal lorry.

'CID.' Connor raised his voice over the din of the worsening thunderstorm hammering the Vauxhall's roof. 'Flying Squad. I put in a transfer request ages ago, but nothing happened until your chief super rang me this morning. I'm on your team until further notice. Apparently my application only just got to him, but I think it's more to do with the shit that's about to hit the fan in Downing Street.' He laughed. 'In fact, things happened so fast that nobody's asked for my gun back yet.'

'You're a specialist firearms officer?' Barclay looked around.

'Murder, shooters and fast cars,' Connor said. 'Everything a boy dreams of when he joins the force.'

Hawkins caught his grin and returned it. Having an armed SFO on the team would be a definite bonus if and when they caught up with the killer.

'This a pool car, is it?' Connor waited for confirmation before he began brushing the water out of his hair onto the upholstery. 'So, tell me what the *Daily Mail* doesn't know.'

'Two previous victims,' Hawkins explained over her shoulder. 'Both female, both killed at home on consecutive Sunday mornings. First was sixty-three-year-old Glenis Ward, who drowned in her bath. We thought it was suicide initially as there were no superficial signs of foul play. Glenis' alcoholism was common knowledge – it was why she had to "retire" from her job as a cook – and the recent diagnosis of bowel cancer was considered depressing enough to have pushed her over the edge. Turns out she was attacked in her hallway before being dragged upstairs to the bathroom.'

Hawkins caught a sign for Belgravia as it flashed past. They were close. 'Then, exactly seven days later, a forty-eight-year-old former care-worker called Tess Underwood was beaten to death with a baseball bat. And when I say beaten to death, think major bones being systematically broken one by one from her shins upwards. The coroner said she didn't die until the killer reached her head, and even then only thanks to an intracranial haemorrhage caused by a direct blow to the face, which rammed a shard of skull into her cortex.'

'Nice.' Connor's tone was suitably disgusted.

Hawkins registered it, pleased with his reaction to gruesome details too familiar to raise eyebrows among the existing members of her murder investigation team.

They hit traffic at the Royal Thames Yacht Club, and Barclay looked at her for approval to use the lights. She nodded, flicking the switch for him. The Vauxhall's siren attacked the air and Barclay kept going, swerving into the empty oncoming lane to clear the jam.

'Proper fucking action at last.' Connor's head appeared between the front seats, like a kid arriving at Disney World. 'So, what's he done to this latest girl?'

'I think,' Hawkins turned to Barclay, 'we're about to find out.'

3.

Oblivious to the elegant living room around them, Hawkins peered into the gaping cavity that had, until the previous morning, contained Jessica Anderton's heart. It looked as though a small volcano had erupted inside the young woman's chest, leaving folds of tattered skin splayed back on themselves all around the wound's edge. The blood pooled in the bottom of the hole had long since formed a crust.

The body was naked from the waist up. The only visible form of restraint that had been used was the black, heavy-duty tape, several layers of which were wound tightly around the victim's head, covering her mouth.

Hawkins inhaled without thinking and caught a lungful of death through her paper facemask. A deceased human starts to smell pretty bad pretty fast, and the intense odour of shit emanating from this one meant the killer had probably ruptured his victim's intestine.

She grimaced and moved back, adjusting her feet in their clumsy overshoes mid-step to avoid the spattered blood patterns on the floorboards.

She stumbled. 'Bollocks.'

Why hadn't she gone with flat heels?

'Careful.' Connor crouched opposite her. 'This is a goddamn work of art. You OK?'

'Yeah.' She rubbed her neck through the crinkly anti-contamination romper suit. 'Tip top.'

Hawkins wasn't the squeamish type, having become immune to the gore of murder scenes early in her career. It was imagining how the event had unfolded that she could never relax with.

And, more importantly, how she was going to prevent the next.

The muted clamour of half a dozen Scenes of Crime officers efficiently dissecting the lavish room around them had faded the moment she and Connor had seen what occupied centre stage. She was glad they'd left Barclay in the other room with the cleaning lady who found the body. He'd looked about ready to puke after seeing Tess Underwood. And next to this, the previous two incidents had been nothing more than tender warm-up acts.

She swore quietly at the damaged corpse, wishing herself away.

Anywhere but here.

'He must have three hands or something, assuming it's just one guy,' Connor continued. 'Hardly spilled a drop.' He motioned to the cup and two large saucepans full of blood on the floor. 'Must have used the mug to scoop the blood out of the chest cavity as he worked. Think it's the same killer?'

'Yep, and I'm beginning to think it might be better for everyone that way. One person doing stuff like this is plenty, if you ask me.'

'Too right.'

Hawkins shook her head, asking under her breath, 'but why remove the heart?'

Connor shrugged, 'Who knows with sick bastards like this? It's probably in a jar in his basement so he can sing to it every night before he has sex with his dog. Did we get much from the first two scenes?'

Hawkins snorted mock amusement, 'Fuck-all forensically, although that's not surprising. These days, anyone who watches enough detective drama on TV has a reasonable grip of basic anti-contamination. We've got some low-res CCTV of a single male leaving the first scene, but he knows what he's doing there, too. Plain, dark clothing and a baseball cap. Keeps his head down, avoids street-lamps. It could be Prince Charles and we wouldn't be able to tell.'

Connor frowned. 'Weapons?'

'No. Whatever he used on the first two he brought and took with him. If he's left anything here, I'll be mighty surprised.'

The Irishman had run out of questions for now, and returned to studying the corpse as nonchalantly as if it were a part-finished jigsaw puzzle, fingers pinching at the neatly trimmed clump of hair beneath his lower lip.

Hawkins' attention also shifted back to the body as she observed, 'you're clearly used to appraising this type of masterpiece.'

Connor didn't look up, 'worked homicide in Belfast for six years before moving to London. But this is the tidiest hack-job I've ever seen.'

'He's no professional, but his techniques are well considered and highly effective.'

Hawkins would have known that adenoidal voice anywhere. She turned to see Gerald Pritchard, the Home Office pathologist, dressed, as ever, the only way she ever pictured him: anti-contamination overalls zipped down just enough to display the top of an immaculately pressed shirt and tie. The combination of nasal tone and conservative dress-sense had long since earned him the nickname Mr Bean.

'Sorry to keep you waiting, Detective,' Pritchard waved his mobile phone at her, 'I just stepped out to prime the lab for our pending arrival. But I bumped into your young constable out in the corridor, and he mentioned you'd arrived.'

Hawkins nodded, acknowledging Barclay's atypically composed presence at Pritchard's shoulder, before introducing the Pathologist to Connor.

'These morning conferences are beginning to feel uncomfortably familiar,' she said. 'Any revelations so far?'

'Nothing yet,' Pritchard replied, 'although that only reinforces the notion that we're dealing with the same individual.' He gestured at the corpse. 'As you can see, the lower half of the body is still clothed, and I suspect forensic examination will demonstrate that, as with the previous two victims, there was no sexual assault or molestation. Also as before, there are no signs of forced entry to the residence itself, indicating either that Mrs Anderton knew her attacker, or that he's capable of bypassing modern security mechanisms, such as they are.'

Connor wore a lop-sided grin. 'Well, at least if we don't get him soon, he'll be enough of a celebrity that *Heat* magazine will track him down for an interview.'

Pritchard ignored the joke, but turned to face the DS. 'Let me show you something.' He crouched beside the body, indicating a particular spot on the torso with a nitrile-gloved finger. 'See the discolouration?'

The mark he referred to looked like a small love-bite, almost hidden against the purple-grey remains of Jessica's chest.

'Do you recognize this?' Pritchard looked up at Connor. 'Sergeant?'

The Irishman stayed silent.

'You should.' Pritchard teased back a flap of skin at the edge of the cavity, moving it into what would have been its original position. 'How about now?'

They all leaned in, staring at the newly exposed detail.

A second mark.

'Jesus.' Connor got it. 'A Taser.'

Hawkins nodded. It was merely confirmation of the fact that: in the last three weeks, serial killing had received a twenty-first-century make-over. Somehow, their quarry had obtained an electrostatic stun gun, currently legal only in the hands of qualified firearms officers like Connor.

The marks denoted points where the Taser's twin projectile electrodes had lodged close to the skin before delivering a massive electric shock, temporarily shutting down the target's central nervous system. Similar marks had been present on Glenis Ward's back: one of the details that had come to light once she'd been removed from the bathwater, and that had led to the revelation she hadn't killed herself after all.

The Taser connection hadn't been established until

now, however, because similar marks found on Tess Underwood's corpse had been rendered inconclusive by the horrific destruction of the skin's surface caused during her sustained beating. But the ones here on Jessica Anderton's chest vastly increased the chances that the same weapon had been deployed on all three.

'Why the excess charring?' Barclay asked.

'Good question.' Pritchard cast an avuncular glance in the trainee's direction before addressing the group. 'Mr Barclay has shrewdly observed auxiliary cauterization around the contact points, exceeding the levels observed on the first victim.'

There were blank stares.

Pritchard indicated the blackened edge of the first mark with a finger. 'This could suggest the use of a more powerful Taser weapon than before, but even in that case I wouldn't expect to see such distinct carbon residue. Standard Tasers have built-in five-second timers, purely to protect the target from overexposure, but many have the option to override.' He stood. 'My professional opinion is that this victim was subjected to a vastly extended electric shock, sufficient to incapacitate for fifteen or twenty minutes; also increasing the risk of heart attack by about forty per cent, incidentally.'

Hawkins swallowed, the nightmare scenario forming itself in her mind. She opened her mouth to speak, but Pritchard continued, his tone solemn.

'Yes, Detective, I believe that Mrs Anderton was cut open while she was not only alive, but conscious as well.'

4.

The silence that followed Pritchard's statement stretched as they all stood looking down at Jessica Anderton's mutilated form.

At that moment, the pathologist was called away by one of the SOCOs, who was on all fours by an ornate marble fireplace. Pritchard made his apologies and moved off.

Hawkins took the opportunity to make some notes, glad to see Connor and Barclay doing the same thing. At least this murder focused their investigation by confirming the consistencies between the first two.

At the top of her page in capitals she wrote SUNDAY MORNING and TASER. Hawkins' knowledge of such things wasn't extensive, but she could recognize a body in the stage between rigor mortis, which abated around three hours after death, and bacterial growth that started turning the skin on a dead body green after about three days. Which put this murder into the right time bracket.

In all likelihood Jessica would have died at the same time as the others: One a.m. They'd know more after the post mortem, of course, but if confirmed this would show the killer had put effort into synchronizing all three deaths. So the time itself obviously held some significance for him, while the source of something as arcane as a Taser might be traceable.

Then she began sketching the room. The forensic scene manager would provide detailed assessments of the crime scene, but Hawkins always found her own rough drawings of more use. There was something clinical and cold about the snow-white, inch-perfect printouts provided by forensics, which somehow made it easier to overlook things that may have seemed obvious in the flesh; things that might be rendered more apparent six weeks down the line by a small detail like, for example, being underlined.

She glanced towards the door, just as a man she didn't recognize entered. He looked vaguely Italian, the wrong side of forty, with wire-rimmed glasses and a black shock of a haircut, most of which was stuffed into a mobcap. She watched his gloved hands searching the outside of his anti-contamination suit for pockets rendered temporarily inaccessible, before settling on being clasped together behind his back.

But those details weren't what drew Hawkins towards him, or what made her suspect he wasn't meant to be there.

He wasn't wearing a crime-scene tag.

She strode over, placing herself between him and Jessica Anderton, cutting off his view. 'Who are you?'

He squinted at her from behind his glasses. 'Who's asking?'

'This is my crime scene. How did you get in here without ID?'

'Oh.' He unzipped his anti-contamination suit, reaching inside. 'You mean this thing?' He handed her a worn plastic sheath. 'Damned clip fell off ages ago, but all the

SOCO guys know me, so I don't usually need it. You're acting DCI Antonia Hawkins?'

Hawkins looked at the tag.

She'd just accosted Simon Hunter, one of the Met's top criminologists, a man she'd never met before because, while he was a regular at high-profile crime scenes like this one, she wasn't.

He should have been asking *her* for credentials.

'Oh.' She handed back the tag. 'Sorry.'

'It's OK, really.' Hunter replaced the tag inside his suit. 'You have an eye for detail. In this line of work, that's never a bad thing.' He held out his hand. 'Simon Hunter – I'll be your psychological profiler.'

She shook it, noticing that despite a voice like gravel and crow's feet like crazy paving, he had the demeanour of a much younger man.

Hunter moved into the room, glancing around at the beautifully co-ordinated seasonal decorations, before shuffling aside to allow a team of six to heave the immense Christmas tree past them and out into the hall. Then he resumed his silent assessment, taking in the corpse before them.

A few seconds later his eyebrows twitched, as if he'd reached whatever conclusion he had been looking for.

'So.' He turned to Hawkins. 'Who else am I talking to here?'

She called Connor and Barclay over and introduced them.

'Hunter,' Connor commented, 'I know that name. You were involved in taking down the Boom Crew gang in Birmingham last year, right?'

Hunter said yes, and they chatted for a few moments about backgrounds and mutual colleagues. The profiler definitely had pedigree.

His profession was largely derided among the Met's ranks as nonsense that earned a disproportionate wage for those sufficiently flagrant to peddle it. But with a strike rate like Hunter's, you had to wonder. He was modest, but Hawkins was already familiar with rumours about the pivotal roles he'd played in several high-profile cases.

'I've been reading the case notes,' Hunter said afterwards, using fingertips to adjust his glasses on his nose. 'Mrs Anderton's demise gives us a bona-fide serial killer which means, I'm afraid, that you get me.'

'Any help gratefully received.' Hawkins nodded towards Jessica's sullied form. 'What do you make of our lunatic?'

'Well,' Hunter replied, his enthusiasm going up a notch. 'Killers like this man are rare, but they do pop up from time to time, and there tend to be common themes within their particular psychological range. Often they choose their victims at random, but there'll be a unifying thread there, somewhere. Most tend to have a specific focus or obsession: it can be anything from religious extremism to emulation of prolific, real-life psychopaths like Hindley or West. This guy hasn't really nailed his colours to the mast yet, but each murder so far seems to have been considerably more violent than its predecessor.'

Connor leaned in. 'What does that tell us?'

'I call it "the gore escalator",' Hunter said, matter of fact. 'It's not the behaviour of your average practising psychopath, but it does happen. So, say you ride the world's fifth largest roller coaster. You probably wouldn't then bother riding the sixth or seventh largest, because after the fifth they'd disappoint. The only way you can replicate the thrill is by riding the fourth biggest, then the third, and so on.' Hunter's glasses caught the light as he looked round at them all. 'Well, the same principle can apply to serial murder, and it looks like this guy agrees. What was probably his first time involved placing someone in mortal danger, then simply standing back and watching her drown. He didn't physically *take* that life; he just chose, at the crucial moment, not to save it. For number two he wants a more visceral experience, hence the increased physical nature of his next attack. Unfortunately for number three here, he's progressing quickly. Anyway, however detached and merciless his actions, you have to admit that his impulses are still undeniably human. We all need a thrill from time to time.'

'Endearing,' Hawkins wasn't convinced. 'but I still don't understand the need for this variety in how he kills them? Why risk changing methods every time, when he could just stick to one?'

The profiler cocked his head, 'Have you considered that he might be experimenting to keep himself interested?'

'What?'

'I've got this friend who's an actor,' Hunter said pensively, 'does theatre. Goes on stage every single night, repeats the same actions time and again. But each day he finds some way to change his performance, just enough to stop himself from going mad. The outcome is always the same, but the intricate details are unique. I know our killer's an extreme example, but I think the comparison stands.'

'Okay,' Hawkins considered his answer briefly, 'but what bothers me is that it's all so *precise*. Why remove somebody's heart, why use the Taser; why such a definite time? Surely the details mean *something*.'

Hunter frowned, 'they'll have significance, of course they will, but you have to remember the type of mind you're dealing with here. Importance is such a personal thing; it's like trying to fathom someone's superstitions. An obsessive compulsive disorder can make a person switch the light on and off any number of times when they leave a room, but the fear they have of what'll happen if they don't is entirely their own. I don't doubt he does these things because they make sense to *him*, but those explanations wouldn't necessarily translate to you or me. One a.m. might be the time he lost his virginity, or the moment he found God.'

'So what are you saying: don't bother with specifics?'

'Not at all. I'm saying that we need to find a starting point; a solid piece of information about this man beyond his actions. Something *factual*. Everything will grow from there; but until we have that, we're drifting.'

Hawkins looked around at the others, realizing that she now appeared to be hounding the man.

She opted to move on, 'So how do we catch the bastard?'

'Let's look at that.' Hunter cast an arm at the room. 'You're finding zero traces at the scenes. That doesn't happen by accident. Also, each murder appears to have been flawlessly planned and – if you'll excuse the phrase – executed. That means you're dealing with an intelligent individual who knows his surroundings. He feels comfortable and confident here, so I'd restrict your search to London, initially at least. And the lack of an obvious connection between the victims doesn't necessarily mean there isn't one. Very few people kill without what they consider to be a damn good reason, no matter how detached from reality their motives might be. So my advice would be to find that reason. Then you'll have a better chance of finding your killer.'

'What do you mean by *reason*?' Connor asked.

'You need to work out why he's doing this.' Hunter responded, 'Are his victims random – irrelevant except as some sort of message to the rest of us – or does he have a list of specific people he wants to kill? Put simply, what's his problem? Until you find out, it'll be impossible to call his rationale.'

Connor stared at him, 'and then?'

'Then we communicate.'

'*Communicate*,' Connor repeated playfully, 'how? Look for bumper stickers with a mobile number and a message that says "*How's my murdering?*"'

Hunter laughed without conviction. 'Not exactly. Granted he won't be in the phonebook, but I promise you he's watching the news. I don't think our friend is finished killing yet and, if he wants to maintain the freedom to carry on, he'll be keeping a very close eye on you detective types. His main source of information will almost certainly be the media, thereby giving you, detective Connor, an open line of communication.'

'OK.' Hawkins cut in, hiding her relief that Connor had asked the question before she had, 'Let's say you're a genius. Tell us why he went for these particular women.

Even if they are random, he's choosing them somehow. And how about predicting the next?'

Hunter didn't bite, except to catch her look and return it. 'I'm here to speculate on *how*, rather than *what* your killer might be thinking, and to predict behaviour given precise future circumstances. As for specifics, Detective, surely that's your department.'

There were uncomfortable seconds of silence as they traded intent.

'Touché,' Hawkins submitted eventually, deciding it was best not to fall out with the profiler on their first meeting.

'Sorry about that,' Pritchard re-joined them, greeting Hunter with the nod of a familiar and respectful colleague.

Hawkins addressed the pathologist: 'Found something?'

'Unfortunately not.' He frowned over at the line of SOCOs slowly disappearing behind the sofa. 'We still haven't established DNA or prints common to both previous scenes, so there's no reason to expect anything different here. We'll keep looking, of course, but none of the genetic evidence so far matches anything on record. So until you can provide us with a suspect, its use is limited.'

'Thanks for the reminder.' Hawkins was well aware that while modern DNA identification could link someone to a crime scene using even the most miniscule trace, you still needed a host to match it with.

She scanned the Andertons' front room. As usual, the place had changed dramatically since Scenes of Crime had arrived. It looked like a second-rate TV make-over show had invaded: great chunks of wallpaper had been torn away, plastic markers had been used to section off search zones, while small pipes protruded through the wooden floorboards, identifying the former positions of two small radiators.

If the killer had left any trace at all, these people would find it.

Connor asked, 'So what are the chances he's just some burn-out we'll find next week in a bed-sit somewhere, having topped himself?'

'Sorry, Sergeant.' Hunter shook his head. 'His mental state appears quite stable. Anyone who can create three scenes like this without leaving traces or getting caught in the process is no candidate for an impending schizophrenic episode.' He brightened. 'But, like I said, once you find that reason . . .'

Hawkins wished she could share his enthusiasm.

After a few minutes discussing the more tedious aspects of investigative bureaucracy, their meeting had finished. Hunter asked for copies of the updated case notes once they were ready, and left, handing out cards on the way. Connor moved across and began talking to his friend from SOC, while Barclay went outside to start doorstepping the neighbours for contact details. Hopefully one of them would know the whereabouts of the victim's husband. So far their attempts to contact the politician had failed. His mobile was unobtainable; his Westminster office unmanned. At least they should be able to get an answer now that business hours had resumed. If the couple's affectionate public image was genuine, he'd be distraught, so they needed to find him before news of his wife's death leaked through other channels. Or before he had too great a head-start.

Hawkins thanked Pritchard, watching him retreat towards a huddle of his colleagues in the far corner. She recognized some of them, like the scientific support officer whose name escaped her, and Pete Munford, one of their regular crime scene photographers. A third man was probably the new public relations official.

Pritchard positioned himself on the far side of the group and glanced over at her.

Hawkins' anti-contamination suit was two sizes too large and hardly flattering, but at least it would prevent Pritchard from indulging his regular habit of staring at her legs. She smiled to herself, resisting the urge to go over and expose his lecherous tendencies in front of his peers. Instead, she turned and walked over to the tall bay window, staring down at an ever-expanding crowd of hacks, neighbours and passers-by drawn like flies to dog shit by the SOCO van blocking the road. She glanced at the sky, annoyed that for the first time that day the down-pour had stopped.

Nothing like a bit of rain to dampen people's enthusiasm for rubber-necking.

Amid the onlookers, Hawkins picked out Frank Todd and Amala Yasir as they moved slowly from face to face: *Did you know the occupants; were you witness to any unusual events here?*

The trick was to gather information without imparting any in return, but those in the crowd who didn't already know who lived there soon would.

And suddenly the nerves were there again.

Hawkins' mind jumped back to her first appearance in a primary school play, watching the audience from the wings, waiting for her cue. She'd just been able to make out faces in the front row, among them her parents: Dad beaming from ear to ear; Mum stoic, so often short of anything that resembled a compliment. Yet she knew, deep down, it was her mother she wanted to impress the most. And she was still having trouble with *that* line.

Hawkins shook her head, evicting the memory. There was no time.

She remembered Kirby-Jones' words from two weeks before: '. . . good opportunity to make a name for yourself on this one, Hawkins. As senior investigating officer, you'll be responsible for getting results. Can your team handle it? Can you?'

Lawrence Kirby-Jones had several dog-eared speeches about equality and developing those he deemed credible. Others might have been fooled, but Hawkins knew a closet misogynist when she saw one. If this investigation wasn't a resounding success, his report would say: 'Secondment fluffed. Do not promote beyond DI level again.'

What annoyed her most was that Kirby-Jones must have known the lack of available resources when he'd offered her the case, but only when the fan had been truly coated had *she* been informed. So far, the investigation had gone from suspected suicide, to murder, to multiple homicide; and now they were looking at a *savoir-faire* serial killer with the apparent ability to butcher half of London, and scare the other half to death, completely unimpeded by anything the Met tried to do about it.

Her first case as SIO was turning out to be a real banana skin, especially as she was lumbered with a makeshift team. Her four current subordinates included a trainee, and someone from the Irish Flying Squad who apparently hadn't been deemed good enough until the situation became desperate.

Until then, Hawkins had believed that developments in the case had taken her boss as much by surprise as they had everybody else. But what if that wasn't true? She'd wondered at the time why no existing DCI had offered to take on this allegedly simple investigation; there were those who could have stretched it to fill two personal development reviews and a bid for promotion.

So had Kirby-Jones warned them off?

Hawkins pushed the thought away: paranoia wouldn't help matters.

She refocused on the case. Inquiries into the first two murders were still underway. Telephone records and interview tapes of family, friends and any potential witnesses were being analysed, and the Police National Computer database was being scoured for the slightest similarities to past murders. Even the Family Liaison officers dealing with the bereaved were on alert for any piece of useful information, however small, that a friend or relative might happen to regurgitate.

Unfortunately, television appeals for witnesses and the interviews had produced few leads, and even fewer potential suspects, although they were still trying to trace a couple of the victims' ex-boyfriends. So far they had nothing.

But the worst part was that this jigsaw still lacked its most crucial piece: motive.

The guy popped up out of nowhere, created his gruesome calling cards, and evaporated.

These murders were far beyond anything Hawkins had experienced. In the past she and Mike had worked on cases involving rival gangs, where games of revenge killing tennis just ran and ran, sending the body count skywards. But for a lone individual to execute a string of apparently unconnected women, in such diverse but clinical ways, was almost unrecognizable as human behaviour. With each attack the killer became more inexplicable to Hawkins.

Her team's ongoing research into his methods was looking more and more futile. They'd already been reduced to trying different combinations of letters in the victims' names, to see if a hidden message might emerge.

Nothing had.

And now the case had escalated around her, along with the need for a sacrificial lamb if Operation Charter wasn't a success.

At one a week, bodies were appearing faster than they could be processed and, unlike other serial homicide cases, they knew almost for certain when the next one would arrive. Sunday – Christmas Day. Less than a week from now.

They needed an arrest. Fast.

Hawkins' attention returned to the crowd outside. An elderly woman had appeared and started shouting at the uniformed officers to tell her what was going on. A younger man was trying to coax her away with offers of a cup of tea.

In the confusion, a lone reporter slipped unseen

through the cordon, tucking his press badge inside his jacket as he sleazed up the stone steps beside the slightly open window.

'Let us in, ay, love?' He addressed the WPC manning the front door. 'Say I'm a colleague. It's worth a hundred to you.'

Hawkins moved forwards and tapped on the glass, edging the window further open and showing him her badge, 'Please move back behind the cordon, sir.' She dropped her voice. 'In other words, take your camera and fuck off.'

Hawkins took a moment to enjoy her victory as two uniformed officers, having heard the louder of her statements, practically carried him back past the front gate.

She returned the WPC's grin.

But she wouldn't have smiled had she known that, from across the street, the killer watched her turn back into the room.

5.

A distant, metallic sound reached his ears through the interference. Its torpid shockwave spread. Memories spun and echoed, the static of recent events choking his senses.

He tried the handle again, but still the door wouldn't open. He looked down at numb fingers. They were no longer holding the key.

He screwed his eyes shut as emotion reared, and steadied himself against the doorframe.

He'd expected this backlash; spent the whole of the day before lying on his bed, waiting for the emotional disorder to arrive. But it had taken so long that he'd begun to think it might have bypassed him altogether. So he had left the house today as normal.

That decision now seemed foolish in the extreme as he'd been overcome, almost collapsing in the street.

He swallowed hard, having to concentrate so his legs didn't give way, until he became aware of something else.

In the distance, his own voice was telling him to pick up the key.

He scanned the ground, not seeing it at first. Then it appeared, partly hidden in the weeds by his feet. He stared at it as he bent, reaching out.

Gripping the key, he instructed his body to straighten. Slowly it complied and, this time, despite hands that felt like they belonged to someone else, the key slotted home in the lock with a dull click.

The door opened to reveal a small kitchen, as unfamiliar to him as everything else had become in the last few hours. He stepped inside, his gaze immediately catching hers.

Jessica Anderton regarded him from the opposite side of the room.

He turned his face away, cowering for a moment, before he lurched over and tore the picture from its pin, angered suddenly by the inequity of his situation. But recent history flared again, and the hands he had managed to control sufficiently to begin ripping the picture in two froze mid-reprisal.

These thoughts were poisoning him.

And still she stared.

He turned the picture away, unable to meet her unwavering gaze, bright and immortalized. Eyes that challenged him.

Eyes of a woman he had killed.

TUESDAY

6.

Hawkins waited while the stragglers took their seats, drumming her fingers on the desk and glaring from face to face. The wall clock said 08:36.

Unfortunately it also showed the date, whose significance Hawkins was trying to ignore. Back in June, when she and Paul were still pretending things were salvageable, they had almost booked a holiday in Barbados over Christmas and New Year. In fact, they might have been in the air at this very moment.

Still waiting for the laggards to settle, Hawkins reflected briefly on her path to acting Chief Inspector, and the moment she'd received fortuitous expedition. The day when, after seventeen years of service with a flawless health and attendance record, her boss, DCI Norman Parr, had collapsed on duty and died. Hawkins' feelings for him hadn't changed, despite his tragic end: she'd considered him a slimy, underhand backstabber ever since they'd begun working together three years earlier. But that hadn't put her off stepping into his role when it had been offered to her.

And so for now, a week before Christmas, she was shackled to a case she wouldn't have wished on a City banker, presiding over a bunch of corpses that looked like props from the *Saw* movies.

Fortunately, her core team understood the gravity of

the situation sufficiently to have arrived on time. Her most experienced DI, a forty-five-year-old Geordie named Frank Todd, sat in the front row, next to the younger and far more exotic Detective Sergeant Amala Yasir. John Barclay and Eddie Connor occupied seats on the other side of the central aisle.

She'd have to explain later to the four of them that the frustration she was about to show wasn't with them. Todd and Yasir had been in early to prepare this briefing room with the latest information, and she had to admit they'd done a great job. Connor had only been here a day, and she'd arrived in her office that morning to find the huge stack of files from another case she'd assigned to Barclay the previous week for analysis. The excerpt she'd checked seemed flawless. She couldn't imagine where he'd found the time to get them all done.

But the rest of her extended team really weren't helping themselves.

The rest of the medium-sized briefing room had filled up fast, with officers of varying familiarity. A small group of uniforms huddled in the far corner, the ringleader holding forth about his shed roof. Opposite them, the analyst contingent consisted of six equally uninterested parties, perhaps in attendance only because it was their goal to suffuse every room in the building with the aroma of over-brewed coffee. Arriving in the remaining space were the three supplementary detective constables that Hawkins had been promised for the middle of last week.

While the initial four days of lateness probably wasn't their fault, Hawkins decided, the last six minutes of insouciance would cost them.

'Right.' She stood, talking loudly to subdue the mouthy uniform at the back. 'I'll open by welcoming anyone who isn't familiar with this ritual I like to call the eight-thirty briefing. The clue's in the name: a briefing given by me, to you, at eight thirty in the morning. Not eight thirty-one, not eight thirty-six, not bloody lunchtime, understood?'

Silence.

'Good.' She waited a beat and then said, 'Welcome to the new faces on the team. It's good to have you here, and I know the others will be glad to get you up to speed as soon as possible.' She smiled briefly at the nods of appreciation around the room, then got down to work.

Hawkins moved around the desk to the whiteboard, where several pictures of the latest victim now flanked those of the previous two. 'Thanks to the discovery of Jessica Anderton's body, Operation Charter is already the biggest real-time serial homicide investigation since Sutcliffe. And it's about to get bigger.'

She explained the three murders, marking the scenes on a large map she'd had printed for the purpose, also adding the victims' previous addresses and places of work. But the resulting configuration only reinforced the apparent lack of connection between them. They hadn't worked, lived or even shopped in the same locations. Normally after three killings of this type, some sort of pattern would become obvious. Here, so far, there was none. Even the latest geo-mapping software, which compared and analysed people's movements over specified periods, looking for event 'hotspots', hadn't produced anything so far.

Hawkins emphasized that, up to that point, they had

released to the media only the most basic details regarding the attacks. The press office had actively played down speculation that the two previous deaths were linked, and no information had been published about the horrific state in which the killer had left the second body.

All that the outside world had known until that morning was that two women had been killed in London at similar times on consecutive Sunday mornings. But, true to form, the papers had made the most of even these scant facts: the past seven days' press had been full of speculation about whether a third successive Sunday would yield a third successive victim.

And now it had.

Which blew a dirty big hole through what was left of the 'freak incident' hypothesis.

Add the fact that the latest body also happened to belong to prominent politician's wife and ex-model Jessica Anderton, and the story suddenly became *big* news.

Once the relentless media machine released her name, Hawkins told the room, all of effing hell was going to break loose. From then on, the killer's notoriety was assured: the remainder of Operation Charter would be conducted in full public view.

Of course, those who lived near the victims needed no such encouragement. Jessica had been the focus of local gossip long before she was murdered, and even though her neighbours held wildly differing opinions of her personality, several had confirmed one thing: a young, Mediterranean-looking man had been seen leaving the Anderton residence on Sunday morning; a matter of hours after Jessica was murdered.

Add in the fact that none of the witnesses knew who he was, and the fact that he still hadn't come forward, he became the closest thing they had to a suspect. Even if he wasn't the killer, he had to know *something*. Now it was just a case of finding him.

She covered her anxiety with a dramatic pause, glancing around at her subordinates. She was a general, impressing on her troops the solemnity of war. As someone who desperately wanted the job into which she was seconded, Hawkins knew the outcome of this case would decide her future, regardless of anything she might previously have done. Usually, when the Met started taking a proverbial kicking for its inability to stop an incumbent perpetrator, someone got fired – or unseconded – pretty damn fast.

Was there a record for the length of time between a temporarily promoted DCI being given a case, and then being taken off it again? Fifteen days would take some beating.

She moved on, listing the individuals they most needed to trace, including Gary Ward, the first victim's less than desirable stepson, currently elusive. Then she doled out initial responsibilities, prioritizing four lines of enquiry: why the killer struck repeatedly at such a specific time on one particular day of the week, the significance of each MO, how and where he had obtained the Taser, and if the victims weren't connected, how they were being selected.

She concluded with, 'Any questions?'

A couple of uniforms raised issues about overtime rates, but everybody seemed to have received the message about the case itself, so Hawkins thanked everyone for their work thus far, made a statement about expecting continuing full commitment from everyone, and left.

She strode along the corridor, head still full of the case.

The two earlier murders hadn't necessarily denoted a regular sequence to come. Deaths on three consecutive Sundays, however, meant this killer, whoever he was, had a plan.

Regardless of whether it was by design or coincidence, next Sunday was Christmas Day, and the Sunday after that was New Year's; the two days of the year when most people were off work, all scratching around for a subject they could broach with the in-laws.

Unless the case was resolved in the next week, Hawkins thought grimly, come Christmas Day it would at least be uniting disparate relatives across the country.

She reached the end of the corridor, looking back as she turned the corner to see uniforms and analysts exiting the briefing room. Her core team weren't among them, which meant they were probably waiting for the others to leave so they could discuss the case.

She knew three of them well enough to imagine how the conversation would go.

Frank Todd would be first in, with hard Northern censure: *Did you see that? Little Miss Promotion was brickin' it. Told you she wasn't up to command.*

Amala Yasir might counter: *You're too harsh, Frank; the chief's doing a good job.*

Barclay, still on trainee's best behaviour, would abstain.

Which left Connor, the new recruit, as deciding voter. Hawkins was well aware of his significance: somehow she had to keep him out of the *No* camp. But that wasn't going to be easy; plenty of officers had listened to Frank Todd over the years. What really worried her was that he could be right.

What if she wasn't up to this?

In reality, this sort of case was incredibly rare, despite what people might be excused for thinking given the consistency with which Hollywood churned out comparable scenarios.

Most murder cases not associated with terrorism or war were simple, isolated incidents, the results of overwhelming desperation or rage that usually burned themselves out within moments, leaving the killer either sated or contrite.

The difference between someone responsible for a crime of passion, and an individual who planned and committed compound homicidal acts over a protracted period, was immense. The latter demanded an almost inhuman state of mind. But it looked increasingly like that was what they were dealing with.

7

'Antonia, it's your mother. Tuesday morning. Your father says you've requested Christmas vouchers for that business-clothing store again. He'd be devastated if he knew I'd said anything, but I think he's hoping this year that you'll spend them on something a little more feminine. Truth be told, I think he's concerned for your health, so please don't stress him out by working right through the holiday period again. Your Auntie Joyce and—'

Hawkins pressed the button on her mobile to delete the message. There were two things her mother would never realize: first, that everybody knew Alan Hawkins was so laidback that he probably hadn't stressed about *anything* since 1978 – especially work-related clothing choices made by his eldest daughter – and second, that unless they apprehended this killer in the interim, for the first time in eight years, her daughter's routine excuse about having to work on Christmas Day might actually be true.

Hawkins dropped the phone in her bag and entered the underground station, heading for Scotland Yard, reminding herself that despite their mildly patronizing nature, her mother's awkward attempts to avoid any bad feeling were pretty harmless. Christine Hawkins was an ex-hospital ward sister and was therefore used to telling people what was best for them. And she'd been completely unable, once retired, to stop doing it.

Hawkins used her Oyster card at the barriers and arrived on the platform as the underground train drew in. Now, post morning rush hour, she found a seat straight away. Unfortunately, the carriage's only other occupants' subject of conversation was a little too close to home.

'Well, I ain't becoming a sad-case hermit just because there's some psycho out there,' the blonde girl said. 'What are the odds, anyway?'

'You're *so* going to die now,' the one with knitted leggings replied. 'That's like someone in a horror film saying "I'll be right back"!' They both snorted with laughter at her witticism.

Blondie and Leggings were seated opposite her. Neither had looked up from their mobile phones during the exchange. Their friend, Bangles, was toying with her heavily braided hair and vast pink earrings, watching herself in the reflection cast against the black void of the underground line beyond the window.

'My mate Sophie lives right near where the second one got killed,' Bangles told them. 'She's scared shitless, hardly left the house since it happened, and then she slags me off on Facebook 'cos I won't go round there.'

'She's paranoid,' Blondie sneered. 'Everyone is. Stick with us and you'll be fine. He only goes after girls on their own, anyway.'

The train began to slow for the next station, and the skinny-jean and leggings brigade moved towards the doors.

Hawkins watched them. For someone who spent a decent amount of her life trying to protect young people like those three, and who was old enough to be any of their mothers, she felt not even the beginnings of a maternal impulse.

Another point of contention between her and Paul.

You're thirty-five, Toni, he would say. *The bloody job will still be there in a few years.*

Patronizing bastard.

She checked herself, putting her bad mood down to the case and her resulting lack of sleep the previous night. She was still hoping that Hunter was wrong about the gore escalator thing, but that hadn't saved her from lying awake. She'd ended up writing full-on development reviews for three of her team, just to keep her mind from generating worst-case scenarios about what the killer might present them with just five days from now.

On Christmas morning.

Even her eventual descent into sleep hadn't provided shelter – she'd had a dream where she'd unwrapped her first Christmas present to find a severed head in an evidence bag.

She shuddered and turned to her paper as the train moved off again. Usually she ignored the media, but this morning every headline felt like a personal attack. There were no details about MOs or pictures of the bodies yet, but now that a third victim – and a semi-celebrity at that – was involved, the papers were full of nothing but.

The *Mirror*'s centre pages were headed **DEATH LOTTERY CLAIMS THIRD VICTIM**, above photographs of all the victims' prettiest sides.

Glenis Ward had probably never been referred to as a stunner – certainly not in the last thirty years – but one industrious researcher had dredged the Ward family album to produce a black and white shot of twenty-four-year-old Glenis wearing the runner-up sash in the Miss Butlin's Ramsgate pageant. What a second Tuesday in July 1973 that must have been.

Stop it.

Adjacent was a picture of the second victim, Tess Underwood. At forty-eight, Tess' relative youth and mildly more glamorous appearance afforded her a slightly larger photo. But what had obviously been one of those make-up-with-a-trowel-and-soft-focus beauty shoots couldn't compete with the image occupying at least 80 per cent of the remaining space.

The tabloids rarely required an excuse to print pictures of women who looked even half as good as Jess Anderton, and now that she was both involved and unable to object, they were making red-top hay.

Unfortunately, the papers hadn't been able to link the three women, either. Instead, the *Mirror* had gone for the random-target theory, printing a map of where the killer had struck already, along with supposedly helpful tips on how to reduce your chances of becoming a mark. Somehow their suggestions of self-imposed curfews, locking doors and joining the Neighbourhood Watch seemed of even less use than bracing yourself before being run over.

Hawkins turned the page.

The next spread was covered with images of the Andertons under the headline **DOWNING STREET'S SHATTERED FAIRYTALE**. There were shots of Charles and Jessica on their wedding day, with the prime minister, and at the Beckhams' most recent party. But the main picture of Charles Anderton leaving his office had been taken yesterday morning, shortly after Hawkins' visit.

Anderton had returned earlier in the day to his constituency home direct from a convention in Bath. He apparently hadn't been back to Hampstead or attempted to ring his wife since Saturday afternoon.

Hawkins had literally bumped into him on his way out of the door. He'd had a face so white that it was obvious her news was going to be no more than confirmation. A man didn't make Culture Secretary without being well connected, and if the press had already known his wife was dead, it was no surprise that word had reached Anderton. But it hadn't made her task any easier.

His pallid physiognomy had remained the same from the moment she'd arrived, along with a Community Support officer, officially to inform Anderton of his wife's demise and to provide personal assurance that the Met would bring her killer to justice.

As soon as they had shaken hands, it had been obvious that the politician's renowned charisma had died, at least temporarily, along with his wife. He seemed to have shrunk inside his tailored suit, his silver hair had started to look grey, and the creases of his face that usually spoke of great wisdom had only wanted to talk about the fact that he was approaching sixty.

Hawkins felt guilty now that her decision to break the news personally had been motivated by hope that he might be responsible for Jessica's murder.

It was the first time she had ever seen a politician cry.

8.

As Hawkins stood in the exit of St James' Park tube station, contemplating the short walk along a soaking Broadway, she wondered why she'd granted Paul custody of their only car without a fight. Admittedly, the fact that he had stronger relationships with most of their mutual friends meant she'd found less need for social commuting since their split, but that wasn't exactly a plus-point in itself.

Not having her own transport was making an already overloaded schedule almost unmanageable. She'd been at the office before seven that morning, cramming half a day's worth of paperwork into three quarters of an hour. At least her administrational autopilot was working as well as ever.

Festive crowds filled the pavement, umbrellas clashing, routes in constant states of adjustment to preserve momentum through the rain. Hawkins backed up as a group of gabbling youths emerged from the crowd and headed for the station entrance. They passed in a whooping haggle, a couple of the taller boys eyeing her up as they passed.

She made a point of looking disgusted, turning away to scan the street for a way that might provide some cover, finding none. There was no time to hang around until the rain stopped; Lawrence Kirby-Jones was waiting. And he was a man who took his role as head of the Specialist Crime Directorate more seriously than Hawkins had ever imagined possible. Of greater concern, though, was the fact she'd been summoned to meet him at New Scotland Yard, instead of Kirby-Jones' office at the Met's Becke House facility in Hendon.

She had already updated him on the small amount of progress in the investigation during their increasingly regular morning phone call. Initial results from the team regarding things like debt and previous interactions with the police weren't exactly encouraging: Glenis Ward had been a hypochondriac; Tess Underwood had missed a few mortgage payments prior to getting married. And Jessica Anderton had recently fielded volleys of mail from a zealous admirer called Derek who, at eighty-three, hadn't proved a plausible suspect, especially after the lengthy consolatory cuddle he'd required from the male detective sent to question him.

In short, the victims' lives remained frustratingly unconnected.

So, apart from being able to link the victims, their best chance of tracing the killer was still via the Taser. *Thinking of which* . . .

She found her mobile and selected Frank Todd's number. She had the DI and a couple of newly recruited constables looking at known suppliers of such weaponry. Their initial research had shown that, while public ownership of stun guns or Tasers was still illegal in the UK, hundreds were ordered online every year, and a good percentage made it through customs. They had replaced conventional firearms as tool of choice in bank robberies, and their use was on the rise.

He picked up on the fourth ring.

'Frank, it's Antonia. Any progress with the Taser?'

'Sort of.' He sniffed. 'We got that firearms consultant in like you said. He looked at the bodies, reckons it was the same medium power Taser used on all three. Some of these things go over two million volts now, but this one's more like eighty thousand. Killer probably went for that type because they sell in higher numbers, and customs don't go Spartacus if they find one.'

'What are our chances of tracing it?'

'Difficult to say. We can be semi-specific about the model now. Apparently it uses detachable nitrogen cartridges to fire the projectiles, although it can also be used in direct contact with the body if no cartridge is attached. He's used three cartridges so far, although they might not have been ordered with the weapon, and they have a ten-year shelf life, so there's no knowing how long he's had any of the gear. And there are loads of online suppliers.'

'OK, Frank.' Hawkins thought for a moment. 'Get the Borders Agency to send over a list of all similar weapons seized in the last ten years, including the addresses they were headed for. The killer may have ordered others that didn't get through. Even if the list's huge, at least we'll be able to check suspects against it.'

Todd agreed and rang off.

Hawkins checked her watch. She didn't have time to ring Yasir, who was looking into whether the killer could have sourced the Taser locally from one of the capital's illegal arms suppliers. It was less likely; those transactions were usually done in person, and he'd been too careful with everything else to make that sort of mistake. But it was possible.

She had less hope for their ongoing battle to discover a link to 1 a.m.

So far, research had produced no particular documented meaning linked to that time of day. Barclay had volunteered to look into whether the killer's MO might have been 'inspired' by music. According to his very thorough report, there had been several music tracks or albums called '1 a.m.' over the years, but he'd listened to them all, and none contained lyrics that pointed towards a potential motive. Apart from that, there seemed to be no film quotes, no Bible passages; no cultural references. The time, if it meant anything, had to be of personal significance to the killer, so they were unlikely to expose its meaning without first knowing who he was.

Hawkins buttoned her jacket and stepped onto the unsheltered pavement, straight into a gust of wind that whipped a stinging spray of rainwater into her face. She cursed herself for having left her umbrella in the office, drawing startled looks from those around her. Ignoring them, she kept moving, trying to shelter behind the biggest man she found going in her direction, still trying to imagine an angle from which the current state of the case would sound positive to her boss.

The good news was that the celebrity angle provided by Jessica Anderton's death had heightened the wider public's awareness of the potential danger. And greater alertness among the killer's target group should at least reduce the chances of losing another one.

Hawkins wiped away the rain dripping from her eyebrows and glanced up at New Scotland Yard. There were few more iconic symbols of modern policing, despite its modest origins as an office block.

Nearing the famous rotating sign, she noticed a group of about thirty people huddled near it, fending off the rain with umbrellas. This in itself was no surprise: the Yard was five minutes on foot from Buckingham Palace, and most guides included it in their tourist walkabouts. But this group was not only larger than usual; it had seen her heading for the Yard's entrance, and was now moving towards her.

Why hadn't she expected this? These people weren't tourists. They were reporters.

She batted away the first couple of Dictaphones, but within seconds she was surrounded.

'Are you involved with the Jessica Anderton murder inquiry?'

'Has anyone been arrested yet?'

'Is any woman in London safe while this killer is free?'

Her second mistake was to confirm that she was working on the case, by making some stupid comment about '… giving official statements when we're ready.' This only intensified the enthusiasm with which microphones were thrust into her face, and further blunted her progress.

Finally, she managed to trip on the pavement and sprawl into the arms of one of the hacks, who leered down at her and commented on how friendly the Met were these days.

By the time she had staggered across, fumbled her

pass onto the electronic scanner and made it through the security doors, she was soaked, angry and shaken.

She stood in the lobby, shivering, staring down anyone that dared to turn a gaze her way. And then she realized what she was doing, unconsciously. There was only one reason why anyone so dishevelled and embarrassed would remain in view of the reporters still laughing at her through the glass doors to her left.

Her next appointment – for which she was now late – was with a boss who hated her even when she was on time.

9.

The Yard's maze of indistinguishable offices was always a headache, but as she read '117-c' on what seemed like the millionth room sign, Hawkins wondered if a subconscious desire not to locate this one had delayed her even further.

She tapped on the open, frosted-glass door. 'Sorry I'm late, sir. It took me a while to find you.'

'Have a seat, Hawkins.' Lawrence Kirby-Jones didn't turn. Instead he maintained his sentry-like stance, towering over a frightened-looking potted plant as he stared out of the third-floor window.

At least if he kept his back to her, he wouldn't notice how ridiculously frizzy the hand-dryer in the ladies' toilets had made her hair.

Copies of all Tuesday's papers were laid out neatly on the desk in front of her. They looked untouched, but the DCS would already have scrutinized every word related to the case.

'What did you think of the press welcoming committee, Hawkins?'

'I think the . . . speed with which information leaked on this one has taken everybody by surprise, sir.'

'Perhaps.' He paused. 'I saw you arrive. Everyone entering the building has been getting that treatment, although

I must say that nobody else has handled it as badly as you did.'

She glared at his back.

Their working relationship had started so auspiciously several years ago, when he'd been installed as chief superintendent, that it was difficult now to remember where it all had gone wrong. Within three months of reading Hawkins' prolific arrest statistics, Lawrence Kirby-Jones' signature had appeared on the certificate of recommendation that propelled her to detective sergeant status; the first in a series of advances he'd overseen. But the higher Hawkins had climbed – ever closer to the glass ceiling designed to keep her from taking his job, perhaps – the further his benevolent-uncle mask had slipped, and the more enthusiastically he had battered her with his rulebook of sanctimony.

Kirby-Jones turned suddenly, breaking her recall. She met his gaze with a penitent smile. At least there was no improvized voodoo doll of *her* at Becke House.

Albeit in Hawkins' desk drawer.

The DCS practically goose-stepped to the chair opposite her, fastidiously twitching his suit trousers up before he sat.

'It's a pity that none of Mike's media expertise ever rubbed off on you,' he said.

Mention of the name surprised her.

Mike Maguire. He and Hawkins had worked together as detective inspectors on a number of successful cases under the DCS, but they hadn't spoken since Mike had been moved to Manchester six months before, on secondment.

64

The move had also ended their affair.

As far as she knew, nobody in the Met had ever found out, but she still confessed everything to Paul – her now ex-fiancé – soon afterwards. They'd tried to patch things up, but their disparities had thrived, and he had moved out three months ago. For a while afterwards, he had maintained a strict regime of calls and text messages aimed at rubbing her nose in her infidelity.

'So now even your—' Kirby-Jones stopped mid-flow, his glare telling Hawkins she had missed a few sentences in between. 'Did you leave the gas on, Chief Inspector?'

Nice work, Antonia. 'No, sir. Sorry.'

'I'll start again. I've spoken to the commander. He's disappointed this business about Anderton's wife got out so fast, because the time scale means the press was probably tipped off by someone on the inside. Which means we're now into damage-limitation. So, until further notice, even your immediate team is on a need-to-know basis. Understand?'

'Yes, sir.'

'Our friends outside are only the beginning.' He nodded towards the window. 'They may not have pictures or MO details yet, which counts out copycat killings for now at least, but it won't take them long.'

He paused, and Hawkins began summoning the courage to ask whether Eddie Connor would be the only additional officer in a murder investigation team still one member short.

Too late.

'Our ongoing media strategy,' Kirby-Jones continued, 'in case you were wondering' – the subtext 'and which you should have asked about' was obvious – 'will now be channelled through a dedicated spokesperson within your team. And based on today's performance, I'm sure it'll come as no surprise that you're off the hook for that job.'

A fresh bout of shouting signalled renewed excitement down in the street, and Kirby-Jones turned his head in response.

Hawkins took what felt like her first breath in minutes as he stood and retraced his steps to the window.

'The one good thing to come out of all *this*' – he turned back to her as he waved a dismissive hand at the noise below – 'is that it's given me some leverage with regard to personnel. Your team is on this full time until you hear otherwise, and I've secured you some support. You've already met the profiler . . . Hunter, is it? He comes highly recommended, anyway. But you need some permanent help as well. I'm sure you'll be pleased with who I've chosen.' Kirby-Jones looked at the crowd outside again. 'In fact, there he is now.'

Hawkins knew what was coming before she stood and walked over to join him.

Thirty feet below them, just about to wade into the seething crowd of reporters, was the only person who could have made her day any worse.

Mike Maguire.

10.

'Are you coming, Detective?' Kirby-Jones hovered in the doorway.

Hawkins nodded. Pretending she'd already forgotten they were going to meet Mike downstairs obviously wasn't working.

She followed the chief superintendent out of the office and along the corridor, struggling to match his long-legged stride as her mind raced. This whole thing was becoming a bad joke: the case alone was nuisance enough, but now she also had to contend with an ex-lover she hadn't spoken to in months.

What the hell did you say to someone after months without communication when your last words to him had been, *Text me your address and I'll post you your underwear?*

She'd picked up a rumour shortly after his move north that Mike wasn't enjoying life in Manchester, and had wondered if he might have returned to the US, where he grew up; his parents still lived in Philadelphia. But Hawkins had been doubtful. Ever since coming to England on an officer-exchange programme, Mike had loved London, and had decided to stay. He'd worked his way up in the Met, despite taking every opportunity to point out how alien to him this quaint little country remained. Now, it seemed, even Hawkins' equivocal ways hadn't managed to put him off coming back.

There was no let-up in Kirby-Jones' pace as they approached the final door leading to the Yard's lobby. The doors swung open and they strode out into the foyer.

Her eyes darted from face to face: a group of suited dignitaries signing in; two Biotech scientists she recognized from a previous investigation; the counter-terrorist officers who occupied the inner security gates like furniture.

'Take note.' Kirby-Jones pointed past her shoulder.

She turned to look at the bank of security monitors suspended above the main desk. On one of the large flat screens, entitled Main Entrance – Broadway, Hawkins saw a shot of the same group of reporters she had encountered earlier. Before them, a statuesque black man with arms raised, was playing to the crowd like some New-Age evangelist.

Mike.

In contrast to Hawkins' experience of them, however, the hacks appeared relaxed and compliant. Notes were being taken, and suddenly the group guffawed like a drunken football team at a comedy club.

Maguire always had been able to make even the most banal report sound to journalists like an invitation to open day at the government's restricted files room.

He'd be crowd-surfing next.

'Don't worry.' Kirby-Jones straightened his tie. 'I've already briefed him.'

A moment later, on-screen Mike moved away from the reporters, who began immediately to disperse. He disappeared from the camera's view and emerged beside the security officers inside the door.

Hawkins watched him being hand-scanned; swallowed

hard as he saw them and waved. He looked even sharper than she remembered, in a casual suit over a plain, open-necked white shirt.

He exchanged a few words with the duty officer, who reacted by laughing out loud and patting the American hard on the back before waving him through. Mike approached them. His smile was warm, and his brown eyes flicked between them alertly.

'Mike, good to see you.' Kirby-Jones' double-handed shake might as well have been a hug. 'Thanks for coming at such short notice.'

'My pleasure, Lawrence. Great to be back. Hey, Antonia.'

Lawrence!?

'Hi.' She nodded as her stomach turned over, trying desperately to keep the dismay from showing on her face when she suddenly remembered how awful her hair looked.

'Well, I must get back to Hendon,' Kirby-Jones said. 'Just wanted to say hello, but Hawkins can fill you in. We must play a round when the case is closed.' He smiled again at Mike and strode off, leaving them in uncomfortable silence.

Hawkins watched him go, wondering how the man always managed to make her feel insignificant. Usually his presence alone was enough; today, however, his exit had achieved the same thing.

And she really didn't have time to deal with ex-lovers, incensed or otherwise.

'Well, then . . .' she looked at Mike, removing the hand that had drifted up to her dishevelled hair, trying to think of something else to say.

Mike studied her before he spoke again, in the melodic Philadelphia accent she'd always found so irresistible. 'How's it going?'

'I'm . . . good.'

'And Paul?' There was no hint of sarcasm.

'He's fine.'

'That's great. You know I heard some rumour that you guys broke up?'

'Oh.' She didn't know where to look. 'We did.'

'For real? Damn, Antonia, I'm sorry . . .' He held up his hands. 'Look, you want to get some coffee?'

Hawkins nodded. Her only regret was when she realized he meant together.

11.

'After you, ma'am.'

Mike held the door of Café Noir for an elderly woman dressed head to foot in tweed before he followed Hawkins in.

They were the first words either of them had spoken since she'd suggested the four-minute walk from Scotland Yard.

There was a Starbucks on the corner, both nearer and less pretentious, but this place made reporters far easier to spot: the combination of discreet atmosphere and sound-absorbent décor attracted everyone from perjurers to mafia bosses. Not to mention higher-ranking cops.

They were shown to an enclosed booth with green velvet curtains and no hint of Christmas decoration, where they were given leather-bound menus.

'Just two strong coffees, thanks.' Hawkins handed her menu straight back to their waiter, who looked more Greek than French.

'Certainly.' The man's expression clouded for a second before he collected Mike's menu, whirled and left. Obviously coffee-only tables weren't big tippers.

'You went brunette,' Mike said without warning. 'That's fresh. Better, I mean.'

'Er, thanks.' *He wanted to talk about hair?*

He grimaced. 'That sounded a lot smoother in my head.'

'It's OK. I certainly wasn't expecting compliments.'

'You know what?' He sighed. 'I messed up, Toni – should've called. I just figured you and Paul deserved a chance.'

She studied him. He appeared genuine enough; maybe it was best to get this out of the way.

'Two coffees.' The waiter broke their eye contact as he leaned across to set out serviettes.

On the other hand, if Mike didn't care enough to be even *token* angry, then why should she?

She took the opportunity to dig in her bag for the investigation file. They'd have plenty of time to discuss their situation later, and not diving into a guaranteed argument now would give her time to think.

The waiter made a fuss of placing their coffees, milk and sugar bowl just so, and checked they had everything they required. His face creased again before he left. Perhaps it was a tic.

She handed Mike the folder. 'So how much has the DCS told you?'

He paused before reaching for the file. 'I got highlights, but I saw the news, too. Those guys are all over this.'

'Yep, they know everything except the MOs, and some finer details we've managed to hang on to.'

'So we're in trouble?'

She exhaled. 'Well, you're here, aren't you? Things have to get pretty desperate before they start dragging people in from all over the country. We're holding the next weekly brief in the canteen because there are too many of us to fit in the meeting room. Half of them I don't even know.' She dropped three sugar cubes into her coffee. 'As for the killer, all we've got is some rough CCTV footage of him leaving the first house, and a few witnesses who saw a man at the scene of the third murder in the right sort of timeframe. We aren't even sure how he's moving around.'

Mike began flicking through the case file.

'It's all the usual stuff,' she volunteered. 'But you should focus on the interview write-ups and the profiles of exes and family members with form. One possibility is that the killer could be Glenis Ward's dropout stepson – Glenis was the first victim, by the way. Gary Ward was the product of her late husband's previous marriage, and probably well past his approach-by date, given his lifestyle. Dad died three years ago, after which Gary lived with her, through necessity rather than choice, mind, thanks to his fondness for short-term loans and amphetamines. He and Glenis never gelled.'

'Could he be the guy seen at the Anderton's place?'

'No; wrong appearance. Witnesses consistently say that man was of Mediterranean descent. We don't have pictures, but neither of Gary's parents had roots outside the UK.'

'So you know where Gary is?'

'That's the thing. Nobody's heard from Gary since before Glenis died. The neighbours say he hadn't stayed at the house in weeks, after a series of late-night rows, but maybe he fancied the place to himself? He returns to facilitate stepmother's trip to the bottom of her bathtub, intending to frame it as suicide and inherit the kingdom as only surviving benefactor in her will. But in the process of knocking her off, he discovers a taste for homicide.'

Mike took over. 'Then he Houdinis his way outta there and starts looking for number two at random. It's neat, right? But you don't think that any more than I do. And it means you guys can't link him to the other victims.'

'It's early days with Jess,' Hawkins countered, 'but, yes, you'd struggle to find three less connected lives. As for area, the crime scenes just about qualify as south-east London, but they're spread out, and two of the three victims came originally from outside London.' She counted off on her fingers: 'Former-model turned socialite; ex-care worker now comfortable jeweller's wife; retired dinner lady stroke school sports supervisor, all of different generations. It's no surprise their paths didn't cross. Until they all got murdered by the same person, of course.'

Mike nodded. 'Any other suspects?'

As they drank their coffees, Hawkins explained about the remaining potentials, like ex-boyfriends or previous work colleagues – they were still trying to trace.

They were just beginning to knock around ideas about how to move forwards when her mobile rang.

'Hello?'

'Antonia, it's Connor. Do you want the good news, or the really shitty news?'

'Good first.'

'It's about the man seen leaving the Andertons' place.'

'Go on.'

'I'm standing in his front garden.'

12.

He needed sleep.

He'd had less than an hour last night, and not much more than that for weeks now. Even when he did go under he woke up screaming. The dreams had been getting worse again; in fact, he had begun to welcome moments like this, when he came round, realizing that his body had simply shut down for a while.

But he couldn't afford for it to happen in public.

He sat back in his chair, blinking slowly, looking around. Everything moved as if he was watching low-quality footage: jerky and out of focus. He rubbed his eyes, even though he knew the problem didn't involve them. He was nearing exhaustion. The number of consecutive hours over which he could function normally had begun to decrease, and recently his thoughts had been all but alien to him.

He couldn't carry on using drugs to stay sharp long term.

As if to emphasize the point, his temperature began to spike. He closed his eyes, all too aware of what would follow.

His body shook and his jaw clenched. It felt like a band was being tightened around his forehead. Rumbling silence built, quickly becoming a roar as he hunched, milling the heels of his hands into his temples. His body locked, and pain set in.

After what seemed like a long time, a level of blackness lifted behind his eyelids, and he felt his heartbeat beginning to slow. He dragged in a deep, tattered breath.

He wiped the sweat from his forehead and stood. His calves burned where they'd been braced against the chair legs, and he bent to massage the muscles.

Suddenly he froze, staring towards the source of the noise.

Someone had knocked at the door.

He waited for confirmation, every sense alert. Had they found him? And, if so, should he try to run, or stay and lie?

Another knock.

He swore silently. The Taser was in his holdall, fifteen feet away in the front room.

He edged into the hallway until he could see across to the glass-panelled front door. Light flooded through the semi-transparent sections, interrupted only by the unmistakeable shadow of somebody standing outside.

But no face appeared at the window, and no shout came. It was a salesman cold calling, something like that. They'd leave . . .

Then the handle dipped.

In seconds he was at the holdall, gripping the Taser's handle as he heard the lock turn.

The door opened. He straightened as the intruder moved out from behind it.

He only just stopped himself raising the weapon.

'Goodness!' His landlady staggered backwards and slumped against the wall, dropping her keys.

'Ms Peterson.' He started forwards, impressed at how naturally his alter ego resurfaced. 'Are you OK?'

The old lady sagged, her dress catching on the raised pattern of the wallpaper. 'Oh . . . yes, dear. You startled me . . . what in heaven's name *is* that?'

'This?' He waved the Taser, nonchalantly. 'It's a, uh, novelty remote control . . . for the TV. You know, *Star Trek*?'

'Well, I never.' She was breathing heavily. 'Oh, dear, I'm sorry to just come in like that, but when there was no answer I assumed you were out.'

'Actually, that's what I wanted you to think. I thought you were a double-glazing salesman.'

'Oh, I do apologize. It's just that I still haven't got round to having a letterbox put in that door and I wanted to leave you this.' She held out a small brown envelope. 'You gave me too much money for this week's rent.'

'How silly of me.' He smiled. 'Come and sit down. Get your breath back while I make some tea.'

She shuffled towards the sofa, frail neck and shoulders looking like they had trouble supporting her head.

He pocketed the Taser and closed the door.

WEDNESDAY

13.

'Antonia, it's your mother. We bumped into Paul in Waitrose yes-
terday, and he said that last time he saw you he thought you'd lost
weight. He still misses you, you know. Anyway, I think your father's
now concerned that you're not eating properly, so I've made you a
lasagne, which I've broken down into portions and frozen, so please
come round and collect them. You must stay for dinner, too, although
we can't do tonight or tomorrow——'

'Message saved.'

Hawkins dumped the phone in the cup holder on the
dashboard of the car, vowing to call her mother back
later. She watched a man with a newspaper wander slowly
past, trying to read as he walked. The car window was
streaked with rain, but she could still make out the bright
SUN EXCLUSIVE header. Today's headline would ensure
champagne bonuses for those involved at the paper, but
she was more inclined to agree with Connor's reaction.
And *really shitty news* was putting it mildly.

Her gaze returned to the wing mirror she'd adjusted to
frame the house thirty yards back, and the garden from
where Connor had called the previous day.

This part of Silvertown, a residential area not far from
Docklands, was also near London City airport, its relative
tranquillity shattered every few moments by the sound
of screaming jet engines. No wonder the locals got up
early.

81

Foot and road traffic was slowly increasing. Unfortunately, none of it had yet carried any sign of their target. She unfolded her copy of the *Sun* and studied the grainy image of Jessica Anderton sitting next to the man they were waiting for.

'You think he's taken off?' she asked the detective inspector in the passenger seat.

'No way. This dude isn't even *expecting* us.' Mike grinned. 'What's the word Connor's buddy used about this guy: a *fuckwit*?'

Connor's contact, Ian, worked at the *Sun*, and had called yesterday to warn them what would be on the next day's front page. Apparently Jessica-bloody-Anderton had been having an affair, and the Mediterranean-looking man outside the Andertons' place was her boyfriend – the same boyfriend who, upon her death, had immediately sold his story to the *Sun*.

So much for grief.

The effects had been instantaneous. Kirby-Jones' ability to convey extreme dissatisfaction without shouting was renowned, but that morning he'd sounded more like a concerned care-home worker.

Please sit down, Miss Hawkins, we have some bad news.

The crowd of reporters at Scotland Yard had tripled in size since yesterday, and the press office was about to implode. And now, supposedly grieving widower Charles Anderton had disappeared 'on important business'.

The fact that Ian had risked his job by giving them the boyfriend's address was small consolation; even smaller now they'd spent almost twenty-four hours staking the place out and the bastard still hadn't come home.

And, as if to compound Hawkins' misery, his choice to sell the story and splash his face across every coffee-shop table in the country reduced his chances of being the killer to almost nothing.

Her hand drifted to the door pocket of the car, to the pack of – as yet unopened – Marlboro Lights. She tapped a couple of fingers on the plastic wrapping and let out a long sigh. Things weren't *that* bad.

Yet.

'Anyway,' Mike offered, 'at least you aren't up on that bridge with John.'

Hawkins forced a smile. Since they'd arrived an hour before to relieve Connor and a couple of the new recruits, who had been there all night, Barclay had been sulking on an overhead footbridge 200 yards behind them.

She felt guilty about sending him up there to cover the opposite end of the street. He'd probably turn up tomorrow with a rotten cold, but she'd tried making allowances for his increasingly bad health before, and nothing made any difference. Since joining the team, Barclay's persistent state of sickness had earned him the nickname 'Maraca', thanks to the number of pills he took on a daily basis. The job soon showed newcomers, in every sense, what they were made of, and yet here he was. At least it had stopped raining. Besides, she'd done her share of purgatory as a junior detective, so why should anyone else get special treatment?

Mike turned to her. 'Remember what happened the last time we staked out together?'

Hawkins looked back at the wing mirror, suddenly uncomfortable. 'I think we'd get *ourselves* arrested for doing that here.'

'It was fun, though, right?'

She'd have to provide her own distraction. Fortunately one occurred.

'Hold on, is that him?'

'Where?' Mike bit, shifting in his seat, trying to follow her gaze. 'I can't see past this goddamn van.'

'Sit still, he's coming straight for us. Thirty feet.'

'We need positive ID before we move. You sure?'

Actually, Hawkins was pretty certain that the perma-tanned, track-suited granddad Mike couldn't yet see probably wasn't their guy, but he'd served his purpose.

'Oh, wait, no. It isn't him.' She did her best to look disappointed.

'No, but *that* is.'

Mike was out of the passenger seat before she had time to react. She turned to look out of the rear window just in time to catch Barclay crossing the road, pointing at something, or some*one*, she couldn't see.

She wrenched the key from the ignition and opened the door, standing up to look back down the street. She couldn't have been more obvious but, thanks to Mike, their cover was probably blown already.

A dark, olive-skinned man had just entered his garden and was making his way towards the front door. He wore jeans and a tan sports jacket over a creased white shirt.

It was definitely their guy. Barclay was closing on him, but she couldn't see Mike. She set off up the street.

'Marcus De Angelo?' Hawkins heard Barclay say as he moved past the gate.

She picked up her pace, although she was still fifteen yards away.

'Fuck off.' The guy struggled with his keys in the door, as if the lock wasn't working properly.

'We'd like to talk to you.' Barclay said.

'You're trespassing, man.'

'Met Police. We need to ask you some questions.'

De Angelo spun round. '*Police?*'

Hawkins saw his fists clench. He was a big guy, looked like he spent a fair amount of time at the gym. Suddenly, Barclay appeared even more wiry than normal. He shouldn't have approached De Angelo alone. She reached the gate just as Barclay went for his badge.

Then De Angelo punched him.

Barclay sprawled backwards into her, and the pair of them crashed to the ground.

'Shit! Are you OK?' Hawkins struggled to free herself from under the trainee, who groaned before launching into a coughing fit. She stood up in time to see the front door slam.

She glanced back at Barclay, who was fighting his way up onto an elbow. It must have been a good shot; he wasn't going anywhere for a few minutes, and there was still no sign of Mike.

She'd have to go in alone.

She ran over and tried the handle, relieved when the door opened into a narrow hallway. 'Mr De Angelo?' she shouted. 'DCI Hawkins, Met Police. Can we talk?'

Nothing.

'I'm coming inside.'

She edged into the hall, checking the stairs to her left. He wouldn't have cornered himself up there. Which left three exits from the hallway: two archways to her right and one door at the end of the hall, closed.

She moved to the first arch and leaned in. A lounge with a leather three-piece, two potted plants, one big-screen TV. But no De Angelo.

Hawkins edged towards the second archway, heart battering her ribs, sliding along with her back against the wall. *What the hell was she thinking?* She'd already broken protocol by entering the house, not to mention the fact she was trespassing, while De Angelo had already shown disregard for police authority, and that he was loose with his fists. He could come at her from anywhere, possibly armed. Plus fifty per cent of her back-up had disappeared, and the other half had been knocked on its arse. Yet here was an exposed Antonia Hawkins, casually chasing a potential murderer into his lair.

Suddenly there were noises from deeper inside the house, and the light at the bottom of the door at the end of the hall showed brighter, as if another had been opened beyond.

He was going out at the back.

She ran to the door and flung it open, but De Angelo was already outside. She saw the concentration on his face through the glass; heard the key in the outer lock.

Shutting her in.

She shot forwards and grabbed the handle, forcing it down. Their eyes met through the glass. He was inches away, but she saw the look of relief cross his face when they both realized it was locked.

'Sorry, darling.' He winked. 'Maybe next time.'

De Angelo turned and ran down the path, leaving Hawkins no choice except to watch their only lead escaping.

But as he opened the tall gate at the end of the garden, his luck changed.

Mike's powerful frame blocked his escape, and this time it was De Angelo's turn to be the smaller man. They both said something she couldn't hear through the glass, and then De Angelo swung at him.

Mike swayed, evading the fist. In the same motion, he stepped into De Angelo's body and, using the flailing arm as a lever, flattened him against the brick wall opposite.

He turned and produced a pair of Plasticuffs, raising his eyebrows at her. Hawkins nodded her approval and watched Mike read De Angelo his rights.

14.

Despite the careers advisor at school suggesting she train as a nanny, Hawkins had never liked the idea of looking after other people's children. And, as she formally introduced the room's occupants to various recording devices, the twenty-eight-year-old sitting four feet away was reminding her why.

'I didn't kill nobody,' Marcus De Angelo repeated as soon as she'd finished. He looked like a defiant teenager, slumped in his plastic chair, staring at the interview room's dirty grey wall somewhere above her and Mike's heads.

'So you keep telling us.' It was the thirteenth time he'd said the same thing since they'd left Silvertown.

'I had no reason to do her in. She was a good shag.'

'How romantic.' Hawkins couldn't resist. 'I can't believe we ever suspected you.'

De Angelo responded with a patronizing smile.

'We just wanted to ask you some questions, Marcus.' Mike leaned forwards in his chair. 'You got *yourself* arrested when you got all Muhammad Ali with our officer.'

'Little prick – eyeballed me all the way here.'

'We'll come to that.' Hawkins took over. 'First tell us if you knew either Glenis Ward or Tess Underwood.'

'Not that I remember.' De Angelo wasn't taking this seriously at all. 'But I've known a lot of girls, if you get my drift.'

'Ever kill any of *them*?' Mike asked.

'Fuck off, mate.' De Angelo's hand returned to the mark on his cheek where Mike had braced him against the wall. 'Or I'll have you done for GBH.'

Hawkins shot a sideways glance at her colleague, warning him to back off. De Angelo still hadn't requested his solicitor's presence, and she didn't want to encourage him, but this display of confidence worried her. He obviously knew they had very little linking him to Jessica's murder, let alone either of the others.

'If you're innocent,' she said, 'why didn't you come forward two days ago?'

De Angelo held Mike's stare for a few more seconds before transferring his gaze back to her. 'Reason's right there in front of you, darling.'

'For the record,' Hawkins said, 'Mr De Angelo is referring to a copy of today's *Sun* newspaper, dated December twenty-first. And why is that, Marcus?'

'I was doing her.' De Angelo smirked. 'And they paid me ten grand to talk about it. I don't reckon your offer would have been so generous. So what else do you want to know?'

She paused, mainly to ensure De Angelo didn't hear the rising temper in her voice. 'We'd like to hear your side of the story.'

'Don't you read?'

Hawkins picked up the paper. The headline shouted: **MY AFFAIR WITH MURDERED JESSICA**, above an image of De Angelo's face. She began flicking through the pages.

'Even the *Sun* gets things wrong occasionally, Marcus.'

She kept her tone casual. 'Sometimes by mistake, other times to sell more papers. Have you read it through?'

Silence.

'Interesting.' She had his attention. 'Shall we check some key facts, just for your peace of mind?' Still no response, but he had started chewing his lower lip.

'This is nice.' Hawkins paused at a double-page spread covered with male-model style shots of De Angelo, and a biographical interview. He certainly had the looks to sell papers, with his chiselled physique and shoulder-length black hair. 'You hide your grief very . . . professionally.'

'I'm used to the attention.'

Hawkins arrived at the centre pages, where another large, flatteringly lit photo of De Angelo accompanied his account of the affair.

She laid the tabloid on the table and sat back. 'Just give us a brief summary of what you told them.'

De Angelo sighed, dropped his head back and stared at the ceiling, as if weighing his options. Then he began to talk, in a tone that suggested he was repeating himself for the hundredth time.

'My company installs air conditioning. I met her about two months ago when I gave her a quote for some work on their other gaff in Surrey. Apparently, good old Charlie was off giving some speech about how good the Olympics were. She was bored.' He grinned. 'So I asked if her old man took care of business at home. Ten minutes later, we were at it.'

Hawkins nodded. It seemed Jessica had been suffering from underappreciated housewife syndrome, despite the Anderton's happy-couple image. She wrote herself a reminder to check the intelligence team's progress chasing up the other 'business' contacts on Jessica's phone records.

'And how many times did you hook up after that?' Mike asked.

'Not many. Four or five.'

'Where at – her place?'

'No, they never did have that work done. Well, not by me, anyway – I only went there the one time. After that she came to mine. Safer that way, with no nosy neighbours watching out for her all the fucking time.'

'So why'd you show up at their home in Hampstead on Sunday?'

De Angelo tried to hide a look of surprise, but his smirk dissolved.

'All right,' he said, after a few seconds. 'We'd arranged to meet that morning, my house, ten o'clock. But she never showed. Usually if something came up she'd let me know, but this time I got nothing. I tried calling, just kept getting the answer phone. Anyway, I knew she was in London and that Charlie boy was away, so I went round there. But there was no answer when I knocked on the door and the curtains were closed, so I left. Wasn't till the next morning I found out she'd been murdered, or whatever.'

'And then you decided to contact the papers rather than the police,' Hawkins said.

De Angelo shrugged.

Hawkins couldn't escape the thought that it wasn't just artists whose true value was often only realized posthumously: Jessica was dead; soon to be followed by her husband's career, and all this arsehole cared about was money. But as she drew breath to ask another question there was a knock at the door. It opened, and Connor's head appeared.

'Sorry to interrupt, ma'am. Could I have a minute?'

Hawkins paused the session, then she and Mike stepped out into the corridor to join him.

The interview suite at Colindale Police Station was unusually quiet even for a Wednesday afternoon in Christmas week, but Connor kept his voice low nonetheless.

'Hope this doesn't mess things up in there' – he held out an A4 sheet – 'but your man has an alibi.'

The faxed image was grainy black and white, but Hawkins realized straight away that it wasn't the topless young woman on the sun lounger she was supposed to be looking at; it was the guy rubbing lotion on her.

Mike beat her to it. 'That's De Angelo.'

'Points for you.' Connor prodded him. 'Ian sent this over just now. The photo never made it to print, but apparently she's the next Jordan or something. It was taken on Bondi Beach in Australia last week – he checked with the photographer. Last Sunday, as it turns out.'

Hawkins studied the bottom corner of the image, and just made out the date signature. The day Tess Underwood was killed.

Mike said, 'So, unless De Angelo is Superman, he can't get back to the UK in time to be our perp.' He turned to Hawkins. 'Looks like your boy isn't the one.'

'It's OK.' She handed the picture back. 'He wasn't a strong suspect, anyway. But we'll need to see the original of this, and check the dates with passport control.'

'I'm waiting for the Home Office to call me back.'

Connor began walking away. 'And John's on his way to collect the full set of photos on disc from Ian.'

'Thanks, Eddie,' Hawkins called as the DS reached the stairs. 'Good work.'

She turned back to Mike with a wry smile. 'But before we give our friend Marcus the great news, let's see what else he knows.'

15.

De Angelo had his eyes closed when Hawkins and Maguire re-entered the interview room.

Mike managed to make him jump by slamming the door. 'Up and at 'em, Marcus.'

'Let's continue.' Hawkins sat down.

De Angelo stretched. 'Get me a coffee and I'll think about it.'

'In a minute.' She held down the red button on the recording equipment until the light reappeared. 'Interview resumed at nine forty-eight. Present are Detectives Hawkins and Maguire, and Mr De Angelo. So, Marcus, if you didn't kill Jessica Anderton, who did?'

'How should I know?' He yawned. 'Isn't it your job to find out?'

'We will,' Mike said, 'but this doesn't need to be tough if we're smart here.'

'Yeah? How's that?'

'Look at it like this. You tell us who you think killed Jessica, then we go do some investigating. We bag the guy, he gets convicted and you're home free.'

'What if I don't fancy telling you shit?'

'That's your prerogative, sure enough. But the faster we eliminate you from our enquiries, the sooner you get outta here.'

Hawkins saw a flicker of anxiety cross De Angelo's

expression. Mike had obviously seen it, too, as he glanced at her before he continued, his voice suddenly softer: 'What's up, Marcus. Don't you wanna go home?'

De Angelo's expression reverted to its original, cocky state, but there had definitely been something there.

'And what made you panic earlier,' she joined in, 'sufficiently that you would punch a police officer?'

'I told you.' De Angelo was struggling to maintain his composure. 'I'd happily go home. Would've been there yesterday except I didn't want to get banged up. No point sitting around where you lot could find me. Plan was to lay low until you lot caught the guy who did it, yeah? No harm done.'

'Well, no harm done except to one of our officers.' Hawkins let her expression become more serious. 'You know this won't be a short custodial sentence. Assaulting a police officer can land you in jail for up to a year.'

'You can't put me away for that long! Not for lamping some little prick!'

'Maybe not,' she continued, 'but I promise you, Marcus, charges for resisting arrest, attempted assault on a second officer, and withholding evidence without a good reason won't help your case. And pretty boys like you are always popular in the prison showers.'

De Angelo sat up a little straighter. 'What do you mean "without a good reason"?'

'Well,' she said evenly. 'Suppose you thought you were putting yourself in physical danger by telling us the truth? That's why you didn't come forward, and why you ran. In that case, the charge of withholding evidence might be . . . overlooked.'

De Angelo's gaze drifted into the distance, before he closed his eyes and his head dropped.

'Come on, Marcus.' Mike's tone was practically that of an older brother now. 'We know you didn't kill Jessica, but let's get this done so we can all grab some lunch.'

When De Angelo's muted reply came, his head stayed down, but the *EastEnders* accent had softened.

'Anderton knew all right? About me and Jess. I don't know how, but he knew.'

No wonder Charles Anderton had looked sick during their brief meeting on Tuesday. He had known news of his wife's affair would surface eventually.

And even though it provided him with a convincing motive for Jessica's murder, he hadn't said a word in his defence.

Suddenly, his important business trip seemed unlikely.

'Go on,' Hawkins coaxed.

'She turned up at mine the other day,' De Angelo continued, 'white as a fucking sheet. When she calmed down enough to talk, she said Charlie had told her he knew. Said he didn't care about us, but if the story ever got out we'd be sorry.'

'Those were his exact words?'

'Yeah, well, something like that. No threats exactly.' He looked up at them. 'But she said there was this look in his eyes, you know?'

'So why did you go to the papers?'

De Angelo shook his head. 'I'd already tried to sell the story once before, but they weren't offering decent money. After she died it was different, though. They called *me*, talking big numbers this time. I thought Anderton would be too caught up in it to worry about me. Anyway, I was booked on a flight to Italy this afternoon.'

'So you thought you'd make a quick ten thousand and disappear?'

'Yeah, couldn't see anything wrong with that. I stayed at a mate's house while we did the interviews and stuff. Just went home to pack my gear, but when your geezer turned up and I realized he wasn't a reporter, I thought Anderton had sent him to do me in. When he reached into his coat I freaked out.'

Half an hour later, Hawkins watched as De Angelo was escorted downstairs, where he would be cautioned and released. They had a video statement and a guarantee from him that he'd testify against Anderton should the need arise. In return, she'd promised to put in a good word when his assault trial came up.

She handed De Angelo's passport to Mike. 'Can you deal with that?'

'No problem.'

'And you can stop looking smug now.'

'Hey, I can't take all the credit – you catch on fast.'

'We're assuming De Angelo isn't just a very convincing liar.'

'No way.' Mike was smiling now. 'Ian was right about that guy. He's a fuckwit.'

'What makes you so sure?'

'I've worked these kiss-and-tell deals before. That story was worth at least thirty thousand.'

16.

The figures lined the perimeter of the room, each silhouette barely visible in the darkness. Some named, others broken; motionless like granite sentinels. His toys.

Outside, lightning made silhouettes of the branches on the dead oak tree. Light flicked across the room; revealing the effigies. He scanned their features and recoiled.

Every face was his father's.

A rumbling sound began. At first he thought it was thunder, but then he realized it was the collective voice of the pack. Then the mob started to jeer and chant, cajoling him to leave the sanctuary of his bed. To begin the intimidating journey towards the landing.

He covered his eyes, willing it to end, but their screams grew louder in response. Then, as suddenly as they had begun, the crowd became silent, allowing him to hear a fragile voice.

'Aren't you going downstairs?'

He lowered his hands and looked at the little girl standing beside the bed. A diminutive child, no older than he.

'You always do,' she said, 'in the end.'

He stared at the door, weighing his options. Eventually, he slid one foot out from under the covers and hung it over the edge of the mattress. But, as he moved, the wooden pillars at each corner of his bed began to change and stretch. He just had time to withdraw his leg and curl into a ball as a cage grew around him, entwining above his head into a tangled mass of jagged, tapering stems.

He looked sideways across his knees, out through the latticework to where the girl remained just beyond.

'Well?' She cocked her head. 'What are you waiting for?'

He sat for a moment, too afraid to move. Then his hands reached out and gripped the most delicate part of the structure. He pulled, but the slender limbs resisted, sharp edges digging into his skin. He stood, bending over in the confined space, and kicked out, twice, three times. But the structure held, while the toy sentries howled mock encouragement.

'Oh, dear.' The girl leaned closer. 'Maybe you should use this?'

She posted a small hatchet through the gap.

He took it, seating the handle carefully in his palm, wrapping his other hand on top, the way his father showed him. So he wouldn't get blisters. He searched the cell's inner surface for signs of weakness. Then he lined up the weapon and drew it back.

He brought the hatchet down, flinching as it cracked into the blackened limb. The blade jerked and dug in, firing splinters as a cheer rose from the horde. In the same instant, his bedroom window erupted inwards, its shattered glass slung across the room by the huge gust of wind that swept in behind, knocking him off balance. But he gripped the wooden handle and hung on.

When the wind had died he steadied himself and pulled the hatchet free. The wood had fractured.

'Harder!' The crowd chanted.

He raised the weapon and took aim again. The toys roared as the blade closed on its target, but then everything switched into slow motion: the trees outside froze at perilous angles; the wind tearing at his skin became a gentle push; and the surface of the cell wall began to change.

He tried to stop, but the hatchet moved on.

The branches were reordering themselves, their craggy shapes blending into a familiar form, becoming recognizable as a woman's face.

Her *face.*

He cried out as the weapon made contact, and her perfect features exploded into tiny wooden fragments that hung before him in the heavy air. The girl's laughter filled his ears for a split second before the rest of the world suddenly reverted to its normal pace.

The spectators shrieked anew, and the wind became a brick wall once more, driving the shards of her shattered face into his skin, where they stung like hot needles. He screamed.

Then, as suddenly as it had started, the pain was gone. The wind stopped and he blinked his eyes open. The wooden cage had disappeared and his toys no longer stood. The sky had cleared, and moonlight glowed gently through the undamaged window. Once more the room looked just how he remembered it.

'Good.' The girl pointed towards the landing. 'Now you can go. Just try not to get scared, OK?'

He stared at her for a second before she nudged him. 'Go on, silly. I won't watch.'

She skipped out of the room, pulling the door closed behind her.

He waited till her footsteps had faded before he climbed out of bed, and stood looking at the door. There was nothing stopping him now. He took a tentative step.

Everything remained still, the silence in the room broken only by the swish of a gentle breeze stirring the fields of corn out on the farm. He looked outside. The sky was calm, and to the south he saw the bridge that marked the edge of his father's land.

His bed socks skimmed the floorboards as he approached the door, but a familiar knot grew in his stomach as he reached for the handle. Would things be any different this time?

There was only one way to find out.

He pulled, and the door swung open.

17.

He stared into the darkness, waiting for his eyes to adjust. It took him a moment to realize he was looking at the ceiling of a room not from his past, but from the present.

Awake.

Feeling now the cold sweat on his skin and the rapid beating in his chest, he lay still, waiting for the dream's intensity to fade. Somehow, he had been spared the harrowing experience that concluded his recurring nightmare. And, beyond its immediate distress, at least his body felt rested.

He began using logic to calm himself. Psychological trauma was necessary; he had begun this campaign for a reason. No individual's suffering was too great a sacrifice. And in order to release his mind from its shackled state, it was necessary to complete the entire sequence.

To eliminate *all* his tormentors.

With that thought his strength began to return, the vision of his future becoming clear once more. He held the image until it dissolved, but it left him energized.

Ready for the next stage.

He glanced over as a breeze lifted the blind away from the window, its knife-edge chill stirring the hairs on his arms. The resulting shaft of synthetic streetlight illuminated the far wall. According to the clock, it was 7:32 p.m.

He powered up the laptop and showered while the ageing

technology organized itself. Fifteen minutes later, he typed the name of the place they met into a search engine, and pressed Enter.

The typical mixture of results appeared, and he scanned them before selecting the second entry. He watched as the Nirvana's Touch Spiritualist Centre website appeared element by element, and he clicked on the 'Meet Us' heading.

For a long time the screen remained blank, but eventually the page appeared. The organization's head clairvoyant, Chris Henderson, enthused at him from the centre of the screen, flanked by photographs of two women; neither the one he was looking for.

The photos were named, and he scrolled down the page, tapping a finger against the table, considering each. The name he remembered, Summer Easton, was not among them; although in her line of work, they probably changed on a regular basis. Instead he studied faces, staring into each set of eyes, past intense make-up and heavy gems, in search of the woman he had not seen for almost a year.

But she wasn't there.

He sat back and chewed a fingernail, suppressing his irritation.

He spent almost two hours on Facebook and similar sites, viewing hundreds of profiles, none of them hers. Then he sat, thinking about how else she could be traced.

She had referred to herself as a psychometrist, a specific type of spiritual medium who claimed an ability to contact the deceased via possessions they had treasured in life. He'd been sceptical, but Easton's charisma was compelling. And if *he* had been misled, there would be others who still believed…

He leaned forwards and typed **Psychic Fan Forum Summer Easton.**

The list appeared and immediately he selected the first result, which contained matches for every word except Easton. He felt a flicker of anticipation as the page opened to reveal a long text conversation between five users.

Three-quarters of the way down, he read the words, 'Set free by Psychic Summer'.

He read the whole string, alert for clues to where any of the meetings had taken place. He banged a fist on the desk. Nothing. All these idiots wanted to do was congratulate the counterfeit bitch.

He rested his head in his palms, slow in, fast out breaths warming the heels of his hands. Suddenly a pinging noise from the laptop dragged his attention back to the screen:

2 other users are online now. Do you wish to join Psy-Chat?

He stared at the text.

If he connected, could he be traced?

There were no details or pictures of him on this hard drive, so even in the unlikely scenario that a police hacker hijacked his system, they would find nothing. And this laptop had no web camera, so neither could he be spied upon without his knowledge. He was also using a dial-up modem, which meant download speed was pitiful but there was no traceable IP address, as there would have been on a broadband system.

So there was no risk.

He clicked on the link and completed the basic membership form using one of his unregistered email addresses, and the random initials he used for his online persona.

Welcome JJ. You have joined Psy-Chat live!

A stream of messages started filling the screen as people flung inane jargon at one another. He watched their dialogue, noting phrases and temperament, preparing to enter their world.

He closed his eyes and assumed his psychological disguise. It became more brittle every time he used it, but it was necessary. His eyelids lifted, while a slight pulse in his jaw was the only other physical sign of his intense concentration. His fingers found the keyboard and the first message began to appear.

He spent a further ninety minutes traipsing through conversations with dozens of other users, ever more frustrated at their inability to tell him what he needed to know.

The next time he looked at the clock it was approaching 11 p.m. And still he had no idea where to find Summer Easton.

He grabbed the laptop, about to launch it at the wall. But he stopped himself, aware that without it he had no chance at all of locating his next target. He replaced the computer on the table and eased back in his chair.

And then he saw it.

The top corner of the screen displayed a list of recent users to join the chat room. He had contacted most of them already, but not the one at which he now stared.

Faith Easton.

He clicked on the name. The attached image was of a much older woman than the one he was searching for, but perhaps that was even better.

He refreshed his disguise and typed.

JJ: Hi Faith, from your daughter's biggest fan!

The message jumped into the conversation window. The cursor blinked, and for a moment he worried that he was being ignored. But then the words he had hoped for appeared:

Faith is typing a reply.

He waited, allowing himself for the first time that day to envisage the terror in Summer Easton's eyes dissolving as she slipped into oblivion.

But without focus and restraint now, that moment would never come.

FE: Hi JJ. How do you know Summer?

Anticipation tugged at him, but he maintained his composure.

JJ: She helped me contact my wife's spirit last year. But I have a friend who needs her gift, too. His sister was killed recently and he feels so sad. I know Summer can help him, but she isn't with the Nirvana's Touch centre any more. Is there any way I can contact her?

Again he waited. Had he been convincing enough in those two short messages? The seconds stretched.

Then Faith Easton replied:

FE: Of course. Summer's with a travelling fair called Old Glad Soul's Roadshow. Here's their website.

He breathed.

JJ: Thanks Faith, you've really made my day. I'll be sure to let you know how it goes :-) See ya!

He clicked the link attached to her last message and watched as a new webpage appeared.

The low-budget site showed an after-dark photograph of around twenty scattered stands, lights ablaze in each awning. Scrolling down, he saw images of the performers: 'Miles the Lion Master' followed 'Spiritplayer' and 'Knife-man Finn'.

He found her three faces from the end.

'Psychic Summer' was almost unrecognizable from the woman he had met the previous year. She had slimmed considerably, almost too far, and had obviously embraced the traveller look. Vivid auburn hair had replaced blonde, and she now had a nose ring.

But his search was over.

He returned to the top of the page and clicked the 'Itinerary' heading, scanning the list of locations and dates. They were coming to London, but not for another two months, and his eye was drawn to the listing for the current week.

Brighton.

He stood and walked a few paces, thinking it through. An attack outside London would confuse the police even further. He could make it to the coast and back without trouble, although he would need to conduct a preliminary visit to locate the fair and assess the vicinity.

A disguise would be necessary throughout both journeys, as they would undoubtedly trawl the transport network's CCTV for images of him once Easton was dead.

This new development would also put extra pressure on his schedule. He needed to dust this place down, and pack a bag with some essentials. Yesterday's unexpected interruption had demonstrated that the need to vanish might arise without warning, and that leaving an apartment full of evidence would be unwise in the extreme. In addition to the disguise, he would wear anti-contamination clothing and gloves whenever he came here once the place was clean. His resulting appearance could be explained as someone carrying out DIY or vermin control should he face another surprise visitor.

Nobody there knew him, of course, so moving on again would be easy. Two homes; two identities. Cash-in-hand lodger status came with many advantages, like the phone line in his landlady's name.

He returned to the laptop and went to the BBC News website. It was no surprise to see he was still making headlines, and he felt a wave of exhilaration when he pictured everyone's reaction to yet another perfectly planned execution.

He scanned the various stories connected to his last

victim, his attention alighting on a video file of that morning's police press conference. He clicked on the link.

After buffering for a long time, the media file opened to show an empty lectern, but the splashy ambient noise suggested every news agency was present in some form. His power was growing: police, press and public; all petrified.

Seconds later, camera flashes accompanied the Met's latest figurehead to the podium. The spokesman was black and, at well over six feet tall, had commanding physical presence. He'd been mildly intrigued when the Met had initially wheeled out Michael Maguire. Media-friendly and sharper than most, the DI had looked like a threat at first. But while broad shoulders and stark assurances might fool the masses, everyone knew Jessica Anderton's death was a major coup. And he saw desperation in the detective's eyes.

His satisfaction grew as Maguire's promises of proaction and results came under fire from the assembled reporters. Then he smiled, as he contemplated the even greater surprises he had in store for the police.

THURSDAY

18.

'*Antonia, it's your mother. There are only three days until Christmas and I'm having a complete nightmare with the dinner. No sooner do I finish the nut strudel than Auntie Irene's on the phone, telling me how last year at Sylvia's they had homemade Apple Jalousie. So now I have to make some, but your father's tried every shop in Bushey High Street and none of them has even heard of vanilla beans. Anyway, if you could just find somewhere to buy . . .*'

Hawkins didn't end the call, but she was no longer listening to her mother's words.

Because Casanova was coming straight for her.

She'd been trying to ignore his smarmy grin from across Gatwick's main terminal for almost ten minutes. Fear halted his progress temporarily when a gang of children with potentially suit-ruining ice creams crossed his path, but then he continued undeterred.

Hawkins looked around, frantically searching for a reason to bolt from her seat without looking like she was simply running away. But options were limited by her need to stay within sight of the arrivals gate, through which Charles Anderton was shortly due to appear.

She missed her chance.

'Hello.' Casanova's accent was straight off the Savile Row peg. 'Mind if I sit down?'

She lowered her phone. 'Would it make any difference if I did?'

He smiled and arranged himself on the seat beside her. Obviously not.

Casanova produced a silver cigarette case. 'Sorry to butt in – don't usually like to – but I'm en route to the smoking area and I seem to have mislaid my lighter. Would you happen to have one?'

'No!' She practically had to shout her reply over a deafening tannoy announcement. 'Sorry.'

'Oh, no problem, I've found mine now,' he said, without seeming to look. He jabbed a thumb towards the exit. 'Care to join me for one?'

'I don't smoke.'

'Come now, I know a smoker when I see one.'

'Well, not any more.'

'Good for you. Trying to give the horrid things up myself. David Hilton, by the way. And you are?'

'Antonia.' Hawkins kept her hands well out of kissing range.

'So what brings you to Gatwick airport today, Antonia?'

'I'm waiting for someone.'

'Right.' He ran a hand over his slicked-back hair. 'Business, or pleasure?'

'Business, sort of.'

'Me, too. Mega busy, always on the run. No time for any of that homemaking or *romance* nonsense.' He was well into his stride now, so no answer was required. 'Eurozone investments are my thing. You know, buy low and all that. Terrible what's happened to the Europeans, but there are still people out there with money to spend. There's plenty still to be made, too, if you know how.'

Hawkins nodded, giving an internal eye-roll. Maybe she should have accepted the cigarette.

'And the perks? Scandalous, really, not that I'm complaining, you understand.'

'Of course not.' She watched him not-so-surreptitiously pull his sleeve up to reveal a huge Omega wristwatch.

'Adaptation's the key. I assist my investors in every way possible, sometimes ethically, sometimes not quite so much.' He snorted. 'But that's where the *real* money is, and in the midst of chaos, who's ever going to know?'

'Well, I've got some friends who might be interested, actually.'

'Really?' Casanova leaned in close. 'But are *you* interested, Antonia?'

'Well, I generally deal with homicide' – Hawkins produced her badge, watching his face fall – 'but I could ring the fraud squad. Do you have a business card?'

'I, er . . .' Casanova shot off his chair. 'I think they just called my flight.'

Hawkins almost laughed out loud as David Hilton took off across the terminal, nearly knocking over John Barclay, who was returning from the service desk.

'Who was that?' her trainee asked, coughing wetly as he sat down.

'Casanova. He thought I'd be impressed by the size of his embezzlement. Turns out I wasn't his type.'

'Shame.' Barclay smiled. 'I thought you'd scrubbed up pretty well this morning, Ma'am.'

'Thanks.' She gave him a sideways glance, gauging the young detective. Some months before, Hawkins had given several lectures to a class Barclay had taken in preparation for his Detective exams earlier in the year. Always eager to learn, he'd often stayed behind to discuss a variety of subjects. Following her final talk, however, John had made an awkward attempt at asking her to dinner. Unfortunately, her refusal had been just as uncomfortably delivered, and she was glad they hadn't seen each other for some time afterwards.

Despite this, Barclay had requested assignment to her team immediately after his six-month post-graduation placement. She'd been moderately flattered, but still suspected his motivation had more to do with an adolescent crush than professional esteem, especially considering the regular compliments he paid to her and no one else. He liked her shoes, her necklace, her hair.

Barclay had joined them two months ago, quickly proving himself to be a competent and intelligent trainee. He had never repeated his invitation to dinner, though, and she didn't want to encourage it.

'So,' she said, 'is Anderton's flight on time?'

'No delays, ma'am. Do you think he'll actually be on the plane?'

'The intelligent ones hardly ever run, especially if they have a face as recognizable as his. He'll understand that disappearing would just make him look guilty.'

Despite her statement, Hawkins was still surprised they'd found Charles Anderton so fast: a remarkably modest amount of arm-twisting over the phone to his office the previous afternoon had traced him to a cultural integration seminar in Scotland.

Hawkins had spoken to him personally, and he'd agreed to catch the first flight home. Their conversation had been short, but Anderton's tone had suggested he already knew the considerable depth of the shit he was due to land in.

'So why carry on working?' Barclay asked with a wry smile. 'Is he staying at full-pelt to mitigate his grief, or doing overtime to pay the hit man?'

She shrugged. The hired-gun theory would explain the consistent lack of sexual abuse or traces at the scenes. And, certainly, details of the real killer's MO could have found their way to a Culture Secretary well connected within the police, allowing him to employ someone to reproduce the scene. The other scenario, that Anderton would order two random murders in advance, just to cover his tracks, seemed equally far-fetched. Either way, the politician had withheld information he must have known would be vital to their investigation.

They sat in silence for a moment before Barclay pointed at the nearest news stand. 'Have you seen the papers, ma'am?'

Hawkins nodded.

Unfortunately, in a rare display of solidarity, almost every front page on the shelves carried the same headline:

THE ADVENT KILLER.

The name itself was no surprise: one of the Met's media team had suggested the same connection after Tess Underwood's demise, although nobody had taken it too seriously at the time. Upon seeing the headlines first thing that morning, however, Hawkins had hauled the constable in question straight into her office, suspecting him of being the source of their leak. His whimpering response had just about convinced her he was innocent, but her attention was now firmly on him.

But the nickname's appearance meant only one thing. With his third murder, the killer had earned sufficient notoriety to merit the consideration of even implausible scenarios, not to mention appellation in the press.

In modern dialect, the word 'advent' meant the arrival of something; in this case, a prolific serial killer. Of greater concern was the religious definition. Christianity classified Advent as, 'The period beginning four Sundays before Christmas, observed in commemoration of the coming of Christ into the world.'

Technically, because Christmas Day this year fell on a Sunday, Advent had actually started a week before the first death. Which raised some worrying questions.

Was there another body, as yet undiscovered? And *still* how did 1 a.m. tie in, when research said it was not significant to Advent? And if the killer had some twisted theological philosophy, were they dealing with a God complex? Or was the Advent thing just media hype?

True to form, most of the papers were pushing the religious angle; a tactic that had only increased their hunger for fresh information.

As a result, Thursday's papers contained almost full details of the first two murders, along with certain elements of the latest death, all of which could mean only one thing: a Met officer or one of their associates had passed yet more classified information to the media.

In truth, she was more disappointed than shocked. For many people, the spoils of covert self-service far outweighed any damage that might in the process be done to their conscience, but this time it really grated. This was a massive case, and Hawkins had made damn sure that her team, and anyone else over whom she held sway, understood the dangerous reaction insider information could provoke in the public. But her influence didn't extend to SOCOs or photographers: people she accepted were underpaid for their constant exposure to the ugliest sides of human nature. Even so, they still had no right to prostitute themselves – typically for a few hundred quid only – to satisfy the equally expedient motives of the tabloid sleaze-merchants.

Internal investigation might identify the culprits, the process for which Hawkins had already set in motion, but it couldn't reverse damage already sustained. And, despite her lack of surprise, she'd been hoping the story would take longer to appear than it had.

They weren't exactly close to a breakthrough.

So far, investigation into Hunter's hypothesis about serial killers' proclivities for increasing gore had provided a few isolated examples, but there was almost no documented research on this psychology. And even though Hawkins had several officers unearthing every word written on the subject, deep down she doubted it would provide a decisive insight.

The small positive was that, if this killer was intent on increasingly horrific attacks, then maybe his focus on not getting caught would falter to a corresponding degree. So, the more ornate each murder became, perhaps the more likely he was to make a mistake.

So far, the killer's targets had been home alone when he

struck, at 1 a.m. each Sunday morning. Glenis Ward because her husband had died four years before, and Jess Anderton because her public-serving spouse was away more often than he was at home. The only time the killer had needed to *engineer* the situation was in the case of Tess Underwood, whose partner had been asleep beside her on the night she died. A phone call from a security firm at half-past midnight had informed Terry Underwood that the alarm at his business, an upmarket jewellery shop fifteen miles away, was going off. As key holder, Mr Underwood had gone to turn it off, returning home ninety minutes later to find his wife beaten to an unrecognizable mess. Subsequent investigation had traced the kid who had triggered the alarm, but his only contact with the person who had commissioned this minor infringement had been via the internet: taking instructions and finding out where the £20 note he had earned for his trouble could be found.

Making matters worse was the news Hawkins had received on the way to the airport. One of the sub-teams had traced Glenis Ward's stepson, or at least the record of his death. For the last three months of his life, Gary Ward had lived rough, until the night six weeks ago when he'd overdosed on crystal meth. His decomposing remains had only just been identified, but the results were conclusive.

Meanwhile, early results from the forensics team working on Jessica Anderton's murder had yielded no traces yet again, while officers trawling hours of CCTV from the Hampstead area early on Sunday morning had discovered nothing of interest. And even though the list of Tasers seized by border control had finally come through, it was huge. Uniform was already working through it although, unsurprisingly, a lot of the people who'd ordered the illegal weapons had already moved on.

But, as a fresh wave of people began to spill through the airport's arrivals gate, something told Hawkins their luck was about to improve.

'Time to get the car, please, John,' she said, as Charles Anderton emerged out of the crowd.

19.

'Thank you, Alan.'

Charles Anderton shook hands with the security officer, who let them into the small office in a staff-only area of Gatwick airport, and then disappeared.

Anderton motioned to one of the shabby wooden chairs there, and Hawkins sat down, trying to block out an aroma of burnt dust and detergents.

Anderton closed the door, removed his grey overcoat, and laid it carefully beside his luggage. Then he took the seat opposite her.

'Alan's a friend,' he said, as if recognizing Hawkins' unease. 'I get him tickets to see Spurs play from time to time. In return, he looks out for me whenever I use his airport.'

Hawkins nodded, glancing over at the shelves on the far wall, where a security radio lay beside a curling sandwich.

Anderton sat bolt upright, his hands clasped on the small table between them.

'Thank you for agreeing to my proposal, Detective.'

'I'm afraid there are no guarantees,' she said. 'I'll do what I can, but we don't have much time.'

Anderton looked tired, even more so than he had two days ago. He wore the expression of a man who'd lost almost everything, and was now being forced to press flush on the rest.

During their telephone conversation the night before, he had offered Hawkins two choices.

If she followed procedure and took him in for formal questioning, he would withhold what he knew for as long as possible. Such a delay would not benefit either party, simultaneously increasing the likelihood of further deaths, and setting the media free to destroy Anderton's reputation and career.

Alternatively, he had offered to tell her everything, *off* the record, in return for her promise to keep his name off the official suspect list. This scenario would allow the investigation to continue unimpeded, with Anderton as grieving widower rather than detainee. He would escape further public humiliation, and he might even hang on to his job. Failing that, he could at least slide into a comfortable CEO position with what was left of his reputation intact.

Hawkins had immediately agreed to the latter. This way they gained vital information when it might still be of use. Her agreement, of course, was on condition that Charles Anderton proved to be as innocent as he claimed.

Anderton's voice interrupted her thoughts. 'I realize my lack of honesty on Tuesday may have damaged your investigation, Detective, and for that I apologize. But neither did I lie to you.'

Technically he was right. He'd spoken very little during Hawkins' visit two days ago, during which she had volunteered to postpone questioning for as long as possible.

That was before Marcus De Angelo had exposed Jessica's affair.

'I left you alone to grieve, Mr Anderton, not to attend a conference.'

He sighed. 'There was no conference, Detective. I just needed time to think, away from the media. Away from home.'

'Fair enough. But you already knew that Jessica was having an affair.'

His eyes dropped. 'Yes.'

'And you told her she'd be sorry if the story ever got out.'

Anderton's interlinked fingers remained motionless, but the whitening flesh around his knuckles betrayed the stress within. 'Yes . . . to my very greatest regret, I did.'

'You do realize, Mr Anderton, that that's motive.'

He looked up, his tone becoming stronger suddenly. 'I accepted the fact that Jessica didn't love me a long time ago, Detective, but I had *nothing* to do with my wife's death.'

Their eyes met, and it dawned on Hawkins what made Charles Anderton such a successful politician: despite having nothing but his assurance, she believed him.

'And if Marcus De Angelo hadn't sold his story,' he said, 'I might have survived, politically at least.' His voice cracked with the final words, and he covered his mouth with his hand, needing a moment to compose himself before he continued.

'Jessica and I had an understanding. Maintaining what appeared to be a happy marriage meant she kept her privileged lifestyle, and I my political credibility. My . . . *threat* was intended simply to remind her of that. I knew that if the truth about her affairs ever came out it would ruin my career, just as it ruined our marriage.'

'Did you say *affairs*, plural?'

'Yes, I'm afraid so.' Anderton exhaled. 'Marcus De Angelo wasn't the first. There were several, others.'

His words suffused the contaminated air, as Hawkins realized their list of potential suspects had just grown.

'Over the years, I took many precautions to keep Jessica's activities from the media, but I promise you murder wasn't one of them. Perhaps I should have worried more about her welfare than I did my career. I guess it's too late for that.'

Hawkins couldn't think of anything to say. Her silence prompted Anderton to go on.

'You assure me that Marcus De Angelo is not the killer, but it could easily have been one of Jessica's other acquaintances, and I wish to help in any way I can. If you'd be so kind, Detective, I'd like to submit a piece of evidence.' He looked over at his Samsonite flight case. 'May I?'

She eyed him. 'What is it?'

'A laptop. Jessica's laptop computer.'

Hawkins' gaze flicked to the security radio on the shelf opposite, all of a sudden acutely aware that it was just the two of them in the room. She had already taken a big risk. Anderton might be nearly sixty, but he still looked in good shape, and even though Barclay knew her rough whereabouts, essentially they were alone.

She rose, 'I think I'd better get it myself.'

'Yes, of course, you're right,' Anderton agreed. 'It's in the upper zipped compartment.'

She kept an eye on the politician as she moved over to the large grey case. There was no way to know if he was telling the truth.

'Are you OK, Detective?'

Hawkins realized she was hovering by the case. 'Fine.'

She began to unzip the compartment, still watching Anderton from the corner of her eye. He stayed where he was, and she glanced down into the widening gap. It looked like a normal laptop.

Hawkins relaxed a little as she pulled the computer out and returned to her seat.

'How does this affect the case, Mr Anderton?'

'Jessica was an enchanting woman' – he sat back, as if being able to talk about her eased his pain – 'but she was also more impulsive than I would have liked. I admit I kept a close watch over her, for both our sakes. More like a father than a husband, I suppose. A couple of weeks ago, she was using the laptop when her mobile rang. She went upstairs to take the call, so I took the opportunity to look at what she had been doing.' He paused. 'Jessica was logged into a chat room, Detective. And, judging by the nature of the exchange up to that point, I think it could be possible that was how she met her killer.'

20.

Hillingdon was nice, Hawkins decided, as she watched yet another park slide past the car window. Charles Anderton had explained, on their way to drop him at a friend's house in Uxbridge, that the borough was the proud home to 239 areas of open space, all protected by green belt laws. They were the main reason behind its status as London's least-populated district. And yet, while Hawkins' home borough of Ealing was right next door, she had never even visited.

She needed to get out more.

Barclay broke into her daydream. 'Where to now, ma'am?'

'Hendon.'

They both fell silent as a commercial radio jingle broke up for the presenter to introduce several items, including a report on the imminent press conference about the Advent Killer case.

Apart from Mike's best attempts to calm the fresh wave of public concern over the latest leaked facts, Hawkins knew it would contain nothing more than a regurgitated version of the same old information.

Hopefully, the laptop she'd managed to squeeze into her bag would help to change that, but recent events suggested that, for now at least, she should heed the DCS' warning about internal disclosure.

Even your immediate team is on a need-to-know basis.

Hawkins had kept details of her meeting with Anderton quiet. She'd told Barclay her conversation with the politician at the airport had satisfied her there was no need to take him into custody. She had, however, warned Anderton to stay local while they tracked down the two ex-acquaintances of Jessica's whose names he had been able to provide. She'd also arranged for him to be placed under covert surveillance until further notice.

What the trainee detective sitting beside her didn't know was that she was now in possession of Jessica's laptop, which she'd pass straight to the technology team back at Hendon, so they could begin extracting whatever information it held about the killer.

She checked her watch before turning to Barclay. 'John, when we get back, I need everyone together in the meeting room for a progress report. These victims link and I want to know *how*. They've bad-mouthed, borrowed from or screwed the same wrong person. Once we find that connection it'll all drop into place, but we're running out of time. OK?'

'Yes, ma'am.'

Hawkins tried not to breathe too deeply as the trainee detective launched into a fresh bout of what had sounded since lunchtime like the early stages of whooping cough.

A news jingle cut in to indicate the arrival of headlines, and Hawkins leaned forwards to turn up the radio. As she reached the control, however, her phone rang. It was a withheld number.

'Hello?'

'Antonia?' A man's voice, one she didn't recognize.

'Yes . . .?' She saw Barclay look over. 'Who's this?'

'You must remember,' the caller continued. 'Danny . . . Danny Burns. We met at the Future Crime conference in June?'

Hawkins paused; June seemed like a lifetime ago. Then it came back to her. A few weeks after Paul had moved out, she'd found herself sitting next to Danny at the conference. The seminar had been dire, but the time had flown thanks to his entertaining company. They'd exchanged numbers that evening, for what Hawkins later realized would have been a rebound-date. Fortunately he hadn't called at the time.

But maybe things were different now.

'Oh, yeah, I remember. How are you?'

For some reason, she was thinking about the 'Two buses come along at once' adage.

'Good, thanks. Listen, I hope you don't think it presumptuous of me, calling like this, but I have something I need to ask you.'

'Uh huh?' Hawkins glanced at Barclay, embarrassed to be arranging a date in front of a colleague.

'You're leading the big serial murder case, right?'

'What?'

'The Advent Killer thing – it's yours.'

Suddenly, more information about Danny Burns came back to her. He might be attractive, but he was also a journalist – one with a particularly salacious reputation – for the *Mail*.

'Oh, I see,' she said, sarcasm-heavy. 'Nice try. Thanks for calling.'

'No, I didn't mean—' was all Danny had time to say before she cut him off.

Hawkins switched the phone to silent and stuffed it back in her bag.

'Fucking reporters,' she remarked to Barclay. 'Shameless, all of them.'

21.

Unsurprisingly, three days before Christmas, late night shopping at Debenhams was a mêlée.

Hawkins fought her way through the outskirts of the crowd, all of whom were too busy gawping at some sort of festive show to be offended by her insolence, and headed for the fragrance department. Sinatra replaced Bublé in the air.

Locating her target, Hawkins joined the queue at one of the make-up counters, behind a harassed-looking couple whose four year old was making it noisily obvious he didn't enjoy Christmas shopping, despite Dad's best efforts to placate.

Mum was deeply engaged with the assistant Hawkins had come for, but she decided not to interrupt as four bottles of perfume were added to their bill.

There was no point in pissing off the subject by costing her commission.

With a few moments to itself, Hawkins brain was straight back at work. The day had been semi-productive. While the techs worked on Jessica's laptop, Hawkins and Connor had chased up Anderton's information on two of his wife's former lovers.

The first was a repulsive children's TV presenter called Douglas Donald. Dee Dee, or Donald Doug, as he was known, turned out to have a cast-iron alibi, having spent the past two weeks locked in a house as part of the latest *Celebrity Big Brother*. He was also the bookie's favourite to be announced winner tomorrow night.

The second was a stronger possibility. All Anderton knew was his name, Thomas Evans, and that he was a private motorcycle courier Jessica often used. The politician had returned home one day six months ago to find them screaming at each other, apparently over a late package. And although he never found out why, Anderton hadn't seen Evans since.

Connor had been working on a current address for the guy, so far without any luck.

Meanwhile, Hawkins had dug deeper into the theory that chat rooms were how the killer met at least one of his victims. She'd despatched Barclay to chase down and interview anyone who might know whether the initial two victims could have been using similar sites. Number two, Tess Underwood, wasn't beyond suspicion in this regard, but the inconsistencies in the theory really began with his first target. Hawkins had trouble imagining sixty-something Glenis Ward on a sleazy internet pick-up site. But you never knew.

At least this collection of leads had ensured that that day's progress report between Hawkins and Lawrence Kirby-Jones had been worthy of such a title.

At the moment, though, that flash of inspiration – the sixth sense Hawkins felt when she neared a breakthrough – wasn't there. Most people assumed that detective work relied on in-depth knowledge of law or criminal procedure, but more often you got nearer the truth via diligence and obstinate intuition.

And Hawkins had always had those.

From the age of five it had seemed perfectly logical to her that, should someone have damaged public property or stolen something, their peers were best placed to perform an investigation. Several classmates had suffered detention after confessing culpability to an apparently deferential Antonia Hawkins, only for her to appear shortly afterwards in the headmaster's office, to report her findings.

She hadn't been popular at school.

But this innate sense of responsibility had led Hawkins to study for a criminal psychology degree, then on to a career in the police force. It had all come so naturally to her, ensuring swift promotion through the ranks. Right then, however, she would gladly have swapped her self-imposed civic duties for something less stressful.

Perhaps the girls in her class that had produced litters by the age of eighteen had a point. *Why start a fight with human nature?*

Hawkins re-joined the present as someone trod on her toe. The man, who was providentially small, mumbled an apology as he battled on through the hordes, weighed down with bags.

Suddenly she felt guilty she wasn't there to buy, and considered capitalizing on the opportunity to purchase a few token gifts, just in case. If she had to make an appearance at her parents' for Christmas, it would be better not to do so empty handed. Present options began flashing through her mind: a Slanket for her sister, make-up for her niece, a home-brew kit for Dad . . .

'Can I help you?'

Hawkins turned back to the counter to find the family with the contra-shopping child gone, and the vibrantly tinted assistant regarding her with seasonal impatience.

'Maybe you can.' She produced her badge, rechecking the assistant's name tag. 'Cherie Riley?'

The woman hesitated. 'Yes.'

'Is there somewhere we can talk off the floor?'

Cherie Riley tutted at the combination lock on the security door, impatiently punching the code in three times before it released. She held the door open for Hawkins, who walked through and stopped, so that the two women stood facing each other in the service corridor; breeze-block walls either side, some sort of air circulation fan humming in the conduits above.

Riley was slender and, apart from the energetic tan, impeccably groomed. She was doing a good job of looking simultaneously bemused and helpful, but she regarded Hawkins with too much suspicion for this visit to have been a surprise.

Hawkins decided to let her speak first.

Riley glanced around, as if her visitor's silence indicated a desire for more privacy, maybe a seat. 'We can talk here.'

'Fine.'

Riley frowned. 'This about Jess?'

'Yes. How well did you know each other?'

'I used to do her make-up for TV and that, but I haven't seen her since July. I know she's dead, saw it on the news.'

'You fell out?'

'I thought we were mates, but she was just a user. What do you want, anyway?'

'We need to speak to one of her more recent boyfriends, Thomas Evans. Do you know where we can find him?'

Riley shifted her feet. 'I didn't know about any of that.'

'Come on, Cherie, you knew Jess was seeing other people. You're not getting anyone in trouble; it's been in the papers all week.'

'Look, just leave me out of it, OK? I don't want any of this shit. Fucking papers trash you, I've seen it happen.' She started moving towards the exit.

'Hold on.' Hawkins blocked her path. 'You'll be helping us catch Jessica's killer.'

'I don't owe her nothing.' Riley tried to step around her.

'What about the other victims, Cherie? This guy's going to do it again, this Sunday. Even if Thomas had nothing to do with it, we need to count him out.'

'You can't make me.'

'OK.' Hawkins gambled. 'If you won't talk, someone else will. Like Marcus De Angelo, for example. The papers would love a reason to extend their coverage of his story, and I understand you two know each other very well.'

Riley looked at her. 'What?'

'How do you think I found you? Marcus told us about you, and that you were friendly with Thomas, as well. Unless we give the papers something new to focus on, like catching this killer, they'll dig for gossip instead.'

Minutes later, Hawkins stood on the pavement outside Debenhams, looking for a less congested position away from the mass of shoppers swarming around her. It was approaching eight o'clock, but if she called soon, most of the team would still be at their desks.

Loading up on overtime.

She caught sight of a side street and began threading her way towards it, thinking about her recent conversation. The truth was that she'd coerced Cherie Riley into divulging information, especially as her allegation had been nothing more than conjecture. De Angelo *had* told them where to find Jess Anderton's former make-up artist, but he hadn't said anything about them being physically involved. Although, technically, neither had Hawkins.

But now they had a lead on Thomas Evans.

Riley didn't have an address, but she knew Evans had moved to the Guildford area six months ago. Which would allow the investigation team to focus their search.

According to Riley, Evans was a bit of a nomad, taking cash-in-hand jobs wherever he happened to find himself. This tallied with the frustrating fact that he hadn't registered with things like councils or employers for years, blunting the Met's ability to trace him.

Which was something Hawkins dearly wanted to do: these behaviours, in someone who had recently been observed rowing with the latest victim, made him a good candidate for suspicion.

And with only three days until the next murder was due, Hawkins definitely needed one of those.

22.

The Central Line train shuddered to a halt at the buffers, and Hawkins inhaled the chill air as she stepped onto the platform at Ealing Broadway station. She had only managed to get a seat a few stops back, but the train had emptied so dramatically since then that human traffic now exiting with her was negligible. She was soon heading north out of Haven Green.

It had been dark for several hours already, although the rain that had seemed entrenched earlier in the week had gone, replaced by cloudless grey skies and arctic temperatures. As a result, the wide pavements were empty and, after unsuccessfully searching her bag for gloves, Hawkins decided to get home before calling Mike about the day's progress.

Five minutes later, she closed the front door behind her and pressed Play on the flashing answer machine.

'Antonia, it's your mother. I need to know what time you'll be here on Christmas Day. I've put you in the corner next to Uncle Pat for dinner, because you have the strongest constitution and won't need to be in and out to the loo. You know what he's like – won't move until the end of the meal. Anyway, we're sitting down around two, so you'll need to be here at one for mulled wine. Call me back to confirm. Ciao!'

Hawkins shed her coat and walked through into the

kitchen, trying to ignore the feeling that she visited home these days only to clean dusty laminate.

She had chosen her new kitchen from a brochure two months ago, in an attempt to spruce up her waning social life by creating a house in which she'd be proud to host. Since then, her secondment and the case still burgeoning around her had ensured that only she and the fitter had admired her sensor taps.

She made a cup of tea before walking back into the living room, fishing her mobile out of her handbag. It felt strange to be selecting Mike's number again, and she stood for a minute, lost in memories of illicit moments spent snogging like teenagers in the storage room at Becke House. Somehow those encounters had never felt sordid.

Then she frightened herself by sitting down on the right-hand side of the sofa. Paul's seat. She shifted to the armchair, sipping her tea and trying to focus on the phone call she was about to make.

It's just work.

He answered after a few rings. 'Maguire.'

'It's me.'

'Antonia.' His voice was warm. 'How's it going?'

'Not bad. We've got some results from Jessica's laptop.'

'I meant how's it going with *you*?'

'Oh, I'm . . . fine, I guess.'

'You sound beat.'

'Thanks. You sound disgustingly well.'

He laughed. 'You eaten yet?'

'Why?'

'Ever since I quit London I've been dreaming about that Chinese takeout near your place. How about I pick up our usual? I can get to you in thirty. We can go over the case.'

She gazed into the kitchen, at the anodized sink that took half an hour to clean and the sculpted fridge that was too small to put food in. Half an hour would give her time to shower, change and tidy up a bit. Plus she wouldn't have to cook. But it was still probably wise to say no.

'Don't forget the spring rolls,' she said.

23.

While they ate, Hawkins outlined her clandestine meeting with Charles Anderton, having decided that the DCS' instruction regarding internal confidentiality didn't extend to Mike.

Maguire endorsed her decision to accommodate the politician's demands, and agreed that even if Anderton *were* somehow involved, he was best kept as an ally until they had some convincing evidence against him.

Hawkins also explained about Jessica's two ex-lovers, and the technology team's progress with her laptop. They had the addresses of several chat rooms Jessica had frequented.

Results from Tess Underwood's home PC had been less positive. The ageing computer had occupied a spare room, vacant since the youngest Underwood daughter had moved out, and was clogged with so many years of the family's web activity that interrogating it would occupy the technology team for the best part of three days.

Isolating the sites used by Tess herself, even during the last few months, presented a challenge. But according to Barclay, her husband and friends had been so shocked at the suggestion she was using chat rooms at all that Hawkins hadn't even broached the prospect of infidelity.

That could wait until they had some evidence to justify such an awkward conversation.

'Geez,' Mike said, when she had finished. 'A psychopath for the digital age. Technology to hunt and technology to kill. At least that gives us our next move.'

'It does?'

'Oh, I forgot; computers scare the hell out of you.' Mike grinned. 'I sure hope this killer doesn't turn out to be Bill Gates.'

'Oh, really?' Hawkins watched him clearing the foil trays. 'It didn't stop me ending up as your boss, though, did it?'

Mike meowed and walked into the kitchen, whistling at the makeover it had received since his last visit, 'All right, *chief*, I'll tell this one nice and slow, just for you. First things first, though. Where's the coffee?'

'Middle cupboard on the left.' Hawkins flopped back on the sofa. 'I'll have tea.'

'*Tea?*' He mimicked her accent. 'What is it with you Brits and this stuff? You go insane if it's not the perfect shade of beige, but you don't mind it comes in a thimble or that you gotta pay for refills?'

'You want me to explain sophistication,' she shot back, 'to a country that can't handle steering and changing gear at the same time, and that still makes houses out of wood?'

'Sophistication.' He flicked the switch on the kettle. 'Still taking three sugars?'

A few minutes later, he handed her a mug and returned to the armchair. 'So you figure our murderer hooks up with his victims online?'

'Yes.'

'Ever used a chat room?'

Hawkins cocked her head and shot him a condescending smile.

'Guess not.' Mike scratched his temple. 'OK, these things are like a . . . digital masquerade party, and nobody's checking credentials at the door. So you got three-hundred-pound truckers with an eye for the kids passing themselves off as twelve-year-old girls. That's grooming heaven, right there. Upside is, if he can do it, then so can we.'

She nodded slowly. 'Catch him with his own net.'

'Right. We magic up a few potential targets and we go fish. Arrange a few dates and take a look at who turns up. Gotta be worth a shot, right?'

'That could work,' Hawkins said, 'but we can't go public. It's the only lead we've got, and if the press gets hold of this and splashes it all over the papers, he'll just find another way of meeting them.'

'I'll do it.' Mike drained his coffee and winked. 'No lady friend to occupy my evenings, anyway.'

An hour later they stood together at the front door. Mike slipped on his long woollen overcoat and Hawkins passed him the list they had created. It contained the profiles of the four fictitious women they would use as bait. 'Just between us, remember?'

'The list, or being here tonight?'

'Both, since you ask.' Hawkins smiled, realizing how narrow her hallway felt with two people in it.

'Just like old times.'

'Yeah,' she said, trying to think of any reason they shouldn't be together. 'Thanks for the meal.'

'Sure thing.' His smile, always so disarming, appeared as he opened the front door.

Cold air rushed in as the *Do we kiss?* moment began. Mike's smile faded. How could he be so calm when her stomach was doing somersaults?

'See you, chief.'

Their eyes met for a few seconds before he turned and walked away down the path.

'Goodnight,' Hawkins called, as he disappeared around the corner.

She closed the door and stood in the hallway, waiting for the distant sound of Mike's car. But she heard nothing. Had he parked too far away for her to hear, or was he sitting out there debating whether to come back? And was she actually about to go after him? There was no real reason why she shouldn't, yet something held her back.

She turned and trudged through into the front room.

'So,' she asked the room. 'Bedtime, or brandy?'

She opted for bed, and had just turned out the lights when the phone rang. Her heart leapt as she stumbled across the room and grabbed the handset. 'Hello?'

Silence.

'Hello?' she repeated. Maybe he had a bad signal.

Still nothing.

Hawkins' fantasy stalled as she realized what was happening. She should have checked the caller ID.

'Paul, is that you?' she said, knowing there would be no response. Silent calls had recently replaced their regular shouting matches. 'Please stop calling me, Paul, it's getting really old.'

She ended the call and unplugged the line from the wall, then stood in the darkness, feeling like an emotional punch bag.

After a moment she replaced the handset, sneering at the soulless chirp indicating it was back on charge, and eased the curtains open. It was best to be sure.

Thankfully, Paul wasn't standing in the garden.

Unfortunately, neither was Mike.

24.

He watched the house from a safe distance as the lights went on and off in sequence, heading for the bedroom. Moments later, the final light went out.

He waited a further ten minutes before moving out of the shadows, keeping his head down. He needed to stay abreast of developments among his opposition's ranks, but his surveillance of the police was becoming harder as time progressed. There seemed to be more officers assigned to the case every day, although that merely verified how intimidated they were. Each new face seemed less experienced, and more reluctant to be involved, than the last.

He reached the end of the road and turned left towards the tube station, from where it would take around forty minutes to get home. Now that the Met's finest were off-duty, he needed to get some rest, too. It had been a long day, and at some point during the next forty-eight hours, the excitement would begin anew.

The station loomed, its dreary brick reminiscent of everywhere else in this shitty town. He paid for a ticket at the machine and walked down onto the platform. It was empty, but only at first.

A woman emerged from the shadows of a seating area and wandered towards him. Her demeanour suggested she had been waiting for a while.

Actually, that wasn't it; her slovenly progress wasn't a sign of boredom. She was a whore.

'All right, darling,' she said. 'Know when the next train's due?'

He shook his head.

'Nah, me, neither. Fucking display's been broken for ages.' She moved closer. 'Cold tonight.'

'Uh huh.'

She leaned back and studied him. 'You're a quiet one, aren't you? They say they're the ones you have to watch.' She cackled.

She was close. Her black miniskirt was heavily worn, and under her tights there were carpet burns on her knees. He wanted to vomit.

'What's your name, then?'

He didn't respond, but his eyes locked on her hands: she was no more than thirty, yet they belonged on a pensioner. The skin was leathery and tired, but he could still make out the indentation left by a recently removed ring. A *wedding* ring.

Hatred flared. He wanted to rip her throat open with his bare hands. Society would probably thank him for it, if they were honest. This slut was probably a Noah's Ark for every STI there was.

'Come on, love, I'm a cheap date. Well, good value anyway, if you know what I mean.' She shifted position, trying to catch his eye.

He scanned the platform; they were almost certainly on camera. He could pretend to accept her offer and take her somewhere more private, but he hadn't come prepared. He'd end up leaving traces, increasing the Met's chances of discovering his identity. And the moment her body was found, the police would certainly begin checking the area's CCTV footage. The risk was too great.

'What are you,' she asked. 'Bent?'

He turned and headed for the stairs.

'Fucking weirdo,' she said to his back. But as he reached the corner he was smiling. He could walk away.

He was still in control.

FRIDAY

25.

She stood by the window, staring at the restless outlines of the trees in Walpole Park.

This part of Ealing usually looked so peaceful in the middle of the night, a fact Hawkins knew because, increasingly, she was awake to witness it. But tonight tranquillity was sporadic at best.

As if to emphasize the point, a tuneless verse of 'Driving Home for Christmas' became audible in the distance, its chorus repeated several times before the five men staggered into view. Yet it wasn't their stewed overtones or the rousing effect they were having on the neighbourhood's resident canines that was keeping Hawkins awake.

Somewhere out there was a psychopath with her name on.

Even when she did sleep, she had nightmares about anonymous calls from the killer, giving the location of his next target. Hawkins would arrive just in time to watch him murder another victim and escape. She had woken in a cold sweat fifteen minutes before; a nightly occurrence since Jessica Anderton's death.

So far she'd avoided the sleeping tablets, but she couldn't go on like this for long. Her heart rate had dropped at last, though, and she took a sip of water before replacing the glass on her bedside table, carefully avoiding her necklace.

As usual it stirred memories of her Grandfather. Hawkins had been too young when he died to remember many details, but her mother's father had always been her favourite relative, and had left her the necklace in his will. The pretty emerald stone was small and chipped in places, but it went everywhere with her.

She closed the curtains and bashed her pillow back into shape before lying down again. After a few moments she found a comfortable position, but it left her facing the bright red figures on her alarm clock. 3.45 a.m.

It was Friday.

Hawkins groaned. In less than seventy-two hours it would be Christmas Day and, at the moment that millions of people were opening their presents, Antonia Hawkins would be opening yet another unfamiliar front door to find yet another maimed body.

She swore, realizing how badly she wanted a cigarette. Perhaps it was a good thing she'd left them in the Vauxhall Barclay had taken home. So far that night she'd resisted biting her nails, a habit that seemed to resurface at times of stress. Not that there was much of them left to save.

She stuck the most painful one in her mouth.

26.

'Well, that was a waste of sodding time,' Hawkins commented, as soon as they were out of earshot.

'Don't fret yourself.' Connor opened the driver's door of his Honda Civic. 'It's not as if it took long, and we got free biscuits. Love a custard cream, me. And, like you said on the way here, dead ends are good.'

'Dead ends are all very well' – Hawkins waved politely to the middle-aged woman still standing at the front door – 'but if your hairdresser found this many, he'd shave your head.'

Connor was right, though. For a hot lead to develop so quickly into such a neat conclusion was unusual, even if it wasn't the outcome she'd been hoping for.

Hawkins had felt more positive that morning when he'd come up with an address for Thomas Evans – the second of Jessica Anderton's 'acquaintances' her husband had known about. Eddie had thought to dig where others hadn't: with social services, whose Godalming branch listed an address for a Mr T Evans.

She'd even dared to hope that their unannounced visit to Evans' Compton home might have provided them with a decent suspect at last.

An hour ago, however, when the door was answered by a dog-eared social worker, alarm bells had rung. Hawkins' hopes had faded further when she and Connor were led into a small front room, to be greeted by a despondent-looking Evans.

From his wheelchair.

A nasty motorcycle accident four months before had left twenty-four-year-old Evans with both legs amputated above the knees. He was more than prepared to talk about it, too, treating them to what she suspected had recently become a rueful life story. This included a string of underpaid jobs, his brief but torrid fling with Jessica, and culminated in a tearful account of the fateful day, accompanied by reports printed in two local newspapers and X-rays of his mangled legs.

All of which ruled him out as the killer.

Connor pointed the Civic back towards London. As they chatted about the case, Hawkins watched him glance repeatedly towards her side of the car.

He'd done it so often on their outbound journey that she'd concluded he was checking his mirrors and asked if they were being followed. His resulting explanation had been altogether more innocent.

This time he lasted until they joined the motorway. 'Open the glove box there, would you?'

'Already? You said twenty miles.'

'Aye. But we've a big case on, and I've pressures at home.'

'OK.' Hawkins flipped open the refrigerated glove box and passed him a Mars bar. 'They're your teeth.'

'Calm your knickers, chief. You can have my spare.'

'No, thanks. Cold chocolate is like eating pavement. You really prefer it?'

'You've no idea. That glove box is the reason I bought the car.'

They were both smiling when a sign for upcoming services caught her eye.

'Lunchtime,' she said. 'Fancy an expensive, salt-ridden, partly-frozen sandwich?'

'Nice to see years on the force haven't tainted you. This might be the finest culinary outlet in all of central England.'

'Flagrant use of optimism? Don't remember the Met handbook entry on that one.'

Connor pulled onto the slip road as a cheerful melody from inside her handbag reminded Hawkins of the voicemail that had arrived while they were at Evans' house.

She dialled her answer phone while he parked.

'Ma'am, it's Amala. I've been to see the people who run the chat room Jessica Anderton was using. I'm really sorry, but the manager says there's too much data for records to be kept of previous conversations, and he can't release details of their privately registered customers. Call me when you get this.'

'If you want something done . . .' Hawkins murmured, ending the call and turning to Connor. 'Sorry, change of destination.'

27.

The offices of Levitt International were spacious and clean, just like the rest of Uxbridge Business Park. Yasir stood quietly in the corner, having been invited to watch negotiations, while Connor waited down in the car, visible through the full height windows across the back wall.

As Hawkins and the sharply suited man behind the desk regarded each other through veneers of grace, the atmosphere in the room was heading decidedly south.

'What can I do, love?' Guy Levitt spread his arms in an expansive gesture. 'I want to help, course I do, but I'm bound by the laws of customer confidentiality.'

Hawkins maintained her composure. 'I understand that, Mr Levitt, but those laws don't apply here. We aren't looking to sell these people life insurance; we're investigating three murders, and at least one of the victims was using your chat room.'

Levitt shrugged, creasing his lower chins.

Hawkins walked over to the framed collection of Levitt company logos. 'You have quite an empire.'

'I know.' He winked at Yasir.

Hawkins pointed at the one for his payday-loan company. 'Has this always been called Levitt-Cash?'

He frowned. 'Yes.'

'That's interesting.' Hawkins retook her seat. 'Because I did some checking on the way over. We have a record of a company called Instaloan, run by a Mr Guy Levitt, which folded in 2008 after being prosecuted for charging double its quoted interest rate.' She paused, watching Levitt flush. 'Now, I'm sure that was probably a different Guy Levitt altogether, but if I have to get a warrant in order to see your client list, I'll specify full disclosure, which means we can scrutinize every aspect of your past and present operations. It might take a while, but I'm sure we can clear up any confusion.'

28.

The wind whipped her hair across her face, and raindrops fell intermittently from the roof's overhang above onto her head. But Hawkins wouldn't have swapped her current position for anywhere indoors.

She inhaled gratefully as she pulled the cigarette from her lips, flicking ash at her feet, imagining the stress of the day being blown away with it across the concrete.

John had chosen the perfect moment to return her cigarettes – as soon as they'd arrived back from Uxbridge to team headquarters in Hendon – with the disk containing Guy Levitt's entire list of registered chat-room users.

After having checked with a couple of the Met's contracted technicians, Hawkins had accepted Levitt's contrite insistence that no records were kept of individual conversations held in chat rooms, partly due to the sheer volume of information; mainly due to privacy restrictions. And while chances of the user list leading them to the killer were almost non-existent, stranger things had happened. She already had people working on it.

Another drag and the tension across her shoulders began to ease. She leaned against the wall of Becke House and closed her eyes.

Mike would crucify her for smoking again, but he was currently talking media strategy with the DCS, so Hawkins had sneaked out for one. Plus, indulging her sordid habit in the face of a virtual hurricane would, she hoped, reduce any residual traces on her clothes.

'You know that'll kill you?'

Hawkins looked around and groaned.

Danny Burns.

'Sorry to sneak up. Got a minute?'

'Not for you.' Hawkins reluctantly stubbed out her cigarette and strode towards the security door. 'Are you not good with hints?'

She'd already ignored three of his attempts to call since yesterday morning.

'Antonia, wait, please.' He tried to block her path. 'I keep trying to tell you – I don't want information. I'm trying to *give* you some.'

She stopped. 'What?'

'That's why I rang yesterday.' He dug in his coat pocket and handed her a folded piece of paper. 'I wanted you to see this.'

Hawkins looked at him, still cautious. 'What is it?'

'Read.'

She took the sheet of paper and opened it. A moment later she looked up. 'We get stuff like this all the time – don't you?' She watched the reporter's face for signs of a wind-up, but there were none. 'That's it? A note from someone claiming to be the killer, containing information that was printed in *yesterday*'s papers? You don't have to be a genius to work out it's a hoax, do you, Danny?'

'Well, normally – and thanks for the vote of confidence – I'd agree. But that email arrived two days before Jessica Anderton died.'

29

Ten minutes after their initial conversation, Danny Burns sat opposite Hawkins in the police canteen, cradling the coffee she had paid for.

They were just ahead of the lunchtime rush, but the queues were starting to build. Conversations among the desk monkeys who hadn't noticed a chief inspector sitting in the corner involved the usual banter, while those who had the best of the overtime ribbed those who wouldn't get to see their children before New Year.

But Hawkins was oblivious as she read the message for the fourth time.

Police,

It is with regret that I involve the media, but everyone deserves to know the truth. And my message must be heard.

It is a sad indictment of modern society that people no longer take responsibility for their actions. The only way to make people listen any more is to shock them. My method is rather effective, I'm sure you'll agree.

I apologize for the use of a Taser, it really isn't consistent with my ethos, but it does allow me to edify my subjects prior to their big moment. Glenis Ward and Tess Underwood have paid for past transgressions, but their deaths will serve no purpose unless others learn from their mistakes.

To reinforce this education, more demonstrations will follow, while this message will ensure that, this time, everyone is paying attention.

My next example will sacrifice her impudent existence this Sunday. She has already sealed her fate, but there is still a chance for everyone else.

Nemesis

The message left only two possibilities. Either information had leaked earlier than they realized and this was a sick joke by someone pretending to be the killer. Or it was real.

Either way, whoever sent the message wanted it seen by the public.

She looked at Danny and pointed to the details at the top of the page. 'This is the email address it came from?'

'Yeah, but it's just some anonymous free account. It could have been sent from an internet café in Delhi for all the traceability of an email like that.'

'Why send it to you?'

'With a reputation like mine, why not?'

'OK, so why don't I have a dozen other reporters lined up outside holding the same email?'

'In my business,' Danny said, 'the more exclusive something is, the more attention it gets. Anyway, everyone knows where to go if you want to stir things up. I do work for the *Mail*.'

'So why bring it to me?'

'You're leading the investigation.'

'Come on, Danny, I know your sort better than that. What do you *want*?'

He returned her stare for a moment, and she saw the

mischief flicker in his striking blue eyes. His sense of fun had enticed Hawkins to offer him her number after their first meeting, but that had been prior to her discovery of what his job was.

She didn't return the grin that appeared on Danny's face before he replied: 'I wanted to check the start of the sixth sentence with you.'

Hawkins read the sentence again. '"I apologize for the use of a Taser." So what?'

'It's the only element not mentioned in any of yesterday's papers. There's nothing in any of them about any Taser. I checked.'

Hawkins read the line again. *Was he right?*

'Earth to Antonia.' Danny waved his hand in front of her face. 'Do you know anything about a Taser?'

'All right, yes, he used a Taser on all three victims. You're sure none of the papers mentioned it?'

'Oh, I'm sure. So it's genuine?'

'Looks that way.' She flicked at a stray crumb and sent it spinning from table top to floor. 'OK, let's assume the note's real. The question now is what we do about it. How many other people know about this message?'

'At this very moment, just you and me.' Danny shrugged. 'By tomorrow morning, anyone who picks up a copy of the *Mail*.'

Hawkins felt her jaw drop. The message referred to events from a week ago, but the killer's promise of further deaths could still create increased alarm among the public in two days' time.

'You're *printing* this?'

'Teed up and ready to go.' Danny sounded excited. 'I

just needed confirmation it was the real thing. The boys in the office are gonna love me!'

'Danny, please tell me you're joking.'

'Reporters never joke about stories this big. That guy increased our sales by nineteen per cent last week. Imagine what *this*'ll do to them.'

Hawkins struggled to stay calm. 'I'm afraid this is evidence now. I can't allow you to print it at all.'

'Sorry, Antonia, we'll have to discuss that one in court. This is far too big to suppress. Nemesis, whoever he is, is bang-on about one thing – people have a right to know.'

Hawkins just stared. Even if she arrested Danny, there was no way to prevent the information from appearing in tomorrow's paper.

'But because I'm a nice guy,' he continued, 'I'll also give you a head start on tomorrow's *main* headline.'

'What the hell are you talking about now?'

'Well.' Danny sat back and looked up at the ceiling. 'Now we're sure this is real, I assume you'd like a peek at the email I received from Nemesis this morning.'

30.

He hailed a cab outside the train station and sat back, thinking about the day's events as Brighton's regimented streets began sliding past the window. It was satisfying indeed when meticulous planning began to pay off.

The cab idled at a junction before they turned left onto a short stretch of dual carriageway.

'Had a good morning, have you, mate?' The cabbie craned his thick neck, trying to make eye contact, but gave up and resorted to looking at him in the rear view mirror instead.

He felt himself smile.

'Oh, yeah? Let me guess. Involves a bird, does it?'

He met the man's gaze for an instant and nodded. *Several, actually.*

'Well, good luck to you. My missus buggered off years ago, said I was more interested in football than I was in her.' He braked sharply, then jabbed two fingers at another driver. 'Yeah, and you, mate!'

'Now,' he continued, 'I'm Claret and Blue to the core, but it's hardly an obsession like she made out. I'd understand if I was one of those armchair types, you know, never been to a match, but I froze me nuts off on them terraces every weekend for years when I was a kid. I've got every single Hammers scarf back to nineteen—'

The driver's inane words faded to a distant murmur.

Soon his message would spread panic across the capital, creating a smokescreen for him to operate behind. As far as the police were concerned, he posed a threat to every woman in London, which meant that by Sunday night their resources would be stretched to breaking point. The Met was already panicking.

But when his next victim fell in a city fifty miles further south, they'd go into meltdown.

He relaxed in his seat and stared out through the windscreen. A stream of queuing cars flashed past in the opposite lane as the cab coasted along. The only sound was a faint rumble from the tyres. It felt warm in the taxi, and he rested his head against the door pillar. Was the driver still talking? He could no longer tell.

Darkness surrounded him, the world asleep. To the right, his parent's bedroom door was closed, and ahead, the stairs stretched down into the lower hallway. Behind him, his bedroom door stood open.

He glanced back at his toys, but they remained motionless. There was no sign of the little girl. He listened again, hearing the wind as it swirled around the building, and the grandfather clock ticking solemnly in the hall. But nothing else.

Downstairs and back without being discovered. It was risky, but his mouth was dry, and he imagined the jug in the fridge. On Saturdays, his father went to the Baxters' farm, which meant the milk he brought back would still be creamy and fresh.

If he made a sound and heard someone get up, he would follow up with a louder noise to ensure both his parents woke. Punishment wasn't generally as bad if his dad was there.

He reached back and eased his bedroom door closed behind him. At least if anyone got up, it wouldn't be obvious that his room was empty. Then he slid forwards, his socks silent against the floorboards.

He took an indirect route to the top of the stairs, avoiding the creaky board that had caught him out in the past.

He paused at the top step, beside the toilet door, peering down into the darkness. The point of no return. If his mother appeared in the doorway now, he could still disappear convincingly into the bathroom. But as soon as he placed a foot on the staircase, that option was blown.

Being discovered at any stage after that meant he'd be hiding the bruises for a fortnight.

After a few more seconds of reassuring silence, his right foot slid gently off the top step and hovered just above the next. He paused, concentrating on the regular beat of the clock downstairs, timing the transfer of his weight onto the lower step to coincide with the louder of its alternate clunks. The first step went well, as did the second, and soon he was making good progress, stepping onto each one of the fifteen stair treads on every fourth clunk.

He reached the ground floor and stood in the hallway, heightened senses divided between the stairs beside him and the corridor ahead.

A few more yards and he would reach the next point of relative safety, when he could close the kitchen door behind him. At that stage, even if his mother crossed the landing, there would be no immediate sign that he'd left his room, and he could enjoy a few refreshing mouthfuls of milk before making the return journey to bed.

But he wasn't safe yet.

He advanced carefully along the hall, keeping to the right, pausing at the steps leading down to the lounge. It was unlikely that his mother would still be downstairs, but it was always best to check. He leaned around the corner and peered in.

The room looked empty, although the main sofa – where she often slept during the day — faced away from him. Was she lying there, hidden from view?

He broke cover and crossed the wide doorway, feeling the vibrations through the soles of his feet as he arrived at the grandfather clock on the far side. He stopped and glanced up at its big white face. 12:47, well past midnight. A time when the likes of him should be fast asleep.

He could hear the mechanism turning inside the case, scrape and whine, back and forth, marking every second that passed. In thirteen minutes it would strike one o'clock. Luckily the chime was broken, so that a small clunk, like a heavy coin dropping into a wooden moneybox, was the only noise it made. If he was caught, it wouldn't be down to the clock. He winced, remembering the last time his mother had found him downstairs at this hour.

But he had come too far to turn back, so he continued, sliding along some floorboards, stepping over others, until he arrived at the kitchen. Where he stopped dead.

For the first time he could remember, the kitchen door was latched.

A door in the house being latched was not unusual in itself, but the mechanism on this particular one was stiff, as it was rarely used.

He paused, trying to work out how seriously to take this minor detail. He hadn't expected this, and it was difficult to predict how loud disengaging the catch would be.

He could turn around now and head back to his room, but the thirst was still there, and the fastened latch probably didn't mean anything bad. He needed to be sure, though, so he leaned forwards and pressed his ear against the wood of the door.

At first he couldn't make out the sound, but then, yes, it was faint, but it was definitely there.

A whimpering, punctuated by short, sharp intakes of breath.

Somebody was in the room.

He took a pace backwards, instinct telling him to leave. But something gripped him.

He glanced along the hallway before he stepped back to the door and listened again. It sounded like somebody was in pain.

Forgetting risk, he reached up to lift the latch.

'*Wakey, wakey.*' A distant voice. '*Oi, mate!*'

The air turned cold.

'*Mate, we're here.*'

Light blinded him. He raised a hand to shield his eyes and blinked, trying to re-orientate himself.

'Take a pill, mate.' The driver stood over him with the cab door open. 'Didn't mean to give you a heart attack. You said the corner of Westfield Avenue, yeah?'

'Yes, just . . . just wait.' He rubbed his eyes. He sensed the man's stare, had to get out.

'Here.' He thrust the first note he found at the driver, pushing past him and out onto the street.

'Fare's only eleven fifty,' the driver called as he hurried away. 'You want change?'

He didn't reply. He knew where he was now, remembering the place he had told the driver to stop: a few minutes' walk from his destination. He cursed the fact he had to be careful; couldn't afford for his plans to be cut short because some idiot taxi driver was able to identify him, and where he had been. He had to calm and re-centre himself. But he was shelterless here: exposed. There were people on the streets and in passing cars. He felt them stare as he stumbled along, head down.

He began humming the tune his father used to whistle

in the fields. It hadn't changed in all the years before he left, and was still comforting somehow.

He walked on, suppressing sickening history, trying to focus on the route he had memorized from an online map the previous afternoon.

Within minutes, his efforts were rewarded as the overtones of music became audible in the distance. And, as the residual effects of sleep faded altogether, he rounded the final corner and stopped.

Before him, a vast plain stretched towards the horizon, interrupted only by a sprawling assortment of canvas and steel.

Old Glad Soul's Roadshow.

A temporary sign saying 'Christmas' was nailed above the name, a clumsily drawn arrow denoting its intended insertion between the final two words.

People rendered minute by distance queued at the entrance, waiting to join others in the confines of the provisional city.

And, somewhere among them, Summer Easton moved inexorably towards her destiny.

31.

He wandered away from Swanny's Urn-Tug and into the darkness, losing himself among the crowd of disparate day-trippers who had provided him with cover for most of the afternoon. They may have shared a coach to get there, but seemed to have so little else in common that he was surprised they'd remained together in a pack.

He glanced back to see Swanny watching them go. The stallholder was at least sixty, but he had already demonstrated hawkish awareness when one of the party's kids had tried to pilfer sweets from the stall during a particularly intense round of urn tugging.

Just as he'd been careful with the cab driver, he didn't want Swanny's, or any of his roughneck compatriots', suspicions raised by his prolonged presence and lack of participation.

His group paused under the central marquee to watch one of the Roadshow's colourful, live performances which was just beginning on the main stage, and he positioned himself with a direct view of one particular tent near the eastern boundary.

The advantage of the fair's layout meant that, once he had located the tent with 'Psychic Summer' emblazoned above the entrance, he'd been able to watch her activities almost uninterrupted since his midday arrival. Not that there was much to report. Easton had left her tent only three times, once to disappear into the unhitched caravan directly behind it, and twice for a few minutes each to use one of the portable onsite conveniences. For the moment, the small queue of punters outside the entrance indicated that she was still inside.

He checked his watch. It was approaching eight o'clock, and had been dark for nearly three hours, but he wasn't yet ready to leave.

His initial goal had been to locate Summer Easton, but now he was more interested in what would happen once this fair shut down for the night.

Where would she spend the night? And would she be alone? Only once he had established the answers to both these questions would he be able to properly plan her demise. But Old Glad Soul's Roadshow didn't close, according to the signs, until 11 p.m.

So he would wait.

He strolled over to a burger van and ordered some food, watching from the corner of his eye as one patron left Easton's tent, to be replaced immediately by the next. He moved across and leaned against an old truck, swallowed by darkness, eating and assessing the scene.

The fair sprawled before him, its uncontained presence in this vast field offering countless escape routes through an ideal collection of dark corners and erratic crowds. Rain fell in a fine haze, extending iridescent beams from massive multicoloured lights that burned against the blackened sky. The acrid smell of diesel generators hung in the night air, while the speakers they drove fired bass lines at volumes necessary to overwhelm their clatter.

Beside the entrance, a huge effigy of Old Glad Soul

himself held arms aloft in perpetual welcome, but only Nemesis mirrored his composure here amid a typical night scene. People clamoured in every corner, a constantly shifting sea of faces, no more recognizable or distinct to one another than enemies at war. They were just like all the others, oblivious to danger, blithe until they realized Nemesis had come for their souls.

A couple of teenage girls approached, laughing. One of them had removed her tiny jacket, and the pair used it as an improvised umbrella against the snow that was now beginning to replace the rain.

'Sorry, mate,' one of the girls squawked as they pushed past. But he made no attempt to hide his already disguised face: identity was irrelevant there.

That was what made places such as London and Brighton such perfect places for him to work. Who would look twice at him in a city? Or a place like this, where every type of freak rubbed shoulders with every other?

Although here, unlike a modern metropolis, Old Glad Soul would not have invested in countless CCTV cameras.

He finished eating and wandered over to join the crowd under the open-sided marquee. On the raised stage between him and Summer Easton's tent, a large man dressed as Father Christmas was throwing enormous quoits over volunteers from the audience. Music blared. The onlookers clapped.

To the casual observer his eyes were on the show, but his mind was on tomorrow.

As usual he had left nothing to chance. The train from Victoria to Brighton had taken exactly fifty-two minutes, the cab ride and walk to his destination a further eighteen. He would arrive at the fair at 9.30 p.m., three and a half hours before Summer Easton was due to die, which would give him time to locate his target, identify any additional weekend security and establish his exit strategy.

And at 1 a.m., as every police officer in the south east of England was looking for him in London, he would be here in Brighton, imposing punishment on his latest victim, and be far away before anyone discovered her twitching remains.

But then Summer Easton did something unexpected.

She emerged from her tent and spent a moment talking to the remaining queue of punters before politely turning them away. Then she rotated the sign above her tent to display a 'Closed' message and disappeared into the caravan behind. A light came on, and her shadow began moving back and forth behind the thin curtains.

Ten minutes later, Summer Easton left the caravan wearing a winter coat and carrying a holdall.

He started forwards in surprise before berating himself for reacting so blatantly. But everyone around him was captivated by the show in front of them, and no one had noticed a thing. He skirted the crowd, keeping his target in view.

Easton stopped briefly to converse with another stallholder, but then she headed for the main exit. She joined the stream of people leaving the venue, looking up every few steps at the snow falling more heavily now, as she began crossing the open area in the direction of the city.

Intrigued and, ensuring that he wouldn't be seen, Nemesis followed.

SATURDAY

32.

People of London

The Metropolitan Police are not being fair to you. There are things they do not want you to know.

You will all be aware of the deaths of Glenis Ward, Tess Underwood and Jessica Anderton. But you do not know why they died.

Their deaths were demonstrations of virtuous justice in a morally neglectful society. How many more follow them will be up to you.

Those who live with integrity have nothing to fear from me, but those who shun the ethical code inherent in their souls deserve to die as examples to the rest of humanity.

I am not a coward. The righteous among you will understand why I cannot show my face until I am satisfied that my message has been heard, understood and acted upon. Therefore, a new demonstration begins. This Sunday, one more of you will die.

Until then, I am the person opposite you on the tube, I am the man walking his dog in the park. Remember me every time you make eye contact in the street.

I am everywhere.

Nemesis

The *thunk, click* from outside the door barely registered as Hawkins sat motionless in front of the projector screen, where the second message was displayed to full, intimidating effect. Only when she picked up the aroma of vending-machine coffee did she open her eyes.

She had known both of Nemesis' messages word for word since the night before.

'Extra sugar.' Mike put down the plastic cup. 'How's the headache?'

'World-class, thanks.'

'Shame the coffee's not.' Mike took a sip from his cup as he sat down. 'Could use a decent caffeine hit myself.'

Hawkins stopped massaging her neck and looked at him. She hadn't noticed until now, but he looked exhausted. She reminded herself she wasn't the only one under pressure; Kirby-Jones had maltreated everyone's eardrums first thing that morning.

The media, who had just started to report other news again, had found fresh enthusiasm for the Advent Killer when the *Mail*'s big news broke. Despite the weather, the crowds of reporters were back, bigger than ever outside Scotland Yard, and now even here outside Becke House.

Snow showers had started overnight and continued through the day. Normally, the media would be going mad at the prospect of a white Christmas, but for now there was only one story.

The public had taken Nemesis' messages seriously, too. Calls were flooding in to the switchboard, mainly through 999. The fact it was so close to Christmas meant that most people not out sledging were at home, televisions on: the perfect conditions in which to cultivate paranoia.

So far, 745 women had seen a man acting suspiciously in their neighbourhood, 268 thought they'd been followed home, and one thought her new son-in-law's dexterity with the hedge trimmer was definite cause for concern.

Panic wasn't the word.

At least Danny Burns had agreed to pass on any further communications from the killer, despite his cringe-worthy attempt to secure exclusive rights to pictures of the next murder scene in return. He'd backed off when Hawkins had threatened to lock him up on extortion charges. Still, she wasn't naïve enough to think he wouldn't reappear as soon as another one was killed. Only *if*, she remembered to hope, *if* another one was killed.

Danny had been right, however, about the traceability of the emails themselves. Hawkins had received a crash-course. After they had contacted its operator, the email account had indeed proved to be unregistered. More sur-prising was the fact that the technology team had been unable to locate the source. Nemesis' emails lacked the usual identification, meaning the killer was either in pos-session of some advanced encryption software, or he was using a dial-up modem.

None of the terminology meant very much to Hawkins, but even *she* could translate the results into just another bunch of dead ends.

The DCS wanted Nemesis caught before he killed any more members of the public. Fair enough, but today was Saturday – *Christmas Eve*, she realized grimly – which gave Hawkins and her team less than twenty-four hours to work out how to stop the Advent Killer before he revealed his next present to the nation's head-line writers.

Hence their crisis strategy meeting.

Hawkins had gathered her core officers to discuss the situation, away from the diluted confusion of a full investigation team briefing.

Hunter had joined them briefly to add his insight to their analysis. After reading both messages, he had snapped shut his notebook and proclaimed that Nemesis was what profilers referred to as a 'mission killer'.

According to Hunter, an individual was able to commit a string of brutal murders, completely free from the constraints of conscience, if he believed himself justified in doing so.

The emails implied that Nemesis was attempting to instruct others, through acts of brutality, and that his beliefs should be esteemed and replicated throughout society. The length of his mission would depend on the results he perceived. Resistance would almost certainly lead to further attacks, whereas hypothetical compliance might prompt Nemesis to simply stop, or hand himself in.

At least Hunter seemed to appreciate the latter was not a realistic prospect.

The profiler had repeated his suggestion that they attempt to engage Nemesis in further communication, via the media if necessary, in a method similar to those used by negotiators in hostage situations. Once open, that channel could then be used to feed Nemesis information, possibly even to suggest that his crusade had succeeded.

What this plan didn't take into account was that the next murder was imminent – Hawkins had reminded him that things like building Rome, and playing disinformation ping-pong with serial killers exclusively through the media, weren't twenty-four hour operations.

She had also speculated that, if the killer was making some Advent-related statement – as the newspapers continued to claim – that night's probable attack might be his last. At least for this year. And if that was the case, they had only one more opportunity to stop him.

As for how Nemesis was choosing his targets, Hunter surmised that the killer's self-proclaimed war on immorality meant he would be selecting victims he saw as having somehow abandoned their inherent ethical obligations; although in a mind as twisted as this, a lack of probity might be demonstrated by something as simple as not apologizing for crossing his path in the street. None of which, Hunter admitted, would help them identify forthcoming targets.

For a prediction on where Nemesis might strike next, they might as well have rung 118 118.

Hawkins had called a coffee break fifteen minutes ago, but only because after three hours of discussion, tempers were beginning to fray. Nobody could quite understand how, after two weeks, three murder scenes and a couple of direct communications from the killer, they were no nearer to an arrest. Plausible courses of action remained in short supply.

She stood and peered out through the blinds, past the exhausted-looking piece of faded red tinsel, strung untidily across the window. In the main office beyond the glass, her team had scattered. Connor and Barclay obviously hadn't anything left to say about the Nemesis case: the young TDC was displaying typical curiosity in Connor's Glock 17 handgun; the firearms officer exercising due restraint, despite his friend's persistence, by keeping the weapon holstered. At a separate station, Todd was motionless, oblivious to the fact that he sat alone beneath a sprig of mistletoe somebody had hung from the ceiling, while just outside the door, Yasir sat reading the extensive notes she had taken throughout the meeting.

At another desk, Brian Norton finished a telephone call. The call-centre manager was based at Scotland Yard, but had taken time out from his considerable workload to join them at Becke House. He looked every one of his forty-three years, had an appetite for cake, an aversion to exercise, and a waistline to prove both. With unkempt brown hair and a tendency to wear the same shirt three days running, he was perfectly suited to the secluded world of the incident room.

As she watched, Brian heaved himself out of his chair and waddled over to stick his head round the door. 'Sorry, Antonia, that was Barry. He's just about holding the fort down at the Yard, what with all these calls coming in, but he says it's getting stupid now. I'll head back if that's OK.'

'No problem, Brian,' she replied. 'I'll update you later. Good luck.'

Norton puffed out his cheeks and closed the door on his way out.

Hawkins watched him lumbering towards the lifts before she turned to Mike with a look of resignation.

Maguire drained his cup. 'Want me to call the others back in?'

'I suppose.'

He moved to the door and leaned out. 'Round two, guys.'

The team stood and filed back into the room. Yasir was first, closely followed by Todd. Yasir smiled; Todd scowled into space. Hawkins watched them retake adjacent seats, confounded as ever by their surprisingly effective partnership: the weathered, middle-aged Geordie and the exotic eastern princess. They were followed by Barclay and Connor, the sergeant carrying an open festive tin of chocolates. They took seats opposite Todd and Yasir.

Hawkins waited while Connor passed the Cadbury's Heroes round, and let everyone settle before she spoke.

'OK, I don't want to end up going round in the same circles as before, but has anyone come up with anything fresh on how to handle tonight?'

Blank faces.

'Right then.' She glanced at Mike. 'We'll go with Plan A: use the public as radar, monitor hotline calls as they come in to Brian's team, and attend as many potential sightings as possible using rapid response teams. The teams will be made up of everyone on duty plus the extras we've got on overtime, supported by firearms officers from SCO19. You four' – she looked at Todd and Yasir; Connor and Barclay – 'will join response teams out in the field to bolster numbers while Mike and I will be at Scotland Yard, taking skeleton transcripts straight from the incident room and coordinating the teams via radio. If we can keep up we might just get lucky. Any questions?'

Todd was straight in. 'We'll have to get mighty fortunate to pick out the right call. There'll be thousands of the fuckers ringing up, mostly to bleat about nothing.'

Hawkins ignored his language. 'Yes, Frank, I imagine there will. But that's to our advantage: the more the better.

If we prioritize successfully, the genuine possibilities should emphasize themselves.'

'"Emphasize themselves"?' Todd repeated. 'Sounds like management speak for pissing in the wind.' He laughed, probably to temper the severity of his disrespect.

Hawkins was glad when nobody joined in.

Yasir came to her aid. 'Hunter thinks the chief's idea is good, and so do I. If we have two hundred officers divided into teams of three, those sixty-six teams should be able to attend two hundred and sixty calls an hour, assuming an average of fifteen minutes per call. Over the peak couple of hours around midnight, if we respond to the statistically strongest alerts, that's over five hundred opportunities to stop Nemesis.'

'OK, Amala,' Barclay joined in. 'But what if reaction time is thirty minutes and there are twenty thousand calls? Don't tell your abacus, but then our response ratio is less than two per cent.'

Connor dug him in the ribs. 'Yeah? Well, I buy a lottery ticket every week, and I won a tenner on Wednesday. I say go with the chief's plan.'

Mike backed him up. 'Five hundred chances are better than nada, right?'

There was a long moment of silence.

'Good.' Hawkins stood. 'Democracy wins. Everyone go home and get some rest, but make sure you're at Scotland Yard for the briefing at nine tonight. I know it's Christmas Eve, but we're here to save lives, so that's the nature of your job.' She crossed her arms to signal the matter closed, but her conscience refused to let her end on such a tough statement.

'Come on,' she glanced around at her team, 'let's get this guy. And if you miss Christmas dinner, I'll cook one for you.'

There were a few thoughtful nods before Eddie and Amala stood, although the others remained seated. Frank was doing his heavy breathing, which meant he really wanted to continue the argument, but was also aware the decision had been made. John seemed lost in thought.

'Smile, boys.' Connor threw a Hero at Barclay, making him jump. 'You're on double time. Go home and jerk off, it's gonna be a long night.'

John grinned and unwrapped his chocolate.

At last they rose, and no further words were exchanged as everyone except Maguire and Hawkins drifted out. She was also glad to see John and Frank, as opponents of her plan, head in separate directions.

She was left staring at the four melamine-topped tables in the centre of the room. On two were copies of the *Daily Mail*, each with its front-page bearing the headline, **ADVENT KILLER: 'MORE OF YOU WILL DIE'**.

The *Mail* already had a styled logo for anything related to the story: it might as well have been dripping with blood like some seventies horror film poster. She pushed the nearest paper away, looking across to where Mike had logged on to the media point in the corner.

'That went well.'

'Yeah.' He turned. 'Least Frank still has the hots for you. Really pulling your pigtails today.'

'Behave.' She unwrapped a Malteser, scowling at him. 'Put your Yankee verve into work for a change, and tell me if you've cracked the chat room thing.'

'Just checking it out.' He pointed to the screen. 'No cigar yet, but these chat room dudes say some scary shit. Look at this.'

Hawkins joined him at the terminal. The forums were full of discussion about Nemesis. And, more worryingly, as many were in favour as against.

'You know bookmakers are taking bets on when we bring this guy down?' Mike covered a flashing Ladbroke's advert with his hand. 'You don't want to know what odds we've got for tonight.'

'What the hell did I miss?' Hawkins said, irritated suddenly. 'When did murder become a form of sodding entertainment?'

'Hey.' Mike gripped her arm. 'Look at it like this – he saved us a job by getting famous. We don't find him soon; I'll just order a signed photo from the fan club.'

'Sorry,' Hawkins relented. 'When did I get so serious?'

'Watch out. People will think you care.'

'Yeah.' Their eyes met. 'Thanks.'

Hawkins looked away first, pretending that something on the computer screen had caught her attention; moving the conversation on, 'So, have you found a place to stay yet?'

'Yes I have, thanks to the good old office bulletin board. Moved in with Johnston from traffic.'

'Well, I'm sure you and Eric will be very happy together.' As she spoke, the boxes lining her hallway flashed through Hawkins' mind. She needed to contact Paul about collecting them, although she couldn't imagine how that conversation would be anything except a disaster.

At least long shifts meant she wasn't home alone, watching some tragic festive TV special, waiting for Paul's next tearful, or worse, silent, phone call. It was nights like these that had brought her and Mike close in the first place. And here they were again. Except this time she had no reason to feel guilty.

She noticed that her hand had strayed onto the back of his neck as she steadied herself on bending down to look at the screen, and removed it quickly, 'Don't you have a press conference to go to?'

Mike looked at his watch. 'Geez! Where'd the morning go?' He stood up and grabbed his jacket from the back of the chair. 'I'll go straight to the Yard after. We can meet there.'

'Keep your head down on the way out,' she called as he left the room.

'Don't have to,' he shouted back. 'Nobody's asking.'

She realized he was right. The inquisitive looks from other officers around Becke House all posed the same silent question: *How close are you really to catching Nemesis?* But looks were all they got.

Everyone wanted to know, nobody wanted to ask.

Officers were being dragged off other cases at an alarming rate: 150 from all over the UK had been seconded onto the investigation so far. Showing interest was the quickest route to selection, but few chose to get involved with nightmare cases like this. Secretly though, Hawkins appreciated the respite.

She sank onto a chair, feeling light-headed. Was it hunger, or apprehension? She watched a full minute tick away on the wall clock. It was coming. They still looked like underdogs and, in just under thirteen hours, the game would begin for real.

She turned to switch the computer off, just as the Sky news headline flicked onto the entertainment heading. She shook her head.

Douglas Donald had won *Celebrity Big Brother*.

33

Two hours, eleven minutes.

'Antonia?'

One hundred and thirty-one minutes.

'Quit staring at the clock.' The American accented voice was more insistent this time. 'You'll wear it out.'

Hawkins sighed and looked over at the room's only other occupant. There was no point trying to deny that for the third time tonight, Mike had caught her calculating how long was left until Sunday began.

'Fine.' She dumped her pile of transcripts on her desk. 'I'm going to get some water. Would you care for some, DI Maguire?'

'Yeah, I'll have mine boiled, with coffee, milk and one sugar. Thanks.' Mike turned back to his radio before she could respond. 'Team 14, we have a possible sighting in Wandsworth, can you attend, over? Ow!'

Hawkins had clipped the back of his head as she left the room. The two of them were using a vacant office near the incident room at Scotland Yard as a temporary operations base. Radios had been set up for them to co-ordinate the sixty-odd response teams, which comprised every available officer from uniform to sergeant level.

She and Mike had already read through hundreds of 'emergency' call transcripts from all over London, without finding a single genuinely promising link to the killer.

They were at full stretch, but if they overlooked a lead that might later prove to have been an actual sighting of the killer, the consequences would be catastrophic.

It was going to be a heavy night.

Hawkins passed the first few windows of the incident room. The blinds were closed, but as she neared the door a young operator wearing a Santa hat flew out into the corridor with a fresh stack of transcripts. He grunted his frustration as he dropped a few from the bottom of the pile, then gathered them up and headed for their office without even seeming to notice her.

The racket from inside the room was silenced suddenly as the door banged shut, but the momentary blast of jumbled noise had suggested that a familiar level of activity existed within. Hawkins resisted the urge to push the door open again for a peek at the chaos, and resumed her course towards the kitchen.

Barking instructions into the radio to co-ordinate dozens of officers under her command should have given her a certain sense of control. If she was honest, though, she felt pretty helpless. The response teams already had a backlog of calls to follow up and, inevitably, that list would continue to grow: they'd have to be even more selective about which calls they responded to as the night progressed.

Voices became audible as Hawkins approached the kitchen area, and she entered the room to find a dozen or so uniforms seated around a couple of the tables, obviously just having finished a shift. Heavy winter coats and festive gloves were being put on, suggesting that a Christmas excursion was about to begin. She caught sight of the vodka bottle as it disappeared beneath the table.

'Don't worry about me,' she said. 'Get out there and enjoy yourselves. That's an order.'

Hawkins' encouragement had the desired effect. The bottle reappeared, and she was even asked if she wanted to join the gang for a drink as they left. She declined, feeling more like tolerant auntie than credible peer.

The young officers filed out, leaving Hawkins alone. Only the hum of vending machines and a wall-mounted television quietly showing the news broke the silence. Outside the window, snow continued to fall.

She filled the kettle and flicked it on before getting herself a glass of tap water. On the TV screen, an image of King's Cross station was overlaid with the caption 'Curfew: London'. . She turned up the volume.

'. . . estimates from the retail sector suggest that last-minute pre-Christmas sales fell by as much as seventeen per cent today, as concerned shoppers avoided the capital. The mayor urged people to remain calm but vigilant in the wake of a second message printed yesterday in one newspaper. Verified by police as "almost certainly genuine", the message claims to be from the person known as the Advent Killer. In it, the author refers to himself as "Nemesis", and promises further bloodshed in the city tonight. The mayor hit back, guaranteeing the Met's response to the threat would be "decisive and unprecedented". . .'

The kettle clicked off, but the familiar faces appearing onscreen held Hawkins' attention. It was the first time she'd seen footage of Mike's press conference from earlier.

Lawrence Kirby-Jones sat beside him at the now familiar press-briefing desk. The man was an intimidating presence in any room, and even on the pixellated display his air of superiority sent a shiver through her. She turned away, distracting herself by attempting to make coffee in a decisive and unprecedented manner.

Behind her, Mike was asking the public to report anything suspicious via the dedicated phone line. She looked back at the screen just as a close-up of Mike's face addressed Nemesis directly:

'The net is closing. Hand yourself in now, and we'll get you the help you need. You're only making things worse for yourself by drawing this out.'

Hawkins cringed. TV Mike sounded calm and in control, but he knew as well as she how far he was stretching the truth. In reality, they were still nowhere near to apprehending the Advent Killer, while the tidal wave of calls continued to create pandemonium just along the corridor.

But disinformation was now part of their strategy. It sought to create a personal battle between Mike and the killer, hopefully getting Nemesis angry or anxious enough to make a mistake.

But as far as she was concerned, Simon Hunter had been optimistic in stating that serial killers typically became complacent after a few successful murders. Unfortunately, there was nothing typical about Nemesis.

Hawkins picked up the drinks before heading back to their temporary operations room.

'Your coffee, sir. Any luck?'

'Nope. Welcome to Paranoid City, have a nice day.'

'Latest batch?' Hawkins pointed to the fresh tower of paper threatening to overwhelm her desk.

'Yeah, and those are just the sensible ones. You wanna see the rest – Brian says read them on screen. They're running out of paper.'

'Fantastic.' She began flicking through the pile. It seemed every lone guy in London had become threatening tonight, from the man sweeping platforms at Liverpool Street station to the bus driver who stared for too long.

At least their current situation could be considered as practice. All three previous murders had happened during the first sixty minutes of Sunday morning, and midnight was still almost two hours away. Even if Nemesis had already chosen his target, he was unlikely to hang around at the scene making polite conversation until it was time for the kill.

She sighed. 'What are the chances that any of these will lead anywhere until after midnight, anyway?'

'Practically zip.' Mike picked up the phone. 'Want me to tell the DCS we've stopped looking?'

'Good point.' She smiled ruefully and levelled a finger at him. 'Maybe I just need a few minutes of not thinking about how far up Shit Creek we are.'

'We deserve a break, anyhow.'

'Won't argue with that.' Hawkins sipped her water as her eye ran down the first of the transcripts on the desk in front of her.

'Why did you take this case?' she asked without thinking.

Mike's eyes narrowed. 'You mean, did I know we'd be working together?'

She hadn't been expecting that. 'Maybe.'

'Well, if that is what you meant, then no, I didn't.'

'Oh.' Hawkins tried to think of a light-hearted response. 'OK.'

'However,' Mike continued, 'if you meant did I *hope* I'd be working with you again, then the answer's yes.' He rolled his chair towards hers. 'And if you meant did I feel like doing a little dance of celebration when you said you'd split up with Paul, then the answer's yes to that, too.'

'But you hardly reacted.'

'I know.' Mike reached out and touched her neck. 'I practise that.'

Hawkins felt the strum of anticipation, but managed to play it down, 'It needs work, really. You didn't fool me.'

'I missed you, Toni.'

He was so close. She reached for the back of his head. 'I missed you, too.'

And, for the first time in three weeks, Hawkins forgot all about the Advent Killer as she gave in completely to the kiss.

34.

The atmosphere in the tube carriage was electric.

Alive with fear.

People crowded around him, the overriding flow towards the city mainly comprising braver members of the public, dressed up for Christmas Eve in the capital. But the average travellers among them provided greater insight: there was something unusual about the otherwise characteristic silence with which people endured their journeys.

The Indian woman a few seats from him had maintained a firm grip on her young son from the moment they got on, scolding him whenever he tried to pull away. Now she had the boy clamped in what he guessed was supposed to look like a hug.

He suppressed a smile: *Who was protecting whom?*

Another woman, Caucasian, younger, was sitting opposite him. She was smartly dressed, as if she had attended a Christmas function, or sacrificed a day off in the name of career advancement. To the casual observer she might have appeared relaxed, nonchalantly reading on the train ride home, but her thoughts were elsewhere.

She hadn't turned a page for ten minutes.

Panic was inevitable, thanks to the terror he had created with help from the media. He'd made the front page of every newspaper, every day, since the first message had appeared.

A copy of the *Metro* lay crumpled on the seat beside him. It carried images of all his victims, and a blacked-out figure behind a question mark, with the headline: **WHO DIES NEXT?**

He had glanced at the paper several times already, expecting each time to be affected by the memories. But tonight his emotions seemed muted, as if the thrill of a new chase had overridden them.

He felt sharp.

Focused.

Propaganda was his ally. Nobody wanted to become the next victim; nobody wanted Nemesis calling at *their* door. And the convenient result was that people were keeping their eyes off each other. Off *him*.

The train began to slow, and the blackness outside gave way to dirty tiles and dim lighting. Faces slid past the window, although none studied the carriage's occupants as they might have on a normal evening.

Seconds later the doors hissed open, but nobody entered, and finally the familiar beeping signalled that the doors were about to close. He had enjoyed the sound several times on this journey already – it reminded him of the movies, the final few seconds before the bomb went off, or as a missile locked onto its target. Except this time, the countdown was his.

The train eased away, gathering speed, back into unlit tunnel, carrying him towards his destination. He swayed as the carriage rocked. Sometimes the lights would flicker and go out for a few seconds, heightening his senses.

He heard the metallic whisper from a pair of earphones, and the tortured screams of wheels on tracks as the train rounded a bend. Being completely in the dark made him smile.

So this was how it felt to be Mike Maguire.

He would definitely enjoy enlightening that American idiot when the time came.

By now the police would be spreading out across London, ready to bounce like pinballs between distressed members of the public in a futile attempt to track him down. That was the beauty of his method. Those calls would be from the careful ones – the people who would never be targets. His victims were ignorant of the penalties imposed upon those who lived without regard for others. They deserved to die precisely *because* they were oblivious to the warning signs all around them every day. Which, poetically, meant they never saw fate coming.

His visit to Brighton yesterday had been even more valuable than anticipated. If he hadn't been within yards of Summer Easton as she left Old Glad Soul's Roadshow, he would never have been able to follow her to the small flat he had since confirmed she occupied here, in London.

Previously, he'd expected Easton to spend Christmas with her colleagues, given the close-knit reputation of travelling communities like hers. He'd assumed, incorrectly, that people who enjoyed such nomadic pursuits were somehow dissatisfied with home life, even though, he considered, his contact with her mother had demonstrated no such animosity. But none of that was important now, because he knew where she was, and had passed the property several times that afternoon to confirm she was still at home.

There was no guarantee she hadn't left in the meantime, but that was a risk he had to take. As far as he could tell, she'd be there tonight. And, judging by the poky nature of the flat and the lack of visitors so far, she'd be alone.

Obviously his impending activities would be more difficult in the terrified capital than they would have been in Brighton, but the disorganization he had prearranged among the Met's ranks would mean he would not be disturbed during the attack.

The carriage's lights flickered again, re-igniting one by one along the length of the coach as the train emerged into Baker Street. He remained seated, taking a final look at those around him.

The Indian woman was already dragging her son towards the doors, moving around a man in ripped jeans who was taking an iPod from his pocket. As the man reached up to adjust the volume of his earphones, his sleeve slid back to reveal a large wristwatch.

He was right on schedule.

SUNDAY

35.

00:00:01

Sunday.

Hawkins watched twenty seconds tick away before she noticed the silence. She waited for something to break it, but nothing did. There was no comment or rustle of transcripts from Mike, no urgent voices over the radio or banging of doors out in the corridor. No cheer to welcome Christmas morning. It was if a minute's silence was being observed.

She dared to look over at Mike. The expression he returned matched her sentiments exactly.

Shit.

Hawkins opened her mouth but couldn't think of anything to say. Any comment about the case would serve only to highlight their continued lack of progress, but nor was this the time to be discussing their personal issues. Suddenly, last night's kiss seemed like a lifetime ago. Her feelings for Mike would have to wait.

Admittedly their timing was abysmal. This was hardly an ideal opportunity to pick through the bones of a relationship neither of them had wanted to end. And, difficult as it might eventually be, that conversation looked easy next to the task they had postponed it for.

Suddenly, her headset hissed into life: one of the teams reporting yet another unproductive lead. Hawkins shook off fatigue and reached for the next sheet in the pile beside her, her voice cracking from overuse when she replied with the next address.

The team leader repeated it correctly, but his tone was glum.

Were they wasting their time?

She rattled off details of the transcript, glancing at Maguire, only to find him still looking at her. For a moment she thought he was going to offer reassurance, but a ringing sound from her desk ensured that whatever he'd been about to say would have to wait. She brought her mobile to her ear without checking the number. 'Hawkins.'

'What's our status, Detective?'

'Sir.' She landed fully back in the present. She'd expected Kirby-Jones to call, but the report she gave hadn't sounded so lame in her head: 'No further progress yet. DI Maguire and I are still working through the transcripts.'

'It's Sunday, Hawkins.'

'Yes, sir, I'm aware of that but, as I mentioned earlier, I believe that now swings the odds in our favour.'

'Why?'

'We didn't expect the killer to make an appearance before twelve o'clock, given that committing the murders on a Sunday is one of his signatures. His MO should increase our chances of getting a positive ID on his location in the next hour.'

'Hmmm.' He was quiet for a few seconds. 'What's our current response time?'

'Twenty-four minutes, sir.'

'And percentage of calls attended?'

'I don't have an exact figure.'

Silence.

'Approximately one in thirty,' she estimated, glancing at Mike, who winced.

There was muffled sound on the line, as if the mouthpiece had been covered.

'Are you still there, sir?'

'Of course. I'm trying to organize some extra manpower from Hertfordshire. Stand by for that, but don't count on it. And, for heaven's sake, Hawkins, get some help for you and Mike on the transcripts. You can't afford for this to fail.' The line went dead.

She replaced her mobile on the desk and slumped in her chair. Suddenly she felt so tired.

'The man hates me,' she breathed, half to herself.

'Hey,' Mike said. 'Don't let it get to you.'

Hawkins almost stood up. She wanted to walk over and collapse in his arms, but before her legs responded, calls came in on both radios.

Thirty minutes later, with any discussion about their relationship dutifully postponed, she and Mike were still at their desks, hunched over respective piles of transcripts, in constant dialogue with their teams. They had adopted similar approaches, with three separate stacks to denote 'promising', 'reasonable' and 'unlikely' leads. Unfortunately, all three piles outweighed the 'attended' stacks. There had been no word from the DCS about reinforcements, and their average response time had climbed to more than half an hour.

The clock read 00:41.

Hawkins pressed thumb and forefinger to her temples. Her head ached, and her throat was sore from giving nonstop direction over the radio. Fantastic – maybe she'd lose her voice *and* her career tonight?

She didn't want to contemplate failure, but her plan to use the public as radar hadn't paid off. Yet.

The response teams had arrested three men already tonight, but two of them had been too drunk to harm anyone except themselves, and the third had been picked up for car theft.

Nemesis was still out there.

To hell with it.

She had just reached into her bag for the packet of Marlboros and her lighter, and was drawing breath to lie about nipping to the ladies', when she was interrupted.

Connor pushed the door open. 'I'm here regarding the call-centre job. Apparently somebody ordered support.'

Hawkins was glad to see him, having called after her conversation with Kirby-Jones to get the sergeant back, redirecting the response team so they could drop him at the Yard. She filled Connor in on their progress before installing him in her chair.

He and Mike manned the radios while she prioritized the calls.

One o'clock on Sunday morning passed.

Hawkins swallowed hard. That was it; they had entered the crucial period when the killer was most likely to strike again, and yet all she could do was sit here in this office, helpless apart from the pile of paper on her desk. She felt an urge to get up and run into the street, waving her arms and shouting at everyone to be careful. But that wouldn't help anybody. Her only option was to press on.

Hawkins placed another sheet on the 'unlikely' pile and

began reading through the next. She sighed as the scenario began to unfold in depressingly familiar fashion, and by the end of the transcript her mind had shifted focus.

Something took her back six days, to the discovery of Jessica Anderton's body and the usual series of harrowing interviews with friends and relatives who had never had to deal with murder before.

Hawkins never knew whether to envy or pity people in that position.

She fought the urge to blame herself for their current situation. Could she have taken the investigation in a different direction? Would Nemesis be locked up by now if someone else had been in charge? Had she missed something obvious?

Connor leaned back in his chair, removing his headset to stretch. He looked round at Hawkins. 'How's it going, ma'am?'

'Oh, spectacular,' she replied. 'We're supposed to be one of the best forces in the world, but this guy gives us the time and day he's going to strike, and we still can't get near him. Not exactly a resounding endorsement.'

'Can't think like that, chief.' Connor turned his chair to face her. 'Sometimes it really is down to luck. Remember Geoffrey Evans?'

'I do, actually.' Hawkins thought back to her dissertation on serial homicide. 'Ireland's most eminent serial killer: went inside in the seventies for multiple rape and murder.'

'That's him – pledged to kill a woman a week. Luckily, they got him after just two, but it was the public who brought him down. He stole a car and painted it himself, then somebody saw it in a petrol station, thought it was weird and reported it. A couple of days later, a Garda patrol passed it in the street, so they picked up the driver. Turned out it was the same guy.'

The same guy.

Suddenly, every thought process in Hawkins' mind froze; a split second later, they were discarded as the spark crystallized into a tangible memory.

Mike and Connor looked startled as she bolted from her chair.

It had to be there. If there was any justice, it had *to be.*

She snatched her bag from the floor and began rifling through it. Connor slid his chair away to give her room as she began dumping files and briefing sheets onto the desk.

Just as she started cursing sod's law, Hawkins found what she was after. Her fingers gripped the ring binder of her previous, now full, notepad. She wrenched it free, thanking habitual disorganization, and began flipping pages.

Mike arrived beside her. 'What's up?'

'Wait,' she told him. 'Just . . . one . . . minute.'

Yes, there was the page. She read down until she found the line. Then she laid the notepad down and stared at it, her fingers trailing slowly across her forehead.

'This is it.' She tapped the page.

'This is what?' Mike asked. 'Come on, Toni, this is *what*?'

Hawkins realized she wasn't making much sense. She handed him a transcript only a couple of calls back from her 'promising' pile. 'This call came in at ten past midnight from someone called Faith Easton. Faith's daughter, Summer, called her a few hours earlier, at ten forty-five. They talked until after midnight, when the daughter's doorbell rang. She thought it'd be a friend, and promised to call her mum back. But she didn't, and now her mum says the line just rings whenever she calls it. At first she assumed Summer had gone out, but then she remembered some random guy contacted her via an internet chat room a few days ago, looking for her daughter, apparently in a professional capacity. So now she's worried.'

'Sounds like every other call we've had tonight,' Connor said. 'What's so special about this one?'

'Trouble is' – Hawkins showed him her notepad – 'I think she might be right. It reminded me about my interviews with Jessica's friends. They mentioned some new man who'd been sniffing around. Look at the name on both these sheets.'

She held up the notepad next to the transcript. Mike and Connor stared at the two documents for a moment before they said the name in unison.

'Jay Jay.'

36.

The lift doors slid shut, sealing them inside. Hawkins hit the button marked 'B1' and stepped back. She crossed her arms and chewed her lip. *The descent didn't usually take this long to begin, did it?* A nightmare scenario flashed through her mind: it wouldn't look great for them if the Advent Killer escaped because the three detectives leading the charge to apprehend him were trapped in a broken lift.

At last a jolt instigated their drop towards the basement of New Scotland Yard.

Hawkins breathed again, turning to Connor. 'You're absolutely sure there's only one Old Queen Street in London?'

'Yes, boss.'

'You've checked.'

'Yes, boss.'

'And how soon can you get us there?'

'Three minutes.' He held up car keys in one hand and waved an *A to Z* map-book with the other.

'Good.' She looked at Mike. 'How long until the first response team arrives?'

'Team 9's closest – they're still fifteen minutes away. Team 12 are four minutes behind that.'

Hawkins checked her watch. Seven minutes past one.

They fell silent as a second jolt was followed by a

pinging sound. The doors opened smoothly, and they moved out into Scotland Yard's underground car park.

It was a mere five minutes since Hawkins had discovered the link that had started the current chain of events. Since then, while Mike had called the nearest response teams and Connor had located the address, she had sourced two radios locked on a secure channel to Brian in the incident room.

Yet the link itself hadn't been the biggest shock. More worrying was just how close to New Scotland Yard the potential victim lived. Old Queen Street was less than a mile north of the Met's headquarters, meaning that she, Connor and Mike could get there well before any of the response teams.

Could this choice of location be intentional? Committing murder on the Met's doorstep would have been bad enough under normal circumstances, let alone on a night when they had been warned. Or was this a shrewd move by a killer who'd always been one step ahead? It was just after midnight on Christmas morning, and Scotland Yard was practically deserted. Had they had left their posts and gambled everything on a duff lead, leaving Nemesis free to kill again with even *less* chance of being caught? She shuddered. It was too late to turn back now.

At least she'd resisted the temptation to summon all their resources to this one address.

Their rapid footsteps echoed off the concrete walls of the below-street car park, and the Astra's lights flashed as Connor deactivated the alarm. A moment later, they exited onto Broadway. Connor and Mike sat up front, while Hawkins switched on the two radios in the back.

They resembled miniature walkie-talkies, and were lightweight enough to be clipped to the user's clothing. The secure channel ensured their messages would not be lost among general radio traffic, and that incoming communication from other units wouldn't interrupt. A couple of quick tests satisfied her that both were working and that Brian was where she had instructed him to wait – beside the main radio – ready to cancel the alarm or call in the cavalry. She turned the volume down on both and had just stuck them back in her pocket when they were all thrown forwards in their seats.

Connor swore at the car that had forced him to skid to a halt at the crossroads, then they were pinned back as he took off again. Hawkins craned her neck to read the road sign: Carter Street.

She leaned forwards between the seats. 'How far?'

'To the end of this street and then right.' Connor's eyes didn't leave the road ahead. 'Less than a minute. What house number is it?'

'Thirty-six.' Hakwins said.

'Park up short of the house,' Mike told him. 'Don't wanna be signposting our arrival.' He waited for Connor's nod before turning to look at Hawkins. His face was blank, but there was reassurance in his eyes.

Or was it exhilaration?

Before she could decide, they lost eye contact as the car jerked violently to the right.

'Shit, sorry!' Connor shouted, unheard by the shocked-looking couple crossing the road, who clearly hadn't expected sixty-mile-an-hour-traffic at one o'clock on Christmas morning.

Hawkins checked her seatbelt was securely fastened as fresh nerves jangled inside her.

Minutes from now, they could be hauling away the biggest arrest of her career, or standing over the body of the killer's latest victim. Or they might simply be explaining to a confused Londoner why they'd interrupted her first night in bed with a new boyfriend.

Two thoughts flashed through her mind: first, that she'd give almost anything to be the one who actually made the arrest, and; second, if it *had* been exhilaration in Mike's eyes a moment ago, maybe they had simply mirrored her own.

Outside, the scenery began to pass more slowly.

They were on Old Queen Street.

Mike and Connor took a side each and started checking off house numbers. Hawkins wiped condensation from the window beside her and strained her eyes, trying to pick out any movement in the heavy shadows that might betray a killer leaving a crime scene.

They were only a few hundred yards from the outskirts of London's beating heart: the Treasury and the Foreign Office were within half a mile; Downing Street itself was two minutes' walk from there. The street appeared deserted, but an eerie sensation descended on her. But the chill Hawkins felt had nothing to do with the temperature.

For at least another twelve minutes, when back-up would arrive, they were on their own.

'Fifty-eight,' Connor said, as he steered into a gap among the cars lining one side of the street. 'Close enough.'

Hawkins pulled her coat tighter as they stepped out of

the car, her breath condensing in the freezing night air. Large white flakes drifted silently around them, dampening the city's ambient noise to create an eerie stillness. Positive temperatures and rain earlier in the day meant the snow had only just begun to cover the ground.

Hawkins took the lead as Connor remote-locked the car.

'OK,' she said, 'nice and easy. We still have the element of surprise here.'

'Small mercies,' Connor whispered.

As they walked, Hawkins quietly cursed every house whose owner hadn't bothered to number, or at least sufficiently light, their door. She picked out fifty-two and forty-six, but none in between were visible. They couldn't afford any mistakes. She also noted the passageways at regular intervals between the houses.

'These cut-throughs should give us access to the rear.' She produced the two handsets and passed one to Connor. 'You take the back. We'll synchronize using the radios. Keep your voices down.' She checked her radio was on. 'And if Nemesis *is* here,' she continued, 'I'll take the heat if you have to shoot him. I want this fucker stopped, OK?'

Connor nodded and clipped the radio on to his lapel while Hawkins did the same.

'There,' Mike said, halting their progress and pointing ahead. 'Thirty-six.'

Their destination had a bright ceramic plaque denoting its number, although the sturdy wooden door made it unlikely they would gain entry by force. The curtains were closed, but a sliver of brightness ran along one edge of the window.

The front room lights were on.

Hawkins looked at Mike. He nodded: *This could be it.*

'We'll wait until you're in position,' she said to Connor. 'Go.'

Connor produced his gun from its holster and moved towards the nearest passage. Hawkins watched him disappear and turned to Mike. 'Ready?' she whispered.

'As I'll ever be.'

They moved closer to the door as a quiet burst of static indicated that Connor had pressed the talk button on his radio.

'Approaching the back now.' His voice was just above a whisper. 'There's a curtain so I can't see inside, but there's no garden. It just opens onto the alley.'

Hawkins heard him release the button, and reached up to press her own. 'Good. Sit tight. Brian, stand by.'

She checked her watch. The response teams would be less than ten minutes away now, but that could be the difference between finding a witness or a corpse. Her eyes locked with Mike's again as she raised her hand to knock.

She spoke into the radio. 'Here goes.'

Hawkins rapped twice on the door, heart pounding in her ears. Seconds passed.

She pressed the radio button again. 'Anything back there?'

'Not yet.'

'Trying again.' She balled her fist to knock a second time.

'Wait.' Connor's voice was tense but in control. 'I've got signs of movement inside the house. I think someone's coming out at the back.'

There was a sound that could have been a door latch being released.

'Armed police, don't m—' she heard Connor say, then: '*Wha—?*'

Static invaded the line suddenly before the signal ended with an abrupt click.

'Shit.' She looked at Mike. 'Taser.'

They turned and sprinted for the passageway, Mike leading, both of them fighting for traction in the snow. Hawkins managed to stay close behind him thanks to the training shoes she had worn since the previous afternoon.

As they reached the corner, the unmistakeable sounds of two gunshots shattered the still air.

'Eddie?' she yelled.

There was no reply as they flew along the passageway, until Mike suddenly stopped at its end. Hawkins fought every instinct to continue headlong into the alley, and flattened herself against the wall beside him. It was possible their quarry was now armed.

'Control, we've got gunfire,' she panted into the radio, as she watched Mike take two short breaths and then lean quickly in and out of the alleyway.

'He's running.' Mike disappeared around the corner.

Hawkins' eyes still hadn't adjusted to the gloom as she followed his lead into the alleyway. It was murky and narrow, hemmed in on either side by tall, terraced houses.

For a second Mike blocked her view ahead, then she heard running footsteps further along the passage and moved to the side, straining to make out detail in the shadows. Then she saw the figure.

Fifty yards ahead, a silhouette sprinted away from them.

Nemesis.

'Oh, hell, no.' Mike pulled up just in front of her. Hawkins tore her eyes away from the retreating figure and glanced down.

The air left her lungs as if she'd been punched.

Connor lay slumped on his side, a crimson halo spreading in the pristine snow. His eyelids were flickering, his throat and one of his temples a gory, gunshot mess.

'Motherfucker!' Mike shouted as he grabbed the radio from Connor's jacket and took off after the retreating figure. 'Antonia, get the car.'

Hawkins couldn't respond. She swallowed hard and crouched over the sergeant, pushing him gently onto his back.

'Eddie,' she breathed, watching helplessly as Connor's eyelids twitched one final time and became still. Even in the dim light she could tell he'd gone.

'Antonia?'

She jerked upright and stared into the eerie stillness, seeing only snowflakes swimming in the black air, exhaling when she remembered the radio. Suddenly, the moment came back to her: she heard the retreating footsteps again, and saw that Mike was approaching the far end of the alley.

'Antonia? Mike?' Brian's voice crackled through the radio. 'What the fuck's going on?'

'Officer down,' she said, searching Connor's coat pockets for his keys. 'Get an ambulance here, and helicopters. It's Nemesis, and he's taken off on foot.'

Brian said something she couldn't make out as she found the keys. She glanced down at Connor once more before she turned and ran for the car. She didn't want to leave him, but the response teams were on their way, and this might be their only chance to stop Nemesis.

'Mike,' she shouted, 'I'm nearly at the car. Which way?'

There was a hiss, then Mike's voice: 'He went straight across Old Queen Street and ... a cut-through.' His speech was broken as he ran. 'Must exit out front of ... St James' Park.'

'Stay with him,' Hawkins replied, aware that Mike's directions were also being relayed immediately to the incident room. 'I'm coming.'

She unlocked the Astra as she approached, clattered into the driver's seat and fumbled with the key. The engine roared into life and slush spattered the bodywork as she accelerated hard out onto the street, activating the un-liveried car's siren.

'Heading ... west' – Mike's breathing had become more laboured – 'toward Buckingham Palace. Think I'm ... catching ...'

Hawkins swore under her breath. She was moving in the opposite direction and there wasn't sufficient space to turn around. She reached the end of Old Queen Street, gunning the engine, slowing just enough to make the corner, perhaps not enough to avoid a collision if there was traffic.

The road was empty in both directions, and she hauled the Astra around another 90-degree left-hander, throwing in opposite lock and skidding onto the road that skirted St James' Park. She accelerated to a steady speed and leaned forwards, turning on the wipers to clear snow from the screen, scanning ahead.

'I'm on the same road,' she shouted over the siren's wail. 'Where are you?'

'Right-hand side.' Mike's voice was tinny through the radio speaker. 'Damn this fucker's . . . fast.'

She squinted through the falling snow, trying to pick out any movement against the whiteness beyond the trees lining the pavement. Two cars passed in the opposite direction, their lights blinding her. But as they moved on, she saw Mike, sprinting along the pavement just ahead. And then, about twenty-five yards further ahead, the form of the fleeing killer.

'I'm right behind you,' she told Mike. 'I'll try to cut him off.'

She changed down a gear and forced her foot to the floor. The wheels span before finding grip, her acceleration propelling her past Maguire.

'Keep going,' she shouted. 'I'll pin him in.'

She moved up a gear and closed on Nemesis as he flew along in the shadows between the trees and the railings surrounding St James' Park.

If Hawkins timed her incision correctly, she could create a blockade, maybe slowing their target enough for Mike to catch up . . . and, considering that Nemesis was probably armed, it wouldn't be a bad idea to hit him with the car in the process.

She held her breath and glanced ahead. No traffic. She pulled into the right-hand lane. She was right with him now; just a few more yards and she could turn in.

He must have heard the siren, known it was her intention to intercept, and yet he didn't break stride or even turn his head.

Milliseconds later, she found out why.

Nemesis had disappeared.

'No!' Hawkins gasped, swerving back onto her own side of the road. 'Mike, he cut into the park. I can't follow him.'

'I'm still on him, central path, heading north,' Mike replied. 'Go . . . round. He won't want to get trapped . . . in here.'

'Be careful.' Hawkins shifted her attention back to the road ahead, bracing for a speed bump. She hit it hard, sending a shockwave through the car as she cursed herself for neglecting to check whether Connor's gun had been left outside the house.

She shook her head. *Focus.* If it was back in Old Queen Street, the ambulance team would pick it up; if Nemesis had taken it, he was unlikely to draw further attention to himself by discharging the weapon again.

She hoped.

'He's going for . . . the bridge.' Mike's voice was a welcome distraction as the Astra crashed over a second speed bump. 'Where . . . you?'

'Nearly at the roundabout now.' She dropped a couple of gears, allowing the engine to aid her braking. There was only one bridge in St James' Park: it cut across the park's central lake, leading to a network of paths on the northern side. It presented Nemesis with an obvious route out of the park – straight ahead.

'I'll head for the north exit and try to cut him off,' she said. 'Mike, if he turns . . .'

'I know,' he came back. 'Try not to make an . . . easy target.'

Up ahead the lights of Buckingham Palace glowed through the snowstorm as Hawkins ignored the no-entry signs at the end of a one-way street, and flung the Astra right along the park's west perimeter.

She eased off the accelerator only when headlights appeared ahead and an oncoming taxi was forced to brake and swerve as Hawkins cut across the opposite lane of the roundabout as she slewed past onto the northern boundary of St James' Park.

'I'm on the Mall.' She released the radio's button and waited for a reply. A second later, she caught sight of the main gate a hundred yards ahead.

'Mike?' She turned the volume control to maximum, straining to hear anything through the speaker.

Nothing.

Suddenly, a lone figure exited the tall metal gates. It turned and sprinted for the shadows on the opposite side of the street.

It had to be Nemesis.

Hawkins floored the accelerator again, letting out the breath she'd been holding as Mike arrived on the pavement. He pointed along the Mall as he saw her, raising a hand to operate his radio.

'Go. I'm . . . right behind you.'

Hawkins set her sights on the figure fifty yards further up the road. Nemesis had cleared the railings, and was heading along the wide footpath set back from the road.

'Suspect is on the Mall,' she reported. 'Heading east. Control, where's our back-up?'

'On the way.' Brian sounded fraught. 'Four minutes.'

'And the helicopter?'

'Observer 2 is en route, but they're six minutes away.'

Hawkins banged the wheel with the heel of her hand. 'We need them here faster than that! If he gets near a busy area, we'll lose him.'

Her heart raced as the gap closed to twenty yards. Fifteen. Then ten. Fortunately, the high walls that skirted the street hemmed him in, leaving only one choice of direction. He had nowhere to hide.

But what the hell was she supposed to do now? The railings prevented her from cutting across directly into his path, and even if she did manage to stop him, he was probably armed with both a Taser and a gun.

Although suddenly she had a new problem.

The Astra lurched to the right and slowed dramatically. Hawkins swore and dragged the wheel across to point the car forwards again. She must have damaged a tyre by hitting the speed bumps so hard moments before.

The steering fought her, and her speed dropped as a grinding sound signalled that the tyre had given up altogether. She was running on the rim.

'Fuck!' Hawkins pulled up in the middle of the road, watching Nemesis reopen the gap.

'Toni,' Mike's voice hissed over the radio, 'what's wrong?'

'Flat tyre. I'm going after him on foot.'

'No, Antonia—' was all Hawkins heard as she clambered out of the car, flakes of snow immediately settling on her face, cold against her sweating skin. She took off without looking back, reassured by the sound of Mike's footfalls that he wasn't too far behind.

She could still see Nemesis up ahead, his silhouette dark against the whiteness now coating the Mall, his pace slowing after the chase through the park.

She was definitely gaining on him.

Her best bet was to maintain pursuit, keeping him in sight for as long as possible without catching up, giving the response teams time to arrive. But her blown tyre had allowed Nemesis to reach the first available exit from the Mall – although that also meant he had to leave the shadows.

Hawkins strained to pick out distinguishing features on her target as he entered the pool of yellow light created by a streetlight. She caught a glimpse of dark blue overalls and baseball cap before he disappeared around the corner that preceded the main steps leading north off the Mall, towards the Duke of York memorial.

Hawkins renewed her efforts and rounded the corner at a sprint. Ahead, Nemesis had scaled the first tier, and was taking the second set two at a time, but his gait was laboured.

At the base, two young men stood transfixed, staring after him.

'Met Police!' Hawkins shouted at them as she shot past. 'Stay . . . there!'

She reached the steps, attempting to clear three with her first leap. But her toe caught the lip of the third step and she crashed sideways, stifling a cry as her knee smashed against the stone. She scrambled back to her feet and carried on, looking up to see how much ground she had lost.

Nemesis had begun the third tier as Hawkins struggled

upwards against the pain in her knee. Her advantage was gone, but she could make out more detail in the streetlight bathing the steps. On top of the blue overalls Nemesis wore a backpack, and around his head was a dark shape that could have been created either by a hood or long hair.

'Suspect . . . heading north . . . off the Mall,' she rasped into the radio. 'Will exit steps near . . . Waterloo Gardens. Attempting to . . . maintain visual.'

But she was only halfway up the second tier of the steps when Nemesis disappeared from view.

She heard distant sirens as she limped to the top, managing to run the last fifteen yards. But as she staggered to a halt beyond the gates, Hawkins' worst fears were confirmed.

Dark, empty streets stretched away in three directions, each lined with trees that had so far kept the snow from reaching the ground. The faint trail of footsteps that might have told them which way Nemesis had gone petered out at the first tree.

Hawkins threw up her arms in desperation, heart pounding as she stared in turn along each of his possible escape routes.

Mike arrived beside her, his breathing also ragged, eyes searching hers. Hawkins said nothing, just let her head drop.

They had lost him.

37.

The sound of sirens faded as he walked casually into the tube station and travelled down on the escalator, keeping his face turned away from the security cameras. And when he lost himself among the crowd of weary celebrants awaiting the final train to run on Christmas morning, the Met's chances of apprehending Nemesis retreated still further.

Moments later, a rush of air from along the tunnel chilled the sweat on his face, indicating the approach of a train. Only when the lead carriage swept into view did his heightened state of alertness subside.

He queued patiently before boarding the train, and headed for one of the few remaining seats. He sat without removing the rucksack tightly strapped to his back, minimizing the chances of it being seen if the police reviewed the footage. The clock display in the door recess satisfied him that he'd be home before three.

He was eager to see the news. Every channel would be awash with speculation about the night's events, but he was interested to see this time how much of the truth would be reported.

He took his first chance to savour this latest victory. He'd enjoyed putting an end to Summer Easton, and had given her an extra long Taser burst, mainly because her delinquency had not been prompted as others' had by basic fear or incompetence.

Summer Easton had such contempt for people that she was prepared to cheat and lie simply for profit and reputation. So she had paid a fair price.

His original plan had been to spend the next day or two resting, in preparation for his final attack, the culmination of his campaign; the moment when he would finally be released from torment. Except the police had genuinely surprised him tonight. He couldn't imagine how they had pinpointed Summer Easton so precisely, almost in time to stop him. But they had, which meant his next attack, his definitive strike, would be even more challenging than expected.

Yet he was still free, and had remained so by ensuring that not even the smallest detail was left to chance. He had shown the Metropolitan Police this evening that they were vulnerable. He'd hurt them, and escaped in the face of far greater resources.

Tonight's second victim was regrettable. He'd opted for a head shot, to ensure the target wouldn't survive, but it hadn't been part of the plan, and would adulterate his message. So now he had to go even further.

It was time to reduce the Met's capability again.

MONDAY

38.

The drawer slid open at waist height, runners silent, plastic-encased cargo ominous. A soft thud marked the end of its travel, and Hawkins fought the urge to turn away, wishing there had been time to do this later.

She took a deep breath of chilled, bleach-infused air, forcing herself to look down at the plastic sheeting as it was folded back to reveal what remained of Connor's pallid features.

She swallowed hard, determined not to react in front of the Westminster Mortuary employee, Arnold, who had yet to show a flicker of emotion.

Mike stood opposite, his expression a mask of controlled professionalism. He must have felt Hawkins' eyes on him, however, because his gaze flicked up to meet hers and the veil of stoicism evaporated, to be replaced with one of sadness.

'*You OK?*' he mouthed.

She nodded, blinking back tears that would have been justified for so many reasons. And yet, greater than sympathy for those who would suffer more than she from these murders, or frustration following their recently dashed hopes of an arrest, the emotion Hawkins felt most was *loss*.

'Remember, no touching.' Arnold's apathetic tone was a welcome distraction as he moved along the wall, checking tag numbers with all the nonchalance of a super-market attendant looking for a certain brand of laundry detergent. He dragged open a second drawer. 'Here's the other one.'

Arnold removed his clear latex gloves and fired them catapult-style into a nearby bin. 'I'll leave you to it. Shout if you need anything.' He ambled away.

'Appreciate it,' Mike called after him.

Hawkins looked down at Connor again. She managed only a few seconds before she had to look away. In the short time she'd known him, Eddie Connor had become not only a trusted associate, but a friend as well.

'Not your fault.' Mike's voice was soft.

'Maybe not, but Eddie wasn't part of his plan. Why kill someone who was already immobilized by a blast from a Taser?'

'He saw the killer point blank, right? Even if he's disguised, he isn't gonna risk letting Connor live. Hunter said it – insane yes, stupid no.'

'I have to meet his wife later.'

'I'll go with you. Seen enough?'

'Yeah.' She replaced the bag over Connor's lifeless form. 'Of this whole case.'

They moved towards the second drawer, and Hawkins tried not to pay too much attention to her surroundings. The odour in these places was enough to turn your stomach, and it clung to you for hours afterwards.

But this was their only chance to see Summer Easton's body in the state Nemesis had left it.

Identification had been immediate, thanks to photo ID found at the house. And because there was no uncertainty surrounding the cause of death, the post-mortem was scheduled for later that morning.

This detailed examination would help to build a picture of the victim's final hours. When and what she last ate, whether there had been any recent sexual contact, and analysis of traces in or on the body that could be tied to a particular location in the surrounding area. Or a potential suspect.

There was even the possibility that, having disturbed the killer, they might have prevented him from erasing his tracks as effectively as before. For the first time in this case, Hawkins was hopeful that forensics may yet produce something of interest.

She eased open the second body bag, this time to reveal a young woman's face. It was the first time either of them had seen Nemesis' latest planned victim. The body had remained at the house in Old Queen Street for the whole of Sunday, only having been moved to the morgue in the early hours, once Scenes of Crime had completed their forensic examination.

Areas around the scene were still being searched for clues, while house-to-house inquiries were carried out with the neighbours. Telephone records were being checked, and a timeline of the victim's last hours was being mapped backwards from the time of death.

An official statement would be released to cover Sunday morning's events, combined with an appeal to come forwards for anyone who might have seen the killer in flight.

But all this would take time. As ever, while interviews with acquaintances and work colleagues of the victim were OK, you had to catch friends and relatives at the right moment, approach them in the right way. Otherwise grief or anger took over, rendering them unwilling or unable to help.

'Summer Easton.' Mike unfolded the interview notes made by Todd and Yasir the day before. 'Thirty-one. Private education and a bunch of jobs she never wanted; jerked around the whole way through, supported by her mom and dad's heavyweight bank account. Only chilled out when she found spiritualism in her mid-twenties; worked as a medium from then on. According to her mom, Summer was in Brighton till two days ago, with a travelling fair she joined as a psychic seven months back. Caught the train to London late Friday, spent Saturday cleaning the house and catching up with friends. She was due at her folks' in Surrey for Christmas dinner, but after her mom's phone call yesterday morning, they were already expecting the Community Support Officers when they arrived at the door.'

'Pretty girl.' Hawkins shook her head. 'What a waste. The research is good, though it doesn't sound like she'll have crossed paths with any of the other victims. We'll have to wait for a full background check. I'm more concerned that she was living outside London.' She looked at him. 'How much wider are we going to have to start looking for potential targets now?'

'She had the house,' Mike offered, running a finger down the page, 'and before the circus, she worked for two years at a psychic centre right here in the big smoke.'

Hawkins conceded the point. She eased the plastic

body bag open further and pushed it down, thankful for the surgical gloves she and Mike had been given upon arrival.

Mouth closed, Summer's face was remarkably undamaged. Beyond that, Hawkins was not keen to see. At one o'clock yesterday morning, jaw muscles debilitated after an extended Taser blast, it must have been easy for the killer to prize open her mouth and slice out her tongue. Then he'd simply taped over her nose and mouth and waited while she choked on her own blood.

The only small comfort Hawkins took from the situation was that Summer's horrific ordeal could have lasted no more than an hour: between the time when she last talked to her mum on the phone, and the moment Hawkins had knocked at the door.

Although the Taser had ensured that, like her predecessors, she had probably been conscious throughout.

Hawkins winced, thinking about the sister who identified these remains, and the family now spending Boxing Day deciding how to dispose of them. It would almost certainly be cremation. Relatives in these situations often saw it as the only way to cleanse their loved ones' defiled remains.

Mike went on. 'Seems the girl liked to party. Wasn't exactly careful who she hung out with. Family and friends have been concerned for a while. Same old, same old.' He sighed and refolded the printout. 'Sorry.'

'We will be,' Hawkins said, 'if we ever repeat yesterday's fiasco.'

The previous morning, following their not-quite-close-enough encounter with the killer, she and Mike had stayed out in the field to assist the returning response teams in their search.

Nemesis would almost certainly have gone straight to Leicester Square, where the crowds provided most effective cover. Their initial search party couldn't have been more than five minutes behind him, but hunting among hundreds of Christmas revellers without even knowing what their quarry looked like, beyond clothing he could have changed, had always been destined to fail.

As more officers had arrived the search had spread, but they'd been forced to concede defeat at 7 a.m., when even the stupidest criminal would have been miles away. After that, she and Mike had returned to the house in Old Queen Street and flashed their badges at the security cordon, only to be stopped and informed that the DCS had left instructions for them.

They were told to return home and get some rest before reporting to Kirby-Jones' office first thing on Monday morning for debriefing. Neither of them was welcome anywhere near the case until then. Todd and Yasir would oversee things in their absence.

Mike had dropped her home, most of the journey spent in solemn discussion about what they would say to the DCS the following day.

Then they had lapsed into silence. Hawkins avoided mentioning their personal situation, which seemed trivial after what had happened to Connor. Mike must have agreed, because he didn't raise the subject either, saying as they parted that he'd meet her at Scotland Yard for the debrief.

Hawkins had spent most of Christmas Day at home,

alone, drifting from one half-finished domestic task to another. At midday, despite not feeling like company of any kind, the pressure of opportunity had driven her into a cab. But as soon as formalities at her parents' house had been observed, she had made her excuses and returned home to solitude.

Although she would have denied it, she kept half an eye on the phone during the remainder of the day. Ultimately, though, she was glad Mike hadn't tried to contact her. They both had a lot to think about.

The meeting earlier that Monday morning had not been fun.

The chief superintendent had spoken to her and Mike separately, denying them the comfort of being interrogated with each other for support; although Hawkins also suspected that Mike's trial had been somewhat tamer than her own.

Kirby-Jones certainly hadn't held back when she admitted to withholding their discovery of Nemesis' possible chat room method for selecting at least some of his victims. She was surprised he hadn't fired her on the spot; although he had taken the opportunity to launch into his *How can we expect to beat crime if we don't work together?* speech.

It seemed that, despite the loss of a team member, Hawkins had just about hung on to her seconded position, and command of the investigation, because they had almost snared the killer. The chief superintendent even advised Mike to maintain his search for Nemesis in the chat rooms. It was made clear, however, that full disclosure was expected from now on. There would be no more warnings.

She was not being held responsible for Connor's death, but so far the investigation into events leading up to it was inconclusive, and would stay open. Question marks remained over her choice of approach, and the number of personnel she had opted to involve.

But while Hawkins' career was intact for now, she feared more for her credibility. To the DCS, maintaining public confidence in the Met's capabilities was everything. An official statement, released yesterday afternoon, sought to minimize embarrassment by reinforcing the Met's promise that, next time, Nemesis would end up in custody.

If he didn't, while Mike's reputation would suffer in the press, Hawkins would be the one clearing her desk.

39.

'Chief, can I in—?'

'Not now, Harris,' Hawkins snapped at the young sergeant. 'Talk to Yasir.'

Heads had turned as she and Mike had entered the main operations room at Hendon, and the noise level had dropped notably in response, but Anton Harris had been the only officer stupid enough to break their stride.

'Sorry, ma'am.' Harris backed away.

'Bloody temps,' Hawkins said under her breath. Westminster Morgue may have been cold and putrid, but at least the inmates didn't interrupt.

They made it to her office and closed the door on the undoubted gossip. Simon Hunter turned towards them from the window, while Frank Todd looked up from his seat in front of Hawkins' desk. Hunter carefully replaced a framed Community Service Award on the windowsill.

'Gentlemen,' she said. 'Thanks for coming.'

The air smelled stale as she moved into the room, probably due to the fact that her office door had been permanently closed for almost two weeks. So far she had resisted the temptation to change the name plate on it for one that said: 'Fuck Off'.

She walked around the desk and sat, checking that the window blinds were blocking the view to and from the main office. Mike occupied the seat next to Todd's, while Hunter remained standing.

Hawkins shifted, trying to get comfortable in the high-backed leather chair she had worked so hard for, realizing after a moment that the seat itself wasn't the cause of her discomfort. She sighed, aware that rank meant the silence was hers to break.

'OK,' she leaned forwards, linking her hands on the desk, 'let's not prevaricate. You all know what happened to Connor, and I don't like deaths on my watch, especially when we're talking about a well-liked and respected colleague.'

She paused to make eye contact with each of her audience. Todd's face was taut; Hunter's blank. Mike nodded.

She continued, 'Yes, we nearly caught the guy, but yesterday turned into a second-rate joke, and those above us with arse-covering options are beginning to take them. Unfortunately, *we* don't have anywhere to hide. Sooner or later, one of the victims' families will go to the Complaints Commission, and once that happens they'll all be at it, which means this Sunday might be our last chance to stop Nemesis,' She paused to emphasize the point. 'I purposely kept this meeting to senior level so we can talk candidly, and come up with a decent briefing for the team. We'll present that later on – the gossip is so strong out there at the moment that most of them wouldn't be listening anyway. And I'm sure that by now you're all on first-name terms with the reporters camped outside, which means the rest of our people are, too, and the last thing we want is another leak. So we'll do an after-action review of yesterday, and then we'll talk about next moves, OK?'

The men nodded. She began by reciting her own experience of the previous night. Her description started with the name on one of the transcripts that led them to the house in Old Queen Street, included details of Connor's death, and culminated in the chase through St James' Park.

The others gave their accounts, too, with everyone taking notes. If nothing else, it looked like all their reports would tally. But one question still bothered Hawkins.

She put down her notebook on the desk in front of her. 'What I really can't understand is why Eddie didn't get a shot off. His gun was drawn, but he lost to a guy with inferior weaponry. Why?'

Todd interrupted. 'I've been thinking about that. What if the killer only opened the door a crack, and fired those projectile things through the gap? Connor wouldn't have pulled the trigger unless he was sure. It's part of their training, like.'

'It's possible, Frank.' Hunter took over. 'But I wonder if there's another explanation. Has anyone checked whether Eddie ever discharged his weapon outside a training environment?'

Hawkins glanced around. No.

'Well,' Hunter said, 'there's plenty of evidence to suggest that some officers – and it's impossible to tell which ones before they're faced with the real thing – freeze in live situations like that. A lot of us just aren't capable of murder.'

Unpalatable as Hunter's theory was, Hawkins had to admit it made sense. Mike offered to trace Connor's duty records once they were done. Then she asked Todd for an update on subsequent events.

'Right.' Todd screwed his face up and stared at his notes as if he hadn't written them. 'As you might have expected, SOC haven't come up with a positive on prints or DNA from the scene yet, although they took a lot of stuff. I've got printouts of all the evidence from the house.'

He reached into a worn Newcastle United folder and handed out sheets from it. 'Tag numbers are next to each item. The list isn't complete yet; there are a few items outstanding.'

Hawkins drew breath, but he held up a hand. 'I'll be on the phone to the lab every half hour. Should be able to let you know about the gun later today.'

'Soon as you can, please, Frank. What about witnesses?'

'Neighbours say they stopped being surprised by blokes turning up at the victim's place ages ago. Nobody saw the killer arrive, but most of the street heard the shots. He was at full pelt after that, obviously, so descriptions are pretty limp – certainly nothing you didn't see for yourself. And the two lads near the steps – we interviewed them, but don't get too excited about the photofit; they'd both had a skinful. Would've been lucky to recognize each other at the time.'

Hawkins rolled her eyes at Mike. 'CCTV?'

'Tapes are on the server if you want a look,' Todd went on. 'But we couldn't make out any detail.'

She held up her palms. 'So we've got nothing new – again?'

'Well, almost nothing.' Frank made an uncharacteristic attempt at a positive tone. 'We know Charles Anderton was home alone all night Saturday. No phone calls in or out. And De Angelo's been tagged. He spent the weekend at home, too.'

Hawkins sighed. 'OK, Frank, cancel the surveillance on Anderton. These aren't contract killings; we're just wasting resources.' She presided over silence for a moment. 'Anything else?' The quiet eventually prompted her to bring up her own mildly desperate suggestion.

'OK, so we know that Summer Easton was a…' She looked at Mike, her hand circling. 'What's that word her mum used on the phone earlier?'

'Psychometrist.'

'Yes, contacting the dead and all that stuff. Well one of the uniforms, Katrina Wilson, found something in her celebrity magazine about Jessica Anderton having hired a personal astrologer. And now I'm wondering whether there's a link. I know it's not much, but we'll kick ourselves if there turns out to be something in it.'

She turned to Todd. 'Frank, get a couple of the guys to look into connections the previous victims had with anything, you know, *spiritual*. Tarot cards, palm reading, the lot.'

'Right-oh.' Todd straightened.

She addressed Mike. 'And it should go without saying, but I want Summer Easton's past torn to pieces. It won't be pleasant for the family, but there's a link here somewhere. This killer doesn't do casual; every detail is planned, so I just don't believe the victims' identities aren't significant. Tell the guys,' she waved a hand at the main office, 'the next person who says the word *random* is in charge of filing reports for a month, OK?'

Maguire nodded.

She turned to Hunter. 'So, any helpful footnotes to add to your profile on Nemesis? As you can see, we're open to suggestions.'

'Yeah.' Hunter scratched his head through the mop of black hair. 'Well, the good news is that I don't think this case will be open for much longer. I believe Nemesis is building towards something, and unless your people intercept, his campaign is likely to end in one of two ways. Scenario one is that he's close to achieving what he sees as the definitive act, as in one that he can't top. In this case, after he's made his ultimate kill, he may just disappear.'

'Which would constitute finishing his crusade.' Hawkins said.

'You think,' Todd interrupted, 'he'll just, like, *get it out of his system*? Are you joking?'

'OK,' Hunter said, 'I admit scenario two is more likely. It could be that he's on some kind of invincibility-trip, where he'll see it as necessary to keep outdoing himself, to prove to everyone, including himself, that he literally *can* get away with murder. We see the pattern building if we look back. At first plain homicide is enough, but the next attack is more gruesome. Then he goes for a celebrity. After that, whether it was planned or not, he decides to kill right on the Met's doorstep. Next . . . who knows?'

'So.' Todd wasn't finished. 'You're telling us he'll go on taking bigger risks each time. Until what, he gives himself an A-star and surrenders?'

Hunter smiled. 'Uh, no, Detective, I don't think he'll do *that*, but there are elements of good news here. You see, the bigger the thrill, the greater the risk. Inevitably, at some point, he'll push his luck too far.'

'His luck's held pretty well up to now,' Hawkins reminded him. 'Anything we can do to speed this along?'

'Actually there is.' Hunter removed his glasses and began cleaning them with a corner of his crumpled white shirt. 'You must appreciate the importance of last night's events.' He came forward and sat on the corner of Hawkins' desk. 'Nemesis is a lot easier to understand than he is to catch. His mind may seem unbalanced, downright deranged, when compared to a healthy mentality, perhaps, but he's behaved logically and consistently so far. That means he should also continue to feel a range of emotion within his own capabilities. Last night, you will have shocked him, don't doubt that. Not only did you come close to catching him, you forced him to kill in the interests of self-preservation. All his victims to that point had been meticulously chosen and screened. But Nemesis didn't plan Sergeant Connor's death any more than you did. He must have known it would become public knowledge, thereby adulterating the message he wants to broadcast.'

'Is there a *point* on its way?' Todd asked.

'Sorry, Frank.' Hunter didn't rise. 'In English, right? Last night you dented the man's pride by messing with his schedule in ways he didn't think you could. You're going to see a reaction one way or another.' He glanced at Hawkins, who tried to hide her apprehension behind a frown. Hunter went on. 'You may have knocked his confidence by nearly taking him down, or you may have boosted it by failing. Either way, my advice would be to push even harder now.'

Mike beat Hawkins to the obvious question: 'How?'

'Well, it may not be the most elegant plan, Detective, but I think you should get back on TV and wind the guy up. Make a big deal of the fact you nearly got him. Tell him that next time you will. Start some proper rivalry; get him angry enough to make that mistake you're waiting for. Let's face it, he's due one.'

'What effect do you foresee?' Hawkins asked.

'Well.' Hunter's brow twitched. 'The idea is to amplify whatever emotion you've sparked. If you've worried him he might ease off, but it's much more likely he'll want to exact revenge.'

'On us.'

'Yes.'

'Put the rest of my team in the firing line?' she snapped. 'I won't do that, sorry.'

'I'm just working with what we have,' Hunter said. 'I wish you had got him last night, Detective, but I'm afraid you just made things personal.'

40.

Hawkins closed her eyes, drumming the fingers of one hand on the windowsill of Mike's car and massaging her temples with the other. Unfortunately, neither action was having any effect on her headache, or helping to organize her thoughts.

She was finding it difficult to remove Connor's ashen features from her memory, especially when every conversation she'd had that day involved the DS in one way or another.

Mike had rung the police records department in Northern Ireland straight after their meeting. They'd called back just before she and Maguire left Becke House to confirm Hunter's suspicion.

Eddie Connor had never fired his weapon in a live situation.

Sergeant Harris had managed to corner Hawkins on her way out. He'd been given the unpleasant task of introducing Connor's swiftly enlisted replacement, Pete Walker.

More commonly known as 'Tank', thirty-four-year-old DS Walker was a former prison officer, six foot seven, with close-cropped, almost translucent blond hair. His sheer size was often enough to guarantee most people's cooperation, whether they were being placed under arrest, or just under pressure to fill a gap in the Met's rugby team.

His arrival was the first bit of good news Hawkins had

received for a while. She had worked with Walker when he was an inexperienced constable; he had sharp instincts, and he got things done.

Antonia now opened her eyes, just as Mike exited a small chemist's shop opposite, followed by an elderly woman. He jogged across the road as the lady raised her walking stick.

'Bloody Johnny-foreigners,' she shouted. 'Ruined our police force, you have.'

'Time to split.' Mike posted a paper bag and a bottle of water to Hawkins through her open window before heading round to the driver's side.

'Making friends with the locals?' Hawkins asked, as he took his seat.

'She saw me on the news.' Mike fired the Range Rover's engine and pulled away. 'Says we should get our act together and stop all these murders.'

'You can't teach common sense like that.' Hawkins removed a pack of tablets from the bag. 'We should get her number.'

Mike watched her wash down three pills. 'You know they're max strength, right?'

'I know.' She popped a fourth blister. 'But as things stand, I'm more interested in immediate solutions than long-term effects.'

They stopped at some lights, as Hawkins assessed the mucky remnants of the recent weather churned up by the Boxing Day traffic. Across the road a convertible Mercedes slewed sideways as it pulled away, its rear wheel drive system struggling in the slush. The snow had stopped falling the previous afternoon, but temperatures still hadn't risen sufficiently to melt what was left. Hence their decision to bring Mike's 4x4.

She sensed him studying her before he spoke. 'You sleep last night?'

'I had my moments.' She turned to look at him. 'You?'

'Same.' He drew breath. '*Man*, this case is crazy.' He paused. 'But I can't stop thinking about our, uh, *situation* from the other night.'

'Oh.' Hawkins was unsure of how to respond. There hadn't been opportunity to discuss their relationship in the day and a half since their kiss. But now Mike had taken the initiative, she found herself remarkably unprepared.

'My head's all over the place, Mike. Do you mind if we get this thing with Eddie's wife out the way first?'

'Hey, bad timing, I get it. Forget I said anything.'

They drove on in silence.

Hawkins thought about picking the conversation up again, but then decided against it. There was just too much going on; one of them would end up saying the wrong thing. Instead, she leaned into the breeze rushing through the open passenger window, trying to appreciate the fresh air, thinking about her pending appointment.

Tara Connor had been so calm on the phone when they'd arranged today's visit, but Hawkins was still dreading what would be their first meeting. Family Liaison officers had informed Eddie's wife of his death yesterday morning, so at least she wouldn't have to deliver the initial hammer blow. But spending Boxing Day returning the possessions of recently deceased husbands to their newly widowed partners was an appalling job by anyone's standards.

What really turned her stomach, though, was the thought that if her superiors suspected incompetence – and more specifically *her* incompetence – was to blame for Eddie's death, then surely it had crossed Tara Connor's mind, too.

But she had no choice; avoiding this duty would only have made things worse. Hopefully the paracetamol would kick in before they arrived.

Mike said they needed fuel as he stopped opposite a garage, waiting for a line of cars to pass. He stuck his foot down to jump through the first gap in the traffic, blurring Hawkins' vision as the Range Rover bumped onto the forecourt.

'Thanks for that,' she said, waving the pack of headache pills at him as they arrived at the pump.

'Oops.'

She saw Mike wince at the price on the pump. 'And don't you *dare* complain about the cost of our fuel when this thing gets through petrol like a refinery fire.'

'Not a word.' Mike began clambering out. 'Your dinky British cars are actually kind of cute, but to get a real engine, you gotta go large.'

She shook her head, making sure he saw; heard him laugh as he shut the door and moved around to fill the tank. They both knew that beneath her fake disdain she loved the 4x4, with its elegant cabin and effortless panache.

Hawkins heard the petrol pump kick in and let her head drop back. She tried taking her mind off Connor by focusing on the case, strategically positioning the team in her mind like chess pieces, the way she always had.

Ploughing ahead with active investigation, Barclay and

Yasir were chasing down the latest leads on Summer Easton's boyfriends. She had Mike primed to incite Nemesis through the media, while Todd had been despatched to re-interview the previous victims' friends and relatives, in case further information had resurfaced now the initial shock had passed. And a small army of officers, including new-boy Pete Walker, was positioned around St James' Park, looking for undiscovered witnesses who might have seen something useful during Sunday morning's chase.

They also had Simon Hunter.

The criminal psychologist had backtracked after claiming that Nemesis would want to take direct revenge on the police, although not sufficiently to set her mind at rest. His revised implication was that he hadn't meant retribution of the physical, shot-in-the-face kind; rather that increased humiliation or dragging the Met's name further into disrepute would be as likely a course of action for the killer now.

But Hunter's reassessment felt more like an excuse made by someone who realized they had said too much. And none of it was moving them any nearer to an arrest. They needed that moment of inspiration, something that would bring them back into contention. Their current lines of enquiry felt insufficient, as if Nemesis had already thought of everything. Unless . . .

'The chat room thing,' she asked, as soon as Mike returned to the car. 'Any progress?'

He pulled on his seatbelt. 'Still zip.'

'Keep going. We have to make the most of our decision not to warn the public. It's a huge risk, but it's only going to work in our favour if we take advantage of the gamble. Think about it. From the public's point of view, the case is falling to pieces around our ears, right?'

'Right. So?'

'So Nemesis gets the same story as everyone else – that's why we kept it out of the papers in the first place. Even if he thought we were on to him, he'd have expected us to release the information by now, don't you think?'

Mike kept his eyes on the road, nodding.

'I'm amazed we managed it,' she continued, 'but only you and me, Anderton, Kirby-Jones, and a couple of the tech guys know about the chat room line of inquiry. If it was going to leak, it would have by now. By keeping it quiet this long, we may just have convinced Nemesis that we missed it altogether.'

'OK, so what next?'

'Well we know he isn't afraid to come right into the city, so if you get anyone promising, try and arrange a meeting somewhere in the centre of town, where he won't notice a few dozen undercovers.'

They discussed possible strategies until Mike turned off the main road into a housing estate. It was a well-presented modern development, almost too charming to host the coming encounter.

'You ready for this?' Mike asked. 'I can go in if you want.'

'No. I should do it.'

She hoisted the box of Eddie's possessions from the foot well onto her lap, thankful there hadn't been long enough for many personal items to congregate in his locker. Among them were two packs of playing cards, a pair of Ted Baker shoes, and six king-size Mars bars. On top was a double picture frame, one side containing a picture of Eddie and a short, attractive woman that must be Tara. They were dressed in hiking gear at the top of a mountain, the angle suggesting a self-timer had been used to take the picture.

Hawkins looked away, composing herself. She turned her attention to the second picture. It showed Eddie holding a certificate in one hand and a rifle in the other, obviously around the time he graduated from firearms training.

But at this point, the Nemesis case barged its way back into her thoughts, as her phone rang.

She pulled her mobile out of her jacket and answered. It was Frank.

Without much in the way of lead up, Todd launched into the final inventory of items recovered from the house in Old Queen Street the previous day.

She shook her head as he reached the end of the list. Of course it wasn't there; life just wasn't that simple.

Connor's gun hadn't been found.

41.

He stared at the kitchen door.

Without his consent, his fingers reached up and found the latch.

His mouth was dry, and he flinched as the stiff mechanism scraped upwards. The sound would have alerted anyone on the other side, but he kept pushing until the latch snapped open.

There was rarely any pattern to his mother's moods, but if she was in the kitchen, one look would tell him what sort of reaction to expect. This was no longer about getting a drink; he was worried about her.

Surely she'd understand that.

He swallowed and pushed, scanning the room as the door creaked open, gradually revealing the farm kitchen. The light wasn't on, but the moonlight filtering through the large window provided light for him to see by. The door swept open revealing the sideboard, then the chairs and table. Still no sign of his mother. Then the back door, cupboards and hob. The sink came into view, and above it the high shelves for plates and cups. Still nothing.

Confused, he listened hard, but the noise of the hinges covered any other sound. He stepped, heart pounding, into the room.

A soft thump broke the silence, and he spun to see that the door had stopped against something.

Then somebody whispered his name.

He reached out and swung the door back the way it had come.

His mother lay slumped in the alcove behind the door, her long red hair pulled back in a ponytail. At first she seemed fine, but as he got used to the shadows he noticed that her make-up had run, and her eyes were glazed. And when she looked up at him, her eyes rolled back in her head. He counted three bottles on the floor. All were empty; one smashed. Glass shards littered the tiles.

She repeated his name, as if trying to wake him. She sounded more tired than angry, yet he couldn't respond.

He'd seen her sleep on or against every piece of furniture in the house, but now there was something different in the set of her limbs, the angle of her head.

Then he saw the bruising and the deep, red furrows in her upper arms.

Gouges grouped in sets of four. Bleeding.

'Please . . . baby,' she whispered. 'Come here.'

His legs felt weak as he stepped forwards, and his cheeks were suddenly wet. But as she reached out to him, he caught sight of the jagged slits in her wrist. Blood ran from the torn skin, and he saw pieces of flesh sticking out of the wounds.

He was barely aware of his attempt to scream as he backed away. His hand found the bench, but it served little purpose as he slid down the cupboard door and curled into a ball.

Then he saw the blood-soaked patch on her skirt under her other arm, and the kitchen knife beside her on the floor. He stared at her through the tears, his breathing rapid and uneven.

He sat, trembling, watching his mother. Her head had dropped back against the wall, but she was still breathing.

He forced out the words. 'Mum . . . what have you done?'

For a second there was no reaction, but then her head tipped towards him.

'Come . . . here.'

This time it wasn't a request.

He stood slowly. 'Why did you . . . cut yourself?'

Her tone hardened, I didn't.'

This reaction seemed to cause her pain, and she shut her eyes tight. But when she opened them again, her expression was softer.

'I'm sorry, baby,' she slurred. 'Didn't mean to up–. . . set . . . I promise, not angry . . . with you.'

He crouched beside her, bringing their faces level.

'I'm here,' he whispered.

'This is . . . it, darling.' Her voice wavered. '. . . you need to listen . . . carefully . . . important.'

Her hand moved, knocking into his knee. She slid it behind his back, leaving bloody smears on his T-shirt. He wanted to run.

'Sorry for . . . hurting you, baby. Don't know what I'm . . . doing, sometimes.'

'It's OK. You'll be all right.'

'Don't . . . think so.' She made a sound almost like laughter, which turned into a wheezing cough.

'I'm scared, Mum. Why did you do this?'

'I told you, darling . . . I . . . didn't. Your . . . father . . . did it.'

'What?'

'Listen, baby . . . in a minute, I want you to . . . call the police. Tell them . . . your father did this to me, and then . . . left. Tell them—'

'Dad did this to you?'

'He did . . . he did it . . . he's done it, before. Lots of . . . but . . . never this bad.'

'Why?'

'Look . . . tell them, he's done it . . . before. They might, not . . .

believe you, but that's . . . what he wants. Promise . . . you believe me, baby . . . please?'

'OK.'

Her arm dropped from his back. He reached down and held her hand.

'They might . . . try to tell you, I did this.' Her voice was almost inaudible. 'Your father . . . did a good job. But you'll always remember . . . it was . . . him, won't you?'

'Yes.' He held her hand tighter as tears ran down his face. 'I'll remember.'

His mother's breathing had slowed, but she seemed calmer. He looked around the kitchen for anything he could use as bandages, but suddenly he realized his father might still be in the house, and he picked up the knife instead. He'd defend them both if he had to.

'Mum?' He touched her shoulder. 'What if Dad comes back?'

'Don't worry.' Her eyes didn't open this time. 'He's . . . long gone. Just, call . . . police. They'll put him in . . . jail . . . if he comes back.' Her head dropped back against the wall, and she made a low groaning noise.

He waited, watching her face in the half-light. She had stopped breathing.

And beyond them, out in the hall, a slow scraping sound preceded a small thunk, as the grandfather clock struck one.

'Mum?' He pulled at her, breathing in bursts. 'Mum?'

But she didn't respond.

He let go of her hand and ran to the phone. He dialled 999 and told the controller their address and what had happened.

Then he ran outside and rode his bike to the deserted watermill where he sometimes went to play. He hid the knife in an old chest he *had buried in nearby woods, so he could use it to scare his father away should he ever return. Then he went back to the house to wait with his mother until the ambulance arrived.*

It was only then that he noticed the pain from the glass shards lodged in the soles of his feet.

TUESDAY

42.

The ringing sound was distant at first, but by its fourth repetition the noise was cacophonous, dragging Hawkins unwillingly into the beginning of another day.

She didn't bother moving; wouldn't make it out of bed and downstairs before the answer machine kicked in, anyway. If it was important they'd try her mobile, which was on the bedside table. Within reach.

The noise stopped and she heard the muffled sound of a message being left, although she couldn't tell who it was. She rolled over and picked up her mobile, expecting it to ring.

Sunlight probed through the thin curtains as Hawkins rubbed her eyes, wondering whether remembering to use the blackout blind would have improved the quality of her sleep.

She felt like shit.

Thirty seconds of silence later she managed to relax, but only until she read the display on her alarm clock.

She groaned and lifted her feet.

Hawkins heaved herself upright and sat there, rebooting. Without permission, her mind began rattling through the day's job list, one piling in on top of the next and then round again, corrupted by a mixture of anxieties and concerns. *Tumble-drying* she called it.

She shook her head and stood; walked across the landing to the bathroom. She stared at her face in the mirror. If mornings felt like this at thirty-five, it was amazing anyone bothered to live into old age. The stress of the Nemesis case was partly responsible, of course, and yesterday's encounter hadn't helped.

Tara Connor had been courteous and controlled throughout her brief visit, but it was obvious the woman was in shock. The delay in her reactions, and the Christmas presents still piled under the tree in the Connors' lounge had been testament to that. Tara had offered tea, which Hawkins had accepted only in order to break the vacant stare Eddie's widow had fixed on the space above her head. They had waited in the front room, surrounded by a sea of photos, each showing two beaming faces. Moments later, her host had drifted back into the front room carrying a single mug of tea, made with stone-cold water.

Hawkins had left feeling more awkward than when she'd arrived; almost wishing she *had* been blamed. Even some yelling would have helped. Somehow, promises of justice being done seemed so empty in response to stoicism.

After that, she had needed some sort of release, although she hadn't realized it at the time. But she found it by unloading on Mike.

During the journey home, Hawkins had blurted out all of her concerns regarding her shortcomings as DCI. Had she lost control of the investigation; pushed too hard for a promotion she didn't deserve?

Was she responsible for Eddie's death?

Mike had listened all the way back to Hawkins' house,

and for a further fifteen minutes in the car outside, before he insisted on making her dinner. He had prepared spaghetti Bolognese while she talked at him from the corner of the kitchen, and for another half an hour as she'd shifted pasta around her plate, before he attempted to respond.

When he had talked, however, Maguire had made a pretty impressive job of giving Hawkins back a degree of self-confidence.

Unfortunately, whether he had known the effect his words would have or not, Mike was also a gentleman. Just when Hawkins was ready to drag him off to bed, he had made a gracious excuse and left her alone to get some sleep.

She pulled at the bags under her eyes, unconvinced that she had actually benefited.

Hawkins showered and dressed. She flicked on the TV while she made some toast, catching the end of a report about the case.

'The Met commissioner says the investigation into the murder of thirty-one year-old Summer Easton is his top priority. But he'll be very much aware that the countdown to the next attack, due on New Year's Day, is underway. So for now at least, the Advent Killer case continues. Back to you, Sophie.'

Hawkins switched off the television and dumped the remnants of her breakfast in the bin.

She walked into the hall and picked up her bag. As she straightened, she caught a glimpse of the new message light flashing on her answer machine, and remembered the call from earlier. She looked at her watch. Her train wasn't due for a while yet.

She pressed the playback button, noticing there were two messages she hadn't listened to.

The machine started reeling off yesterday's date and the time the first message was left. Hawkins made use of the wasted seconds by running her hand along the top of the hall mirror. She tutted – the whole place needed a good clean.

At last the message kicked in.

'Antonia, it's your mother. Your father and I just wanted to make sure you're OK. It was nice to see you on Sunday, though it would have been nice if you'd stayed for dinner. We know work runs you ragged. Anyway, I hope you haven't forgotten your dad's birthday. We're having a get-together three weeks from Saturday, so I'll cross my fingers and put you down as a maybe.'

Hawkins wiped the message, making a mental note to call back on the way to work. But her eyes locked on to the machine as the second message began. There was no mistaking that voice.

Paul's tone was more positive than she'd heard it in months.

'Hi, Ant, it's me, pick up if you're there . . . OK, I guess not. Look, I wanted to apologize for not being around recently, and for the way I acted after, well, you know. I just needed time to get everything straight in my head. But I've done that now, really, and I wanted to clear the air. It's high time I picked my stuff up, too. Don't want you charging me for storage, ay? OK, call me when you get this. Bye.'

The machine beeped and said there were no more messages, but Hawkins remained rooted. Was this some sort of ploy, a change of tactics now she'd lost patience with his attention seeking?

She played the message again, listening for inflections – any indication that Paul's apparent mood wasn't genuine. There were none.

She glanced at the nearest box. If he was going to collect them, she'd have to put back his *Star Trek* DVDs. And the cycling helmet.

She stood there, trying to make sense of the situation. Then another glance at her watch convinced her she'd have to think about it on the way to work.

43

Hawkins paused at the top of the west stairwell in Becke House.

Directly ahead were the double doors of the serious incident suite; its purpose to house, in one place, officers drafted in from all over the country to work on major investigations like Operation Charter.

Currently, an average day would find nearly a hundred officers in the room, split into four teams of twenty-five, comprising every rank from detective inspectors down to typists. Hawkins' destination, the main operations room, lay opposite this entrance, beyond the open-plan desk area.

The thirty-yard walk was something she'd been so proud of five months ago when she'd first made DCI. She used to feel like the guest of honour at some big award ceremony whenever she strode along the central walkway. Recently, though, it felt more like a walk of shame. Every day, the distance stretched as she sped through, expecting the arrival of rotten fruit hurled by once loyal subordinates.

The investigation surrounding Connor's death, and especially her prospective culpability for it, was supposed to be a secret. Unfortunately, in the real world, there was rarely such a thing, and Hawkins had noticed changes in her colleagues as the rumours got around. They weren't obvious, but they were there. Some people overdid courtesy or politeness, while others would become suddenly distracted in her presence, thereby avoiding the need to acknowledge her.

All of this lay beyond the double doors. But while opaque glass panels prevented her from being seen by those in the room, they also gave no indication of how busy the place would be.

She took a deep breath and smoothed her jacket. Time to go.

Hawkins broke cover, pushing open the door, thankful that she'd arrived fifteen minutes before most officers rolled in. The office was only sparsely populated, with just a few analysts and indexers dotted around. And most of them appeared too preoccupied with whatever they were catching up on to notice her arrival.

She bowled along, bidding as nonchalant a greeting as she could manage to anyone crossing her path. She reached the operations room and breathed again as she pushed down the handle. She entered, scanning the room for Mike.

To her left, a large map of London dominated a whiteboard, stickers marking the locations of major incidents in the Nemesis case, thick annotation lines leading out to photos of the victims, crime scenes and post-mortem reports.

At first Hawkins thought the room was deserted, but then she noticed her trainee detective constable at his workstation.

Barclay sat hunched forwards over his desk, staring blankly at the tabletop. His diminutive frame was lost inside his ill-fitting black suit, and his mousy hair obviously hadn't been brushed.

She'd have to talk to him. They were all feeling the pressure of this case, but they'd never catch Nemesis if the team fell apart now.

'Morning.' She moved towards him. 'All alone?'

Barclay nodded without making eye contact. She noticed his eyes were red, although that wasn't surprising given recent events. Connor's death had been a blow for everyone, but he and Barclay had become friends immediately.

'So how's it going?' She arrived at his desk. 'Any leads . . . John?'

Barclay flinched, as if he'd just woken up, and looked at her. Neither of them spoke, until he broke eye contact and sagged, as if somebody was letting the air out of him.

'Look,' Hawkins began, 'I know you and Eddie were . . . friends.' She trailed off, wishing she'd considered the end of the sentence before launching in like an idiot.

A noise from behind her dragged Hawkins' attention away. She glanced around to see Amala Yasir entering the room.

'Ah, chief, I'm glad you're here.' Amala came towards them as Hawkins looked back at Barclay, whose gaze had returned to the middle distance. 'Not interrupting, am I?'

'No.' Hawkins turned to face her. 'What's up?'

As she spoke, she heard Barclay push back his chair, and he drifted past them, out of the office.

'Is he OK?' Yasir asked, as the door closed.

Yasir's demeanour, Hawkins was reassured to notice,

was as bulletproof as her appearance: both were sharp as ever, despite the recent death of their colleague.

'He's just feeling the pressure, I guess. Like the rest of us.'

'I understand, ma'am, though I always think you deal with everything so well. There aren't enough strong women in positions of responsibility like yours. How do you stay so focused?'

'Amala.' Hawkins resisted shaking the sergeant, not wanting to damage the faith this young woman obviously had in her, 'Everybody feels pressure. I *definitely* feel pressure. And if you end up like me, honestly, you'd be taking a step backwards.'

'But,' said Yasir, looking confused, 'how could I . . .? You're so—'

'Enough.' Hawkins held up her hands. 'We'll have to do this another day. What did you want?'

'Of course.' Yasir's professionalism returned as if someone had switched her back on at the mains. 'I have good news. Frank said you wanted us to look into possible connections between the first two victims and spiritualism. Well, it didn't take long for us to find one. It turns out that Tess Underwood's cousin was what they call a "spiritual healer". She claims to use spells and charms to cure people's ailments.'

Hawkins perked up. 'What about Glenis?'

'Tenuous,' Yasir admitted, 'but according to some of her former AA acquaintances, Mrs Ward placed a huge importance on her daily horoscope.'

Hawkins felt her brow contract.

Yasir must have seen it, because she rushed to qualify: 'They say Glenis lived by the things. Wouldn't make a choice without reading at least two different astrologers.'

It was enough.

'Great work.' Hawkins smiled. 'Let's get after this. Speak to Frank. Put a few teams together and talk to every London-based spiritualist you can find. Start with Faith Easton – see if she knows any of Summer's mentors or colleagues. Then move onto celebrities and advertised businesses. It's probably an occupational hazard for these people, but ask about former clients they'd describe as notably unusual. Or threatening. Keep me informed, OK?'

'Yes, ma'am.' Yasir moved to leave.

'Amala?' Hawkins waited until she turned back. 'this needs to get done fast. We're running out of time.'

44.

Hawkins positioned the telephone receiver a few inches above its base and dropped it as sarcastically as she could manage. As if in retort, the handset clipped the edge of the unit and clattered away across the desktop. She retrieved it and banged it back on the hook.

The latest update from Yasir's team wasn't good.

She stared into space, resisting the notion that randomly pursuing every spiritualist in the capital – with fingers crossed that one of them might happen to be the killer's next target – was pretty futile. Their opening line might as well be, 'Hi, I'm from the Met. We're missing a particularly nasty murderer. Carries a Taser, responds to the name Nemesis. Have you seen him?'

Even Faith Easton, despite her online contacts in the clairvoyant community, hadn't come up with anything useful. Okay, so she might not have been 'gifted' like her daughter, and shock would undoubtedly be playing a part, but all the hours she spent on psychic chat rooms should at least have provided a *few* leads.

No such luck.

But the spiritualist angle was still the best anyone had come up with to link the victims so far. And at least it meant they were doing *something*.

Hawkins sighed and reached for her mobile, deciding

that now was as good a time as any to ring Paul about collecting his stuff. Whatever happened in the Nemesis case, things at work weren't going to calm down in the next few days. So she might as well get it over with. Mid-second ring, however, she ended the call, because Mike had walked in.

She couldn't help herself: 'Where the hell have you been?'

'Busting my ass, actually.'

She relented. 'Sorry, ignore me. How was your morning?'

'Real productive.' He seemed to relax. 'Found something big. Call it a late Christmas present.'

He reached into his coat and produced a worn-looking videocassette.

Hawkins eyed him, remembering Mike's passion for photography, 'I hope this isn't some sort of confession.'

Hawkins massaged closed eyelids, trying to relieve the strain of staring from close range at a television screen. So far, she and Mike had watched the tape he delivered an hour ago five times. Unfortunately, during the last three viewings, she had noticed nothing new.

She rewound to the right place again, swearing at the dilapidated technology when it ejected the tape as soon as she pressed the stop button. She grabbed the warm cassette from its slot and banged the wood-effect side panel of the television.

'Stupid thing.'

The clunky old set rocked. Its fuzzy, low-resolution picture and wheeled trolley reminded Hawkins of science lessons at school, but this junk was the only apparatus capable of playing their aged bounty.

And without it, they wouldn't be watching footage of Nemesis.

It was probably an idea to let the whole system cool down.

They'd borrowed the video set-up from the sympathetically entitled Media Suite, which was actually a converted storage cupboard on the floor below. You weren't supposed to remove equipment from the area, even stuff as arthritic as this, but Hawkins ranked highly enough to ignore that particular rule.

Even the cleaners avoided spending time in the Media Suite, which these days smelled permanently of takeaways and sweat. You could never be sure who had used the desk in there last or, more sordidly, for what. Affairs between colleagues were common, and window blinds and an internal twist lock made this room popular.

Hawkins pushed back her chair and walked over to the window, gripping the cassette, reminding herself to be thankful they had it at all.

It was the best news she'd had in weeks.

The tape came from a lady called Doris Hicks, who had recently converted her house into two flats. And then sold the lower half to Summer Easton.

Ms Hicks had been visiting friends in Corfu until the previous evening, when she'd returned home to find her property garnished with crime-scene tape. She'd immediately called the number provided for enquiries, and ended up talking to Mike; at which point she had mentioned the motion-triggered security camera above her old front door.

Images from the camera were recorded on a three-hour tape by a VCR in what was now the upstairs flat, where she lived. Her call had come just in time: the system ran on a loop and, once full, the tape simply rewound and started again. And because nobody had noticed the camera hidden behind ivy above the door, the flurry of police activity over the past two days had given the system plenty to record. The critical footage was almost the oldest thing on the tape: if Ms Hicks had called any later, they'd have found nothing but images of forensics officers wandering in and out.

Hawkins was still watching raindrops edge down the window when Mike interrupted her thoughts.

'You gonna play that thing, or marry it?'

Hawkins realized she was clutching the tape to her chest. She lowered it, noticing that the plastic had cooled.

She returned to the VCR, hoping it would survive at least one more viewing. A digital copy had already been made by Anton Harris, who also happened to be a skilled video editor. Harris thought he could clean up the pictures, but that was going to take a while, so in the meantime they were making good use of the original.

What concerned Hawkins was that he couldn't retrieve what hadn't been there in the first place. It was hardly Sky HD.

She pushed the tape into the slot, waiting as the machine groaned and gulped it down. She winced at the appliance's various mechanical protestations, hoping the noises weren't being made by the tape permanently tethering itself to the electronic stalagmites within.

At last it settled, and she pressed play.

The display illuminated blue for a second before a grainy image appeared, difficult to make out while the tracking adjusted itself.

The end of the previous recording appeared; an overture to Summer Easton's final hours as she returned home for the last time. It was already late evening in the clip, and Summer's vibrant hair contrasted with the dark pavement below.

A moment later she passed out of shot and entered the house, followed by a ten-second still of the front step, as the system made sure that whoever had set off the sensor had gone, and wasn't just standing still.

The image flickered, and interference lines ran up the screen as the scene changed.

A pair of feet entered from above.

They both leaned closer and Hawkins raised a hand to shadow the screen, determined to capture every detail the poorly defined image had to offer.

The figure moved fully into frame. Once again she recognised the overalls, rucksack and baseball cap that obscured most of the killer's face, inscribing every visible element on her memory, noting again that the shape she'd later seen around his head was indeed created by shoulder-length hair protruding from under his hat.

But the shaky monotone picture made it impossible to determine his features, and the high camera angle meant it was difficult to determine height or even build.

The killer produced a bunch of flowers and a clipboard from his bag. Then he shouldered the backpack and reached for the buzzer.

They heard the electrical chime that had brought

Summer Easton to the door, and watched as Nemesis waited.

Hawkins felt her stomach turn over, as it had every other time she'd seen the tape. Watching the killer's controlled behaviour from the safety of her office emphasized just how dangerous this man was; something she hadn't had time to consider when they were only metres apart on Christmas morning.

On screen, a shaft of light fell across the pavement, indicating that the door had been opened on the chain. Then the killer spoke.

'Twenty-four-hour flowers, love.' The sound was scratchy and distorted, but the accent seemed local. He raised the clipboard as if to check it. 'From your old lady.'

Nemesis turned to look up and down the street as the shaft of light vanished momentarily, before reappearing when the door was opened fully.

Hawkins swallowed as Summer's shadow fell across the scene.

'Just need a signature, darling. Mind if I step into the light?'

The shadow in the doorway slid aside, and Nemesis moved out of shot. The door closed, leaving the scene empty again. Ten seconds later the image flickered, instantly skipping the time gap between that clip and the next. Hawkins watched herself and Mike enter from the top of the screen.

She pressed stop, retrieving the cassette when the machine finally spat it out.

'The guy's smart,' Mike said. 'Gotta give him that. If he

dresses up like that every time, even if the victims know him, they're not gonna recognize him till it's too damn late.'

Hawkins nodded.

'Let's run this through,' Mike went on. 'It doesn't matter if he follows her home or if he already knows where she lives. He waits till after midnight, then knocks on the door and pretends to be delivering flowers from her mom, right?'

Hawkins took over: 'She's taken in by the gesture and doesn't feel threatened by the delivery guy because of the twenty-four-hour flowers stuff, so she lets him in.'

'Then she gets Tasered and . . .' Mike shook his head. 'We've seen the rest.'

'And because she lets him in, any neighbours who see aren't suspicious enough to raise the alarm.'

'Right. The overalls pass for a uniform, but it's really an anti-contamination suit – same as we got, just blue instead of white. I know it ain't clear in the video, but I *guarantee* he got black overshoes and clear plastic gloves on already. All available to Joe Public, right off the shelf.'

Hawkins asked Mike to prime the investigation team. She wanted them to look into where the flowers used by the killer might have come from. If they were real, they must have been sourced in the last couple of days. Perhaps from a local florist. If they were fake, perhaps they were of a recognizable make.

While Mike was gone, Hawkins rang the press office and told them to contact *Crimewatch*. Their timing was fortunate. The team said they could get the tape broadcast on the upcoming show.

Mike returned while she was making her second call, to check on Harris' progress with the recording.

She hung up, turning to see Mike replacing one of the pictures on the shelf behind her desk. It showed the two of them at the Met's Christmas party last year, towards the end of their affair.

'I forgot about this picture,' Mike said, 'Why wasn't it here the other day?'

'It was. The first digitally enhanced copies of the tape will be ready in an hour, and the recording will be shown on tomorrow night's *Crimewatch.*'

'Great. So why's this frame not coated in dust like all the others?'

'OK, Poirot, I came across it in a drawer yesterday. Anton says they're doing well on cleaning up the sound and the picture. We can help Yasir and Todd take it round to all the victims' friends and relatives later.'

'Cool. Where's that snap I took when you made DI?'

'It's there somewhere,' she replied, hoping that Mike wouldn't remember the picture of Paul she'd removed to make space for the dustless frame.

Hawkins walked over and prised apart the dusty blinds on the internal windows of the room, peering out into the operations room beyond. Barclay still hadn't reappeared since his dramatic exit first thing, but Amala Yasir sat at her desk with the phone pressed to her ear. Her hunched pose suggested she was conscious of being overheard by Frank Todd, the room's only other occupant.

She was probably apologizing yet again to her boy-friend about her negligible chances of being home at a humane hour. Hawkins had asked her and Todd to play the tape to every officer involved with the case, as soon as copies were available.

It was good that the footage would appear on *Crimewatch* tomorrow night, but the thirty-odd hours before that was also a head start for them over Nemesis, who wouldn't know they had it until then.

Seconds later, Yasir replaced the handset, before she and Todd gathered their respective belongings and left, probably to get some food.

She turned back to Mike, suddenly feeling light headed. 'Have you had lunch?'

'No.' Concern entered his voice as she steadied herself on the desk. 'When did you last eat?'

'I'm fine,' she said, not even sure she had convinced herself. 'I just need to get out of here. You know, forget the mess I'm—that we're in with this case.'

'Hey.' Mike rubbed her shoulder. 'Just keep doing your thing. We'll get this guy, I swear.'

Hawkins picked at a splinter on the edge of her desk, nodding as enthusiastically as she could.

'Come here, girl.' Mike put his arms around her. 'Don't lose it on me now.'

She lowered her head to his chest and closed her eyes, brought her hands together behind Mike's back and breathed deeply, inhaling his aftershave.

Hawkins was barely aware of the light knocking sound, and was still in Mike's arms when she heard the door open. She pulled away, looking up to see Barclay in the doorway with a shocked expression on his face. His jaw hung open, but only his eyelids moved, flickering as if locked in complex calculation as he stared at them.

'John—' Hawkins began.

Barclay said nothing, but his stare broke away. Then he was gone, banging the door closed behind him.

Mike watched him go and then turned to look at her. 'What the hell just happened?'

'What do you mean?'

'Come on, this ain't a big thing. You find your boss hugging a colleague, you apologize, right?'

Hawkins was about to respond when it hit her. She looked down at her desk, silent as the answer arranged itself in her mind. Suddenly, it seemed amazing she hadn't realized before.

'Oh, bloody hell.' She slumped into her chair.

'Hello?' Mike stepped closer. 'Bloody hell *what?*'

Hawkins sighed, unable to think of a convincing reason not to tell him the truth. 'I thought he was just upset about Eddie, but maybe he suspected . . .' She trailed off, realizing she needed to start at the beginning. 'Look, John . . . asked me out when I was lecturing here last year. Obviously I refused.'

'Obviously,' Mike parodied. 'And that's it? Nothing . . . happened?'

'Oh, please. Of course nothing *happened.*'

'And he didn't give you any sign he's not OK with that?'

'No.' Hawkins pinched the bridge of her nose with thumb and forefinger, feeling the exhaustion of the past twenty-three days washing over her. 'Not until just then.'

'John's got a crush on you,' Mike reiterated. 'Why didn't you tell me?'

'I don't know. I suppose it was around the time everything blew up with Paul.'

276

'Oh, and by *blew up*, you mean when you did exactly what I warned you not to and told him everything.' He looked at her. 'You gotta get John back in here, Toni – you can't let this kind of shit go on.'

'So now you're running my team *and* my life?' Her voice rose as she stood. 'John's *my* responsibility, not yours. I'll deal with him because *I'm* in command. That's something you'd do well to remember, by the way.'

Mike's lower jaw shifted slightly as he conceded the point.

His voice was quieter when he spoke again. 'I still can't believe you didn't tell me about it.'

'We had our own problems, remember?'

'I mean since I got back. Doesn't it bother you?'

'Not really, no. And this is hardly the time to be addressing some schoolboy crush.'

'He's hardly a schoolboy.'

She didn't reply.

Mike frowned. 'Or *did* you do something to ask for this?'

'What are you suggesting?' Hawkins heard her voice rising again. 'That I led him on?'

She stared at Maguire, waiting for him to retract the question. When he didn't she turned away, running a hand through her hair, unable to comprehend how things between them had turned so bad so fast.

'Just go,' she said to the wall.

Mike breathed at her for a few seconds before she heard him move. She blinked as the door slammed, and stood looking at the photo of the two of them. How could these emotions still be so raw? It was as if they had simply paused the argument six months ago, and now that Mike was back, it had started right up again.

She sighed and sat down at her desk, picking up the phone to call the techs, but she pressed down the receiver button after dialling only half the extension number: it had been only minutes since she'd last checked, and they'd promised to let her know as soon as copies were made.

She held the receiver for a moment before she started to dial Mike's mobile, cut it off, then tried again. On the third attempt she completed the number and held her breath while she waited for it to ring. She exhaled when his voicemail kicked in. Hawkins replaced the handset and let her face sink into her hands.

It was a long time since she could remember feeling so alone.

45.

She stared back at him.

The photograph was old and battered, but in it her expression was one of satisfaction. Yet her current mood was of discontent. He knew because he had been watching, furtively tracing her regular paths, conscious of the locations from where he could observe without risking detection.

Her face told him everything. She was rich in so many ways: attractive, and gifted with compassion and grace. Traits that precipitated his infatuation. But, recently, she had become sullen and withdrawn.

So he had a decision to make.

He dug a hand in his pocket and touched the folded paper, taking comfort in its well-worn softness. He didn't need to read its contents; they were etched in his memory. Simply having it to hand gave him strength.

He remembered the moment when he had received the letter, shortly after his eighteenth birthday. The day the authorities delivered it, and also informed him of his father's death.

A decade's worth of anger at the man had prevented him from opening the letter, addressed so clearly in his father's handwriting. It would be almost two months before he tentatively broke the seal. The words played themselves back in his mind . . .

Son,

I hope this letter finds you well. I realize that to expect a reply would be unrealistic, but I have been granted a very different perspective on life in recent months, and I want you to know the truth.

It shames me to think of the tortured childhood I did nothing to avert or improve for you, yet I believe there were injustices perpetrated against me that you deserve to understand.

Your mother was once a rational, compassionate person. We were happy for many years, until she gave birth to you and your twin sister. She had always wanted a girl, but your sister died before taking her first breath. The experience left your mother emotionally disfigured, the worst expression of a parent. This, unfortunately, was the woman you knew.

I was aware of her subsequent alcoholism, and of her violent nature towards you. I'm ashamed to say that I was too weak to confront either. I stood by, despite her repeated adultery; in the hope that eventually the woman I loved would resurface. Perhaps that was an impossible dream.

One day she told me I was no longer welcome in our home, and that if I didn't leave, she would kill you in your sleep. Shamefully I did as she instructed.

I don't want you to forgive me. I will never forgive myself. But I wanted to behave like a parent at least once in my life.

If this letter is to have any positive impact at all, you must learn from my mistakes. If you see injustice, fight it. If you know what is right, act.

Don't let your life be filled, as mine was, with regret.

Dad

*

280

He had known immediately that every word was true. But his father's absence – the lack of a voice of reason – had rendered his mother's lies so believable.

His father hadn't killed her; hadn't even known of her death during all the years he remained elusive. *She* had been the evil one.

She hadn't wanted him or his father, hadn't even wanted to live. But neither had she wanted them to have each other. She'd forced her husband to leave, and turned his son against him before ending her own life.

At 1 a.m. that Sunday morning, when everything changed.

The ambulance crew had dragged him out of the kitchen and away from his mother as he screamed at them to make her better. The police had looked after him until the next day, when a social worker had arrived to take him to the first in a long line of juvenile care homes.

At first he'd struggled to cope with his mother's death and his father's disappearance. There had been no police enquiry. He followed events on TV as far as he'd been able, but the coroner returned a verdict of suicide and the case was dropped.

And as soon as it became clear his father was not going to return, he'd been absorbed fully into the care system.

He found interaction difficult, soon retreating into mute isolation. And throughout his time being shunted from one communal home to the next, it seemed all any-one wanted to do was fix his damaged, juvenile mind – they did nothing to protect him from the constant vio-lence of older boys, interested only in eradicating the psychological trauma caused by his abusive mum and his abandoning dad.

And those that talked to, rather than *at*, him, had wanted only to convince him his mother's death had been self-inflicted.

He hadn't listened, any more than they had when he repeated her lies.

After a while, he had simply acknowledged everything they said; repeated everything they wanted him to say, knowing that eventually they would lose interest. And they had.

He had learned to live with the torment, the nightmares, the pain. But he had neared adulthood with trepidation, aware that he would soon be required to choose a path in life.

Then his father's letter had arrived and, while he could not forgive, the man's words gave him direction at least. He'd walked out of his final care home determined to make a difference.

For a long time he foundered, his attempts to improve the lives of those around him having little impact. Then he had met *her*, and for a while he had thought that perhaps they could be happy together, a paradigm of solidarity and love.

But she had desecrated him, just as his mother had.

He had decided that, whatever failings men like his father demonstrated, women were always worse. They led society's decadent march towards destruction. Morality and justice hung on the precipice. He knew then his destiny.

Nemesis was born.

He'd hoped that his initial acts of retribution would make society listen; and sate his ravenous pain. But they had not.

Which meant there was only one possible course . . .

Suddenly everything slotted into place, and his eyes snapped back to the picture of his prey.

Forfeiting her *was* the answer. He would condemn his former love to oblivion, forever aware of who had served sentence on all who tried to crush or undermine his cause. With her death would come recognition and release.

And, at last, his torture would ease.

He stared at the picture, envisaging her pain, dismissing the remnants of compassion tugging at his core. She was the last, the crescendo of atonement.

Only the ultimate sacrifice was enough.

And *she* would be his.

WEDNESDAY

46.

The doorbell went at 07:19.

'Oh, for fuck's sake,' Hawkins killed the hair dryer and dumped it on the floor. Recently restructured post routes meant her mail had started turning up at this time of day, while early exiting neighbours with mail-order obsessions meant the packages often weren't even for her. But if she didn't answer, she knew the postman would be back at the same time every morning until he ruined her weekend lie-in.

Even though she'd be lucky to see one of those before summer.

She groaned, adjusting the towel around her damp, naked body and shuffled towards the stairs. The doorbell rang again when she was halfway down, this time followed by a knock.

'*Coming,*' she shouted from the bottom of the stairs, checking her bedraggled appearance in the mirror as she passed.

Hawkins arrived at the front door and fumbled with the lock, bracing herself. On the right day her postman's insensible enthusiasm was entertaining. Today it was going to be hard work.

Her mood after the argument with Mike was not the best. In fact, she'd stewed all night. But as the cold air began attacking her extremities, Hawkins reminded herself it really wasn't Royal Mail's fault.

She freed the lock and, determined to maintain decency at least, clamped the end of her towel with one hand as she opened the door.

To Paul.

'Hi, Ant.' Her former fiancé stood on the front step, apparently unfazed by the dreadful condition of his ex. 'Not a good time,' he stated, once it became obvious she wasn't going to say anything. 'I'll come back.'

'No,' Hawkins spurred herself as he began to turn away. 'It's OK. I'm not really awake yet and I wasn't . . . expecting you. What's up?'

'Sorry, didn't mean to intrude, but I was passing and, well, I left a message . . .'

'Your stuff.' The penny dropped. 'It's here.'

She moved aside, and Paul stepped past her into the hall with all the civility of someone on a first visit; so credibly, in fact, that Hawkins had to remind herself that, less than three months ago, he'd lived there.

Over his shoulder, she caught a glimpse of a new-looking Jaguar saloon parked out on the road.

'Blimey.' She pointed. 'That yours?'

'Yeah, well, sort of. Company car. Just got it.'

'Nice. Promotion?'

'Don't be daft, Morrison's don't do Jags. I'm with John Lewis now. Store design, don't you know.' He pulled his posh comedy face.

Hawkins laughed. It was refreshing to see this side of Paul again: it had been missing in action for the last six months they'd lived together; presumed dead once she'd told him about her and Mike. But here it was, back and convincing.

She shut the door, feeling somewhat less self-conscious than she'd expected, despite her attire.

'So what happened to the Peugeot?'

'Oh.' He looked sheepish. 'Sold. You don't mind, do you? I'd have offered it back, but we weren't really speaking.'

'It's fine.' Hawkins smiled, determined not to fall out with two ex-boyfriends within twenty-four hours. 'I still owe you a percentage of this place, after all. We'll have to sort that out at some point.'

'No rush.' Paul crouched beside one of the boxes and pulled out a *Star Trek* DVD. 'Bloody hell, I thought you'd have had these away by now.'

'It's all there,' Hawkins said with dignity, opting not to tell him the majority had sat exactly where it was since the day he'd left. 'I'd give you a hand loading up, but I can't risk flashing the neighbours; I'm on my final warning.'

Paul stood, grinning. 'Wow, the old routine, ay?' He looked at her, his smile slipping a bit. 'I didn't think we'd ever get to do it again.'

'Yeah.' She nodded.

'Anyway' – Paul picked up the nearest box – 'I guess we both have work. I'll load up and be out your way.'

'Sure.' She opened the door to let him exit, noticing as he passed that not only did he smell great, he also seemed to have gained some weight; although the extra bulk looked like the result of increased fitness rather than indulgence. And while he'd never been tall, his posture was straighter, somehow.

His dress sense had improved, too; something she'd never successfully been able to influence. The jeans looked expensive and, contrary to his traditional approach, the nicely cut jacket definitely wasn't supermarket own-brand. Even the hard-soled brogues he'd always insisted on wearing everywhere had gone.

Hawkins propped the door open and went upstairs to dress, keeping an eye on his progress out of the upstairs window, and noticing that the last remnants of Sunday's snow had gone.

She went downstairs as he finished loading the car and came to the front step. 'Well, that's it. Had to use the back seat, but at least it's done in one trip.'

'Great.' For the first time Hawkins realized his hair had changed, too, and was now cropped, instead of the scruffy mess she remembered. Was it ironic that this was the version of Paul she'd always wanted?

Her mind flashed back to Mike as she remembered whose fault the split had been, 'Anyway, we'll have to arrange a time to talk about your share of the house and, you know, catch up or something.'

'Definitely.' He smiled. 'I'd like that.'

'It's good to see you looking so well. New job, new car.'

'New house, too, actually; just across town. I'll text you the address.'

They stood for a moment in appreciative silence.

Paul broke it first, fishing a card out of his wallet. 'By the way, here's my new mobile number. Don't be afraid to use it, OK?'

'OK.'

He headed for the car, and Hawkins actually found

herself checking out his backside before he turned again halfway down the path.

'Hey, why don't you come over and see the new place? I'd love you to meet Nancy.'

'Nancy?'

'The soon-to-be Mrs Shefford. Bring someone; we'll have a blast.'

'Wow,' Hawkins tried to cover her shock, but managed only to make her next statement sound a little forced, 'Congratulations.'

'Thanks,' Paul didn't seem to notice, 'so you'll come for dinner?'

'It's a date.' Hawkins waved the card, indicating that she'd call to make arrangements. 'Take care.'

She watched Paul drive away before shutting the door, and stood in the hallway, feeling distinctly outdone. If the new house and the new 'soon-to-be Mrs Shefford' were anything like the car, Paul's life was going a lot better than she'd expected.

And a thousand times better than hers.

47.

Hawkins pressed the buzzer and turned back to face the group of boys. They hadn't ventured up the path behind her, but they had followed her around the building from where she'd left the unmarked Golf.

There were six of them, all unnaturally tall for their age, which she estimated to be around eleven or twelve. The housing estate itself didn't appear run-down, but the afternoon light was fading fast, and there was a biting chill in the air, which was probably why the streets were empty. Except for these kids.

The boys huddled for a moment, apparently determining a nominee. Then one of them stepped forwards.

'S'cuse me, miss,' he said, a cheeky grin on his face. 'My mates want to know . . . do you give *head*?'

She almost smiled with relief as the boys ran off crowing, amid much backslapping for their mouthy counterpart. Manners might have deteriorated, but apart from a few extreme exceptions, at least kids were still kids.

She turned back to the panel and pressed the backlit button for number 3 again. She hadn't heard a response through the speaker, but this type of intercom system rarely worked.

She checked her watch. 4.15 p.m. She was due in Buckhurst Hill in half an hour to show the enhanced video clip from Summer Easton's place to Glenis Ward's daughters. She could still just about make it – not that there was much chance of them recognizing the man on the tape, of course. They'd already shown the recording to just about every friend, relative and neighbour of the four victims during the last eighteen hours. Headshakes and frustrated apologies were all they'd received so far.

Obviously there was an outside chance that the Wards might surprise them, and if not, there was always *Crimewatch* later tonight, when the video would be seen by millions.

The intercom remained silent.

Hawkins checked the note she had made of John Barclay's address. This was definitely the place.

The buzzer panel showed that the block contained only four flats. She peered through the security glass into the entrance hall, where two doors faced each other just inside, wearing numbers 1 and 2. A central staircase led to an upper landing, where the remaining flats must have shared a side each.

She stepped back and looked up at the two-storey building. Eighties-style grey stonework and red steel railings framed each of the front-facing windows. There were lights on in both upstairs flats, and she knew the TDC lived alone. Either John wasn't bothered about his electricity bill, or he was in.

Communal intercoms were one thing, but Barclay's non-compromising attitude at work told Hawkins his home phone would not be so neglected. Pulling her mobile out of her bag and selecting his landline number, she hit dial.

As it began to ring, Hawkins looked up at the window, watching for signs of movement. Her concerns had been roused by his strange behaviour yesterday in the incident room. He hadn't been eager to talk, but without Yasir's interruption Hawkins suspected she'd have found out then and there what the problem was. And then there was his reaction to her and Mike. Perhaps the shocked expression was understandable if he was jealous, but a hug was hardly sufficient to merit storming off as he had. Something was definitely wrong. His actions were those of someone under pressure. But pressure from what?

Her anxiety hadn't peaked, however, until Barclay had failed to appear at Becke House that morning. She hadn't expected a great day's work from him, or even an apology, but she had expected him to be there. But there had been no croaky phone call; no message to say he'd been delayed, and no answer when she'd tried any of his numbers periodically through the day.

With one team member in the mortuary, and the remainder as disheartened as she was, further disunity needed to be dealt with straight away. She had to rally her team; remind them they had the moral high ground here. Locking up twisted killers was something to be proud of, well worth the long hours and relatively meagre pay. So she'd taken this detour to Barclay's Enfield flat, determined to get him back on side.

Yet there was still no evidence of movement, and

she became more concerned with every unanswered ring.

There was a good chance Barclay was simply ignoring her. Trainees exhibited high dropout rates once they realized the sacrifices police work demanded. And it wasn't going to be easy convincing John, or anyone else for that matter, that *she* was completely behind the job at the moment.

Hawkins ended the call and stood, blowing into cupped hands and shifting her feet to fend off the cold. She could wait longer, but she was tired and there was nowhere to shelter from the icy wind. The garden was empty apart from some patchy grass and a Haart estate agent's SOLD board. Plus it was starting to rain.

Best to force the issue.

She stepped back to the intercom and pressed the buzzer for number 1, the downstairs flat with a light on.

A short pause preceded a hiss.

'Hello?' An elderly woman's voice.

'Hi,' Hawkins said. 'I just bought the flat that was for sale here, but my husband has the only outside door key, and he's at work. Could you let me in, please?'

It sounded as if the old lady tutted, but a few seconds later a buzzing sound signalled that Hawkins' sham had worked.

'Thanks,' she called towards the speaker as she pulled the security door open.

She stepped inside and waited in case the old lady wanted to meet her new neighbour.

The entrance hall was lined with cheap beige carpet,

but it was clean, and smelled far better than some. Lino-faced stairs led up to her left, flanked by black iron railings

Once she was certain that the door to number 1 would remain closed, Hawkins moved towards the steps. She pressed the timer switch to light the upstairs landing and climbed slowly, keen to minimize the echo of her heeled boots on the metal kick plates. There was no point announcing her arrival until she was ready.

She reached the landing. A battered number 3 hung at a slight angle just below a peephole in John's cream-coloured front door. A television audience clapped and cheered across the hall, but she could hear nothing from inside Barclay's flat.

That wasn't a good sign. She hadn't known the trainee detective to go more than two minutes without a coughing fit in the last few months. Either this door was more soundproof than the neighbour's or, if he was there, John wasn't keen on company.

She waited until the rapid clicks of the timer had expired and the light flicked off. She'd look pretty conspicuous standing there in the dark should one of the other occupants of the building step into the hallway, but she wanted to check for shadows in the light escaping under the door.

Nothing.

Hawkins leaned back and pressed the plunger to relight the landing. She checked her watch again, aware that if Barclay did answer the door, he was likely to require a lot more than a five-minute pep talk.

She raised a hand and knocked, but as her knuckles made contact with the door, it moved. It didn't open, but neither was it secure. She looked around, senses suddenly razor sharp.

She checked the frame for signs of damage or forced entry. There were none.

Instinct told her to walk away, to return with some back-up at least. But then pride kicked in. Did she really want to throw away twelve years of the reputation that had brought her a DCI's badge – at least temporarily – because she was scared of an unlocked door? The taunting didn't bear contemplation.

Her heart rate leapt as she pushed the door. It resisted a little at first, but opened freely once it cleared the frame, to reveal a narrow hallway. The light she'd seen from outside came from what was probably the living room, straight ahead.

'John? It's Antonia.'

Silence.

She stepped over the threshold and switched on the hallway light, glancing through the archway to her left into a small kitchen. Everything looked normal. She checked the first room on her right. Bathroom. Nothing amiss.

'Hello?' Anyone home?'

She waited, still aware of the television noise drifting across the landing through the open front door, still hearing no reply. Only two rooms remained, judging from the size of the place.

Hawkins edged closer to the archway leading to the lounge, next to what had to be the bedroom door. But as she reached for the handle she froze, her eyes locked on the scene before her.

In the centre of the front room, the television lay

screen down on the carpet, surrounded by broken glass. A small dining table was on its side in one corner, and on its flat surface, there was no mistaking the most alarming element of all.

A smeared, bloody handprint.

48.

Hawkins ended the call to Amala Yasir and glanced across the corridor for what must have been the hundredth time in twenty minutes. The door remained closed, its smart silver plaque engraved with the words: 'DCS L. Kirby-Jones'.

Hawkins was the sole occupant of the glass-fronted waiting-cum-meeting room that had been installed opposite Kirby-Jones' office as part of a recent refurbishment at Becke House. Visitors were treated to a view of the corridor wall, punctuated only by a large painting of a seventeenth-century warship, and the plain wooden door leading to somewhere infinitely worse.

'Damnation's waiting room', as Hawkins called it, was silent except for the noisy wallpaper and the distant hum of air conditioning fans. A suspicion that the DCS had a button marked 'Nerve gas' in his office, to dispose of those inside had always amused her. But she wasn't laughing today.

Kirby-Jones wanted to see her. He hadn't said why, but it didn't take a genius to guess. She continued pacing, as she had been since her arrival, too nervous to sit in any of the poor-quality leather armchairs surrounding the glass coffee table in the centre of the room.

She had to get things straight before he called her in,

but her thoughts were chaotic, jumbled, falling over themselves.

'Get a grip, Antonia,' she said to the empty room, reassuring herself as a man strode noiselessly along the corridor outside that the floor-to-ceiling plate glass was soundproof. The man was tall, which made him appear thinner than he was, and he walked with an elegant confidence possessed only by those with power. He wore a dark suit, and his auburn hair was fashionably styled. But Hawkins wouldn't have noted these details, or the fact that his eyes were both sharp and blue, if he hadn't been staring straight at her.

She stared back, unable to read his expression, hoping he wouldn't enter the room as she tried desperately to place him. Instead of approaching the waiting room door, however, the man did something more worrying: he stopped outside Kirby-Jones' office and knocked.

A second later he entered and the door closed, leaving Hawkins even more unnerved than before. *Who the hell was he, and what was he doing here?*

Could he be a witness, or some sort of official come to take her badge and walk her off the premises? She shuddered as the three Ds flashed through her mind: discipline, demotion, dismissal. No, she had to be warned if it was any of those, so she would have time to arrange counsel.

She took a deep breath and blew out her cheeks as she exhaled. *Don't go in there looking like a bag of nerves.*

But that wouldn't be easy. As the Nemesis case stood, she had four dead women, one dead sergeant and still no suspect. Now she had a missing trainee detective constable, too; a situation made extremely concerning by the bloody handprint in his ransacked apartment.

She could think of no explanation other than that John Barclay had been abducted by Nemesis.

After finding the handprint, Hawkins had searched the rest of Barclay's flat, establishing beyond doubt that the place was deserted. Then she'd called it in.

It hadn't been long afterwards that Eleanor — Kirby-Jones' personal assistant — had rung to inform Hawkins that the DCS had 'requested' her presence.

So here she was, charged with explaining a two-hour-old situation she could barely grasp, to a superior officer she could barely stand.

First he'd want to know what she had found at the flat, and how she came to find it. Then what subsequent progress had been made, and what she planned to do next.

She tried to concentrate on the facts. While she had waited for the SOCOs to arrive, she'd used the anti-contamination suit from the crime-scene kit in the pool car to search the place in more detail.

The clothes in the bedroom were undisturbed; there was an empty suitcase under the bed. Not even the tooth-brush had gone from the bathroom. Even if you ignored the scene in the front room, it didn't look like John had been planning to go anywhere.

She could explain her presence at Barclay's flat as a result of his absence from work and her inability to contact him, but what would she say when asked about her most recent encounter with him? The fact that he'd stormed out of her office after finding her in Mike's embrace was bound to come out once Barclay resurfaced.

And she had to hope that was still possible.

And what of his erratic behaviour? Was it simply the pressure of the case and the death of a friend, or had he been threatened somehow?

Scenes of Crime were still at the flat. They'd already collected samples, but it would take time to separate the jumbled who's who of DNA typically found in short-term rented accommodation. John had moved in shortly after joining the team, just three months ago according to the building owners, so there would be plenty of residual traces from previous occupants, not to mention their visitors. In addition, she had four previous scenes that told her Nemesis was more than capable of keeping his DNA to himself.

And if Nemesis *had* taken John, it was a behavioural development she needed to discuss with Hunter as soon as possible. What did it mean if a serial killer started kidnapping people instead of murdering them? Or at least kidnapping them *first*.

Was he now targeting her team? The thought sent a chill through her.

Hawkins had spent the remaining time between leaving Barclay's flat and now, speaking to every officer she could contact, unsuccessfully trying to defuse the situation by locating her missing TDC. Nobody had seen or heard from John since lunchtime yesterday.

Nor had Hawkins' most recent conversation, with Amala Yasir, done anything to improve matters. Following her unexpected delay in Enfield, Hawkins had asked Yasir to take her place and show the tape of Sunday's footage to Glenis Ward's daughters. She'd had to blow proverbial smoke up Yasir's back end for several minutes in order to convince her she could handle it alone.

The sergeant had just left the home in Buckhurst Hill, where blank responses had extinguished that small glimmer of hope, too.

Plus, every development was still making headline news, so it looked very much like someone on the inside was continuing to leak information to the press.

Hawkins sighed again, resisting the temptation to turn exhalation into scream. She stared up at the ceiling, as if the answer might be hidden amongst its patterned tiles.

Think.

Her gaze settled on an innocuous grate on the wall just below ceiling level. She studied it for a second before shifting her stare, deceitfully scanning the room for the clock she knew to be on the opposite wall. If Kirby-Jones had a camera hidden in the room, there was no point winding him up by glaring at it.

She sank into the nearest armchair, conscious of every motion, unsure whether she cared any longer that her despondency would be apparent to anyone watching. The door across the hall remained closed.

Then her mobile rang.

She sat up and fumbled inside her jacket. *Please be John.*

Her fingers found the phone and she pulled it free, hitting the answer key before she had time to read the caller display.

'Hello?'

'It's me,' Mike. 'I got your messages.'

'Oh.' It took Hawkins a second to realize this was the

first contact between them since their terse conversation about work earlier in the day. 'Where have you been?'

'I had some stuff—'

'Look, it doesn't matter. Have you seen John since yesterday in my office?'

'Barclay?'

'Yes, have you seen or spoken to him?' She paused, waiting for an answer. 'Mike?'

'Why do you want to know?'

'Because he's gone, Mike, he's disappeared. Nobody knows where he is, there's blood in his flat, and the place looks like a sodding war zone. That's why.'

'Shit.' He paused, then, 'Can we talk about this face-to-face, Toni? Where are you?'

Hawkins lowered her voice. 'I'm in the bloody waiting room at Becke House. Kirby-Jones wants an explanation and I don't have one, so, no, we can't discuss it face-to-face.'

She heard Mike swear again under his breath before he answered, 'I don't know where he is, but' – he drew a breath – 'I went there last night, to John's flat, after our argument. But nothing happened, Toni, the kid wasn't even there. I would have told you.'

Hawkins found herself out of the chair, pacing.

'Toni? You there?'

'Why did you go?'

'I was cranked, OK? Ready to knock the guy out. But on the way over there I calmed down. I just wanted to talk, smooth things over.'

'You didn't see him?'

'No. I buzzed over and over. There were lights on, but

if he was there, he didn't answer. I left. You believe me, Antonia – you trust me, right?'

Hawkins lowered the phone and ended the call.

Lawrence Kirby-Jones was standing in his office doorway.

She switched her phone to silent, swallowed hard, and stood.

49.

Kirby-Jones' office was panelled in the same dark wood as the door, dimly lit by small lamps mounted on three of the four walls. The only window, to the rear, was covered by a heavy roller blind.

She stopped a few paces in as the chief superintendent closed the door and walked past her to the oversized teak desk in the centre of the room, sitting down in the huge executive chair behind it. Despite the presence of two, more modest seats opposite the desk, Hawkins was not invited to follow.

From the corner of her eye, she could see the tall man standing slightly behind and to her left. He made no attempt to introduce himself, and Kirby-Jones didn't acknowledge his presence. Instead the DCS studied Hawkins, as his wife and kids stared disapprovingly down at her from inside a wall-mounted frame.

The day's events swirled around her head. Should she try to soften the impact? Was Mike's confession relevant, or even true? She felt sick.

Kirby-Jones spoke at last. 'I'm informed we have a missing officer, Detective. I don't suppose you have sub-sequently located John Barclay?'

She shook her head.

'I see.' He glanced at the unidentified man, then back at

her. 'I don't want your focus taken off the main investigation, and we have to at least consider the possibility that his disappearance is not related to this case. So I've organized another team to find Mr Barclay, and a direct replacement will be sourced. Thankfully the media haven't been on the phone yet, so it may yet be possible to manage how the incident is reported.' He looked down at the desk for a second before going on. 'My concern is that, while Eddie Connor's death was almost certainly unplanned, it's probable that John Barclay's disappearance was anything but. In that case, every one of your team is a potential target, so safety takes precedence. No one working on Operation Charter is to spend time alone, at home or at work, until the case is resolved. Those who live alone will need to co-habit with other officers. For tonight, I've authorized surveillance teams to protect you at home, but from tomorrow I want you all to pair off. Do you understand?'

'Yes, sir.'

'Good.' He regarded her for a few seconds before glancing across at the unidentified man, who stood and moved around behind the desk. 'This is Superintendent Tristan Vaughn, one of the founding members of the special enquiries outfit, now a government consultant for COBRA.'

Hawkins eyed Vaughn. He certainly had the look for special enquiries – the cutting-edge unit for high-fliers, set up to deal with victims or criminals deemed to be in the public eye.

It was rumoured that most of their time was spent schmoozing celebrities who had fallen from grace.

The DCS sat back and drew a deep breath. 'Do you know what elevates someone into my position, Hawkins? Results,' he said, before she could answer. 'I deliver. Except that the higher your post, the more you rely on those in your charge to help you do so. And I, as your commanding officer, rely on you.' He paused, and Hawkins tried not to let the panic show on her face. 'Unfortunately' – Kirby-Jones steepled his hands in front of his chin – 'I'm no longer sure I can do that. I've been concerned about the progress of Operation Charter for some time.'

They stared at each other across the desk.

'However,' he continued, 'I appreciate this has been something of a baptism of fire for you, and that I put you in that position by recommending you for the role. I'm also reluctant to alter the team any further than it has been altered for us. Therefore, to preserve stability, you will retain chief investigating status, but I must act to stop any further degradation of the service we provide. To that end, Superintendent Vaughn will oversee this operation from now on, reporting directly to me. You are to brief him fully, and refer to him on *all* further proceedings. We'll review your position once the case is closed. Do you understand?'

Hawkins just stared for a second before she found her voice, the words almost catching in her throat. 'Yes, sir.'

'I'm not interested in your explanation of what happened today, but I need to get this circus under control before it destroys the Met's reputation completely.' He glanced at Vaughn. 'The superintendent will meet you in the SIS tomorrow morning at nine. Have your briefing prepared.' Kirby-Jones motioned towards the door. 'That's all.'

Hawkins nodded and turned. Closing the office door behind her she walked away, head up, determined to maintain composure.

Her nerve held until she'd established that the ladies' second floor washroom was empty. There, she slumped on the seat in one of the cubicles and brought a trembling hand to her forehead. She fought the urge to shout, to batter the walls with her fists; the same urge she had felt in the chief superintendent's office when he'd effectively relieved her of command on the Nemesis case.

Kirby-Jones' reason about not wanting to alter personnel at this stage was bullshit: there was more to it than that. Maybe he wanted further ammunition against her, or maybe he'd known the case was a career-killer right from the start. Why introduce a second scapegoat, when there was still life in the original?

Hawkins had heard before about cases where people like Vaughn had been drafted in to 'oversee' things. Those supposedly still in charge remained so until the cases were closed or forgotten, but resulting sideways moves or redundancy packages ensured they weren't around for long afterwards.

She rested her head against the cubicle wall, waiting for her heartbeat to return to normal. If the DCS wanted her demoted or thrown out of the Met, there was very little she could do about it. She had to make the best of this mess, by putting Nemesis behind bars. But how was she supposed to make progress when her team was falling apart?

She took out her mobile and saw three missed calls from Mike. She tabbed to his number, but her thumb hovered over the key.

She should call him back, apologize for cutting him off. Plus she needed to talk things through with somebody and, under normal circumstances, Mike would have been the perfect confidant. But something stopped her, and it wasn't just yesterday's argument.

Her mind drifted back to Barclay's flat. When she'd arrived, the door had been on the latch. It seemed inconsistent with the theory that the killer had taken John against his will; it was almost as if someone Barclay *knew* had rung the bell. He'd buzzed them in, and left the door open because he trusted them.

He wouldn't have done that with someone unfamiliar, but he might have done it for a colleague. Especially someone of a higher rank.

Someone like Maguire.

Twenty minutes after leaving Lawrence Kirby-Jones' office, Hawkins drifted out of Becke House. She stood forlorn in the damp, cold blackness of the car park, contemplating the train journey home, before remembering she still had the keys to the pool car. She turned towards the Golf, glad that she wouldn't have to suffer the tube ride home.

Hawkins dumped herself in the driver's seat and pulled on the seatbelt, started the engine and put the car in reverse.

Her phone rang.

She knocked the car out of gear, but left the engine

running. She rotated the heating knob all the way into the red before searching her bag, weighing up how to conduct the coming conversation with Mike.

She retrieved the handset, relieved to see Yasir's number.

She answered. 'Hi, Amala.'

'Ma'am?' Yasir sounded excited. 'I think we may have something.'

'Go on.'

'We've been interviewing various psychics all afternoon, dozens of them. No good until half an hour ago, but you might want to talk to this one yourself.'

Hawkins sighed, looking at her watch. 'Why?'

'In the last three months, she's the only one to have received a death threat.'

50.

Hawkins stepped out of the Golf onto a raked gravel drive, which was lit by ornate metal lamps dotting the area. She looked up at the lustrous greenery framing the parking area, and the attractive five-bedroom house covered in leaves.

The police-liveried Astras ahead of her on the driveway would have delivered Yasir plus the two uniforms, and the three security officers Hawkins had summoned. The brand new Alfa Romeo sports car and BMW saloon beyond them obviously belonged to the house's owners.

Two years ago, according to Yasir, Emilia Jeffries had married a successful lawyer called Winston Pare. It had afforded her the twin luxuries of being able to live between several houses like this one, while at the same time dabbling in whatever pseudo-career she fancied. And, since July, she'd fancied being a psychic. In contrast to her previous enterprises as style consultant and interior designer, Emilia had shown an intuitive skill in her latest vocation and, after experimenting with several stage personas, Emilia Jeffries had realized her own name had become synonymous with her talent.

She'd quickly developed into something of a local celebrity, having astounded a number of her husband's high-society friends, along with the local media, and was reputedly on her way to stardom. Except that in the process she'd upset someone sufficiently to induce a death threat. Which begged one critical question . . .

Was that someone Nemesis?

Hawkins threaded her way among the assorted vehicles to a marble-floored porch, mildly impressed to see her reflection in the flawless black paint finish on the door. She pressed the smart doorbell, unable to hear any resulting carillon from within, but reluctant to risk appearing impatient by ringing again. She waited, inhaling the brittle December air, laced with the scent of whatever potpourri occupied the delicate receptacles either side of the entrance.

After a moment, the front door swung open to reveal a young uniformed officer. Hawkins recognized his permanently flushed cheeks from the control room at Becke House, but couldn't dredge up his name.

'Come in, chief.' He stepped aside. 'Everyone's in the front room.'

She followed him along the hall, past the biggest mirror she'd seen in a while, into a cavernous front room. Everyone looked up.

The three security officers stood in a stoic line behind a long floral settee, while the second uniform, Steve Judd, hovered by the fireplace. Amala Yasir sat in one of the leather armchairs flanking the coffee table, while in the other sat a striking woman in her early forties, with long ebony hair.

'Emilia.' Hawkins shook hands with her, avoiding potentially incorrect use of Miss or Mrs. 'DCI Antonia Hawkins.'

Jeffries didn't stand. 'Chief Inspector, is it? I assume that means you're in charge, so perhaps you'll make a better job than this lady of explaining why my house is full of policemen.'

Hawkins cleared her throat, determined not to rise to a woman who'd managed to put her offside within a sentence. She explained that Sergeant Yasir had been instructed not to divulge the specific reason for their visit but, now that both Jeffries' profession, and the fact she'd recently received a death threat, might be linked to the Nemesis investigation, it was time to inform her of the potential danger.

In other words, love, you might be a target.

Her words had transformative effect.

Jeffries lost eye contact with Hawkins for the first time, and there was silence among the eight people in the room for a long moment.

'So,' their host's voice wavered, 'you think the death threat was from this . . . killer?'

Hawkins drew breath, feeling that her attempt to make the woman back off had been a little too successful. 'It's possible.'

'Oh.' Jeffries reached for the glass on the table that Hawkins had previously assumed contained water. But the way she slugged it back, and her resulting expression, suggested otherwise.

'I'm going to be murdered,' Emilia Jeffries breathed, apparently to herself.

'Look,' Hawkins reassured her, 'there's no guarantee we're even right about this, but if you're a target we can protect you. And the more information you can give us, the faster we'll catch this lunatic, OK?'

Jeffries glanced at the drinks cabinet on the opposite wall, then at her empty glass, then back at Hawkins. 'OK.'

For the following thirty minutes, Hawkins and Yasir took notes on Emilia Jeffries' explanation of events leading up to the threat on her life.

Three months before, she had performed one of her earliest psychic readings for a woman named Karin. During the session, Jeffries had picked up negativity surrounding Karin's partner, Curtis, who, her subject admitted, had recently attacked her, leading Jeffries to suggest that she curtail the relationship.

Afterwards, as she showed her client out, Jeffries had opened the door to find a man standing on her porch. Karin hadn't introduced them, but her timid reaction and the short, pseudo-polite conversation between the three of them suggested that he was Curtis, and that he'd followed his partner without her knowledge.

Jeffries had no idea whether the woman had acted on her advice but, a week later, she'd received a telephone call late in the evening. A muffled voice had said: *You should have kept your pious mouth shut, bitch. But you didn't, did you? So now you're going to die.*

As she finished writing the sentence in her notebook, Hawkins felt a sense of hope for the first time in days. OK, so this whole thing was circumstantial, and Jeffries knew only Karin and Curtis' first names and that they were from the Newington area, but the links were there: the psychic connection and a recent history of violence.

Plus, Hawkins reminded herself, instinct had already taken them within millimetres of stopping the killer.

Trust your gut.

51.

Headlights arced lazily across the hedges to his left, two brilliant searchlights among the columns of precipitation beginning to drift silently from sky to ground. He aligned himself with the largest tree trunk as the Bentley limousine swept past.

Every property in this road had tall, manicured foliage separating one immodest resident from the next, but he'd selected this particular grove because its owner had been especially liberal with their festive decoration. The lights surrounding him were insufficiently radiant to make him visible among the trees, but their glow would engage the eye of any onlooker, obscuring the figure hidden in the darkness behind. And, of course, this vantage point had another critical attribute.

Its view.

He'd been there since before the first police cars had arrived, to observe his prey and gauge her disposition in the run-up to their pending encounter. And his patience was rewarded.

Thirty yards away, the front door of the house opened. And there she was, leaving the house flanked by two uniformed police officers, her frame bent gracefully against the rain.

The woman he'd once loved.

The group distributed themselves among the assembled cars, exiting the drive in sequence.

As her car reversed to a halt before accelerating away, he caught a glimpse of her through the window. His final victim's expression was suitably reverent.

She knew their paths were destined to cross.

THURSDAY

52.

'Do you mind if I call you Antonia?'

'Please.'

Vaughn smiled. 'Believe it or not, Antonia, I'm on your side.'

Hawkins studied him. He looked genuine enough; certainly lacked the supercilious air of their commanding officer.

He wanted her to call him Tristan, insisting from the off that they ignore rank in this meeting. His voice was warm, his tone reasonable, and he'd demonstrated nothing but desire to work *with* her on this.

All the underhand tactics she'd expected.

In the ten minutes since their arrival in the meeting room adjacent to the serious incident suite, Hawkins had filled the gaps in Vaughn's knowledge about Operation Charter. Obviously he knew what was going on in the media, and Kirby-Jones had given him an outline of proceedings, but now he was asking about Hawkins' plans for progress.

Part of her was reluctant to respond. If her every move was to be reported and scrutinized, maybe it was best to say nothing. Or perhaps saying nothing would get her fired even faster. Or maybe she should just admit she didn't have a definite plan.

'I can understand if you don't trust me,' Vaughn said,

eventually. 'You want to be sure I won't report anything I don't agree with to the DCS.'

'The thought had crossed my mind.'

She hadn't told him about Emilia Jeffries.

'Fair enough.' He signalled surrender with both hands. 'I was trying to avoid appearing to dictate, but how about if I tell you what I'd do in your position?'

'Go ahead.'

'OK.' Vaughn picked up one of the newspapers from the desk and held it up. The headline read, **DID SOCIETY CREATE NEMESIS?** 'These are part of our collective nightmare, right?'

'Yes.'

'So what's our main problem right now?'

'I thought you were telling me.'

'Right.' He laughed. 'Well, at the moment, Nemesis is giving them all the best lines. We, meanwhile, have a leak. So we're clamping down on what we tell our people, and on what Maguire's allowed to say to the press, because we're afraid of making things worse. So I say turn the thing on its head and grab some headlines of our own.'

'Media mind games. A profiler once told me the same thing.'

'Hunter, I know. And you ignored him because you had a plan to find Nemesis by posing online as a potential target. Hell, I might have done the same thing, but the situation's changed.'

Hawkins decided not to interject with an update. Mike's online search for Nemesis had led to several speculative 'meetings'; mainly with the sorts of people Hawkins could imagine at dogging hotspots. But none of them came sufficiently close to the physical appearance of the man caught on tape outside Summer Easton's house the previous week.

Vaughn went on, 'We're two-nil down: one officer dead, another missing. At the moment, the Met look like bungling fools, and Londoners don't back a loser. Public perception, that's what concerns the chief superintendent. So I say be honest, neutralize the mole and win back some support from the public.'

'And the rest of the investigation?'

'Keep doing what you're doing; there's nothing wrong with that. The reconstructions on *Crimewatch* last night should bring in plenty of new leads, just keep me informed. But if we're going to stop Nemesis, we can't afford to lose further ground here; this type of media-facilitated exchange is about saving face and gaining a psychological edge at the same time. So I'll put something together for the papers, and we can talk it over before sending it, OK?'

Hawkins left the meeting room deep in thought. Tristan Vaughn was sharp, on first name terms with everyone in the media she'd asked about him, and he seemed to be genuinely trying to help. His strategy, albeit focused as much on institutionalized politics as saving lives, showed promise. Yet he remained a minion of Lawrence Kirby-Jones, with whom his loyalties inevitably lay should further conflict ensue.

Anyone who didn't expect that was a fool.

53

Hawkins re-entered her office holding the case file in one hand and a cup of brown liquid that the vending machine said was coffee in the other. She kicked the door closed and headed straight for her chair. She sat down and closed her eyes, rolling her shoulders, breathing deeply.

Amala Yasir had just introduced her to DS Aaron Sharpe, who had been drafted in to fill the latest gaping hole in her immediate team.

She probably should have been thankful to replace a trainee with a sergeant, but everything from the guy's limp handshake to his tacky suit screamed *underachiever*, while a long service record coupled with low rank for his age – which had to be in the region of forty-five – backed up her assumption. It was the look in Sharpe's eyes as they had shaken hands, however, that convinced Hawkins he hadn't volunteered for the position: he was as shit-scared as every other officer in joining a team being systematically exterminated by a psychopathic killer.

She pushed the thought from her mind and switched on her computer, sipping the drink while the PC booted up. She logged into Outlook, deleting the regular mix of emails about the previous night's crime reports and figures, and various internal circulars about overtime adjustment and New Year rotas.

Hawkins saw an update from the missing persons team and clicked in. As expected, it was too early for anything solid, the mail detailing instead preliminary information about John's family and his recent work history. Nothing she didn't already know.

She sat for a moment, thinking about her trainee detective. Did she dare hope that the killer would spare him, given the option? Even *that* scenario left him scared and alone, tied up in some dingy basement. Although that was better than what had happened to Connor.

Hopefully the full interviews with John's neighbours scheduled later in the day would provide a lead or two.

She returned to her inbox and scanned the remaining mails for anything of interest, finding little except a message from Brian Norton entitled, Touching base and one from Tristan Vaughn headed, What do you think?

She opened it and read a few words before shaking her head. It was the press release. The message had arrived thirty-three minutes ago, which meant that either Tristan Vaughn was a very fast worker, or it had been prepared prior to their meeting.

The content looked fine, however, and would certainly grab some of the headlines Vaughn was after. She spent ten minutes typing out suggestions for some minor adjustments – ostensibly to prolong the illusion that she still had a say in Operation Charter – then she replied to say that otherwise she thought it was fine.

Hawkins sat back and drained her cup, thinking. She needed a break, anything to give her back some credibility.

She looked out into the main incident room, realizing

that the cleaners must have left the blinds open earlier, having broken time-honoured tradition and dusted them. Yasir and Walker sat at their desks, working on some of the leads thrown up by last night's *Crimewatch* reconstruction.

There was nothing solid yet, but Todd had taken DS Sharpe along to look into a prospective sighting of Nemesis from the previous Sunday morning. Even if the lead came to nothing, it would allow the two of them to bond. After all, the two men would be getting to know each other whether they liked it or not, thanks to the chief superintendent's buddy scheme of no one working or living alone.

She'd gone straight from her meeting with Vaughn to give the morning briefing. As she'd expected, Kirby-Jones' plan wasn't universally popular, although she suspected at the same time that most of the squad were secretly relieved. There had almost been a stand-up fight to decide which of the men would move in to 'protect' Amy Scott, an attractive young DC seconded to the murder investigation team mid-week. Disappointment had followed when Sue Drayton, a middle-aged detective sergeant had offered her spare room, and Amy had swiftly accepted.

Despite Mike's absence, Hawkins had then gathered her immediate team – those most at risk – to discuss their options. It was established that Yasir's live-in boyfriend was a martial arts instructor; while Walker's burgeoning family home currently housed his equally large brother. That left Sharpe, whom Hawkins hadn't been surprised to discover was a bachelor, with no choice other than to move in temporarily with Frank Todd, whose wife had walked out three years ago. That was, of course, after Hawkins had started rumours by mentioning that Maguire would stay with her. In the light of current events, though, speculation about her and Mike living under the same roof seemed pretty harmless.

Now all she had to do was ask him.

She thought for a moment about calling him straight away to get it done, ripping off the proverbial plaster, but decided it was best left until later. Apart from anything else, she hadn't decided whether to admit why she hadn't been in touch.

After spending the previous night turning things over in her mind, Hawkins had put her suspicions about Mike's involvement in Barclay's disappearance down to paranoia, and their recent argument to stress. There were few enough people she trusted on the force these days, without questioning Mike's loyalty, too.

She turned back to the PC, almost logging off before she remembered Brian's email. Opening it, she read:

Hi Antonia, have been trying your mobile all morning. Please call me asap on my personal number when you get this. Have something that may interest you. Brian.

She dug her phone out of her jacket, seeing the missed call messages, cursing her luck. She'd switched it to silent before her meeting with Vaughn, and had purposely left it that way afterwards to give herself transitory peace to think, purposely not checking the screen.

She unlocked the phone, ignoring its voicemail icon, and selected Brian's number. He answered after a couple of rings.

'Antonia, bear with me. I'll find somewhere I can talk.'

Hawkins waited, listening to Norton wheeze as he walked. Initial background noise on the line suggested he was in the incident room at Scotland Yard, but he obviously didn't want their conversation overheard.

'Sorry about that, boss, but it's probably better I don't broadcast what I'm about to tell you. Might lead to complications.'

'Sure, Brian, what do you have?'

'Well, I know the guvernor's been giving you a rough time recently, so I was looking for an opportunity to help out.'

'OK.' Hawkins began wondering how much he knew, but couldn't suppress a quiet surge of gratitude that someone still believed in her.

'I've been searching our incident room files like you suggested. Seems you were right about nobody ever remembering to include them in standard back checking. Anyway, the names you got from Emilia Jeffries came up together in an emergency call we logged a couple of months ago. Someone called Karin Shelton rang the nines in distress, saying that her boyfriend, one Curtis Rickman, had attacked her. Uniform responded, but the show was over by the time they got there.'

'Fantastic!' Hawkins wanted to hug him. 'Do we have an address?'

'Not for him, but we have one for Karin Shelton. And Rickman's address might not be on file, but his greatest hits are. Take a look.'

'I'm with you.' Hawkins was already logging in to view his file. 'Where can I find Karin?'

'Camberwell. Flat 424 in the Heygate Estate. It's just

across the river, so it shouldn't take you more than twenty minutes to get over there. I thought you'd want to be first to check it out, so I haven't raised a call on it yet. We don't even have to link it with Operation Charter because he's already wanted for other stuff. All we need is for you to be in the vicinity when I put out the radio announcement that we've got something on him.'

'I know the area. I'll call you back when I get near. Thanks, Brian, I owe you one.'

She hung up and studied the notes that had appeared on her screen. Thirty-eight-year-old Rickman was no stranger to the inside of a cell, but that owed more to his proclivities for vehement protest than anything as mundane as burglary or fraud. As a teenager in the nineties, Rickman had been heavily involved in almost all the prominent demonstrations of the time, against everything from the poll tax to the first Iraq war. An apparent tourist of dissent, he'd been arrested multiple times for causing damage to public property. Following several such brushes with the law, however, he had disappeared from the scene for ten years, not being apprehended once, even under a different name.

His return to notoriety in 2005, however, had been spectacular, when he'd nearly killed a man in a fistfight outside a restaurant in Hounslow. The victim had been a drug dealer and extortionist, roundly despised by everyone in the area; now reduced to consuming blended meals through a care-home straw. Rickman had earned sixteen months inside for that, but also sacks full of laudatory mail from the dealer's previous victims and their families.

She'd seen the type before: militant vigilantes who saw themselves as dispensing the sort of upright justice the law had legislated its way out of. *The extremist moral high ground.* Hawkins felt her pulse quicken.

Since his release in 2007, however, it seemed that Rickman's grasp of the judicial system had grown. He'd been investigated in connection with a number of attacks, some perpetrated in person, others by proxy, mostly against local hate-figures with smug demeanours and expensive legal teams. But almost none of these alleged assaults had culminated in anything beyond a caution, mainly due to a lack of evidence.

The exception was the stabbing of a known paedophile, of which Rickman had been convicted in 2012, after he was caught in the act by officers who happened to be exiting a neighbour's house two doors along. Again his target survived, otherwise he'd have gone down for a lot longer than the paltry fourteen months he'd served.

Rickman had recently been released, four months early due to overcrowding, and had kept regular appointments with his parole officer until a few months ago. According to the officer's records, Rickman had spent most of the visits trying to convince him that he was a changed man.

That he had goals.

Apparently his protestations had been reasonably convincing, right up to the point when he'd disappeared from his registered address in Clapham. Probably to stay with Karin Shelton.

What really compounded Hawkins' excitement as she left her office, however, was the photo of Rickman. It was a mug shot taken upon his latest release, showing his narrow eyes, oblique jaw and sullen countenance.

And, just like the man captured on CCTV outside Summer Easton's house, his brown, shoulder-length hair.

54.

'OK, control, we're two minutes away. We'll check it out.'

Hawkins released the talk button on her Airwave handset and tucked it back in her coat, silently thanking Brian again, knowing he'd enjoy the box of Krispy Kreme doughnuts on their way to his office.

She moved out of the alley and took up the agreed position in full view. She thought better of leaning against the wall, her desire to blend in overpowered by her wish to avoid taking away a souvenir print on her clothes of what looked like recent graffiti.

Words like that were recognizable even when reversed.

Instead, she pulled a Marlboro from the pack, ambivalent as she raised the lighter, guilty as she savoured the first drag.

A woman appeared from around the corner to Hawkins' left, laden with Lidl shopping bags that looked like a week's worth of supplies for a small family. She was about Hawkins' age, but her head hung low and she moved the same way as everyone else around there – as if all the hope had been sucked out of her. The woman edged towards the stone steps leading into the tower block and disappeared from view.

Hawkins drew on the cigarette again and looked up at the Heygate Estate. The seventies-built council flats were scheduled for demolition to make way for 'regeneration projects'. Hawkins remembered reading a local newspaper article about a number of the Heygate's 3,000 residents who were campaigning against its destruction. They said tearing this place down would 'destroy the area's sense of community'.

Not to mention its endemic lawlessness and rampant drug-trade.

It was exactly the type of place where a cunning fugitive like Curtis Rickman might hide: at the bottom of a proverbial barrel even social workers thought twice about scraping.

But today, thanks to Brian, Hawkins had the chance to do just that. Bring Rickman in for breaching parole; hopefully nail a killer in the process. There were enough unaddressed blemishes on his record to justify holding onto him for a few days. And if Sunday morning began without another murder . . .

Events had unfolded just as they'd planned, with Hawkins responding to Norton's low-key radio message as nearest available officer to Rickman's suspected location.

Just then, she caught sight of Maguire as he picked his way through the mid-morning traffic further along New Kent Road. She crushed her cigarette underfoot and set off towards him, fastening her coat against the icy drizzle that was starting to fall.

She had called Mike before leaving Becke House, given him a brief outline of her meeting with Kirby-Jones, and told him about the added complication of Tristan Vaughn. She'd also apologized for hanging up on him the previous evening, and for her part in their latest argument.

There was no point complicating things further by telling Mike what she'd suspected him of.

He spoke first. 'Thanks for calling. Look, I was out of line—'

She held up a hand. 'It's forgotten. We're both tired and under pressure.'

'So we're good?'

'What I mean is, can we discuss it later?' She gave what she hoped was a reassuring smile. 'We're on a tight schedule here.'

'Uh, since we're talking about it . . . you sure this is a good idea?'

'By *this*,' Hawkins dropped her voice as two hooded teenagers passed, 'I assume you mean apprehending Curtis Rickman, and yes, I'm sure. The DCS currently has my reputation filed somewhere between 'Fawlty' and 'Hitler'. And yours is taking a hit in the press, too. But if we collar Rickman and he turns out to be the killer, we can both take our pick of promotions out of this mess.'

'I get that. But if we're right about this guy then he's armed, Toni, and we don't have back-up.'

'Yes, but he's not going to gun us both down on the doorstep in broad daylight, is he? And requesting back-up means our babysitter finds out. Then you can say goodbye to any credit for this.'

She decided not to mention that neither Rickman's name nor this address was on the list of mail-order customers whose illegal Tasers had been intercepted. That didn't mean he didn't have one of the weapons, of course, but if Maguire knew, he might withdraw his assistance anyway.

'Besides,' she turned and headed for the entrance, 'I've got you to protect me.'

'Great.' Mike followed. 'What if he's got ten of his buddies in there with him?'

Hawkins waited for him to catch up. 'If it's that bad, we'll say we're Jehovah's Witnesses and come back with an army. But he skipped parole, Mike – there are points just for bringing him in.'

'OK, Sheriff. I just hope you're right.'

They entered the Heygate Estate and began ascending the stairwell. Bags of rubbish almost blocked the first landing, most torn open by rats or mice. The smell of urine was mild but constant.

They reached the fourth floor. Even at this modest altitude the wind had increased substantially, howling as it whipped semi-frozen drizzle into their faces, making them squint. Flat 424 would be around two-thirds of the way down the walkway, according to the sign.

The narrow balcony was deserted except for two blackbirds fighting over a takeaway food bag, and a scruffy-looking dog tied to a drainpipe. The mongrel, which had appeared to be asleep, stood and emitted a low growl as they passed.

Even the canine residents of this place had police-radar.

'I'll knock,' – Hawkins pointed out the spy-holes mounted in most of the doors – 'you stay out of sight. He's more likely to answer the door to a woman on her own.'

'That's what worries me.'

As they passed, a heavy bass line became audible from inside one of the neighbouring flats. Hawkins wasn't a fan of dance music, especially at this time of the morning, but at least the thumping beat would help to mask their arrival.

Mike backed up against the wall to her left as Hawkins approached the door. A single window faced outwards from what looked like the kitchen, but she detected no sign of movement from inside.

She rapped firmly on the faded blue door and moved back against the balcony wall. It was only a few feet, but it would appear less threatening to whoever might answer. Plus it gave her vital extra seconds to respond should their reaction be aggressive.

Nothing happened. Hawkins knocked again, louder this time.

'Who is it?' A woman's voice, tentative, just inside the door.

'Met Police.'

A pause. 'He isn't here.'

'Please open the door, madam.'

More silence preceded the noise of two serious-sounding deadlocks being released before the door swung slowly in.

'He doesn't live here anymore, OK?'

The woman in the doorway must have been some-where in her thirties, but she wasn't at all what Hawkins had expected. Dress code on the Heygate Estate was usu-ally velour tracksuit or mucky jeans, unwashed hair and a skin condition. But the person now facing her looked quite out of place. The woman's accent was more Home Counties than inner London, and she had a natural beauty unadorned by make-up, further subdued by a shapeless grey jumper and floral skirt. A large necklace with wooden beads hung around her neck.

Hawkins ignored her statement. 'Are you Karin Shelton?'

'Yes.' The woman flinched as a fresh round of bass heavy dance music kicked in from next door. 'Sorry about the noise.'

'I'm DCI Hawkins, and this is DI Maguire.' Hawkins raised her badge as Mike moved in beside her. '*Who* isn't here?'

'Curtis.' Karin's eyes dropped as she said the name.

Hawkins noted her reaction. 'OK, but we need to find him urgently. Do you know where he is?'

'No.'

'When did you last see him?'

'Months ago.' Karin's hand moved to her stomach, as if she felt sick. 'What's he done?'

'We need to discuss it with him, really. Where else could we try?'

The woman eyed her for a second before there was a faint bang from inside the flat. Instinctively, Hawkins tried to peer past her into the hallway.

'He isn't here,' Karin repeated. 'Come in and look if you want.'

Somewhere behind her a baby started to cry.

'Well, if you don't mind.' Hawkins glanced at Mike, who shrugged.

They stepped inside and poked around while their host tended to her daughter. The dingy hallway had doors for a bathroom and single bedroom, and then opened into the living space with a tiny kitchen stuffed in one corner. There was clearly no room in the flat for large amounts of storage space, but they checked cupboards and corners big enough to hide an adult, alert for stray clothing or possessions; anything to suggest that Rickman, or any other man, had been there recently.

'Satisfied?' Karin asked when they returned to the poky front room.

'Yes, thanks.' Hawkins scanned the room in more detail. At first glance the place looked like it was mid-decoration, the top layer of wallpaper removed to reveal patchwork generations of tastelessness beneath. The ceilings harboured years' worth of cigarette staining. But there was no refurbishment going on here: this was *home*.

Mike squatted beside the baby's bouncer. 'Who do we have here?'

'Olivia.' Karin smiled as her daughter grabbed his finger.

Hawkins watched them for a moment. Perhaps this answered the question that had been bothering her since they'd arrived: if Rickman was an unscrupulous killer, then why was Karin, as someone who could conceivably help to convict him, still around?

She addressed Shelton. 'Is Curtis the father?'

'Of course.' Karin frowned. 'Though it didn't stop him leaving us, just after she was born.'

'That the last time you saw him?' Mike stood.

Shelton nodded. 'Four months ago.'

Hawkins softened her tone to match Mike's. 'The more you can tell us about him, the better.'

'Right.' Karin sat on the arm of her tatty sofa, fingers

working away at the beads on her necklace. 'I'm sure you've seen his record, and I won't try to say it's all lies, because it's not. But Curtis isn't the monster people label him as; he's just, sort of . . . *intense*. The stuff he cares about is all really important. It's why I liked him.' She looked at her daughter. 'What's all this about, anyway?'

'I'm afraid we can't tell you,' Hawkins replied, realizing that if Shelton had seen Mike on the news, she might make the connection herself. She checked the room again; relieved to confirm there was no TV. She turned back to their subject. 'Was he ever violent with you?'

Karin shifted uncomfortably. 'Towards the end it was like he stopped seeing us, me and Olivia. So I confronted him. We argued and he lashed out.' Pain entered her expression. 'It was the only time, honestly. And he'd already gone when the police arrived, so I told them I'd over-reacted, because I knew the parole board would put him away again.' She sighed. 'I thought he'd come back.'

'Look, Karin.' Mike picked up a toy Olivia had been reaching for and passed it to her. 'Curtis might not even be involved in this case, but if he is, it's real serious, you understand?'

Shelton reached down to stroke the baby's hair. 'Will you do what you can to help him?'

'I promise we'll try.' Hawkins glanced at Mike. 'But the best thing for everyone is if we find him.'

'OK.' Karin turned her head to stare out of the grubby window. 'There was one place he used to go, some protest group above a snooker hall in Deptford. Masters, I think it was called, on the High Road.'

'Good,' Hawkins pressed. 'Any others?'

'He used to disappear for hours, but he'd never say where he was going. The only reason I know about *that* place is because he took me there once. I couldn't stand it; everyone was so full of hate.'

Minutes later, once Hawkins had extracted them as fast as politeness would allow, she and Mike walked back to the stairwell.

Mike asked, 'So, what now?'

'Ah.' Hawkins turned. 'I've been meaning to talk to you about that. I think we should grab some food on the way to yours, so you can collect some clothes and a toothbrush, then head back to mine.' She held up a hand to silence Maguire, whose eyebrows had shot skywards. 'It's not what you think, but you're staying with me for a while.'

55.

Another shot cracked the air around him. He turned full circle, scanning the trees.

Still nobody approached.

To his left, a red flag on the hill relaxed, indicating that the wind had dropped. Behind it, the sun dipped below the horizon. The light was fading.

He raised the gun again, releasing the safety catch.

He adjusted his stance, positioning his feet, hefting the weapon's mass and bracing himself for the kickback.

An explosion this time, off to the right. He aborted the shot, conscious of limited ammunition.

He pulled the creases out of his plastic gloves and checked the area again. Still clear. Then he steadied himself once more, lowering the gun into position, aligning the sight.

His target stirred briefly, but then became still. The air around him seemed to solidify.

He pulled the trigger.

The plank leapt, splintering.

He drew back into the copse, checking the ridges all around for signs that the shot had betrayed his presence. But there were none.

Soon he was certain that, even if anyone heard his gunshot, they weren't coming to investigate. At that moment, as if to reassure him further, a burst of distant gunfire rang out to the west.

His trip to Longmoor Range had been a success. The military training ground covered a vast expanse of heath land, and its regular live-firing exercises meant that nobody in the vicinity would be surprised to hear gunshots while red flags were in place. The risk was that he might be seen by servicemen in the area, but the facility offered the perfect place to test-fire a gun without raising alarm.

Best of all, his third and final shot had been perfect, hitting the thin piece of wood dead centre from almost eight metres.

He'd already used the weapon to kill, of course, but that had been from close range. And he needed to be confident with it, should circumstances arise where he was forced to fire from a distance.

He collected the spent cartridge casing and replaced the gun in his bag, scanning for any evidence he'd been there. Satisfied, he moved away, retracing the short route to the edge of the red flag area. Then he began the thirty-minute walk back to Liphook station.

He checked his watch. He could be home within a couple of hours, which left plenty of time to write and send his next email.

Keeping the public on high alert so far had served him well, while adherence to a strict pattern had maintained not only his freedom, but his notoriety as well.

And people still needed reminding there was good reason to be afraid.

FRIDAY

56.

'I'll walk from here,' the suited man shouted over the pneumatic drill's clatter, 'and you can stick this up your arse.'

He slammed the cab door and thrust his money through the open passenger window. Then he vaulted the railings near to where Hawkins stood.

'Fucking traffic,' he barked to nobody in particular. 'Evolution moves faster.'

He strode away, pausing to vent at the workmen and their equipment blocking both of Victoria Street's westbound lanes.

Then, as if choreographed, the temporary lights changed and the traffic moved on. Hawkins watched the black cab cruise past the suited man, no more than a hundred feet from where he had exited. She grinned when an arm appeared out of the driver's side, at the wave that turned into a V sign.

She scanned the fresh set of gridlocked cars when they came to a halt; traffic heavy on the last working day before the New Year break, but the black Mercedes she was waiting for wasn't among them. She checked her watch: still five minutes early. She returned her attention to Friday morning's *Daily Mail*.

Thanks to Danny Burns, the *Mail*'s front page screamed

its exclusivity almost as loudly as its headline: **KILLER TARGETS BOYS IN BLUE**. She cringed at the media term used whenever they wanted to paint the police in a positive light. It wasn't even accurate, given a detective's lack of uniform, but it got the point across. Below it were images of Connor and Barclay.

Inside was Vaughn's message, signed off by the commissioner himself. The message was aimed at a public readership whose affection for all things celebrity now seemed to extend even to serial killers. It confirmed that Nemesis was known to be responsible for the death of one officer, and was believed to be behind the abduction and possible murder of a second. It sought to remind them that, for a man who claimed moral incontestability, and one who courted media hype with such success, Nemesis was still a murderer.

Its primary function, of course, was to piss the killer off.

Having accepted the strategy's merits, Hawkins would have preferred to see the message carried by every paper. But she'd suggested that Vaughn contact Danny Burns, aware that every message from Nemesis so far had been sent to him at the *Mail*: they couldn't afford to wait for the killer's future messages to appear in print, simply because they hadn't offered Burns exclusive rights to their own.

Maybe Nemesis was right about morality being dead.

Inevitably, Vaughn had accepted; he knew there was no point throwing away a day's head start. And, as frustrating as Danny's terms continued to be, the reporter had stayed true to his word. Hawkins had received a call just before 6 a.m. that morning.

Danny had another email from Nemesis.

That fact alone pretty much confirmed that the killer wasn't some religious nut, for the simple reason that Advent was over, and therefore any sufficiently obsessive perpetrator would have stopped with Summer Easton. Thankfully, however, it also made it doubtful there was an as-yet undiscovered victim from the first Sunday of Advent.

But it also meant that, unless they stopped Nemesis, there were likely to be more attacks.

The lights changed again and the traffic crawled on. Seconds later, a horn sounded to her right, and Hawkins looked up to see the Mercedes CLS draw to a halt fifteen yards away. She raised a hand to let the driver know she'd seen him, then folded her paper before picking her way through the stationary vehicles to open the passenger door.

'Am I late?' Tristan Vaughn killed the radio, cutting Bruno Mars off mid-chorus.

'Not at all. I was early.'

They filled a few moments with idle chatter about the impossibility of trying to get anywhere during rush hour, before the lights changed and Vaughn eased the car forwards. He cleared his throat as they passed the road works.

'So, how's the case?'

Which one? Hawkins nearly said. But while the baby-sitter's expression was pleasant enough, she sensed cracking jokes would still be premature. 'Fine.'

'Any news?'

Hawkins' instinct said only an idiot would mention the Curtis Rickman lead. Yasir and Walker had spent all of

347

yesterday evening at the snooker hall in Deptford that Karin had told them about, asking after him. Explaining why she hadn't called Vaughn at the time about such an important development would be difficult enough even now, let alone if and when they got him.

But she needed that arrest on her record instead of Vaughn's, especially if Rickman turned out to be the killer.

She explained her suspicion regarding the spiritualist link between the victims, and their discovery of Emilia Jeffries. She also mentioned that, in light of the death threat, she'd convinced Jeffries to move into a local safe house, where she was now under the protection of armed police. But she carefully avoided mentioning the two names provided by the prospective victim, or the resulting lead on Rickman.

She finished by telling Vaughn they'd also gained a few more potential witnesses thanks to *Crimewatch*'s screening of the security video from Summer Easton's house. There was nothing solid yet, but they'd know more when the team reported back at the morning briefing.

A sultry woman's voice interrupted, telling Vaughn to keep straight ahead onto the A302 through Grosvenor Gardens.

'And,' Hawkins continued once the sat nav had finished, 'I'm sure you know about the DNA reports from Barclay's flat.'

Vaughn's raised eyebrows said he didn't. Hawkins marked down a mental *one-nil*, despite having called in another favour at the lab to get the results early. The call had come twenty minutes ago.

She explained that, despite extensive sample analysis from Barclay's flat, the most recent traces were all from one individual, presumably John himself. This included the blood on the table top. Given the degradation of other forensic evidence from the address, it looked like nobody else had been there since August at least.

If Nemesis was to blame for Barclay's disappearance, the killer clearly hadn't forgotten how to cover his tracks.

The results also indicated that, thanks to their recent workload, the trainee detective constable probably hadn't had social company since he moved in; which, Hawkins omitted to mention, made his private life tragically similar to her own.

Vaughn listened intently until she finished, but made no direct response.

Hawkins swallowed as the lull stretched, willing something to break the silence in the whisper-quiet Mercedes. Even Marilyn 'sat nav' Monroe would have done.

Was Vaughn simply digesting the information, or was he aware of the Rickman lead? Obviously the news about Barclay was tempered by the fact that the missing persons team had gleaned nothing from John's neighbours the previous day. Bearing in mind their average age was above sixty, no one had seen visitors come or go, nor heard a commotion on the day he disappeared.

She bit her lip and stared out of the window.

'OK.' Vaughn spoke suddenly. 'I'm sure something'll break soon.' He pointed up at a large, art-deco style building. 'I think this is the place.'

He turned left onto Derry Street, and then right into the entrance of an underground car park. They stopped at the barrier, where a security guard stuck his head out of the control cabin.

Vaughn lowered his window. 'We're here to see Danny Burns.'

'Hold on, mate.' The guard walked round to the front of the car and checked the Mercedes' plate against his clipboard. Then he returned to his post and the barrier began to rise. His head appeared out of the window. 'Go to the back of this level. Mr Burns will meet you by the lifts.'

Vaughn nodded and drove on. Hawkins saw the reporter waiting towards the rear of the car park and pointed him out.

Danny picked up the briefcase standing beside him and wandered over to meet them.

'You must be Tristan.' He shook Vaughn's hand through the window. 'Hi, Antonia.'

'Good to meet you.' Vaughn nodded at the back door. 'Are we OK to do this here?'

'No worries.' Danny opened the rear door and climbed in. He leaned forwards between the front seats. 'Sorry you had to come down here, but it's all kind of top secret. These days I have to get written permission to take a piss if it's got anything to do with Nemesis. Emailing this message is a sackable offence.'

'It's fine,' Hawkins replied. 'We understand how valuable these exclusives are.'

'Exactly.' He pointed to her newspaper. 'So what do you think of our coverage?'

'Just what we wanted,' Vaughn said. 'It's good to have you on side.'

Danny grinned. 'Everyone's a winner, right? And by

tomorrow, every other paper will be talking about your message instead of his.'

'Speaking of which.' Hawkins was keen to move things on. 'Do you mind if we see it?'

'Sure. Sorry.' Danny pulled the briefcase onto his lap. 'I have to say, the man knows what he's doing. The messages arrive between 5 and 6 a.m. every Friday morning, comfortably too late to make that day's headlines, but giving us plenty of time to reserve the next day's front page.'

He produced a sheet of paper from the case and held it up between them. Hawkins forced herself to let Vaughn take it.

'And he knows you won't release details to the TV news people until after the paper's gone out, so he gets synchronized coverage, thereby creating a more intense reaction.'

Vaughn finished with the message and passed it to her. 'At least we get our timing right sometimes.'

She began to read.

Police

> *I assured you my message would be heard.*
> *I hope you now realize the futility of trying to deter my campaign.*
> *As I have demonstrated, those who attempt to do so will be dealt with.*
> *My next target has already been selected.*
> *This Sunday you will witness my greatest demonstration yet.*
> *Nemesis*

57.

'I think you should consider dropping the case.'

Hawkins spun. 'Where did *that* come from?'

'Whoa!' Mike nearly ran into her with the trolley. 'Look, I'm just saying, we're all at risk here, even you. And we've already seen what this asshole's capable of.'

'Keep your voice down,' she hissed, smiling apologetically as a scowling mother ushered two young kids away from them down an adjacent aisle.

They were in the fruit and veg section of Hawkins' local supermarket. She'd offered to cook dinner for them both, hoping to get their differences patched.

It wasn't going well.

'Sue me.' Mike held up his hands. 'But someone's gotta watch your back.'

'I'm not going through this again, especially not in bloody Sainsbury's.' Hawkins leaned towards him, her voice hushed. 'I'm serious about my career. I'm certainly not about to give it up because some fruit-loop threatens my team, or because *you* want me to play house.'

She strode off towards the meat aisle.

'Toni, hold on.' Mike caught up with her.

'Are these all right?' She held up a pack of chops, her tone more curt than she had intended.

'Forget the damn pork. This isn't about you and me. I

said *consider* dropping the case. But you tell me your mind's made up, then I'm behind you all the way.'

'It is.'

'All right, but we gotta come clean about Rickman if we don't get him soon. This lying business isn't fair on the others.'

He had a point. Tristan Vaughn had insisted on attending the morning brief after he and Hawkins had collected the new email from Nemesis. She'd only just managed to collar Yasir and Walker in time and convince them to keep a lid on the search for Rickman.

They hadn't been impressed.

'I know,' she conceded now, 'but I've only got one basket left, and I'm running out of eggs to put in it. Rickman's my only chance of coming through this with any credibility. If we don't get him, I'm probably out of a job anyway . . . are you listening?'

Mike didn't respond. Instead, he was staring into the distance over her right shoulder. 'No way.'

'What?'

'Is that your *ex*?'

Hawkins spun, catching sight of Paul's back as he queued for the basket-only checkout.

'No,' she lied. 'That guy's too tall, and the clothes are all wrong. Come on, we need peas.'

'It *is* Paul. We should say hi.'

Hawkins dumped the chops in the trolley, using it to block his path. 'And rub his face in what we did, while we're *shopping together*? Could we look any *more* like a couple?'

Maguire accepted she was probably right, and allowed himself to be dragged to the frozen foods aisle, where Hawkins prevaricated until she was sure her ex-fiancé had gone. The delicate peace between her and Mike wouldn't last long if Paul mentioned his early morning visit before she did. She'd have to explain the lack of boxes in her hallway at some point, but it would be better if Paul weren't actually there at the time.

They paid, and headed out into the dimly lit car park. Hawkins' mobile rang as they reached Mike's car. She searched her bag. 'This had better be good.'

But her hunger evaporated when she looked at the display. She answered as they both climbed into the car.

She hung up after less than a minute. 'How soon can you get us to Hounslow?'

'Twenty minutes if busting the speed limit isn't a problem for you. Why?'

'Dinner will have to wait. I think we just located Curtis Rickman.'

58.

Eighteen minutes later, Maguire pulled up outside a row of mid-range semi-detached houses, near to a dark blue Vauxhall Insignia. In the pale glow from a nearby street-light, Hawkins made out two familiar faces in the front of the other car.

Mike locked the Range Rover, as they crossed the road and climbed into the back seat of the Vauxhall.

Hawkins went straight to business. 'So which one of these lovely residences is Mr Rickman's?'

'Number 29.' Yasir pointed over the steering wheel. 'About forty yards down on the left.'

'Good.' Hawkins was relieved to see they had kept to a safe distance. 'Any action since we spoke?'

'Nothing.' Walker rotated his considerable bulk in the passenger seat. 'Unless you count fast-food delivery drivers. The whole street must be overweight.'

'Take it from a Yank,' Mike said. 'Makes 'em easier to catch. How solid is this lead?'

'Looks good,' Walker replied. 'We got the tip from a mate of Rickman's who showed up at the place above the snooker club where the protestors meet. He was dismissive at first, but he came over all reasonable when we started showing an interest in the group's activities. Turns out this protest lark's like the bloody Masons. The guy who owns this house, along with half a dozen others, said Rickman could use the place as long as he looked after his dog while he's abroad.'

Hawkins leaned forwards. It was difficult to make out exactly which property was which, but nearly every downstairs window in the row was lit.

'Good enough for me,' she said. 'Let's get him.'

'Er, chief?' Yasir's tone wavered. 'If there's a chance this man's armed, shouldn't we order some back-up?'

Hawkins knew she was taking a huge risk: four unarmed officers were about to attempt the arrest of a known violent criminal, who may also be a serial killer in possession of a powerful Taser weapon and a Glock 17 handgun. The odds of success weren't good, which made this action difficult to justify, but she wanted the arrest.

Walker intervened before Hawkins had a chance to reply. 'Come on, Amala, the chief's trying to see some credit where it's due here. By the time you get authorization for armed response, the bureaucrats will be all over it. We'll be lucky to get a ruddy commendation.'

Yasir stared into space for a moment before she agreed. Hawkins made eye contact with Walker and nodded her appreciation.

After a short discussion to organize their approach, Walker produced from the boot two extra sets of body armour, which Hawkins asked him to organize in advance, and passed them through the rear door to her and Maguire, before he and Yasir headed for Rickman's house.

Hawkins watched them go as she and Maguire removed their jackets and shrugged on the protective vests. She noticed that the temperature had fallen further when they stepped out of the car, the clouds having moved on to reveal a sheet of stars. She lowered her gaze to the two officers twenty-five yards ahead: Yasir's diminutive frame dwarfed by Walker's tall, broad one.

The sergeant would be an imposing presence in any situation, but Hawkins' pulse began to race as she saw them cut left along the path leading to the back of the houses. Memories of the night Eddie Connor died reared in her mind. At least this time none of them was alone.

She and Maguire reached number 29, the house where Hawkins desperately hoped they'd find not only Curtis Rickman, but in doing so, Nemesis as well.

Discovering Barclay tied up in the shed would be a bonus.

The seventies-style home appeared to be undergoing light renovation work: parts of the shallow roof were covered by gently flapping sheets of clear plastic, held down with planks of wood, while the garden contained various polythene-covered piles of bricks and other building materials. A light was on somewhere towards the back of the downstairs area, its glow visible through the front window. Otherwise the house was in darkness.

'Your turn to knock,' she told Maguire.

Mike led the way past a stack of what looked like dismantled kitchen units to the entrance. The whole front door assembly was held in place by wedges driven into the gaps around its edge. If nobody answered, it looked almost loose enough to lift out.

Mike blew into cupped hands before knocking firmly.

For a moment nothing happened, but then the light from inside brightened as a door opened and a shadow emerged into the hallway, its edges distorted by the patterned glass. The figure stopped.

Hawkins watched, senses alert. *Could this be Nemesis? And was he contemplating another break for freedom?*

Suddenly the figure moved again, but not evasively as she'd expected. Instead, it came towards them.

She glanced at Mike. 'Ready?'

Maguire nodded.

The figure arrived at the door, one ethereal arm reaching for the handle. It swung open to reveal a narrow hallway and a thin man wearing black jeans and a dark grey T-shirt. His hair was tied back in a ponytail.

Hawkins recognized Curtis Rickman from his file.

Rickman's eyes narrowed. 'Yes?'

Hawkins held up her badge. 'Met Police. Sorry to turn up unannounced, Curtis, but if you will insist on being ex-directory . . .'

Rickman's response was an attempt to slam the door, but Mike was too fast, jamming a steel-capped boot into the gap. The pinned door frame creaked, but it held as Rickman braced himself against the other side, managing temporarily to resist Mike's strength.

'Harvey,' Rickman shouted from behind the door. 'Here, now.'

Over Maguire's shoulder through the glass, Hawkins caught sight of a second silhouette entering the hallway. Except that Harvey wasn't some lackey with a crowbar; he was a dog. A big one.

'Mike,' she warned.

'I know.'

Rickman was starting to lose the shoving match, but his next statement swung things in his favour.

'*Burglars.*'

A sharp bark and a scrabbling of claws on wood preceded a snarling black and brown snout full of teeth appearing in the widening gap.

Rickman suddenly released the door, which swung open, Mike releasing his weight just in time to stop himself from falling forwards. Before them a Doberman stood rigid, emitting a low growl, daring them to advance.

Rickman backed away, reaching the understairs cupboard and releasing the latch. He leaned in and pulled out a black holdall.

Hawkins reassured herself that, even if the bag did contain Connor's gun and the Taser, Rickman was less likely to use either now that his identity had been established. He could have no idea how many officers were here and, even if he escaped tonight, his face would be on every TV screen in the country within hours.

Leaving the cupboard open in his haste, Rickman instructed the dog to hold them as he moved past and began to climb the stairs.

Hawkins saw Maguire start forwards and put a hand out to stop him. If they attempted to enter, Harvey would take chunks out of them both.

'Back up and shut the door,' she whispered. 'Slowly.'

Mike turned his head. 'What?'

'I know what I'm doing.' She watched Rickman disappear onto the upstairs landing. 'Just don't close it fully.'

He nodded and edged the door shut. The dog seemed unsurprised by their apparent retreat.

When they were safe Mike asked, 'So, what's the plan?'

'You know what they say about a good offense.' Hawkins walked back to the nearest tarpaulin and fished out a cupboard door. She handed it to Mike and grabbed one for herself.

They moved back to the entrance and eased the door open again. The dog hadn't moved, and resumed its threatening stance.

Hawkins and Maguire lined up their doors and advanced. The dog appeared confused by this and backed away. Held low and together, the doors spanned almost the entire width of the hallway, and by adjusting the angle and height in response to Harvey's evasive efforts, they were able to maintain forward momentum.

Seconds later, they had backed the dog into the understairs cupboard, and Hawkins eased the door shut with her foot before clicking the latch closed. The dog began barking from inside as Maguire arranged the doors side by side on the floor to jam the cupboard closed, in case Harvey decided to test the latch.

At that moment, they heard the sound of a toilet being flushed.

Evidence.

Mike turned towards the stairs, but Hawkins stopped him, telling him to check the other downstairs rooms in case Rickman hadn't been alone, while she let Walker and Yasir in through the back.

When the downstairs area had been confirmed clear, the four officers advanced up the staircase to the sound of another flush.

Maguire and Walker reached the top first, with Hawkins and Yasir close behind.

Three doors led off the landing: two were open; one closed. Maguire quickly checked the first, a shake of his head confirming it was empty.

Hawkins also checked the other bedroom. A few bits of furniture were piled in the middle of the room, wearing the same paint-spattered dustsheets that covered the floors. But there was nowhere suitable for anyone to hide among them, and the windows were latched from the inside, eliminating the chances that anyone else had escaped. She quickly moved back to join her colleagues on the landing, in front of the final door.

Maguire and Walker positioned themselves either side of the frame, while Hawkins guided Yasir into a corner.

This was it. She just had to hope that if he had a weapon and used it, he'd go for the torso. Beyond that, she'd have to rely on Maguire and Walker's self-defence training.

She took a deep breath and nodded at Mike.

'Open the door, Mr Rickman.' Maguire's tone was loud, authoritative.

Hawkins held up a hand, instructing them to wait. Any immediate reaction in this type of situation was likely to be violent. But there was no response. Downstairs, Harvey continued to bark from inside the cupboard.

'Stand back, Mr Rickman,' Mike shouted. 'We're coming in.'

The toilet flushed again. Maguire and Walker looked at Hawkins. She signalled for them to go in.

Walker raised his foot and Mike placed his fingers on the handle. Walker nodded, and Mike pulled the lever down as his colleague's foot smashed into the door just above the handle. The door flew inwards, accompanied by a crunch as the lock surrendered.

Hawkins couldn't see into the room as Maguire followed Walker in, but the sounds of the ensuing scuffle were short. Seconds later, the officers emerged, restraining Rickman by an elbow each, his hands cuffed behind his back.

'Curtis Rickman,' she told him, 'you are under arrest for breaching the conditions of your parole.'

She led the way outside as Mike read Rickman his rights, waiting while Yasir collected the car.

Hawkins studied Rickman, noticing for the first time that he wasn't wearing shoes; only socks. His feet must have been freezing against the pavement, yet he seemed oblivious to the cold.

He hadn't said a word since his arrest. Nor had he resisted once the cuffs were in place. Killer or not, he was unfazed by his arrest, and Hawkins was trying hard to take that as a positive sign.

The Insignia pulled up at the kerb with Yasir at the wheel, and Walker followed Rickman into the rear seat. Hawkins watched the car leave before she turned to Maguire.

'What was he getting rid of?'

'Sorry, didn't see. Wanna go back in?'

'No, it can wait. We'll call forensics in a minute.'

'Think it's him?'

'Not sure. But if there's evidence for that, I don't think we'll find it here.'

'Why not?'

'Well, I'm not convinced that guns or Tasers will flush.'

59.

The fly circled above his head, retracing its path again in the restricted space. The insect lacked the capacity to understand that the door and small window would remain securely closed for hours yet.

For the fly, an extended period in this enclosed room would result in death. For him, it was merely essential preparation for his definitive act. The irony was that, just like those of his human prey, the fly's instincts told it to panic rather than adapt. And flaws like that inevitably led to the perpetrator's demise.

He closed his eyes and concentrated on the forthcoming task, focusing his mind.

He pictured the people his message was designed to reach, the ordinary individuals he observed in the street. Their faces told him everything. They were beginning to understand.

But it was always to the strongest emotion that people responded first, which meant that most of the changes so far were due to fear. And those emotions were also those most quickly forgotten once danger had passed.

The seeds of change were planted. But if, as a by-product of his campaign, an ethical revolution was to be sustained, people needed to believe in it. Nemesis' part was to continue highlighting the problem in a way that society could comprehend, to make discussion essential, action imperative.

The modern world accepted injustice as part of life, and dealt with it by apportioning blame after the fact. Most people thought nothing of the way they treated others, which led to erosion of their self-respect. And so it went on.

Sacrifices were unavoidable if the circle was to be broken.

Once everyone had accepted that Nemesis could not be stopped, that their actions once again had tangible consequences, change would begin to spread. His only regret was that he hadn't started earlier.

He'd been exposed to the depravities of human nature at a young age, to the suffering caused by abuse he was unable to repel. For a long time he'd accepted it, convinced that compliance would eventually pacify his abuser.

Then his mother had self-destructed before his eyes. Her last words had been indistinct, but she left him in no doubt as to her message: beware the absent enemy, for he is the most dangerous.

He remained determined not to repeat his parents' mistakes, keen to impress on others the dangers of moral ineptitude. His words were often ignored, although he was content to be spreading a message of hope.

But everything had changed that day, nine years after his mother's death, when his father's posthumous letter revealed the true delinquencies she had orchestrated. He'd read the words over and over, stopping to think only when every one was etched in his memory.

Suddenly past events had become clear. His mother

had been evil in a way he'd never contemplated. But by ignoring a moral obligation to expose her, by condoning immorality through inaction, his father's conduct had been just as destructive.

From that moment onwards, his view of the world had changed. The only way to fight injustice was through direct action – to force moral decline into reverse. He had begun straight afterwards with renewed enthusiasm. Making a difference felt good.

And then he had met *her*.

He'd been enchanted by her beauty, inside and out. Their ideals matched. The answer had appeared to be in their partnership, a flawless paradigm for society to follow.

But she had not shared his vision. She had defiled him, just as his mother had defiled his father.

Only then had his true calling become obvious. He wasn't supposed to live in harmony with her. She'd been a test, a temptation for him to overcome. His destiny was to demonstrate to others that true morality demanded sacrifice.

He had turned his back on her, to begin his campaign. If society no longer enforced ethical behaviour, he would use targeted demonstrations to dispense justice to the morally corrupt. To lead others, however unwilling, by example.

Immediately, he'd known who his victims would be: five perfect examples of immorality at its worst. And with the four deaths so far had come recognition.

But while others were starting to listen, his personal torment had grown, ethereal flashes of memory arcing across his mind like electricity. He gripped the thin mattress on which he lay, feeling the anger rising within – the unstoppable force that sustained his resolve.

He saw her face, every line in vivid detail. But while the image had once given him strength to believe she could be his, now it reminded him only that he was strong enough to dispose of her.

The fly buzzed onto the windowsill beside him, the sound of its wings lazy, as if nearing exhaustion. It bumped against the windowpane a few times before coming to rest.

He struck, crushing the insect, lifting his hand to reveal its broken, dead form.

A punishment similar to the one he would impose in two days' time.

On *her*.

SATURDAY

60.

Hawkins slammed the receiver down. 'Shit!' Then she picked it up and slammed it down three more times. 'Double, fucking, *shit!*'

She slumped forwards on her elbows, letting her head drop towards the desk. To anyone entering her office she would look like some ridiculous, abandoned puppet. But after the way her morning had gone so far, Hawkins couldn't have cared less.

It was 8.40 a.m.

The phone call had been from Kate Foster, an old acquaintance who worked at Hendon forensics lab. The fact that Foster owed her from years back, when Hawkins had breathed on several of her dissertations, was the only reason Hawkins had been able to coax her into work on what was not only a Saturday morning, but New Year's Eve as well.

The results she'd been waiting for had come back fast, but uncomfortably conclusive. It had been a long shot to hope they would get a match for Rickman's DNA on traces taken from any of the four murder scenes, mainly because the killer didn't leave any. If he had, the connection would already have been made, because Rickman had been on police record for a long time.

However, fuck-ups occurred from time to time; records could be misfiled or lost. So Hawkins had watched as fresh samples were taken from their suspect, and then sent them to the lab herself. She'd been hoping desperately since then for a positive match.

But that hope had just been extinguished.

It didn't mean Rickman wasn't the killer, just that Hawkins wouldn't have any evidence of that when she met Tristan Vaughn in half an hour's time for a pre-morning-briefing catch-up.

She'd have to come clean about having withheld information about Curtis Rickman, too. And without proof, her unauthorized apprehension, even of a troublemaker like him, would appear arbitrary and petulant.

More bad news was that Rickman had managed to secure the services of Steven Colt, a defence barrister with a solid reputation for getting banged-to-rights career villains off major charges. Thanks to Colt's swift intervention, Rickman was steadfastly exercising his right to remain silent.

Rickman's retreat to the bathroom prior to his arrest hadn't filled Hawkins with hope at the time, and whatever he had flushed away before they broke in had gone for good. The search team had, however, recovered from the bath a hurriedly rinsed plastic box containing ricin residue. They'd also found traces of the lethal powder in the kitchen, and retrieved a bottle from a neighbours' bin that tested positive for acetone: a volatile liquid used in its manufacture.

The problem was that ricin, nasty as it was, seemed a little tame for Nemesis. And while this evidence could put Rickman away for possession of a biological toxin; simply taking down an aspiring terrorist, plus his mates from the protest group once investigated, wasn't going to save her on this one.

Because a thorough search of the property had yielded nothing connected to the Nemesis case. No John Barclay; no Taser.

No hairy great knife.

Hunter said a serial psychopath like Nemesis wouldn't hide his murderous tools anywhere particularly inaccessible: first, because he'd want immediate access to them; and second, because he wouldn't be expecting to get caught.

So there wasn't much point looking further, which would have entailed tearing plaster off the walls and digging up the garden.

She had bugger-all chance of getting authorization for that kind of operation anyway.

In fact, the only positive was that details of another property leased to Rickman had been found at the house. Frank Todd was on his way there now with a second forensics team, and would arrive at approximately the same moment she was due to meet Tristan Vaughn. But Hawkins knew better than to hope they'd uncover evidence suitably incriminating, in time to defuse what was certain to be a roasting.

She had gambled her entire reputation on Rickman being the killer; on the strength of what she now had to admit was pretty flimsy evidence. It was the classic cautionary tale – the officer who let a case become personal.

She'd been so sure about Curtis Rickman. He had the right build, the right hair, the right *mind*. And yet, from the moment she'd arrested him, something had felt wrong.

Worse still, if they couldn't prove he was connected to

the Nemesis case in the next fourteen hours and twenty minutes, they were obliged to hand him over to the parole board. And there would be little chance of the Crown Prosecution Service granting the usual twelve-hour custodial extension after that. It was common knowledge that the board's recently appointed chief executive was already under pressure, which meant he'd have Rickman back in their custody faster than she could say 'prime suspect', but getting to him after that would be a painstaking process of tertiary access hearings and accompanied interviews, overseen by more bureaucrats than nature could ever have intended to create.

At least he'd still be detained, although they'd have to wait until Sunday morning to see if his incarceration co-incided with the absence of another body.

Her train of thought was interrupted by an abrupt knock at the door. Hawkins caught her breath as Tristan Vaughn appeared.

'Hi.' She managed to retain her composure. 'I thought we said nine o'clock.'

'We did.' Vaughn's tone was unpleasant. 'Circumstances have changed. Come with me.'

61.

Vaughn knocked and waited for a response before he opened the door and stepped aside, allowing Hawkins to pass. Then he followed her in.

The chief superintendent looked up from behind his desk as they entered, closing his laptop screen with a characteristically precise movement. He made no attempt at a greeting, but his eyes remained fixed on her.

Instead of the usual scowl, however, Lawrence Kirby-Jones' expression conveyed something she hadn't expected. It looked like sorrow.

His gaze flicked to the chair in the centre of the room and then back at Hawkins; a barely detectable movement, but one she interpreted as an instruction to sit, and obeyed.

Vaughn took a seat to the side of Kirby-Jones' desk, his body language equally ominous, except that he was being careful not to make eye contact with her at all.

Hawkins heart pounded. Things were even worse than she'd feared.

Still nobody spoke.

She began to glance around the room, trying to regulate her breathing. There were times in the past when she'd broken silences in this office and then wished she hadn't.

Oddly, the room seemed darker in daylight than it did

under artificial illumination: even the hazy sunshine creeping through the rear-facing window seemed intimidated by the prospect. One notable difference created by the natural light, however, was that the upper parts of the walls, normally left in darkness by the down-turned lighting, were currently visible.

For the first time she noticed a shelf filled with books, mounted high and towards the rear of the room. She could read a few of the titles: *Understanding Criminology: Current Theoretical Debates* and, further along, *Criminological Perspectives: Essential Readings*. At the far end was a large volume named *Police Ethics: Crisis in Law Enforcement*.

She looked back at Kirby-Jones, realising suddenly where she'd seen his expression before. Family Liaison officers wore it when they rang the doorbells of the soon-to-be bereaved. It was the look of someone about to tell you something you really didn't want to hear.

'Was I unclear, Detective,' he said quietly, 'the last time we spoke?'

She hesitated, aware of the risks associated with her coming question, but equally determined not to make this too easy for him.

'Unclear about *what*, sir?'

The reaction was almost imperceptible, but Hawkins saw his cheeks twitch ever so slightly before he replied in the same, controlled manner.

'About your instructions regarding Superintendent Vaughn's involvement with the remainder of Operation Charter.'

Hawkins looked down at the desk. How much did he

know? However much it was, she'd gain little by attempting to confuse the issue.

'No, sir, your instructions were clear.'

'Then why was he not involved in the decision to arrest Curtis Rickman?'

'Mr Rickman wasn't wanted only in connection with Operation Charter, sir. He was in breach of his parole conditions for an entirely separate case. His arrest became a formality as soon as he was located, and his place of residence was identified during the course of routine enquiries. I felt it . . . unlikely that superintendent Vaughn would disagree regarding the need for immediate action, and that a delay to obtain permission might jeopardize our advantage.'

Kirby-Jones stared at her in the same way an infuriated parent might regard a disobedient child. 'I'm not questioning your actions with regard to Mr Rickman's detention, but I do wish to know why the superintendent was not *informed* of them.'

'Well, sir, things moved pretty fast, and although we suspected initially that Mr Rickman might have been linked to Operation Charter, it now looks more likely that—'

'Please, Detective.' Kirby-Jones held up a finger, silencing her. 'Don't lie to me. You purposely neglected to notify superintendent Vaughn of Mr Rickman's potential involvement, or your subsequent decision to apprehend him, because you wanted sole credit for the arrest of a man you hope will soon be identified as the killer.'

Hawkins opened her mouth, but no words came out.

'And you were prepared to risk the lives of your team in

pursuing a potentially armed suspect without appropriate support – a bad enough decision had it been made by a fully fledged DCI, but you seem to have forgotten that your position in this role is both temporary, and due more to circumstance than my better judgement.' He paused. 'Do you wish to submit anything at this point in your defence?'

Hawkins hesitated, then realised her voice had returned, rising as she spoke. 'In my defence? Is this a *formal* disciplinary, sir?'

'No.'

She felt heat run up the back of her neck. 'Then I don't see why I should be subjected to this biased and derogatory treatment *yet again*. Either I'm competent to lead this investigation or I'm not. But you think it's acceptable to leave me with SIO status, along with responsibility for the eventual outcome, while in reality I'm barely authorized to sit down when I feel like it, let alone make major decisions.'

Kirby-Jones' eyes widened noticeably, but he made no attempt to respond.

Hawkins glanced at Vaughn, who still refused to meet her gaze, before she continued. 'So with all due respect, if I'm no longer in command, I don't see why I should remain under this sort of pressure. If you want a scapegoat, fine, but at least allow me to make my own mistakes.' She paused, heart pounding, before deciding to leave it there. 'Sir.'

Lawrence Kirby-Jones blinked several times, as if he couldn't quite comprehend what had just happened. Then he leaned forwards, linking his hands on the desk before him. His reply, when it came, was controlled, but thick with candour.

'You may be surprised to hear, Detective, that I agree with you on several points. As I mentioned last time we spoke, my major concern, apart from stopping this killer, was for the reputation of the Met. I now believe our current situation to be working against that interest. What you interpreted as revoking your command status was an attempt to preserve your self-tarnished reputation. Now it's clear that to allow your continued involvement would be a mistake. I'm sorry to say, Detective, that I am bound by the Metropolitan Police Code of Conduct. And by disobeying direct orders, withholding information from a superior, demonstrating insubordination, and failing repeatedly to protect officers under your command, you leave me no option but to move toward disciplinary proceedings.'

Hawkins just stared, afraid to ask for absolute confirmation of what her superior officer appeared to be saying.

But his final words on the matter still hit her like a wrecking ball.

'I tried time and again to help you out, and when that was ignored I risked my own reputation to cover the cracks in your approach. But you've thrown it back at me as if you refute the inevitable consequences of your repeated mutiny. Therefore, and with immediate effect, Detective Inspector Antonia Hawkins, you are hereby suspended from active duty.'

62.

'We should talk about this.'

Hawkins sensed Maguire looking at her again. She turned her gaze away to the A406 skimming past the window, and the immense grey façade of Ikea just beyond.

'You gotta get this stuff out,' he persisted. 'It helps.'

She sighed. He wasn't going to let it rest. 'I'm beyond help.'

'Come on, Toni. You bet everything on going behind Vaughn's back, and you wiped out big time, I get that. But it was your only option. All or nothing, right?'

He fell silent, obviously waiting for an answer, but Hawkins wasn't ready to start looking on the bright side. On top of her suspension, she was still mourning Todd's phone call of ten minutes earlier, which had dashed her one remaining hope that they'd find something at Rickman's other address.

She rested her head against the door pillar, feeling the thrum of the engine resounding through the bodywork into her skull.

What conversations were going on at Becke House right now? Her reputation would already be mulch among rank and file: she pictured Frank Todd offering around glasses of champagne, explaining how he'd always said she was a walking liability. Aaron Sharpe would probably have a glass to toast someone else's underachievement for a change. At least Amala Yasir might finally have accepted that she wasn't sodding Superwoman.

She leaned forwards and grabbed her bag from the foot well, digging around in it for her packet of Marlboros. She put one between her lips and raised the lighter.

'No, you don't.' Mike snatched the cigarette.

'Don't be so bloody precious,' she snapped, reaching for another. 'It's only a stupid car.'

'Fuck the car. Think about your damn lungs.' He wrestled the pack from her and threw it in the back. 'Talk to me, please?'

'I'm off the case,' she breathed. 'Suspended.'

'OK, so take a sabbatical, on full pay. Chill out, read a book; they'll assign you something else when you go back.'

'What about the formal disciplinary, Mike,' Hawkins heard her voice hollow, 'when they demote me to toilet cleaner?'

'They won't demote you, Toni, that doesn't happen above DI level. You go sideways at worst.'

'Maybe, but it'll be sideways into a job with no future, with a reputation that nobody will ever be able to see past. Look, I appreciate the whole cheering me up thing, Mike, but there's no point. Kirby-bloody-Jones put me in an impossible position and I messed up, just like he wanted. Now he has me on four serious counts of misconduct.' She sighed. 'I was on track to make superintendent in two years, now I'll be lucky if they let me make tea. Career over. Goodnight.'

'It isn't—'

'And what about Eddie and John?' She cut him off. 'One of my officers is dead; another abducted. There's a damn good team out there looking for Barclay, and they've found precisely fuck all. How do you think my conscience is dealing with the fact I presided over both?'

She crossed her arms and slumped in the seat. Mike took the hint and they travelled on in silence.

They crawled through the A40 underpass in heavy New Year's Eve traffic, but eventually Hawkins saw the sign for Southall and Greenford.

They weren't far from her house, but she realized suddenly that, once she got there, she had nothing to fill her afternoon.

So what the hell was she going to do for two whole weeks?

Inspiration seemed to hit Mike suddenly. 'Maybe it's a sign?'

'What?'

'A sign, you know, that it's time to try something new?'

'You mean quit.'

Mike rolled his eyes and shot her an exasperated stare. 'It isn't like that. You spent nine years fighting a war that can't be won, where two criminals replace every one you bust. So maybe it's time to let somebody else take over? I'm saying don't push your luck. Look what happened to Eddie and John .'

Hawkins sighed. 'Don't start this again.'

'Listen to me.' Mike steered the Range Rover onto a slip road. 'Whenever we talk about this you get all bent out of shape, thinking I want you to stay home reading *Take a Break* and looking after a bunch of kids. But you can have whatever you want, Toni. I'm just saying you don't have to risk your life to get it.'

'You're *still* trying to protect me.'

'So what if I am? And not just you, either. I've been thinking about leaving, too.'

Hawkins stopped mid-retort. 'You'd come with me?'

'Yeah.'

She paused, unconvinced that the commitment she wanted could be so easily attained. Would he really do it?

They'd reached her street, and Mike waited for a couple of cars to pass before he parked outside her house.

He pulled on the handbrake and turned to her. 'Well?'

'I . . . don't know.'

'I want *us*, Toni, you and me. Only reason I left before was to give you and Paul a chance, but that isn't an issue any more, right?'

She shook her head.

'So?'

She released her seatbelt. 'Let's talk inside.'

'Shit, Antonia, I can't . . .'

'Can't what?'

'Come in. The case, it's Sunday tomorrow, you know? There's a briefing in an hour. Vaughn wants to—'

'Vaughn? What happened to "I've been thinking about getting out"?'

'You can't expect me to walk away just like that.'

'What if that's *exactly* what I want?'

'You know I can't.' Mike shook his head. 'Come on, Toni, I'll do anything for you, but I gotta finish this. I need you to be safe.'

'Is that why you took this case? You didn't think I could handle it?'

Mike sighed. 'Look, you're tired and emotional. Go inside and pack some things, then go straight to my place.

Makes sense for you to stay with us now you won't be coming into work. Eric's on leave so he'll be there, but he said it's cool—'

'Cool for *you*, maybe,' she cut in. 'Just bundle the little woman off to your mate's house while you go and save the fucking day, is *that* how it works?'

'That isn't fair.'

'Fine.' Hawkins was halfway out of the car. 'Whatever.'

She slammed the door before Maguire could respond, and stamped her way around the front of his car.

Mike lowered his window. 'So it's like that?'

'Just go,' she shouted back. 'I'll go straight to Johnston's. Tell Vaughn I said congratulations on getting me suspended.'

She reached the front door of her house and dug in her bag for the keys.

Behind her, Mike fired the Range Rover's engine. 'I'm sorry, Antonia,' he shouted. 'I'll call you later.'

Hawkins stepped inside, turning to watch him drive away, regretting everything she'd said.

She closed the door and stared at the empty hallway, feeling the tears build.

63.

Hawkins picked up her mobile from the coffee table and pressed a button to light the display. Still nothing.

Where the hell *was* he?

The on-screen clock said it was after 8 p.m., nearly six hours since Mike had dropped her off.

And he still hadn't called.

She dumped the phone and sat back, berating herself.

She had almost dialled Maguire's mobile at several stages during the afternoon, partly to apologize, mostly to find out what was going on with the case. Pride had got the better of her every time.

But she still hated to admit that, without a case to obsess over or a semi-boyfriend to fight, she was basically lost.

She'd tried making plans for things to keep her occupied during the two-week suspension. Obviously she needed to prepare her defence, but what apart from that?

She realized she finally had the opportunity to catch up with long-neglected friends and family – providing that any of them still remembered her. And she could always do some of the hundreds of jobs around the house she'd been putting off for months. It was only natural that she'd need some time to adjust.

Yet all she could think about was work.

She kept catching herself preparing tomorrow's morning briefing, or making mental notes of people she needed to chase up about this or that. Then she would feel absurd, and chastise herself for being such an idiot.

That anger, in turn, would be redirected towards Lawrence Kirby-Jones.

Finally, after using every derogatory term she knew at high volume, Hawkins ended up reminding herself that daylight was long gone and that really she shouldn't still be at home. Alone.

She swore, well aware that she should have left for Eric Johnston's house hours ago. Except that every time she got up to leave, another damn good reason not to go had occurred to her.

Initially, just a plain desire not to go was enough. When that had worn off, she'd spent an hour telling herself there was no point. In her experience, Eric Johnston was a petty bigot who spent most of his time spouting lines from the police ethics handbook. OK, he was harmless, but by this time of night – if their previous encounters were anything to go by – he'd be half-cut. Which made him less than ideal protection.

Anyway, she could handle herself.

And besides, John had gone missing mid-week: Nemesis would be far too busy to deal with the likes of her tonight. If history had taught them anything it was that, as far as he was concerned, Saturday nights and Sunday mornings were reserved for the main event.

In the end, it was her memories of the bloody handprint in Barclay's flat that convinced her otherwise, and she'd started to pack.

*

An hour later, a bag containing enough clothes to last her a week dominated the hallway, and Hawkins had promised herself just one cup of tea before leaving. Her final mistake had been to switch on the TV.

She'd flicked through the various news channels, looking for updates on the case she should still have been leading. She'd settled as usual for BBC News, which was currently filled with only two subjects: endless coverage of the lead up to New Year was interspersed sporadically with reports, speculation and punditry about Nemesis.

Normally even the biggest news stories started to bore the public after a month or so but, five weeks into Nemesis' murderous campaign, its allure remained.

The Advent Killer had everyone's attention, and nothing made people panic like the national media telling everybody they'd be stupid not to. Now that darkness had fallen, reporters dotted residential areas and town centres around the capital, each highlighting unusually deserted streets and the feeling of unease that permeated every suburb.

Yet even the knowledge that a breakthrough was unlikely hadn't stopped Hawkins hanging on each new promise of an update or fresh information.

The current loop ended, and a newsreader with cheeks like a hamster's began reciting other headlines. Hawkins glared at the phone lying on the coffee table.

Still not ringing.

She pictured Mike and the rest of her team gathered around Tristan Vaughn like sycophantic disciples, all aware of her mistakes, none eager to repeat them. And Curtis Rickman, presently a tenant of the holding cells but who, if no evidence could be found by 11 p.m., would soon be out of their hands.

What if nobody thought to inform the parole board of why Rickman was being held? Releasing a potential killer into the custody of the usual, unarmed two-officer team would be asking for trouble. She reached instinctively for her mobile, only to groan when she realized there was no point: she had to accept that the others knew what they were doing. Apart from that, any attempt to influence the case now would mean disobeying another of Kirby-Jones' direct orders. And even *she* wasn't stupid enough to go there.

'Idiot.' She let her head drop back to stare at the ceiling. 'Idiot, idiot, idiot.'

She stood and walked into the kitchen, opening one or two cupboards, aimlessly looking for comfort food she knew she didn't have. Anything to take her mind off today. Was it possible to rescue a career that had been flushed so comprehensively down the toilet? And, if so, was that even the right thing to do?

What if it's a sign, Mike's voice repeated in her head, *that it's time to try something new?*

She slammed the cupboard door. Who the fuck was *he* to make her question the part of her life she'd worked harder for than anything else? But if even Mike didn't understand her, then who the hell did?

Paul?

She thought about it for a moment before walking to her bag and digging out the card he'd given her, feeling its silky finish, admiring the tastefully rounded font. After six months away, did Paul *really* seem more like what she wanted than Mike did?

She shook her head as she dropped it in the bin, remembering the nuisance calls, and the fact that she wasn't in the right state of mind to be making decisions about careers – or anything else.

Looking over, she realized that the clock on the microwave she'd been trying to ignore now said 20:16. She sighed in resignation and pulled a small, magnetic card off the fridge door. The cab company's number was printed in lurid rainbow coloured letters across the top, but even the friendly driver she'd had last time didn't make her want to call now.

Mike would probably be out all night, and she couldn't realistically ignore Eric Johnston on her first night of taking advantage of his hospitality. She needed to relax if she was going to survive a night there in her current mood.

Maybe she needed a glass of wine.

Or two.

She could call a cab in the next twenty minutes, sink a couple of glasses and still be in Wood Green by just after nine.

Hawkins reached for the fridge door again, but this time opening it to produce the chilled bottle of white she'd been saving for an evening in with Mike. She took an oversized wine glass from where it had spent a couple of nights on the draining board and set it down on the countertop.

She gripped the cool bottleneck and twisted, anticipating the first sip, expecting to hear a crack as the seal broke.

After a moment's wasted effort, however, Hawkins realized what was wrong. She banged the bottle down on the work surface and began rifling through the kitchen drawer, her search growing ever more frantic.

In the end she conceded that Paul must have taken the corkscrew.

And she'd managed to buy a bottle without a screw top.

64.

He crouched in the shadows, watching. Alert.

Assessing the scene.

The house itself did not appear protected: there was no evidence of an alarm or other security measures, although he couldn't take that for granted. Neither was there any way to determine exactly who or how many were inside.

Yet these factors would not deter him.

No one had entered or left since his arrival, while the late hour and plunging temperatures ensured the area was likely to remain deserted.

According to his most reliable police informant, *she* was here. And he would not let such an extraordinary opportunity pass.

He checked the mobile phone again, as he had done regularly since switching it to silent. The signal was strong, but there had been no further messages from any of his sources. Still no news that contradicted his current information.

Not that the informant knew what he had done. There were several Met officers willing to take cash in return for inside information on Operation Charter. But as far as any of them understood, they were simply providing leads for an underhand journalist: ironically, he was responsible for the information regarding the case, strategically leaked to the media throughout. The beauty of the situation was that, because his police informers had already broken the law by selling classified data, none of them would confess, even if they later came to suspect that their actions had assisted a killer.

His original plans for tonight had been uncertain, fraught with complication. But the Met had inadvertently helped him out.

He placed the handset back in his pocket without switching it off. Despite the fact that phone companies could triangulate the location of a modern digital handset to within a few metres almost instantly, they'd have no reason to investigate this particular signal. It was also a pre-paid voucher system, purchased from a busy supermarket a month ago.

No contract; no trace. Like a single spit of rain against the pattering background of a billion distant others, he remained an enigma to them. Unpredictable. Unstoppable.

One drop in the deluge.

He checked his watch: 11.45 p.m. His pulse quickened in anticipation of coming events. He closed his eyes, resisting the excitement, forcing himself to remain calm.

He studied the gun. It seemed fine, although he was no expert. There were five bullets left in the clip, five more than he hoped he would need, because it was the component in which he had least confidence, despite his recent excursion to test-fire the weapon. That had given him a feel for the firearm, but it had been difficult to assess the absolute accuracy of his aim under volatile conditions.

He adjusted his crouching position, ignoring the

sensation of pins and needles in his right foot. It would soon be time to instigate his final attack.

He could not see inside the house, but he felt her presence.

Suddenly his mind clouded, as if the very thought of her had poisoned his intent. Emotion flared, casting its spectre over his resolution. Ambivalence. *Doubt.*

He shook his head, resisting its onslaught. *No.* He had repelled these sensations; they no longer controlled him. He inhaled deeply, driving out compassion, fortifying his resolve.

He looked out over the undulating cityscape to the south. Dull, charcoal shapes hung in the sullen air, portending rain over London's blurred, shadowy skyline.

It had to be tonight; otherwise the chain would be broken. And the moment he failed to deliver on his guarantee, those who had come to respect him would lose faith. There were supporters out there, believers. He sensed them growing in number and conviction every day.

He wouldn't let them down.

SUNDAY

65.

Hawkins woke with a start and was sitting bolt upright before she had time to stop herself.

Light seared her retinas, forcing her eyes shut, followed by a tidal wave of nausea that drew her elbows back to the table top and a shuddering breath from her lungs. Her mouth tasted like she'd eaten a whole pack of cigarettes. She groaned and brought her hands to her temples. Had her brain been replaced with a brick?

She fixed her position, massaging closed eyelids, waiting for the sledgehammer to ease its assault on her head. When she felt confident that opening her eyes wouldn't cause her skull to explode, she looked around, blinking.

Beside her, a well-populated ashtray and the empty wine bottle accounted for a fair percentage of her queasiness. She'd managed to open the bottle around half-eight and had finished it in less than an hour. That, combined with fatigue, had obviously been sufficient to put her to sleep, even here at the kitchen table.

The lights overhead bathed her in stark whiteness, a dramatic contrast to the blackness beyond the kitchen window. Opposite, lit by a sea of shifting colours from the muted television, the doorway framed her sofa – where Hawkins would have been, given possession of any sense. Instead she was there, inebriated and spot-lit in her kitchen.

She squinted at the clock. 12:08 a.m.

New Year's Day.

The knocking sound made Hawkins whip round, eyes wide, body taught, to stare at the black sections in the back door where somebody had just tapped on the glass.

She saw nothing.

She stood, suppressing her panic, desperate to see who was in the garden. She edged backwards, eyes locked on the door, groping behind her for the light switch. She had to turn and look before she was able to flick off the light.

She turned back again to the door, staring at the form now becoming visible beyond the glass. Her heart rate began to slow as her eyes adjusted to the darkness, her alarm turning to confusion when she recognized the stooped figure outside.

Could it really be him?

Hawkins let out a huge sigh of relief and crossed to unlock and open the door.

'Are you OK?'

'I'm sorry, ma'am.' John Barclay's voice wavered as he looked around nervously. 'I didn't know where else to go.'

He wore grubby jeans and a torn jumper, and he had what looked like a mixture of dried blood and dirt on his neck.

'It's alright,' Hawkins told him. 'Come inside.'

She stood back and the trainee detective moved slowly up the step and into the kitchen. Hawkins leaned out and glanced around the garden before she locked the door and switched the light back on.

Barclay was acting like a frightened animal. His eyes darted anxiously and his jaw chattered as Hawkins encouraged him to sit at the table.

'Wait there,' she instructed, and ran to get a blanket, stopping briefly to check the front of the house through a crack in the curtains. Everything seemed normal, but she checked the door was secure before returning to the kitchen, where she wrapped the blanket around Barclay's shoulders.

Physically he seemed OK, but he was clearly traumatised, staring into space as if the wall and the housing estate beyond were invisible. Had he been held captive? She wanted to ask, but the panic in his eyes said he needed some time to settle, first.

'John?' She crouched, trying to make eye contact. 'You're safe here, OK? All the doors are locked.'

Barclay didn't respond directly. His gaze alighted on her for a split second, but then slid away, as if in submission. There was clearly something very wrong.

'Are you injured, John?' she asked carefully, waiting for a response that didn't come. 'Are you hurt?'

His head made the smallest of shakes. *No.*

'Good. Just sit there and relax. Would you like something to drink?'

Another shake.

'OK.' She straightened up, feeling her headache resume its thumping assault. 'I'm going to make some coffee. Let me know if you change your mind.'

She filled the kettle and set it back on its base, cursing under her breath when she opened the drawer to find no clean teaspoons, and then the cupboard, to find no cups. She began lifting day-old dishes out of the sink.

Her headache was back to full strength now, and she steadied herself against the worktop.

'Ma'am?'

She turned her head, but Barclay wasn't looking at her. He still stared into the distance.

'I have to tell you something,' he said quietly, 'and I need you to understand.'

Hawkins swallowed. She wanted to know what sort of ordeal he'd been subject to, and help if possible. She thought about calling for an ambulance straight away, but he seemed physically okay, so it was probably best to try and calm him down a bit first.

'What is it?' She moved towards him. 'What happened to you?'

'I . . . I was confused . . . trapped.'

'OK,' she coaxed. 'Take your time. Who trapped you?'

He looked up at her suddenly, his expression a mixture of fear and confusion.

'I was . . . I came to tell you, but . . .' His eyes dropped. '*He* was there.'

He was clearly confused, so Hawkins avoided leading him; not offering the name that sprang to mind, '*Who* was there, John?'

Barclay stared at the floor for what felt like an eternity before he said the name.

'Maguire.'

Hawkins frowned, crouching down again. She had to keep the conversation going, get something coherent out of him.

'Mike? What does *he* have to do with this?'

Barclay's narrowed eyes focused on her at last. 'He . . . took you from me.'

Hawkins just stared, her head thumping. 'I don't understand what this has to do with me or Mike, John. Where have you been?'

'I just needed . . . space. Time . . . to think.'

Hawkins tried to repeat her question, but managed only to shake her head, mouth open. Had he disappeared through choice? But what about the flat, the handprint?

'We can start again, Antonia,' Barclay said. 'I can forgive you.'

Hawkins shrank away as his words finally started making sense. She remembered the day Barclay vanished, the same day he'd walked in on her and Maguire in her office. She remembered the look on his face.

She stood, suddenly uncomfortable.

'Don't you see?' Barclay's words were no longer whispered. 'We should be together.'

'Look,' she said, edging away. 'I don't want to sound insensitive, and you're clearly not . . . feeling well, but we've had this conversation before.'

'I know.' He looked directly at her, his expression now more one of frustration than fear. 'But things are different now. *I'm* different.'

'John, this is ridiculous, I'm your comm—' She broke off, remembering that, as of that afternoon, she wasn't in command of anything at all. 'It's just not going to happen, OK? I'm sorry if that sounds harsh.'

Barclay's head dropped, and Hawkins saw the muscles

in his jaw moving under his skin. He obviously wasn't thinking straight.

Then his shoulders sagged and he started to sob quietly.

Embarrassed for them both, Hawkins turned her back and clicked on the kettle, trying to think of something conciliatory to say. When she glanced around again, Barclay was composing himself, wiping his eyes. She felt a stab of pity; perhaps he was just lonely. She sighed and turned to face him.

'Listen, John, you're a nice enough . . .' She didn't want to say 'kid'.

Barclay's head lifted and he stared at her. He was breathing heavily.

'I was worried about you,' Hawkins continued. 'We all were.'

He blinked several times in quick succession, as if he didn't understand. 'I didn't want you to be worried.' His tone was more indignation than concern.

Behind her, Hawkins heard the kettle coming to the boil. She wanted to turn around, but something in Barclay's demeanour held her fast. 'I wanted you to be *afraid*.'

'Afraid?' An icy finger suddenly ran down Hawkins' spine. 'Why?' She eyed her mobile six feet away on the countertop, thinking fast.

Barclay was still sitting down as Hawkins began to edge towards the door, but he seemed to notice her movement and stood suddenly.

'You're all such fucking idiots,' he sneered. 'Don't you get it? Fear is the only reason people do anything decent these days.'

'What are you talking about?' Now she was looking for a weapon.

'Nobody gives a shit any more. Nobody listens. But everyone's paying attention now, aren't they? Thanks to me.'

Something fell in the pit of Hawkins' stomach as she made the final connection.

'John,' she managed to say. 'Please tell me you're not responsible for—'

'Responsible?' He cut her off. 'I'm the only one who demonstrates anything *like* responsibility.'

He began to advance on her. His eyes were wide, and Hawkins recognized the same merciless glare she'd seen too many times in her career.

The look of a killer.

In the seconds it took Barclay to cross the room, Hawkins had turned and grabbed the kettle. She released the lid and thrust the open end towards him. A wide arc of boiling water flew across the kitchen.

Barclay raised his hands, wrenching them away as the water made contact with his right forearm. He hissed sharply and stepped back.

Hawkins lunged for the door, but he was too fast.

She felt a hand grip her trailing wrist with alarming strength, and another on her shirt. Her forward motion was pivoted through ninety degrees, and she was thrown towards the kitchen table. She skidded across the smooth surface, scattering objects as she went, before crashing with stunning force head-first into the cupboard doors on the other side of the room.

Her immediate instinct was to get up, but her vision

blurred and her head swam. She slumped face down and closed her eyes, breathing heavily.

'You burned me, you fucking bitch.'

The voice sounded muffled. It came from the opposite side of the room, as far as she could tell. Then she heard the familiar sound of the back door being unlocked and she forced her eyes open.

Everything was still distorted, but Hawkins saw Barclay open the back door and step outside, closing it behind him.

She blinked hard, attempting to clear her vision, relieved that when she looked again, the room was not only in focus, but empty. She tried to get up; to run, but energy had deserted her.

She lay still, breathing hard. How long did she have? There was no way to tell.

Barclay could return at any second.

Hawkins scanned the kitchen for something she could use to defend herself. The empty wine bottle lay against the wall on the floor under the table, unbroken despite its fall. But it was too far away to reach quickly, and would be relatively ineffective as a weapon. She turned her attention to the cutlery drawer, where there were three or four sharp knives.

She steeled herself and attempted to push up into a crouching position. Pain erupted in her head as if it she'd been hit by a cricket bat. She dropped back to the floor, fighting nausea, looking around for something nearer.

Then she saw the penknife.

It lay beside her on the ground. For a second, Hawkins thought she had imagined it, but then she remembered:

she'd used its corkscrew to open the wine a few hours ago, and must have knocked it onto the floor on her way over the table.

She just had time to reach over and palm it before Barclay re-entered the kitchen and locked the door again, pocketing the key. He let down the window blind and pulled the curtain across the door before turning to leer at her.

He held a black ruck sack.

He set the bag on the table and reached inside to produce what looked like a toy gun. Hawkins' blood almost froze in her veins when she realized it was a Taser.

'I'm sorry.' Barclay levelled the weapon at her. 'I never wanted it to end like this.'

Hawkins' mind raced. She had to keep him talking.

'But what happened to your flat? The handprint in your blood?'

'What *happened*?' he repeated. 'I was angry. Haven't you ever destroyed something out of anger?'

Suddenly everything started to make sense. Barclay's flat hadn't been turned over in a fight; he had simply vented his frustration prior to disappearing. And they had assumed the rest, probably just as he had anticipated.

Her train of thought was broken as he raised the Taser.

'John, wait . . . please.' She struggled to sit up. 'Maybe I was being unfair. Maybe there is a chance for us.'

Barclay didn't react immediately. He continued to stare, but after a second the Taser dropped a couple of inches.

'I was suspended this afternoon.' Hawkins kept her

voice calm. 'Which means I'm no longer your boss. So I suppose we could . . . try, you know – see how it goes.'

Barclay took a step forwards, and the Taser dropped again. 'Really?'

'Sure.' She held his gaze, picking open the largest blade on the knife behind her back. 'You could . . . move in with me. I'll tell Mike it's over, OK?'

Barclay's eyes drifted away for a moment. Was he going for it?

'John.' She felt the blade click fully open. 'What do you think?'

He moved closer and crouched right in front of her, his eyes searching hers. He still held the Taser, but it would be difficult to fire at this range.

She kept going. 'Nobody has to know about what happened here.'

Barclay's eyes narrowed suddenly. 'You want to know what I think?' He leaned closer, his face almost touching hers. 'I think you're a *fucking liar*. And I'm here to make you pay.'

He began to move away.

It was now or never.

Hawkins summoned all her strength and kicked out at his wrist, knocking the Taser from his hand. Barclay reached instinctively after the weapon and Hawkins saw her chance. She grabbed a handful of his jumper and launched the penknife at his jugular, putting all of her strength behind the blade.

She felt the knife make contact and puncture skin as Barclay screamed.

Hawkins let go of the penknife handle in an attempt to

push him away. To get to the Taser. But she hadn't accounted for Barclay's free hand. What must have been a fist made contact with her jaw so hard that she crashed backwards into the cupboard door, her vision blurring. She tasted blood almost immediately.

'You *bitch*!' Barclay's voice was distorted by anger and pain.

She glanced up, but everything looked like a badly tuned television picture. The Taser was in his right hand again, as far as she could tell, and she could hear him breathing heavily.

If she'd punctured an artery, he wouldn't be standing for much longer.

But her optimism waned with every second Barclay remained upright and, as her vision cleared, Hawkins saw the penknife. Only the handle was visible, but the blade wasn't lodged in Barclay's neck as she had intended; it was in his left shoulder.

She had missed.

Panicked, she fought her way up onto one knee. Barclay's feet didn't move, but she sensed him watching her as she paused, gasping for breath, willing her head to clear. She tried to stand, but her strength had gone again and she collapsed into a sitting position against the cupboard door.

She looked up at him, shaking her head, her voice a ragged whisper. 'John . . . don't do this.'

Barclay stood over her, rocking slightly. His eyes were unfocused, but he no longer seemed to be aware of any pain.

He glanced down at the penknife handle protruding

from his shoulder before a thin smile passed his lips as he raised the Taser.

And pulled the trigger.

There was a faint hiss as Hawkins felt the twin darts land on her shirt. She had time to snatch a breath before the electricity crashed in.

For an instant only her chest tightened, but then the shockwave lit up her entire nervous system. Her muscles screamed and her body hunched, instinctively trying to rid itself of the assault. She heard the crack as her head jerked against the door behind her, but the feeling was lost in the frenzied maelstrom of shrieking nerve ends. A high-pitched whimper was all that escaped as she tried to scream, and then she was lying face down, cramped, twitching. Powerless.

And still the fire burned through her. It felt like being trampled by a herd of elephants. Every muscle was taut, and her teeth began biting through her lower lip, but she couldn't stop them any more than she could stop the sensation. Tears welled in her eyes, obstructing her vision, and when she tried to blink, her eyelids were no longer hers to control.

She became aware of the clicking sound made by the Taser and tried to focus on it, on anything but the torture ripping through her.

And then it stopped.

Hawkins slumped, her ears ringing violently. She blinked several times, relieved to find her eyes and eyelids working again. She could feel her tongue, but not her jaw. She tried to move.

Nothing.

She strained to turn her head, but her face pressed against the floor like a tonne weight, and her limbs were unresponsive. She wanted to cry, or to scream, or to get up and fight. But the Taser blast had reduced her to mere observer.

She strained her eyes sideways, looking for Barclay, seeing only his shadow. He was standing right above her.

'I really didn't want it to be this way.'

His words were clipped and emotional, but there was conviction behind them. He was simply repeating a process he had proved several times he was more than capable of.

The shadow moved, and footsteps, three of them, placed Barclay near the kitchen table to her right. A zip opened, followed seconds later by a familiar rustle that told Hawkins he was putting on an anti-contamination overalls. Then she heard the snap of nitrile gloves.

He obviously wasn't thinking straight; traces from his clothes and bleeding shoulder would already be all over the room, too many for him to remove. If he was losing it she might still have a chance.

She closed her eyes and tried to tune the noises out, to concentrate on her body. Her automatic functions were operating normally. She was still breathing, albeit in brief, rapid bursts, and the blood raced through her veins, its sounds mixing in her ears with the thumping of her heart. But still her muscles ignored her.

If she remained immobile, she had no chance of making it out of this situation alive. Even moving a finger would be a start. Hawkins strained against the invisible force disabling her, sending every ounce of willpower to her right hand.

Her eyes sprang open again as she heard Barclay approaching. His shoes appeared near her face, covered by black, slip-on overshoes. Her breathing quickened further, approaching hyperventilation, but she fought to bring it down. She couldn't afford to give in to the panic threatening to overwhelm her.

Barclay crouched down and leaned in towards her, touching her, flipping her over. She tried to resist, but her body hung limp and heavy. As she was raised, Hawkins saw the blood pooling on the floor from her torn lip. Then she was on her back, staring up at the man she now knew as Nemesis.

His jaw twitched as if he was grinding his teeth, and he glared down at her with angry, vindictive eyes.

She tried to speak, but no words followed.

Barclay put gloved hands either side of her face, and turned her head towards him. 'There's no point attempting to move.' His eyes bored into her. 'You're not going anywhere.'

He watched as a tear crept out of the corner of her eye.

Apparently in response, Barclay stopped breathing for an instant, and an expression that could have been pity ghosted across his face. It was replaced a split second later, however, with the original, hate-filled stare.

Hawkins was having trouble keeping her eyes open against the resounding pain in her head.

Barclay leaned in close and put his arms around her neck. At first she thought he was going to kiss her, but after a moment he moved away, and she saw her necklace swinging between his fingers.

He paused for a second to look at it before closing his fist around it.

He reached out to stroke her hair. She screwed her eyes shut and tried to block everything out, to think clearly, but her head pounded worse than ever.

Barclay was talking again. 'You rejected me at training school, but I learned to live with it. I thought we could make a difference working together, enforcing the law. But that wasn't enough. Society needs reminding of what really matters. And I was doing that, despite your best efforts to stop me.' His voice began to tremble. 'I was going to tell you about my plans, when I found you and Maguire . . . together. And that hurt. I needed time to get over it, but I decided to offer you one last chance. And you rejected me again.'

Barclay's expression hardened once more, and he stood and picked up her mobile. He tapped the keys for a minute before holding it down for her to see. She read the text on the screen: **Hi Mike, hope case is going ok. Off to sleep now. Speak in the morning X**

He sent the message and turned off the phone.

'I'd love it to be Mike that finds you.' His voice had become morose, suddenly matter of fact, as if his behaviour was the only reasonable course of action. 'But I don't want him turning up before time.'

He reached for the cloth on the draining board and began wiping down the kitchen surfaces.

Erasing the evidence.

As he turned away, Hawkins realized this would be her final opportunity; the last time John's attention would be on something other than her.

She stared up at the ceiling, concentrating hard. The worst of the pain from the Taser had subsided now, although its embers still danced through every nerve ending in her body. And she could still taste the metallic tang of blood in her mouth.

Don't give up.

She shut her eyes, trying to ignore the shattering pain in her head and the rapid, relentless, thumping sound that filled her ears. She concentrated on her right arm, urging it to obey, feeling her eyelids flicker as she strained against invisible bonds. But when she opened her eyes, there was the ceiling again.

Her hand wasn't in front of her face.

Tears reduced her vision to a kaleidoscope of colour and shadow, spilling over and running down her face into her ears. It was no use.

What the fuck was she going to do now?

Saliva caught in the back of her throat, making her gag. She tried to swallow, but failed. Instead she coughed, her head rocking back and forth against the smooth tiled floor.

Movement.

She strained again, suddenly expecting a different result. But this new hope faded when her neck muscles refused to turn her head. The coughing had been nothing more than a reflex action, her body keeping itself alive.

She fought fresh despair; had to find a way to communicate. The inability to move her jaw made speech impossible, but if she could produce even a ventriloquist-style whisper, perhaps it would be enough.

She had no control over her rate of breathing, but her

mouth hung open slightly. She attempted to hijack one of the outward breaths by humming. Her muscles ignored her. She tried to blow, and then inhale faster. Anything that could make the beginnings of a word.

Just a whisper.

Nothing came out.

And then her chance dissolved.

'It's time,' she heard him say.

His tone sent an ice-cold sensation of pure dread through her.

His face reappeared above her as he crouched next to her again. 'I know what you're trying to do, but it's too late to repent now. You made your choices.'

He watched her for a few seconds before reaching down for something, lifting it into view. A roll of duct tape.

'I understand you're finding it difficult to make noise at the moment, but this may take a while, and I can't have you screaming halfway through.'

He picked at the corner of the roll before ripping a length free. He laid the tape across her mouth, leaving her nose free so that she could breathe. Then he gathered her hair in one hand, using it to pull her head off the floor, and started winding the tape around her face and neck, pulling it tighter and tighter.

He finished with the tape and tore off the end. Then he reached down again, raising his hand so that she could see what he held.

Her pulse reacted, racing faster than ever, and she felt herself starting to hyperventilate.

She didn't recognize the knife, but she could see from

the way it reflected the light that it was heavily sharpened.

The same knife he must have used on the others.

She wanted to close her eyes, but even that was beyond her control now, and she merely stared at the blade, her heart pounding and her breath coming in tattered bursts. Tears streamed down her face as she still fought desperately to regain some sort of movement, but her limbs were still unwilling to respond.

He moved closer, rubbing the knife-edge between thumb and forefinger. Suddenly, his face trembled and he began to cry. For a moment she thought he was going to back away, but then he wiped his eyes and raised the knife.

With his movement, she realized how unimportant everything was: her bank balance, her career, the hair cut she kept meaning to book. Things that had seemed so relevant yesterday.

'I know you're scared,' he said, as he leaned towards her, 'but one day my actions will make sense to everyone. Things are clear now; change demands sacrifice. You have to die, for the greater good.'

She saw the lines of his face tighten, watching with terror as all the humanity drained from his eyes. Time was up.

He ripped open her shirt.

And, as buttons scattered across the kitchen floor, regret like she'd never felt flooded through her.

Panic won.

Her heart was racing so fast now that it hurt. Blackness crowded her vision, blocking out everything except his face and the anticipation of death.

She tried to scream again as the knife made contact

with her flesh and she felt the blade break her skin. Her vision blurred. A gurgling sound crept out from somewhere in the back of her throat.

Then the pain came, and so did the rasping seizure of air in her thorax.

66.

Mike Maguire leaned back in his chair, stretched, and sipped his coffee.

'Mmmh!' he protested, pulling a face and peering across the desk at Frank Todd and Amala Yasir.

They both looked up, and Yasir asked, 'What is it?'

Maguire forced himself to swallow the tepid mouthful, raising the mug. 'About an hour cold.'

'Oh.' She laughed. 'I thought you had something then. Whose turn is it to make?'

Todd was straight in. 'Well, you're the only lass here. I think that makes it your turn again. Right, Mike?'

'Tell us again why you're single, Frank—?' Maguire stood. 'What can I get you, Amala?'

He took orders, returning minutes later with two coffees and a tea, threading his way between empty desks. Apart from the three of them, the incident suite inside Becke House was deserted, angle poise lamps in their work area creating an isolated pool of light in the vast darkness.

'Hey, guys.' He distributed the drinks. 'Any inspiration yet?'

Both heads shook.

'No difference, one report to the next,' Todd complained. 'Whose stupid idea was this, anyway?'

'It was the chief's, Frank.' Amala got in first. 'And it's

brought us closer to catching Nemesis than anything else so far.'

'She's not my bloody chief anymore,' Todd shot back. 'Or yours.'

Maguire bit his tongue, aware that direct reaction to Frank's antagonistic humour would only encourage him. But he was pleased when Amala continued to demonstrate uncharacteristic fight.

'We could all do a lot worse,' she said. 'What do you know about Tristan Vaughn, anyway?'

'What I know is that the whole operation was mishandled before he arrived. At least we might get some action now, instead of her standing about, spouting some textbook flannel, expecting us to do all the bloody work.'

'Oh, shut up, Frank. Rather her flannel than yours.'

Amala's response stunned them both.

Mike suppressed a smile. He rolled his shoulders and adjusted the laptop in front of him, preparing to settle in for another round of transcripts. To his left, a second screen showed a map of London, overlaid with real-time markers indicating the location of every response team.

He was two lines into another statement when the text came in.

He checked his cell, seeing that the message was from Antonia. *Shit*, he should have called. Of course she'd been in his thoughts all afternoon – pretty much the same as any afternoon, really – but today he'd been so caught up in the case that he hadn't even thought to check on her. Sometimes he was such a self-absorbed asshole.

He'd left Antonia's place earlier that day, pissed that he'd dealt with things so badly considering the pressure she'd been under, and her suspension from work. He could have spared ten minutes, gone into the house with her at least.

She was probably texting to call time on their on-off relationship altogether.

He opened the message.

He read the text and smiled, relieved that her tone appeared conciliatory. Perhaps there was still a chance for them. He considered calling her back, opting instead to send a happy but rhetorical text, carefully minimising any mention of the investigation. No need to disturb or stir things up.

Maguire put the phone back in his pocket, already feeling more positive. She was safe now. Eric Johnston wasn't the most amazing host, but he was tough, and he wouldn't let her come to any harm.

At least now he could focus properly on the case. OK, so it was only a half after midnight, but their chances of repeating last Sunday's major stroke of luck in locating Nemesis were tiny.

Their approach, at least, had evolved. Calls from the public were now being sent electronically to their laptops, where they were read and assigned a priority level. From there, complex software plotted each location on a map, and sent over the nearest response team. Meanwhile the program was also choreographing the network of units, ensuring that any location in London could be reached within ten minutes. The idea was to eliminate dead zones like the one left around Scotland Yard last week, which had allowed the killer to escape.

This meant that as soon as any marker, even the

smallest clue to the killer's location surfaced, they mustn't let it . . .

Suddenly, Mike was frantically searching his pocket for the phone. He pulled it free and accessed the SMS menu, staring at the message from Toni.

Hi Mike, hope case is going ok. Off to sleep now. Speak in the morning X

He thought for a moment before opening her previous text, from a few days earlier. He scanned the words, confirming his recall that she rarely wrote a message without abbreviating at least a few words: *speak* was normally *spk*; *hope* normally *hp*.

Was something wrong?

He began checking back, message after message, going beyond the last couple of weeks to the messages he'd kept from when they were seeing each other six months before. *Why hadn't he realized?*

Whenever she ended the message with a kiss, it was always 'Ax'. Never just 'X'.

Instantly, he was off his chair, sprinting out of the control room, ignoring confused shouts from Walker and Todd. He didn't have time to explain.

He stumbled as he reached the corridor, trying simultaneously to run and dial Antonia's cell. Straight to answer phone. *Fuck*. He selected Eric Johnston's number, barging aside two uniforms exiting one of the offices just as Eric answered.

'Y'ello?'

'Eric, is Antonia with you?'

'No sign yet, dude. Why?'

Maguire cut him off, immediately selecting her landline

instead. *Please be at home, please be* OK. But after a few rings the machine cut in.

Maguire reached the parking lot, landing in his car and firing the engine before roaring out onto the street. He slotted his seatbelt in place as he reached the first corner; not for safety, but because it would hold him in the seat.

It was eleven miles from Hendon to Antonia's – twenty minutes under normal driving conditions. But Maguire still cursed every second of the eight minutes it took him to clear the North Circular and A307 to Richmond.

He used the time to order an ambulance and two of the response teams to her address, hoping to hell that he was wasting everyone's time. But as he hit the kerb outside her house and ran for the door, Maguire was more afraid than ever that his suspicions were right.

He launched himself at the front door, hearing the plastic flex and crunch. But the framework held. He tried the handle, banging his fists against it and ringing the bell.

No answer. *What if she wasn't even there?*

He stood for a second, desperately watching the windows for signs of a response before he remembered the emergency key she used to keep hidden in the back yard.

He turned and sprinted for the alley, hearing sirens in the distance, reaching the garden and clambering over the fence, looking up at the house.

Kitchen light was on, blind down.

Maguire almost ran straight for the back door, but forced himself to divert, clambering on his knees by the shed, using the light on his mobile to search among the stacks of old plant pots.

Come on. It had to be there.

Twice he almost gave up, desperation dragging him towards the house, but after what seemed like hours, he found it. The key was rough with rust, and he rubbed it with his fingers as he stood and ran for the house, clattering to a halt against the door.

Terrified, he suddenly noticed the empty wine bottle on the floor under the table in the kitchen, and the kettle lying on its side on the worktop.

Fuck. Something *had* happened.

His hands fought one another as he tried to force the rusted key into the lock. It took three attempts, but finally the metal scraped home. He twisted and pushed, falling forwards to his knees on the kitchen floor.

The sound of sirens and screeching tyres came from the road outside, but the knocks and rings at the front door went unanswered as Maguire knelt in the kitchen, unaware of anything except the horrific scene that had now become visible in the corner of the room.

67.

The last few steps were torture.

Across the street in front of his flat, through the pool of light under the street lamp, and up the path. Just another member of the public: a New Year reveller, returning home. Nothing more.

Nothing more.

He'd managed to maintain his composure and pace, slow but definite, all the way back. Somehow instinct had guided him, unseeing, along the twenty-minute walk from her door to his, but tonight he had had no impression of how long it had taken, or which route he had used.

And as he reached the entrance and let himself in, the façade collapsed.

He stumbled across the front room, tears welling. Into the kitchen. A room that held nothing of her, no trace at all.

It was no good; they were still there.

The poisonous thoughts.

How could he have expected to ignore these feelings?

He needed shelter, to suffuse himself with her. He fumbled in his pocket for her necklace and held it tight. Then he hauled himself to a chair and collapsed onto the seat.

He looked around, seeking anything that could offer solace. But this place mocked him. He had previously kept a few of her personal items, stolen from her office at work, but he'd been forced to dispose of them, realizing that their discovery in his possession would become incriminating once she was—

He clutched the pendant, rubbing his thumb hard against the smooth emerald stone. He didn't hear the chair creaking as he jerked back and forth, or his own whimpers of distress as the tears came again.

He glanced frantically around the room, unable to rid his thoughts of her.

The half-done washing-up was not hers; nor the mud on the floor from her shoes. The empty glass on the table had never touched her lips.

And now it never would.

Then he saw her, just as she appeared in his dreams, standing at the far end of a long passageway. Lights blazed at regular intervals, lining the roof between them. He waved. She smiled and gestured him on.

He began to walk, eager to meet. But as he passed the first light it went out. And so did the second. He sped up, trying to stay ahead of the lights as they extinguished in time with his progress. Soon he was running along the corridor, closing rapidly on his destination, but the lights increased their rate, too, and then the darkness overtook him. He tried to go faster, straining to catch up but, seconds later, he was trailing badly. He shouted at her to get back, away from the advancing shadows, although she didn't seem to hear, and stayed where she was, smiling, waving.

And then the last light went out.

Blackness surrounded him. He kept going, but something tripped him and he fell, crashing to a halt.

He dragged himself upright, reaching out in the darkness to find the wall. But as his fingers felt something, the lights came on.

And he recoiled.

She lay on the ground in front of him, pallid and motionless, both colour and life draining from her. The way he'd left her tonight.

His mind flashed back to the first incision. Normally it was so *easy*, the pleading eyes of his victims just a reminder of how effective his methods had become. They were so *afraid*. But with her it had been different: his hands had been trembling and he had hesitated.

As he had forced himself to cut her, as the knife sliced into her flesh, he'd seen the fire in her eyes. That familiar mixture of pain, fear, and shock.

Hatred.

And for the first time, he'd felt those things, too. His tears had mixed with her blood and he had broken down, bent over her body, sobbing. It had taken all his strength to leave her for the final time.

He tore himself from his thoughts, opening his eyes, looking down at his hands. A thin trail of blood crept across the heel of his clenched fist and dripped onto his shoe. He stared at it for a moment until his brain fired. He released the necklace, freeing the clasp from where it had punctured his skin.

He didn't get a chance to say goodbye.

Was this *his fault*?

He clawed at his forehead; he didn't want these thoughts. Why did it have to end this way? She should have been *his*.

But now she would never betray anyone ever again.

He stood and snatched the glass from the table, launching it across the kitchen to where it erupted against the far wall. But as the fragments scattered, his strength deserted him and he dropped back onto the chair.

He fumbled inside his jacket for the picture and held it up to look at the face of the woman he loved.

This wasn't right: the pain should have been banished now, yet he felt no release. He clutched her necklace to his chest and searched for answers in the tattered photograph. Was this as close as he had ever truly been to having her?

He shuddered, reliving their last moments together in her kitchen. She'd been pleased to see him after their time apart, and he had been encouraged. He'd even tried to explain his mission. But her eyes had given her away; she hadn't been able to understand. There had been no chance of reconciliation.

And as he'd described his achievements, she had attacked without warning. He saw her expression now, contorted with rage. Heard her ragged breaths. The scalding water seared his arm once more, and the penknife tore into his shoulder.

The penknife . . .

Suddenly, physical pain re-entered his sphere of consciousness. He became aware of the intense burning sensation in his left shoulder and realized that he hadn't been using the arm, cradling it instead against his body. Adrenalin and distress must have masked the effects until now.

Slowly he lifted his coat. The penknife handle lay flat

against his skin, which meant the blade, probably a corresponding three inches of it, was hilt-deep in his muscle.

She had put up quite a fight.

Fortunately, his clothing had soaked up the small amount of blood escaping from the lesion, and the bulk of his jacket had both secured and hidden it since. He touched the skin around the knife, tentatively, in assessment of how painful it would be to remove. The area had swollen, and the flesh was tender.

He scanned the kitchen for something to clean the cut, before awkwardly tearing off three sheets of kitchen roll with his good hand and folding them into a pad, which he placed on the table. He shrugged off the coat, wincing as its cloth grazed the fresh burn on his right forearm, and sat breathing deeply for a moment. Then he gripped the handle.

Withdrawing the blade at a steady pace would provide the best compromise between tolerable pain and the risk of causing further damage.

He closed his eyes and pulled.

His body shook and his teeth ground as the blade moved inside the wound, the metal grating against bone. Sweat broke out across his forehead, and his jaw clenched as he suppressed the urge to scream.

Eventually the knife came free, and he dropped it on the table.

Blood began to ooze immediately from the gash, validating his choice to leave the blade in place when he left her home. Not leaving traces of his blood at the scene was critical.

He stripped to the waist and pressed the pad of paper

over the cut, turning his attention back to the weapon. Apart from his blood, it appeared to be clean and rust-free, although there was no way to tell what sort of invisible contamination it carried.

He needed to clean the wound with some kind of anti-septic, and apply a sterile dressing, neither of which he had. Venturing out in public was something he'd planned to avoid for at least a few days, but this left him no choice. The burn on his right forearm was painful but superficial, and he could use bulky winter clothing to cover whatever makeshift bandages were necessary for his shoulder, thereby reducing the likelihood of unwanted attention.

A tickling sensation ran down his left arm. Blood had already overwhelmed the kitchen roll pad, and was nearing his elbow. He pressed down harder on the pad and walked towards the sink.

Something in the next room caught his eye. The tele-vision – he must have left it on. He moved to the archway and stared across the room at the screen, its colours vivid in the darkness. It took him a moment to register exactly what was being displayed, but then he scrambled forwards and grabbed the remote, jabbing at the volume button.

A caption at the bottom of the screen heralded break-ing news. Above it, a reporter stood in the entrance to a darkened street. As her voice became audible, he was cap-tivated, oblivious to the blood now dripping from his fingers onto the carpet.

'Yes, Stuart, this is the road where the attack took place. Details are sketchy at present, but it appears that another Met police detective working on the Advent Killer case has been attacked, in all likelihood by the murderer himself. Antonia Hawkins, a thirty-five-year-old detective chief inspector, was stabbed here at her home in Ealing less than three hours ago . . .'

Before the reporter had finished her next sentence, his attention had shifted again, this time to the unregistered mobile phone. He selected his informant's number and hit dial, hurriedly composing himself as the line connected and started to ring.

He needed inside information, details the news channel did not currently have. And he needed it *now*. If what the reporter said was true, he had made a catastrophic error.

She had survived the attack.

68.

He checked the phone's display: 3.42 a.m.

No further messages had come in; nothing to contradict the information he had received from the two different Met informers.

He turned off the handset to save its battery and stared up at the tall structure of Ealing Hospital, looming above him. He'd arrived there by taxi within an hour of hearing the news.

There was still time.

It was New Year's Day – a Sunday morning – so the hospital would be minimally staffed, and as peaceful as it would ever get.

His short conversations with his informants had proved invaluable, confirming also that he'd been lucky. So far.

His sources verified that she had indeed survived the attack, and that she'd been transferred here by ambulance two hours ago, before undergoing surgery. She was still in critical condition, however, and had not yet regained consciousness. But the doctors were hopeful.

And so it was time to go in, and take the biggest risk of his campaign.

Everything hinged on the coming hour.

He cursed, frustrated that his own carelessness had forced him into this course of action. All his other victims had died in his presence; he had been certain of that. But in his traumatized state just hours ago, he had left her lying in a pool of blood in her kitchen without making sure she was actually dead.

He'd merely assumed his fervent attack had been a success.

And if the doctors *had* managed to save her, as soon as she became conscious she would divulge his identity. With every passing moment, it became more likely that she was saying her first words since the attack. And those words would be 'John Barclay'.

He began crossing the road towards the entrance, stifling a cough, recognizing the irony: he'd been using the pretence of poor health to avoid compulsory overtime for so long that his cough had become automatic.

He glanced upwards as he neared the threshold to the building. Only half the moon was visible, so the night was dark enough that he still had a good chance of escape, even if the alarm was raised.

The doors slid open as he approached, and he walked into the reception area, relieved to find the desk unmanned. Suddenly conscious of the bulge created by the gun tucked into his belt, however, he disguised it by lifting his hands into his coat pockets.

Pain erupted through his damaged shoulder, flashing like lightning beneath the bandage. For a moment he considered looking for a doctor. If small movements were this painful, despite the heavy dose of painkillers he had taken, the wound probably required antibiotics and stitches. But he dismissed the idea; he had to strike now.

He drew himself up, vowing to let neither emotion nor injury deter him from his goal. And, as he caught sight of a sign for the trauma recovery ward, he felt his strength return.

He retrieved the photo of her from his pocket. Her creased and faded image smiled back at him. The picture had been taken a few years ago, before they met. Still her face elicited an emotional response. But, whereas it had once invigorated his desire to be with her, his current reaction was entirely different.

He crushed the picture in his fist.

69.

He carried the flowers, taken from a sleeping patient's bedside, calmly past the double glass doors, looking over at the nurses' station inside. A lone woman sat in the softly lit area. She was around thirty, with natural brown hair pulled mercilessly into a ponytail, and a compact demeanour that suggested she wouldn't be easily misled. Her blue uniform and tired features were illuminated by her computer screen. She didn't look up.

Just before he passed the doorway opposite she raised a cardboard cup and took a sip.

He stopped a few yards past the doors and crouched, pretending to re-tie his laces, checking the corridor in both directions, soon satisfied that he was the only person there. Night traffic on the ward was almost non-existent.

He made a return pass, this time concentrating on the door at the rear of the room. On the wall beside it was an electronic security lock, and beyond that he saw at least two of the secure rooms designed to keep at-risk patients safe, or dangerous patients contained.

And in one of them, his target.

The relative lack of fortification still didn't make his task easy, however, partly due to the camera visible in the far corner of the room, but mainly because he didn't know whether she would be alone. Armed guards were a distinct possibility. But his hand was being forced.

Whether he struck or not, his liberty was at stake. But she deserved her fate, and he was prepared for this to be his final act of freedom.

Tonight he would take her life, even if it cost him his own.

He found a secluded corner and shed the cleaner's overall he'd taken from a storage area on the ground floor, which had allowed him to roam the hospital unchallenged. Then he walked back to the secure area reception and through the double doors, just another confused first-time visitor entering the area.

The nurse – Sarah, according to her name badge – looked concerned. 'Can I help you?'

'Hi.' He held up the flowers, 'I know it's not exactly visiting hours, but a friend of mine works in A and E, and she said I could drop these off.'

'Oh, OK,' Sarah relaxed slightly, 'who are they for?'

'Am I allowed to say?'

She smiled at last. 'It's fine as long as I don't tell you.'

'Great.' He arrived at the desk and produced his police identification, 'They're for my boss, Antonia Hawkins. How's she doing?'

Sarah studied his ID. 'Pretty good, considering. She's had a hefty operation, so we haven't rushed to bring her round, but she's doing OK.'

He feigned relief. 'That's good to hear. Everyone at work will be so worried; at least I can tell them something. Have any other night shifters been in?'

'Not yet.' She sipped her drink. 'So far it's just the guy who arrived with her. He was so distraught that we put him down as next of kin so he can sit with her. He's in there now, fast asleep in a chair, poor bugger. Mike, is it?'

Revulsion wrenched at him, but he covered his shock with a hacking cough. 'Sorry. Damned nights play havoc with your health.'

They chatted for a few minutes about the difficulties of shift work.

He checked his watch. 'Look, I have to get going, but could I ask a favour? Don't disturb them, but would you set my mind at rest by checking on her before I go?'

'Of course.' Sarah rose and moved towards the security door.

He watched her remove the security pass from around her neck and hold it to the sensor. Then she pressed a concealed button underneath the plate and twisted the handle until a green light illuminated on the panel.

As soon as she stepped through the door, he produced a small plastic bottle from his pocket, leaned over the desk, and squeezed the contents into her coffee. The solution contained a mixture of powdered sleeping tablets and Rohypnol, easily potent enough to render her unconscious, but insufficient to kill.

There was no point disposing of someone who had done nothing to bring death upon themselves. He still regretted having to silence Eddie Connor by such a measure.

He stepped back, aware that his actions were being filmed. But people tended to relax as soon as they knew a camera was observing on their behalf, and it was unlikely anyone was watching live. It would soon be obvious if they were, but that risk was unavoidable.

Sarah reappeared through the security door. 'She's hanging in there. Try not to worry.'

'Thanks for doing that.' He handed her the flowers. 'I'll tell the guys.'

He retreated to the canteen on the first floor and waited impatiently for a full ten minutes, reassuring himself that, as Sarah had confirmed, the next shift wouldn't arrive until six o'clock.

He returned to find her slumped over the desk, and considered briefly the merits of dragging her out of sight, before deciding against it. Anyone observing her at the moment would likely assume she had come to work poorly prepared for a night shift and flaked out at her post. Only if someone tried to wake her would subterfuge become apparent.

But he didn't have long.

He walked to the desk and gently removed Sarah's pass from around her neck, before approaching the security lock and repeating the sequence she had used. The door opened first time and he stepped inside, noting another camera in the adjacent corner.

Three windowed doors lined the back wall of the area, and he checked the view through each from left to right. The first two rooms were unoccupied, and his senses bristled as he approached the last.

In a bed against the left-hand wall, she lay motionless. Myriad wires and tubes joined her to various machinery and screens. And in a chair beside the bed, Maguire sat awkwardly, asleep.

But they were the only people in the room. Obviously, the fact that nobody was supposed to know where she was hidden had been enough to convince the Met of her safety.

As he raised the security pass to unlock the door to her room, he couldn't help but marvel at their negligence. Apart from a potentially troublesome escape, this really couldn't have worked out any better. Here was the perfect opportunity to finish them both. He could even make her watch Maguire die first.

He removed the Taser from his pocket, but left the knife in his coat and the gun tucked in his belt, before he repeated the unlocking sequence. When the green light came on, he eased the handle down and pushed. He stepped into the room and closed the door, hearing the powered lock re-engage.

Maguire stirred briefly but he was ready, lowering the Taser only when he was sure the American hadn't woken.

He paused, exhilarated by the imminence of his definitive act, enjoying the serenity of the darkened room, its silence unbroken apart from the quiet electronic pulse of monitoring equipment.

His instincts urged him towards her, but he resisted, instead moving closer to Maguire and studying his former colleague in the pale radiance of the weak bedside light.

His hands were sweating, so he pulled at the sleeves of his gloves, lifting the grips to allow air to reach his palms. He toyed with the idea of waking the American, aware that he would still be unaware that his younger colleague was Nemesis. The expression when he realized would be one to savour. But he needed to avoid anything that might necessitate use of the gun, whose noise would expedite attention.

He took a moment to select the ideal point on Maguire's body for the Taser strike, reluctant to deploy its projectiles in case he should require them later. He unclipped the canister section, leaving the electrodes exposed. He also wanted this experience to be as visceral as possible, and looking into the American's eyes as he endured a thirty-second blast would be an exquisite start.

He lined up the Taser and positioned his feet, satisfied that the chair appeared sturdy enough to withstand the forthcoming onslaught. Then he filled his lungs and depressed the trigger to awaken fifty thousand volts.

And drove it into the centre of Maguire's chest.

For a split second his target didn't react. Then Maguire's body tensed and his eyes flicked open, their frenzied apertures conveying the obliteration of peace, his mouth gaping in silent shock.

He renewed his efforts, drilling the weapon into his victim, ignoring the pain in his shoulder, determined that contact would not be broken. The chair legs chirped against the polished floor as the opposing forces of his strength and Maguire's weight brawled. In odd contrast to the nature of events, their struggle remained almost soundless.

And in the midst of their quietly clicking dance, he maintained eye contact, searching for that ineffable clue that Maguire might have recognized the features beneath the long hair of his wig, and realized who was delivering this torture.

But Maguire's face showed no such emotion, something that might have frustrated him if he had intended to kill by prolonging the Taser strike. But he wasn't going to let his two greatest opponents off that easily.

He completed his thirty-second count before forcing himself to release the trigger and step away. Freed from the tensioned state, Maguire slid straight off the chair and slumped to the floor.

He almost laughed.

A glance to his left told him she hadn't stirred, and a second into the corridor satisfied him that nobody had yet found the nurse unconscious at her desk. But he added a further level of protection by jamming the chair, recently vacated by Maguire, under the door handle. Now, even if they were discovered by someone with a security pass, nobody would enter the room till he was ready.

He returned to the bed and crouched in front of Maguire.

'Mike? Can you hear me?'

The detective's eyes were half-open, although there was no way to know if he understood. The dealer who had supplied the Taser had explained that any discharge longer than twenty-five seconds risked permanent brain damage for the target. He'd never tried it before, but he was happy to let Maguire test the theory.

Brain damaged or not, the American was definitely still alive, because his lower lip was shaking ever so slightly, as if trying to voice whatever sentiments he felt in his prison of nervous disability.

He bent, gripping Maguire by the neck with his good arm, and dragged him across the room to prop him against the far wall.

Then he returned to the bed and looked down at her.

She lay on her back, upper body raised on the adjustable bedstead, covers folded down to her waist. An oxygen tube ran from her nose. Sensors peppered her chest. Bandages were visible beneath her robe, hiding the wounds left by his previous attack. She looked dead already, although the quiet rhythm of the monitoring equipment suggested she was anything but.

And yet he felt nothing.

He was free, purged of the irrational affection that had once threatened to neutralize him. She was just another deserving victim, soon to pay the price for sustained and latent contempt.

But he wanted her to *know* that.

He examined the hospital apparatus, aware that it would incorporate alarms to warn of asphyxia or disconnection. Which meant if she was to be roused, full disablement was the best option.

He identified the two main power cables and traced them to the wall, where he found secure plugs that required a key for release, to ensure they weren't removed by a negligent cleaner. Deciding not to test their strength, he wheeled the two machines away from the wall and followed the cables back to where they entered each box. Then he drew the knife from his belt and pulled the first cable taut across the blade, keeping his fingers on the wooden handle, away from the steel.

He jerked the knife, cutting the cable, hearing the electric fizz as power was disconnected, watching the glow from the screens evaporate. Immediately the unit emitted a tiny, high pitched whine, but this died after a few seconds, and he moved on to repeat the process.

With the second cable cut, he stepped back to the bed and pulled the tube from her nose, and the sensors from her chest. Then he leant over and listened to her breathing.

This was the moment. Without the machine's help, she'd either slip quietly away, or she'd wake. He waited, watching her face, oblivious to everything else in the room. Seconds passed.

And then her eyelids flickered.

70.

'*Antonia?*'

The voice was distant and muffled, but it was definitely there.

'*Wake up.*'

Her head rolled towards the sound as her lungs dragged in air. A dull ache filled her chest.

'*I have something to show you.*'

Her eyelids lifted on dark colours and unfocused, murky shapes. But before she could make sense of anything, a wave of nausea hit, stronger than any she'd ever felt. Her vision blurred and she clamped her eyes shut, as her head filled with disorder.

She waited, breathing heavily, slowly concluding that she must have been asleep. As for where she was, or any information regarding the previous day, *any* day in fact . . .

She coughed and swallowed. Her throat felt so dry it was painful. The nausea had abated, though, so she braced for another onslaught and opened her eyes. There was no pain this time, but the darkness remained, and it took Hawkins a few seconds to recognize that the bed in which she lay was not her own. Neither was the room. Then she noticed the person looking down at her.

Her eyes moved first, then her head rolled slowly to face him. It took a second to make out his features in the dim light, and a few more for recognition to come.

Suddenly she was trying to sit up, to get away, as memories of the attack in her kitchen streamed back into her mind. But her body resisted, and pain flared in her chest. Then he was gripping her shoulders, locking her down, his face in hers.

Barclay's breath was putrid. 'Nice to have you back.'

She tried to shout for help, but the sound jammed in her throat. And when she attempted to push him away, her arms felt like they weighed a tonne each. She slumped, breathing hard.

'Having trouble?' Barclay released her. 'You're still under anaesthesia, apparently, but I do have something that'll liven you up.'

He turned away, and immediately she moved her eyes, searching the room for anything she could use to her advantage.

'Look who I found.' Barclay's voice came from the far side of the room. Lifting her head took Hawkins three attempts, and her eyes wouldn't focus until . . .

Mike.

He sat crumpled in the corner. His head hung, and he didn't react when Barclay nudged his shoulder. *Was he . . .?*

Barclay caught her expression. 'Oh, he's alive, for the moment. Just feeling a little dazed after being woken up with the Taser, aren't you, Mike?'

Hawkins' neck muscles seized, and she couldn't stop her head from dropping back onto the pillow.

'No, you don't.' Barclay's footsteps moved towards her. 'You're going to watch him die whether you like it or not.'

Hawkins forced herself to concentrate. There had to

be a way to save Mike. She turned her head, realizing that they were in a hospital room, and that she must have been here since he attacked her. She scanned the wall for a way to raise the alarm. But before she found one, Barclay re-appeared above her.

He picked up a remote control attached by a cable to the bed, and pressed one of the switches. A motor whined, and the mattress began to lift. A few seconds later, Hawkins was sitting almost upright, staring straight at the corner where Maguire lay, still not moving. She groaned. Her torso felt like it had been run over by a truck.

'Good.' Barclay dropped the remote on the bed in front of her. 'Here's the plan. First you're going to watch me kill your boyfriend, and then I'll put you out of your misery, too. *Any questions?*'

Hawkins glanced at the door. Where was the hospital staff? Surely somebody would check on her soon? She and Mike had to survive. Right now, they were the only people who knew the Advent Killer's identity.

She coughed again, clearing her throat. She had to stall him.

'Why?' she croaked.

'*Why?*' Barclay seemed surprised to hear her speak, but conviction rose in his voice as he continued. 'All this time and you still haven't worked that out?'

Suddenly, Hawkins' attention was drawn past him. Had Mike just moved?

'Sorry, John.' She dragged her eyes off Maguire, desperate to hold Barclay's attention. 'I don't ... get it.'

'Detective *Chief* Inspector,' he mocked. 'How the *fuck*?

You want me to justify my actions? You really think I would do these things to people who didn't absolutely deserve every second of their pain?'

He brought a fist down onto the sheets, just missing her leg. 'This is about fucking *respect* – is it really that hard to grasp? You fuckers have shown me nothing but contempt, but this time you picked the wrong man. I'm not one of those idiots who just takes it any more. If you cross me you're going to pay, and if I teach everybody else a lesson in the process, then all the better.'

He paused, face reddening.

This was good, he obviously wanted her to understand, and the longer she kept him distracted . . .

'You want details?' Barclay leaned closer. 'You want to hear that I almost drowned at school because Glenis Ward thought pushing a five-year-old into deep water was the best way to teach him to swim? That I was put into care when my mother killed herself, where Tess Underwood turned a blind eye to the bigger kids who beat the shit out of me every other day? Or Jessica Anderton, who humiliated me in front of the entire school because she didn't want to date me? *Sad little motherless runt.*'

Suddenly everything began to make sense. The attacks had been impossible to connect because they related to disparate negative encounters spread throughout John Barclay's life. And he'd killed each victim in the way he perceived her as having mistreated him. He had drowned Glenis Ward because she had almost let that happen to him, and beat Tess Underwood to death for the same reason. Jessica had broken his heart.

And so had she . . .

Barclay turned away, shaking.

'John.' Hawkins tried to grab his arm, desperate to keep him away from Mike. She risked a glance past him, and this time she saw Mike's leg move.

He was definitely recovering. She had to keep it going.

'What about ... Summer Easton?' Her speech was broken by the worsening pain in her chest.

Barclay spun back, tears in his eyes. 'Summer Easton? The woman who said she was in spiritual contact with my mother? I threw away my father's watch because of her, because she said it was conducting negative emotion.'

He reached inside his coat and produced a knife. The same weapon, Hawkins realized, he'd used to cut her before.

'Enough talk.' He brought the blade to her throat. 'It's time for your boyfriend to die.'

Hawkins turned her face away, feeling the same terror as she had during their last encounter. Her eyes came to rest on the bed's remote control.

And its triangular emergency call button.

She looked back at Barclay, who stared at her for a second longer before he stepped backwards and started to turn.

Just as Mike crashed into him.

The two men sprawled noisily into the equipment to her right. Immediately, Hawkins reached out and jammed her thumb onto the button, seeing it light up in response. Somebody would be here within moments.

On the floor beside the bed, Barclay knelt above Maguire, who lay on his back with both hands clamped around the younger man's wrist. But he was clearly still impeded by the effects of the Taser blast, and Barclay was gaining the advantage. The knife was slowly moving nearer to Mike.

'John,' Hawkins shouted, gambling on his previous statement. 'Your father wouldn't have wanted this.'

Barclay ignored her, and continued driving the blade towards Mike's throat.

A bleeping sound drew everyone's attention to the door. Through the glass a man and a woman could be seen outside, obviously having released the electronic lock. For a second Hawkins thought they were saved, but then she realized the chair under the handle was preventing them from entering the room.

She looked back at Barclay, who was reaching with his free hand under his coat. She recoiled as he produced a gun and took aim at the people outside.

'Get back!' she gasped as Barclay fired twice, shattering the glass.

The faces disappeared, and Barclay turned the gun on Mike. But the distraction had allowed Maguire to recover strength. His fist crashed into the side of Barclay's head, sending him skidding across the room on his back. The knife clattered to the floor and disappeared behind the grappling men, but the gun slid in the opposite direction.

Straight under her bed.

Mike clambered to his knees and launched himself on top of Barclay.

Hawkins summoned all her strength and lifted herself towards the edge of the bed, just in time to see Barclay land a punch in Mike's face.

Her limbs shook and she was nearly sick, but she held it down.

This was their only chance.

The pain in her chest felt like fire now, and she was having trouble focusing. But after two juddering breaths she was ready. She concentrated everything into one absolute effort, and launched herself over the edge.

She tried to get an arm down to break her fall, but she landed heavily, hearing a sickening crunch from somewhere in her side.

She looked up, ignoring the conflict behind her, to see the gun wedged between the wheels of the bed.

Connor's gun.

She reached out and grasped it before heaving herself onto her back, then elbowing over onto her right side, bringing the gun to bear on the two silhouettes still brawling in the shadows across the room.

A combination of blurred vision and lack of light made it impossible for her to distinguish between them, and she couldn't risk hitting Mike. She closed her eyes and rubbed them desperately with her free hand.

Somewhere beyond the shattered window voices were screaming, although nobody reappeared in view.

But her vision had cleared, and she was able to make out detail on the two figures before her. One sat with his back to her, astride the other, and in the upper man's hand the Taser hovered, its naked electrical light dancing, ready to strike.

The gun leapt in her hand as she fired two shots into the back of the upright figure, and a second later it slumped.

She waited for any indication that her aim might have been off, ready to fire further shots if necessary.

Then, suddenly, the only sound she could hear was of blood thumping through her veins, and the images being processed by her brain lost stability, before jagged black and white lines invaded her vision completely.

She clung to consciousness for a full ten seconds before passing out.

EPILOGUE

'How are you feeling?' the nurse asked. 'Want more pain-killers?'

'I'm OK,' Hawkins replied grimly, 'but could you not use the word *killer*?'

She winced as he checked her latest damage, asking her to raise her left arm and keep still. Apparently, thanks to her fall off the bed, she could now add two fractured ribs to the multiple stab wounds on her injury list, even though the anaesthetic still in her system at the time had saved her from the immediate pain.

She was lucky, he said, not to have burst the stitches holding her recently operated-on torso together. She might even have agreed with him, had it not been for the intense, burning sensation now pervading her chest.

She waited as he poked about, and took her mind off the discomfort by studying her fresh, much busier sur-roundings. She'd been moved to a bed on a standard ward, apparently as the shots she had fired earlier in the day had ensured that John Barclay wouldn't bother anyone ever again.

Hawkins had asked to authenticate this personally, but the polite doctor who assessed her insisted that he was qualified to identify a dead body. And besides, Barclay's corpse had been removed from the hospital a long time before Hawkins awoke from the twelve-hour sleep brought on by her exertions.

'Hey, chief.' Maguire's voice precipitated her first genuine smile for two weeks, as her deputy was wheeled into view. 'How's our hero?'

'Good, thanks. You're not such a lousy sidekick yourself. How do you feel?'

'Won't complain about being woken up by my alarm clock any more, that's for damn sure.' Maguire glanced back at the nurse pushing him. 'Don't let the chair fool you, though – I'm fine and dandy.'

The nurse parked him by the bed and smiled at Hawkins. She'd obviously won the battle to keep Mike in a wheelchair, at least until the residual effects of the Taser had worn off. He had no serious injuries, so it probably wasn't necessary, but then Maguire always had been a sucker for pretty girls.

In truth they were both alive thanks only to Barclay's deteriorating mental state: Hawkins, because he'd been easily distracted during their final encounter; and Mike, because the Taser hadn't been operating at full efficiency. It turned out that, because stun guns were designed to operate in short bursts, if you bypassed the timer as Barclay had, the unit's generator soon wore out. After six prolonged uses, his was pretty much wrecked.

Mike's joke also reassured her that their friendship was undamaged. They'd already spoken, six hours before, when Hawkins had come round for the first time since that morning's drama.

Mike had explained his own experiences of the previous

night's events. He described the text he'd received from her phone, and his ensuing mad dash across London; how he'd found Hawkins on her kitchen floor in a pool of blood, alone and close to death.

Fortunately, however, thanks to the same warped logic that precipitated his actions it seemed that Barclay hadn't been trying to kill her directly. His aim appeared to have been exsanguination; a method of knifing around the vital organs to induce bloodletting, which allowed the victim time before their inevitable demise to rue whatever actions led to such a fate. It had been well on the way to working, too. Except that she'd been found just in time.

Mike's call to the emergency services on the way to her house had saved her life: the medics estimated that her wounds were only around twenty minutes old by the time they arrived; the sole reason she was still breathing.

Despite their expertise, she'd been only a cigarette paper's thickness from death, thanks to a nick in her right lung, and a punctured vein next to her heart. She'd beaten the odds by recovering at all, let alone without long-term damage.

The ensuing hours, Mike admitted, had been a living hell for him. In Maguire's mind, it was *his* negligence that had placed her in such a vulnerable position, and therefore his fault that Nemesis had been able to catch her alone. He'd been so focused on saving the day that he'd completely overlooked the fact he'd left a potential primary target unprotected.

Ironically, however, it was Barclay who had delivered her back to him. The doctors said that being disconnected from the breathing apparatus had forced her system to self-sustain. Had she stayed plugged in, the more likely alternative would have been a coma, where her body would have become reliant on life support. But because the chances of resuscitation following straight disconnection weren't favourable, the professionals would never have risked it.

Fortunately, Barclay had had no legal concerns or Care Trust to satisfy, and had made the impossible decision for them.

Mike, of course, was a little way behind her in the enlightenment stakes. Things were still adjusting themselves in his mind, falling into place. He realized now that targeting the investigation team itself had never been Barclay's intention. Instead, he'd seen Connor's death as necessary to protect his identity, while his own disappearance *had* been due to Nemesis, but not in the way they'd assumed. And Hawkins had, of course, been marked right from the start. At least now they had an answer to why Eddie had frozen when Nemesis opened the door.

He hadn't expected to recognize his killer.

Mike had also spoken to Lawrence Kirby-Jones and Tristan Vaughn. They were ecstatic that Nemesis had been stopped; less enamoured they'd now have to admit publicly that the killer was, until very recently, a serving Met officer.

The nurse finished his inspection and stepped back. 'I think you're going to be OK, Antonia, but you have to rest.'

'Great.' She looked up at him. 'Can I go?'

'I don't think so.'

She turned to Mike. 'Looks like I'll be in here for a while.'

'I'll stick around.' He grinned. 'So, how about jacking in this detective garbage and getting a real job?'

'After today?' She caught the wink that told her he was joking. 'Thanks, but I think I'll stick at it a while longer.'

THE DI ANTONIA HAWKINS SERIES
By Alastair Gunn

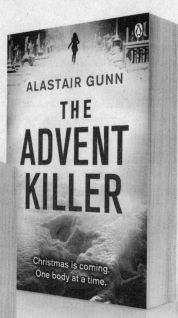

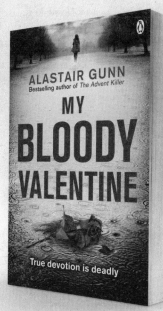

THE HALLOWEEN KEEPER
Available October 2016

He just wanted a decent book to read ...

Not too much to ask, is it? It was in 1935 when Allen Lane, Managing Director of Bodley Head Publishers, stood on a platform at Exeter railway station looking for something good to read on his journey back to London. His choice was limited to popular magazines and poor-quality paperbacks – the same choice faced every day by the vast majority of readers, few of whom could afford hardbacks. Lane's disappointment and subsequent anger at the range of books generally available led him to found a company – and change the world.

'We believed in the existence in this country of a vast reading public for intelligent books at a low price, and staked everything on it'
Sir Allen Lane, 1902–1970, founder of Penguin Books

The quality paperback had arrived – and not just in bookshops. Lane was adamant that his Penguins should appear in chain stores and tobacconists, and should cost no more than a packet of cigarettes.

Reading habits (and cigarette prices) have changed since 1935, but Penguin still believes in publishing the best books for everybody to enjoy. We still believe that good design costs no more than bad design, and we still believe that quality books published passionately and responsibly make the world a better place.

So wherever you see the little bird – whether it's on a piece of prize-winning literary fiction or a celebrity autobiography, political tour de force or historical masterpiece, a serial-killer thriller, reference book, world classic or a piece of pure escapism – you can bet that it represents the very best that the genre has to offer.

Whatever you like to read – trust Penguin.